YESTERDAY'S MAGNOLIA

Betty J. Vaughn

TotalRecall Publications, Inc.
1103 Middlecreek
Friendswood, Texas 77546
281-992-3131   281-482-5390 Fax
www.totalrecallpress.com

ISBN: 978-1-59095-555-0
UPC: 6-43977-45552-9

Library of Congress Control Number: 2015954555

Printed in the United States of America with simultaneous
printings in Australia, Canada, and United Kingdom.

FIRST EDITION
1   2   3   4   5   6   7   8   9   10

With gratitude to those who have believed in me and encouraged me to pursue my dreams, to those who have been my friends through the vagaries of life, and to my family who gave me roots and love, I owe you all. Although you go un-named here, I hope that you will find yourself in these lines.

Fiction Award NC Society of Historians 2010

NC Society of Historians
Established December 1941

AWARD WINNER

Prologue

I'm old now and I'm lonely. Everyone I knew is mostly gone, at least the ones from my generation and those before me. The young ones don't have time for someone old and wrinkled...don't have time for someone who just wants to talk about the past. They live for tomorrow. I don't know if I will even have a tomorrow. I guess that means I have begun to die. I always said if you stop dreaming, stop looking ahead, you begin to die. Now I just look down at where I am and back at where I've been. It was quite a story. Once I couldn't tell my story...when I could still dream about tomorrow and worry about what people would think if they knew. Now it doesn't much matter. I just want to tell it to put my own mind at ease before I join the others in eternal dust.

It's a wet day out. Rainy days have always been days to make me want cleanliness, order, thought, and peace. Lazy days they are but with an undercurrent of throbbing energy. There's something about the rain just dripping down from the eaves that causes my mind to begin turning to past days of rain and sunshine. I find myself thinking of all the good times and the bad...old happinesses, worries and joys. Too, it's a good time for dreamy, melancholy, poignant melodies to come in merged succession from a tiny transistor radio I received as a gift years ago. It's old; it's cheap but terrific in tone, but then mine is not a refined ear. It's my old friend, a companion being.

Somehow those yesteryears of mine seem so remote, so dream-like...perhaps just a fantasy I tell myself...there's just today, no more. Do yesterday and tomorrow exist only in my imagination, are here but not, are clear yet vague, are pleasant but tinctured always with the sadness of the ephemeral...old loves, old wants, old faces flash fleetingly across the screen of my heart, striking mellow chords of tunes I thought long since dead...old hurts casting new daggers against old wounds causing new pain, feelings dulled by the scarring of time but still there and capable of welling tears.

Almost against my will, my thoughts relentlessly pick from memories vague mass, the face of my college sweetheart, my first love, the first man to kiss my lips and awaken the dormant and unrequited throb of life's mysterious force to mate. He would hold my hands against his chest to warm them on clear starlit nights as wordlessly we ambled a pine studded campus, enjoying the warped shadow images across our path, the clustered needles above, and the bleeding perfume of grass newly bruised by relentless blades.

He won my heart, while I in naive wonder and joy but knew untouched happiness. I sensed this newness inside was a dear and precious thing, a treasure above all others. I felt the subtle wash of its fleeting wings beating past me. Clutching wildly at the future, I hoped to carry with me this new sensation not yet recognized as love. I ached in every embrace with some deep inner awareness that it must end with its birth, to be replaced by a cold loneliness. That delicate, gossamer thing, that hauntingly beautiful spring of my freshman year seeped inexorably across my heart and was gone. Thus it was in early bloom, rich and cheap with its lavishness, innocent and joyful awakening love and then like yesterday's magnolia.

He picked me one once. It was a huge, majestic thing, an oriental temple of cream-like ivory against leaves of deep, shiny unfathomable green. I kept it until the next day when its sharp, clear, rejuvenating scent turned into stagnant repulsion and its color browned in prodigal death. Yesterday's magnolia: but the faint suggestion of what was, now left in that withered thing.

The years have flown since those spring nights of slow kisses, youth and magnolias opening under a full-blown circle of lunar gold to offer their heady incense to a heedless heaven. Years have passed and I have known new loves, new joys and deep sadness. And now, on rainy nights alone, my thoughts conjure the faces of others who entered my life and my heart, each in their own way, long after that magnolia was but a distant memory. Two are now dead and the other just a beautiful dream that soured with the rising sun.

Now I live with just the memory of them as my days tick past. I will tell you about the time they wove like threads across the fabric of my life giving it richness and color and bringing new dreams and experiences that now begin to die even in my memory.

And no, not all of it is melancholy. There were moments of giddy pleasure, foolish play and child-like romps. Those memories bring a smile and quiet joy. I'm glad I have them...all of those memories, the good and the bad...for that is the way of life.

Chapter 1

The post cards read: "you'll always be the girl in the Casa Valadier." As I sit here holding it, I remember so clearly all of those special rare moments that marked the days we shared. Moments that stand out in the album of one's memory, like snapshots of frozen time, are rare...rare, and oh so precious. What is it that makes them as dazzling, as memorable as jewels? Is it the perfect coming together of place, people, and events? Or is it when one of you has the wisdom and sense of temporality to heighten the experience, savor the moment and present it wrapped like a gift under the Christmas tree? I've often wondered if he had known he was dying or if it was just his special genius to celebrate the small and perfect times in life, to snip them from the total fabric, and forever frame them under the glass of memory.

"The girl in the Casa Valadier"...Rome. I first met Maurice de Beaubourg there in the spring of 1984. I was in a brief and crumbling marriage and Maurice had experienced the end of his engagement to my sister who had left him for the glamour and power of another man, one of the best known in the world. We were united in our mutual losses and personal unhappiness, but more than that, from the first words between us, Maurice and I had shared a special kinship of spirit, and had the same aesthetic interests, both artists. Even when he had been obsessed by Margot, her vivacity, beauty and personality; and she fascinated by his life of aristocratic wealth and grandeur, the old world cultivation he represented to her, a farmer's daughter from Eastern North Carolina, Maurice and I had been friends. He had often talked to me from Europe while Margot would wait for him to get off the line so she could talk with me as well. He had sent gifts of art books from various locales in Europe. Some of them were quite rare, one his own personal copy of an out of date volume of Henry Moore, his favorite sculptor. From that early beginning until I first met him over three years later and in the years after that, our rapport was deep and unique and not without frustrations.

As an art teacher, I had planned with my best friend, also an art teacher, to take a group of our students to Italy and Greece during Spring break. Maurice had phoned frequently since he and Margot had broken up and we had become close. It was only natural, when he learned that I was coming to Europe, to make arrangements for us to meet. Wanting it to be somewhere special and romantic, he selected the Casa Valadier in Rome for four o'clock on the last Saturday afternoon of March 1984.

Not long after arrival in Rome, I hailed a taxi from the Hotel Genoa where I was staying. Just as in the stereotypical movies, the taxi tore madly through the twisting, crowded streets of the area near the Palatino taking me past the Spanish Steps, then the building on the right where Napoleon had established the school for Prix de Roma art students, and then on up the pine crowned hill to the park of the Casa Valadier. I climbed out of the taxi near the entry steps and looked up at an impressively grand, faded ochre colored villa of a past era. It had been a private home, but now was converted into a tony outdoor cafe and restaurant. From the terrace of the cafe, I looked over the roofs of Rome, across the Tiber to the Vatican and from there to the distant hills that encircle this celebrated old city.

I was early, typical for me, and Maurice...as I would learn...was typically and woefully late. To kill time and allay a growing nervousness, I wandered around the grounds near the house, glorying in the experience of having at last made it to Europe, a life-long dream of mine. Afraid that I might miss him and not knowing what he looked like, I decided I should wait in an obvious and prominent place. The steps to the porch on the side of the Casa that overlooked the parking area seemed perfect.

Following a futile attempt at a nap and a reviving shower, I had dressed carefully. My hair, long and brunette, was swept up Gibson girl style. I was wearing a turquoise blouse that enhanced the honeyed tones of my complexion, along with a beige silk skirt and over blouse that I had found at a local designer outlet. I had bought it instantly when I saw it flattered my figure which I had dieted to a new slimness: long legs trim, breasts high and firm, and waist small...but then that is true despite what I might weigh. Mine is not a typical beauty: cheekbones almost too high, lips full, nose prominent but not overly so. Artist that I am, I've learned to paint the canvas to best advantage so I look a bit exotic, or so I'm told. In fact most people think me foreign and even in Europe, I am rarely taken for an American...unless I open my mouth. Then the jig is up.

God was I nervous! I wanted Maurice to find me pretty because I suppose I was already half in love with him, a rather late schoolgirl fantasy for sure. Pacing the porch, I nervously fingered the filigree of the railing, rueing the fleeting of those precious hours allotted to Rome. I both longed for and curiously enough, dreaded this meeting. I had treasured our telephone friendship and wanted nothing to bring that to an end. I didn't know if he would like me in person, if I would prove nothing like what he had envisioned and too, I didn't know if he would meet my own expectations.

I sensed his presence, felt the force of his personality, even before I turned and saw him climbing the steps toward me. The first thing that struck me was the way he moved...with the grace and restrained power of a leashed jaguar. Dressed in black slacks, black shoes and black knit shirt, he exuded that same lithe, sinuous strength. Not even the red sports jacket he had zipped against the late afternoon chill took from the sensation of primal force. Pride, massive intelligence, knowledge of his physical appeal, a confidence native to Europeans of aristocratic heritage, and a tremendous aura of will-power combined to make him a compelling, striking man. The opaquely dark sunglasses added an air of glamour tinged with mystery. His face was like a Roman statue...a classical one, colored by the ravages of time and life. The only dissonant note was his hair. It didn't fit: stiff, peppered gray with a bizarre tinge, and not quite kempt. It gave that quixotic touch. Later I would learn that it was the result of this god-awful, messy mud he combed into his hair to prevent it graying and thinning. He was convinced it worked. It did change his hair from gray to that indeterminate hue and he wasn't balding. But for a day after an application, his shoulders looked like the leavings from a Saharan dust storm and his hair was as stiff as the tines of a fork. It was obviously newly applied for our meeting and it for sure provided that eccentric touch.

He walked up to me, smiling warmly into my eyes as he approached. "Maurice?" I inquired.

"Jo!" Laughing, he swept me into his arms in an intense embrace. His body was hard and lean against mine. I looked up into his chiseled face realizing he was tall. In heels, I'm nearly six feet and he towered over me by several inches. Releasing me, we turned together to the stairs. He smiled at me. "I would have known you anywhere."

Again I was struck by his English, no accent, and an incredible vocabulary...both slang and proper. Laughingly I responded, "But you have the advantage. I look a bit like Margot." Margot and I were much the same height, had the same complexion and hair color, but whereas hers was very fine, straight and thin, mine was longer, thick and wavy. Typically we both wore our hair up. Her eyes were blue and mine green, her nose small and slightly retroussé. My figure was more hourglass, whereas she had larger breasts and waist that tapered into those slim hips I so envied. However, from a distance we had been mistaken for one another on frequent occasions.

"Did you not ever see a photograph of me? I gave your sister several."

"I'm sorry, but I haven't." Looking provoked, he took my elbow as we ambled along the graveled path into the park. I was curious in retrospect that she had not shown me any, as I had been with her frequently when she was at home in Coral Gables. But then we never spent much time in the house, as we were usually out and about enjoying the liveliness of the local scene.

As we walked in the park, I babbled nervously and despised myself for it. I wanted to say something frightfully witty and intelligent, and yet, there I was discussing the weather and jet lag. He didn't say much...just listened and occasionally looked down at me. As we walked, I glanced down at the path and caught a glimpse of his shoes. The two-inch heels he wore certainly were contributing something to the commanding height. After several minutes of silence, I resumed my monologue with a description of my recent bout with flu. Just wonderful, I groaned to myself. If he is not going to talk, I need to shut up as I sound like a blathering idiot. I suppose he decided he had finally heard enough.

"Would you like something to drink? The outdoor cafe here is excellent and the view is fabulous. Don't you just love the way the city is surrounded by the misty hills and how it is all laid out at our feet? I want to take you to those hills there," he remarked as he swept the horizon with his hand. "While you are in Rome, I'm your own special tour guide. Is it possible for you to leave your group and be with me?"

As I slid into the metal ice-cream parlor style chair, I replied, "That's not a problem. I've already told the group that I will be with a friend of mine while we're here. My friend, Jaynie, who's also an art teacher but with another school, is going to cover both my group and hers. I'll give her a break when we get to Athens as she has a friend there she wants to spend some time with."

"Good! Now what would you like? I recommend the 'arancia spremuta.' It's made of the blood oranges that grow in the volcanic soil near Naples. The flesh is very red and the juice is superb." Obviously he was a man accustomed to control as he didn't wait for my agreement but immediately signaled a waiter, "*Cameriere! Due arancia spremuti, per favore.*"

That done, he leaned back to bask in his chair, face to the waning sun, eyes closed to the meager warmth. Maurice chatted then about Rome, his trip there and his recent travels on business. He was fluent

in Italian, Spanish, English and German. In his native French he had
the power of language possessed by the poets. I'd had French in high
school, southern American variety, and Latin that I'd never had the
chance or reason to speak and had I done so, it would have been with
the Michigan twang of my teacher. In college I had taken four years
of Spanish with refugee Cuban professors who'd fled Castro, so even
that was to prove virtually useless when I visited Spain several years
later and was exposed to Castilian Spanish. I spoke English fluently
and nothing else. Then and there, I decided change was in order.
Now I can manage fairly well in French, can speak restaurantese and
shopping in Italian, and read Spanish. Everything else is Greek to me,
including Greek, which I had tried to learn with a Berlitz traveler's
dictionary prior to that trip, since it included both Italy and Greece.

What the heck! I figured I might as well relax and enjoy myself.
He would just have to like me "as is." After all, he seemed to have all
those months on the phone. I grinned at him, my sense of humor
restored and my thrill at finally being in Rome and meeting him
adding sparkle to my eyes. Catching the subtle shift of mood and
body language, he responded.

"Ah, Jo. It is so good to be with you here. It brings me so much
peace. You cannot know how I have needed this...needed to see your
face and know you as something beyond a voice." I noticed the harsh
lines beside his mouth as he talked and knew that he carried deep
pain.

The orange juice had arrived and I found it delicious and as red as
he had described. I was glad he had chosen for me, as I liked the fun
of learning new and exotic things. "This is great. Thanks for ordering
it for me."

"I'm glad you like it. It's one of my favorite drinks when I come
here." He pointed to the rosy sky that was bleeding a warm glow
onto the ochre walls of Rome. "The sun is beginning to set. I love the
way it lights the sky behind the dome of St. Peter's. Lets drive to the
hills above the Tiber. I know a beautiful building there and a park,
which provide a fabulous overlook of the city. If we go now we can

get there while there's still enough light to appreciate the view."

Maurice may have been poetic, romantic in his soul, but I decided after that ride he was one frantic poet. When I climbed into the silver BMW that he had triple parked, I was in for a Roman traffic experience that reduced my earlier taxi trip to the equivalent of a sedate trot on an old Shetland pony as opposed to one on a run-away, terror crazed bronco. He was a maestro behind the wheel, controlling and making love to that powerful, purring, darting machine. We barreled over cobbled, twisting streets so fast we couldn't catch the bumps. Down narrow, one-way, convoluted streets, the passing buildings became a blur. A quick beep at a blind corner and we were tearing around it, Maurice blithely chatting and gesticulating and me all but breathless as I clung to the door handle to brace myself and bite my lips to keep from screaming in panic. I wanted badly to tell him to please keep both hands on that wheel and slow down. I had much the same feeling I had when against my better judgment I allowed a friend to drag me on to a roller coaster...an ordeal to be survived. I cut my eyes at him. He seemed confidently in control and he was certainly old enough to have made it through many years of such driving. So with a sanguine sigh, I decided to relax, endure and wait for it to be done.

Maurice was a witty and well-informed tour guide and a natural teacher. He loved to share his knowledge and his love for the beauty of Europe. In the years ahead he became my mentor as he opened the beauty and charm of Europe to me, granting me entree into the grandest of homes, the most luxurious of hotels and restaurants, as well as picturesque and quaint by ways. Those memories of all he gave me to experience are among my most treasured.

The view of Rome spread below me in the last rays of the setting sun was thrilling, soft and mellow with the dusting of thousands of twilights. The air whispering through the Pina Parasola trees sounded as though it carried the sighs of lovers, the moans of the despairing, the laughter of the joyous all captured through the millennia in the embrace of those needled branches.

He turned to me and took my hand, "Listen to the music in the trees. Do you hear it...like soft voices murmuring to one another?"

"I think you must be a wizard. You read my mind too well. I think I should watch my thoughts as well as my words or I'll have no secrets."

He laughed and squeezed my hand, "So, Jo...do you want to keep secrets from me now?"

"Ah mystery: it's always more intriguing don't you think?" I teased.

"Oh, are you trying to intrigue me? Don't you think maybe I already was? He cocked one eyebrow, smiling down at me.

"Hmm" was my noncommittal answer.

Putting his arm around my shoulder, he pulled me to his side, as we stood there bathed in the magic of the moment. He smiled again and softly asked me, "Are you hungry, my Jo?"

"Yes! I'm absolutely starving. I had only a roll on the plane for breakfast and no lunch. I was too excited to eat."

"My poor darling, I must feed you. Come. I'm hungry, too and I know the perfect place, the Girarrosto Toscano. You'll love it. The food is marvelous and the atmosphere is charming. It's also quite a meeting place for the international set." He smiled with a twinkle in his eye. I could have just melted on the spot at the sight of those chiseled Latin features focused on me. I told myself: hold on old girl; don't go jumping off that particular cliff. Holding hands we walked back to his car, past the gypsy souvenir stands that cluttered the parking area. They were dark and shuttered now as they awaited the return of light and the hoards of tourists that come here to the Gianicolo for the panoramic vista.

The restaurant was as charming as he promised. Situated on the Via Campania, it faced the ancient walls of Rome just down from the Porta Pinciana. Entering the inconspicuous door at street level, we immediately descended to the vestibule where a grill on the right provided a tantalizing aroma redolent of the gustatory pleasures to come. Procuitto, cheeses, garlic and peppers hung in the semi-open kitchen area. The dining room itself was divided by low partitions into three spaces, with banquette seating, warm paneled walls, and bottles of wine sitting on a ledge that surrounded the upper walls. It was beautifully appointed with pink linens topped by white cloths, sparkling crystal and the glint of well-polished silverware. The antipasti and dessert dishes on rolling carts that we passed on the way to our table had my mouth watering in anticipation.

Maurice proceeded to teach me something of the pleasures of Roman cuisine: recommending the small fried baby artichokes, a risotto of spring vegetables and a lovely fish dish, followed by a salad of baby arugula which I had never eaten before as it was not then available at home. When he ordered the small woodland strawberries with zabaglione, I knew I was in a diner's heaven. By the time we finished the meal, it was nearing midnight and I was as stuffed as I was pooped. He drove back to the hotel at a more relaxed pace much to my relief and with a brief hug and European air kisses on both cheeks, left me in the lobby to make my way to a long awaited bed.

The next day Maurice had reserved for exploring Rome. I arose early to breakfast with my group, made sure they understood the day's itinerary, and then returned to my room to await the appointed hour. He met me in front of the Genoa at 11:00...he told me he was never out and about any earlier...and we hastened to the Vatican intent on seeing the Sistine Chapel, ostensibly early to beat the tour buses and crowds. On subsequent trips, I discovered, to really arrive early, it is necessary to be in line at the entry no later than 7:30 or 8:00 and then stand there patiently until it opens at 9:00.

"Jo, darling, look: the view is absolutely ruined with all those damned tour buses!" Maurice apologetically exclaimed as we neared St. Peter's. He was right. The place was as swarming with buses, vans, and people as an overturned beehive. Wheeling into the street on the left side of the colonnaded piazza, he found a parking space just a block down by a flower stall. I was enthralled by the lush array of fresh, colorful flowers spilling from the bins and paused to admire them as we passed.

"Darling, I would buy you a bouquet but I fear they would never survive the Dutch tourists in the Vatican."

"Oh, don't worry. It's okay because I wouldn't want to have to carry them all the way through the Vatican." I looked up at him puzzled by his remark, and laughed into his amused eyes. "Why are you being so hard on the Dutch?"

He chuckled, "The last time I was in Rome, I had friends of mine from California with me...Bill and Sherry. They wanted to come here so I agreed to give them the tour. Unfortunately, we arrived in the midst of a hoard of Dutch tour buses. We could barely push our way through. Bill knows I hate to get caught up in crowds so he started to tease me about my guide services at about the same time we were caught in the midst of a huge group of very fat Dutch ladies..."

"You did say *huge*?" We both laughed and I could see he was pleased with my sally.

"...So, I took the arm of one of them, introduced myself as a guide since they seemed to have lost theirs, and led us all through the museum approach and into the Sistine Chapel, often with rambling and *inspired* commentary. Bill and Sherry were laughing so hard they were crying. That little performance was the only thing that made it bearable for me. See: you had no idea what an experienced guide I am." We grinned at one another as we paused to admire Bernini's imposing colonnade before rounding the corner to face the line for tickets.

"Well now, I suppose if any Dutch ladies get in my way, I'm going to have some competition for your services, aren't I?"

He wiggled an eyebrow wickedly, and responded in a sultry voice. "I would be happy to service you, my dear. Dutch ladies aren't my type."

"Did I mention that I have Dutch ancestry on my mother's side?" I couldn't help teasing him. And it is true. I had grown up with stories of my great, great, great something grandmother, Polly Blitha, and seen the wooden sabots she brought from Holland as a young girl. According to family legend, she was kidnapped by Indians at the age of eight and lived among them for two years before being rescued and returned to her family where she lived until marrying my great something grandfather.

Gaily, arm in arm, we entered the museum with Maurice feigning the tour guide role and I madly trotting behind to keep from being separated and lost in the crowds. As it was, it was the Sistine Chapel that was lost. We were practically propelled across the space of the Chapel by the pushing throngs. There was so many people and so little time, that I felt as though I barely glimpsed the ceiling. By the time we reached the haven of the far exit door, I was breathless. Maurice had successfully elbowed and nearly trampled several nuns in his haste to get us there. It was obvious to me he was not thrilled by the whole process.

Tactfully, if a bit secretly woeful and hoping to spare any more hapless nuns, I suggested, "If this is any example, I'll forego the Pieta this trip. I'm starving and it's nearly half past one. Let's have lunch."

"Wonderful!" His relief was tangible and I could see that he hated to be caught in crowds even more than I. Since that trip, I have returned to the Vatican more than a dozen times, and always make it a point to visit the Pieta, that fabulous pink marble statue of the Virgin and crucified Christ by Michelangelo that rests in a small chapel just to the right of the entry into the Basilica. It is worth all of the crowds to stand in the presence of this masterpiece, the only one of his works that the artist ever signed.

We walked past the flower stall and reclaimed the car he called "Battleship."

That seemed highly appropriate to me at the time, as behind the wheel, he was like an implacable admiral leading his vessel against the enemy. Holding my breath to prevent an involuntary gasp and trying not to grip the armrest too obviously was a struggle when we wheeled into traffic, tires squalling and irate Romans honking at us. Maurice said he knew the perfect place for a tranquil lunch that was quite near the Vatican. At what must have been sixty miles an hour on a narrow twisting city street, it seemed really close and frankly much too far.

The street we entered was cobbled, the buildings, Roman-austere in style. The Antica Pesa Restaurant was on the left, mid-block just past a police station. With only a simple sign on the pale, dusty red exterior, it would have been easily missed. On entering the ceiling was low; tables on either side were spread with an array of delectable looking freshly cooked vegetables, antipasti, rustic loaves of bread and sinfully rich desserts. The tables were centuries old and the walls behind, more so. When we entered the Maître'd met us, warning us to duck our heads as we penetrated through a low arch into a narrow hallway. At the end of which we descended a couple of steps to find ourselves in the dining room where the right side walls were covered in murals, the left banked with French door style windows and the far wall centered with a massive stone fireplace. The country style tables were draped in pristine pale yellow tablecloths and set with fresh bouquets of spring flowers. Through the open windows we could see a small courtyard redolent with the aroma of flowering lemon and orange trees.

We were charmed as we sat at the table enjoying the best calamari I had every eaten, but then I had never had any except frozen and encased in a thick covering of batter. I commented on one of the murals that faced me, remarking that it reminded me of the Dead Toreador by Manet. When I mentioned it, Maurice grabbed my hand and pressed a kiss on it; sighing, he said how uncanny it was that so often our thoughts paralleled and just as he started to say something, I would say it for him. I could feel his bemusement and knew he was delighted with me.

After an assortment of antipasti, the calamari, fresh arugula salad, a luscious pear sorbet and two bottles of chilled and very dry white Frascati wine from Lazio, the region around Rome, we were mellow, relaxed and happy. In that quiet, age steeped place we had sealed our friendship, finally achieving the same level of comfort in person as the one we had previously established by phone. We laughed and teased and it was not until nearly four in the afternoon, when all of the other patrons had long since departed, that we reluctantly ended the bliss of the moment. Arm in arm we strolled back to "Battleship."

When we left the restaurant, Maurice drove to the area above the Baths of Caraculla where we found a delightful, old monastery. Both of us furiously snapped photos of its gateway and ivy walled street leading to it as the sun at last flickered from behind the clouds lighting everything in dozens of warm hues. From there we drove down the hill to the Terme di Caraculla where Maurice parked on the edge of the street, again oblivious to the blaring horns of those blocked behind us. He never worried about such things, whereas I, with inbred American concern for the other fellow's opinions and rights, was constantly to be appalled by his disregard for such niceties of politesse.

He grabbed his camera from the trunk and I posed in tipsy delight with those marvelous old and ruinous walls of ancient Rome's most glorious public bath looming behind me. Laughing we dashed back to the car, Maurice blithely ignoring the various gestures directed our way that I strongly suspected were of vulgar implication. With happy contentment and a sense of being attuned to one another, we drove from there to the Campidoglio, Rome's ancient capitol sited on the Capitoline hill, one of the seven hills, which hosted the ancient city.

As the sun sank low in the sky, we stood in the square designed by Michelangelo and stared in mute and mutual horror at the center. There, where we had anticipated the famed equestrian statue of Marcus Aurelius, stood a cardboard cutout of the statue proclaiming that it had been removed for restoration.

Taking it as a personal insult, I groaned, "Oh god, Maurice. How could they do this to me? I wanted to see it so much!" Disappointed, we left for a driving tour of some of Rome's other glories before the fading light marched into darkness: the Column of Trajan, shrouded in scaffolding; the Arch of Constantine, hidden behind green restoration framing and netting. When we reached the Trevi Fountain only to find the entire upper right corner of the sculptural backdrop draped in restoration materials, we began to laugh.

"Well, it looks as though I'd better toss some coins in the fountain. If I'm ever going to see the 'Glories of Rome,' I'll have to come back when they are through restoring it."

"Alors, ma Chérie, I should have warned them you were coming." As the city lights winked on, we drove away.

Dinner that night was in the Cesarina, close to the Via Veneto and the restaurant of the previous night. There I ordered a grilled Scamorza mozzarella made from buffalo milk. I loved it. Following Maurice's example, I covered it in olive oil and freshly ground pepper, as he explained to me, "During the last century, Italy's cattle suffered a disease carried by the water which decimated much of the cattle population. In order to work the fields, water buffalo were imported from Asia because they had been found to be resistant to the blight. Today Italy has the second highest population of water buffalo in the world, exceeded only by India." Glancing at my rapidly diminishing plate, he inquired, "Shall I order more, Jo?"

"No, please. You already have me eating too much. Pasta, bread, cheese, wine...I am just glad I don't have to weigh in and out of Italy and pay a fine on the increase!"

It had been a long day for me: jet lag, a strange diet, trying to monitor my group, hectic dashing about and a late evening were taking a toll. "Maurice it will be almost midnight when I get back to the hotel. Let's go, shall we?"

"Of course, darling. You must be exhausted. Jet lag is always worst the second day, isn't it?" I didn't answer, as I had never flown far enough before to warrant the malady.

The drive back to the Genoa proved to be the 'scenic route' as we promptly were lost in the maze of streets. Maurice could not seem to find the right way and I was of no help. By the time we finally arrived, I was so tired I could have screamed with frustration.

"Jo, tomorrow I want very much to take you shopping and then I need to have a

talk with you about a serious matter that plagues me very much." I groaned inwardly and not at the shopping. "You're very tired now.

Go to bed and in the morning I'll pick you up at eleven."

"That's fine. I truly am exhausted." I turned to open the door...it surprised me that he never offered to do that. He reached over to stop me and pulled me back to him to kiss me fiercely and lingering on the lips. I was too shocked to respond. With cupped hands, he caressed my cheeks. "Goodnight, my darling."

Flustered, I stammered my own goodnight in return. I went up to my room, puzzling that he would kiss me in that way when he had stressed repeatedly how happy he was to at last meet his 'sister.' In my family, brothers and sisters don't lip kiss. I couldn't deny that I was attracted to him but somehow it just didn't click. He was handsome, sophisticated, *French*, brilliant, witty, warm, romantic, wealthy, the everything-in-one-package kind of man on the surface. But under that veneer, I sensed deep rage, bitterness, loneliness, frustration, and the passion without sexuality that Margot had alluded to. However, romantic fool that I am, there was a part of me that was titillated by the hope that he might be attracted to me. I wondered if it was some kind of suppressed jealousy of Margot and the glamour of the life he had provided her. From what she had told me, he had loved her madly and lavished a fortune in gifts on her. I was no gold digger and she wasn't either, but the idea of being lavished on was appealing on a materialistic level and the prospect of being panted after had a certain charm as well.

The following morning at seven, I had gone down to breakfast with my group, checked to make sure there were no problems, and everyone knew the day's program. I bade them goodbye from the steps of the Genoa. They were on their way to enjoy a day in Florence and I was rather sad that I would miss that because of spending the day in Rome. At eleven I was waiting on the steps of the hotel anticipating his promised arrival, at eleven thirty I gave up and returned to my room. He called not long after to say he was running late and he would have the hotel call me when he arrived. I was exasperated that my precious hours in Rome were rapidly ticking past while I frittered away my time in a hotel room. Finally at half past twelve, the front desk called to summon me to the lobby where he waited.

"Ah, Jo, it is a lovely day. I suggest we have lunch and then I'm taking you shopping. It is not good for a lovely woman to come to Rome and not enjoy the wonderful fashions. I want to buy you a pair of shoes. I just love high heeled shoes on girls with lovely legs." He gave me an exaggerated ogle that had me laughing at him, the frustration of waiting started fading. He knew I was upset that he had arrived so late and he was determined to charm me.

Not far from the Piazza D'Espagna we lunched at a very 'in' cafe, Nino's, on the Via Borgognona. I was enchanted by the old world aura of it.

"Maurice, I love it here. Rome is all that I dreamed it could be. There is such magic, such grace, such drama and poetry in it. I'm fascinated by the fusion of the old with the new...not just an old building beside a newer one but often layers of age in the same building, from ancient Roman to Renaissance to Baroque."

"Yes, Rome has a rare charm. I've loved it since my days here as a young man when I came to study painting following my graduation from Harvard."

"Harvard and Rome, too?"

"Yes. When I finished at the University in Paris, I went to Harvard next for three years to obtain my degree, a Doctorate in International Law, which my father insisted I earn. Afterwards I rebelled. I never wanted to enter the family business, although I knew, as the only child and a son, I eventually would be compelled. It's a hundred year old family firm and it's my duty to perpetuate it, but back then I wanted to be an artist. So I came to Rome and lived here for a year and I painted. My father was furious with me and always retained a certain anger against me for that period of defiance. After I left Rome, despite his demands that I return to Marseilles, I went to Paris and continued painting. I was successful enough that some of my paintings were accepted into museum collections. I even met Picasso through mutual friends and he said that I would be his heir, meaning that I had the potential to stand with him in the world of art. Unfortunately, that wasn't to be, as I succumbed to the pressure of my family obligations. But, I have always regretted it and wondered what might have been."

"Margot told me that you have a Doctorate from Harvard, but I didn't realize that you had studied in Rome as well. How I envy you that. Do you still paint?"

"Some, but most of my time goes into the business. What little of my art is left, I have sublimated into photography. And I love that and would really like to be able to do just the photography, but business affairs are much too demanding and there is no one to run the company for me the way it needs to be done. I hate it! I never wanted to be a businessman, never. And sadly I know that because of my temperament, I am not as good as either my father or grandfather at running the business. At one time, we had plantations in Africa and Indonesia as well as Provençe. The firm was the largest French importer and exporter of spices and herbs. We no longer have the plantations, so I contract for spices and herbs from farmers both here and abroad. It's a constant struggle to get the right products, have them shipped, assure the quality and then process and package them for reshipment and marketing."

Taking an awkward bite of the pasta, Spaghetti a la Vongole Veraci made from tiny little clams from the bay of Naples, I complimented him on his menu choice for me.   Eating in companionable silence, we enjoyed our meal.

"Maurice, would you excuse me please?" As I rose, the Maitre'd came to assist me by sliding back the table. It was typical of European restaurants in that the tables were so closely packed as to leave only a narrow passage for the waiters and those entering and leaving. I was proud of the few phrases of Italian I had learned from a pocket Berlitz and here was my chance.

"*Dov'è la gabinetta, per favore?*"   I grandly inquired.   I was inordinately proud of myself when the waiter responded in Italian. Unfortunately a great truth then dawned on me: the book could teach me the questions to ask, but no book can teach the infinitely variable answers in such pat format. I hadn't the foggiest notion what in the heck he had said to me, but I was determined that neither he nor Maurice would know, so I set off with feigned confidence and without a clue as to the proper direction. I approached a waiter who grinned and pointed. He was a saintly gentleman, I was sure. I smiled, "*Grazie,*" and then took off in the indicated direction. About the time I reached the door the Italian sank in. I realized the Maître'd had said the door on the left, *a sinistra.* Later I was to discover that *gabinetta,* while understood, is an outmoded word not typically used, as *toiletta* is more current and W.C. more universal.

I walked in chuckling at myself only to have the chuckle turn into a strangle in my throat when I noticed a person of the gentlemanly gender washing his hands at the lavatory. Oh great, I told myself, you've found the men's room you idiot. I started to apologetically back out when I saw two doors beyond the lavatory, one for men and one for women. It was a typical European restaurant facility, a common wash area with two separate W.C.'s. Experience would teach me that W.C.'s could run the gamut from truly luxurious like the huge suite for ladies at the Villa d'Este in Cernobbio, equipped with a private room containing your own toilet, bidet, sink, chair and various designer toiletries, to a Turkish toilet consisting of an ordure encrusted hole with foot slots on either side. *That* only the direst of emergencies can induce me to use. On this occasion, prudish American attitudes toward such facilities were the predominant force in my experience and I was nonplused.

I arrived back at the table to find Maurice chuckling at me. "I see you found your way, Jo. I didn't know you could speak Italian."

"All right, all right. I found it, didn't I?" I grinned impudently.

He roared with laughter, attracting the attention of our elbow-rubbing neighboring tables. "Well, I don't *know* but I'm hoping you did! After all, it is a standard European joke that American ladies hold the record for the smallest bladders in the world. They almost always go to the restroom in restaurants, whereas European women rarely do."

Whether that was true or not I didn't know. "Have you paid the tab? We might better leave before I have to go again, small bladder, you know." He nodded. I grinned.

"Ah, ha! You want those shoes, do you?"

"Well, yes I do. Tall, spiky ones. Sexy, too. Where do we find them?"

"The perfect place. It's on the Via Veneto, so we'll need the car. You are going to love it."

And did I ever. It was the Rafael Salato store with marble floors and butter soft tan leather banquettes, big panes of sparkling clean glass show windows and absolutely gorgeous leather goods: skirts, jackets, slacks, belts, wallets, bags and such shoes. It was raining when we arrived and I mistakenly propped my sodden umbrella against the leather sofa. The clerk reprimanded me with an English butler sniff of superiority and requested I remove it at once. Embarrassed at my thoughtlessness, I hastened to comply. I was uncomfortable anyway. While I was not opposed to the idea, I was unaccustomed to a man taking me shopping and buying me things. After that trip, I decided there are some real positives to be said for it. Raleigh had not exactly prepared me for shopping in Rome either as at that time, J. C. Penny's set the middle standard and Belk's was about the limit for the upper. So there I sat, blushing while Maurice and the 'snooty butler style' clerk discussed my feet, my *figure*, and what to put on me. I had only to provide the feet.

"Try these, Jo. They're absolutely perfect for you."

"They're beautiful!" I gasped at his choices. They were the best in the shop. One pair had very high heels, black with white skin insets on the toes. The other was medium height, beige with crossed bands of matching skin on the toes and heels. I slipped my feet into the black pair and stood to test them.

"Jo, your skirt's too long. Pull it up so we can see your legs." I blushed again, hesitating.

"Go on. Nice legs should be appreciated." Obligingly I hiked my skirt while he and the clerk analyzed legs, shoes, and legs and shoes together. The procedure was repeated for the second pair, with instructions to hike my skirt higher as the heels were lower. Oh well, I did.

Maurice and the clerk, who by this time was exuding a great deal more charm, conducted a whispered conversation followed by Maurice extracting a paper bag of money from the leather bag he carried. From a huge roll of bills, he began extracting lire. When the countertop was pretty much littered with money, I realized just how expensive those shoes were. I was going to be afraid to wear them.

"Madame, would you like forms?" The clerk turned imperiously to me. I wasn't sure what he meant, but what the heck, I figured why not. It was one sure way to find out without giving him the satisfaction of having me ask. At my nod, he quickly produced black plastic shoe forms that he adjusted to fit perfectly in the shoes to hold their shapes. Both pairs were then dropped into flannel bags with drawstring tops; one for each shoe and then all went into a beautifully designed, lacquered bag. Eastern North Carolina was impressed. I hoped the clerk didn't know, but all I got in Raleigh was a cardboard shoebox with paper. Now with the influx of more and more people, many of foreign origin, such amenities are more commonplace.

I held my pretty bag like a little kid with a sack of candy. As we exited to the Via Veneto, Maurice took my elbow and escorted me out like I was a princess royal.

"I don't want to leave Rome tomorrow. There is so much to see and I've seen so little."

"Jo, we can resolve that problem: we'll go to the Trevi Fountain again since we didn't stop last time and we'll toss in coins to guarantee our return."

"Great! I don't know if I've got enough coins, but I intend to litter that place with enough money that I can come back until I'm sick of it, if that's possible. By the way, if I put in a quarter, is that twenty-five trips or one trip per coin? In which case, pennies will do."

He shook his head and laughed. "You are a delightful breath of fresh air. Don't ever change and don't ever stop being my friend."

At the Trevi, I posed for him as I had done on numerous occasions since our first meeting. He was an exacting, demanding and perfectionistic photographer, an artist who knew his craft and his vision. I now treasure those photo memories but at that moment I was impatient at the chunks of time it chewed from those few hours in Rome. The main advantage to the continued posing was he wanted shots of me tossing coins into the fountain, and having long since run out of my own, he continued to supply me. I figure that if I live to three hundred and twenty six, I cannot get all of my trips in from that one excursion alone. It gives one a certain ambition. Since then, I have been in Rome at least thirty times, and each of them has found me back at the fountain with more coins to toss. Hopefully I will return many, many more as I still love it.

The sun was beginning to sink as we ambled along the Via Boca di Leone admiring shop windows. At the Spanish Steps, the pellucid light of Rome enfolded us in its warmth as we savored these last hours together. I felt a growing sadness in me and an increasing tension in Maurice. He wanted to tell me something he had said. In his own time and way he would. I waited and did not pry.

It was nearly nine when we stopped walking. I was bushed. He asked me where I would like to go for dinner and because I had loved the charm of it that first night, I selected the Girrarosto Toscano. As we entered, the lady who manned the door and directed things at the restaurant like a German general deploying troops, smiled and with hands extended to me, palms up, exclaimed: *"Bella, bella madonna!"*

"Grazie." I was both delighted and amazed. I felt so bedraggled I couldn't believe that anyone would call me beautiful.

We were led to a table in the far right corner. After a look at the menu, I decided I wanted nothing so much as a simple green salad and an omelet. I was gorged from so much food. Maurice was a big eater: two full meals a day, not counting the continental breakfast. And he liked meats, lots of meat. It was not uncommon for him to order two entrees if he was particularly pleased with the first. I on the other hand, generally ate just one meal a day and never a great deal of meat, preferring seafood or chicken to beef and pork. This new routine was not compatible to my system. Hoping for some salvation for my digestive tract, I'd begun to drink a Fernet Branca, a bitter herbal digestivo. Margo had suggested it to me when she learned I was doing a tour of Italy. I had not told her that I was meeting Maurice in Rome. I knew her well enough to know that she'd be furious had she known. She didn't want him anymore as she had made abundantly clear, but maybe she liked the idea of him waiting patiently in the wings, an insurance policy against her current affair. I didn't feel any resentment against her for that. It's a pretty common human failing...especially in women, which I know about...for all I know, in men as well.

As we sat there waiting for our food, it was apparent that the dam that had contained his anger, resentment and pain was about to be breached. He began to talk about Margot, gaining momentum as he went. I loved her and I treasured my friendship with him, and could see the fundamental incompatibilities between them and the impossibility of any true relationship. I did truly regret his pain and anger and could feel the basic righteousness of his outrage. He felt he had been used. Even so, he would not understand that my first loyalty was not to him but to my sister.

My eyes filled with tears and I was embarrassed when the waiter brought the food, thinking he would suspect we were having a lovers' quarrel. I did not have Maurice's blithe disdain for the opinions of others. And his remarks about my sister were hurtful.

"Please, could we eat now? We can talk more after we leave." I attempted to change the subject and to soothe him as we were beginning to attract stares from the other diners. He subsided like a pot that has been lidded and the heat reduced, but I knew he was seething beneath that veneer of polite restraint. I also knew that I was in for an emotionally exhausting evening and that it would be hours before I could at last collapse and rest.

Leaving the restaurant, I was so tired I wanted only to go to the hotel and my bed. It had been so hectic, trying to get up at six every morning to breakfast with my tour group, chase around Rome at his intense and madcap pace...jet lagged as I was and without sleep. I was too wired to relax. Too, I was saddened to know that I had to leave Rome in the morning. Despite his anger at Margot, I would miss him. I was extremely attracted to his intellect, his love of art, his powerful personality, and I enjoyed being with a man who expected to be the man. It made me feel deliciously feminine to have a man take care of me, as for most of my life, I've had to fend for myself. He was strong but as I came to know, he also had great weaknesses. Too, I felt my heart go out to him in his pain and I wanted to help him. I asked myself, why is it I always think I've got to be the great *earth mother*?

I think I have never know a more gifted man: physically, intellectually, financially, nor have I know a more tormented one. He was deeply miserable. It went beyond disappointment in a love affair. I knew from my sister that the relationship they had had was not the typical one.

Margo and I had been very close until she began dating Tony Marconetti. Tony was possessive and did not seem to want to share her with anyone including her family, so we were becoming less close on a daily basis. Eventually my sister, Katerina, and her husband, Clint Phillips, would become friends with them as a couple, but in the beginning they were excluded as well. During the two years course of her time with Maurice, we had talked by phone at least every other day, sharing our most intimate thoughts and secrets, including the nature of her relationship with Maurice. She had told me that they attempted sex only twice during those two years and that those attempts were relatively futile. It seems he had no trouble in becoming aroused, particularly by erotic attire, but once because of premature ejaculation and the other time because of an inability to sustain an erection; he failed to achieve a satisfactory coupling with her. She had dated him for some of the same reasons that I admired him. Also he had been exceedingly generous with her: furs, jewels, designer clothes from the best of Parisian boutiques, Gucci luggage, a lavish expense allowance and at the end, he had financed and helped to furnish a home for her in Coral Gables. It was to have been a vacation home for them after they married. While they were dating, I once asked her, if despite all of the material positives, had that kind of relationship not been terribly frustrating?

"Jo, don't be naive. Maurice is just too good to me, and too much fun to be with, to simply give him up. What he cannot provide, I can find elsewhere. Besides I give him what he needs and wants of me. It works for us."

I snorted derisively, "The ultimate courtesan, hmm? What *do* you give him?"

"He wants to be with a pretty woman. He likes it when others admire me and envy him for having me. He likes to buy me things and then have me model them for him. He gets off on that. Besides, it probably keeps his mother happy. I think she wants him to marry and he wants to please her. I've already thought about that. There is just no way I could go through with a marriage...dating yes, marriage no. He's strange, not quite right, if you know what I mean?"

"Why don't you spell it out?"

"I mean, I think he likes to 'play' with the boys. He told me when he was a boy one of their maids made him have sex with her. I think it must have turned him against women. Maybe that explains why he doesn't perform in the sack."

"He's *gay*?" I was astonished and skeptical.

"Well, obviously I can't *prove* it. But something's not right. We'd be having sex if things were normal."

"Probably. So, what are you going to do?"

"For the moment nothing. I will probably go on seeing him when I'm in France, but I'm going to make sure to include one of the other stewardesses when I do. I don't want to be alone with him. It makes me uncomfortable. Besides, I have met someone else that I really like. He's very famous and I think he's interested in me too."

"Who is he? Have I heard of him?"

I gasped when she told me. I had for sure heard of him and seen him a number of times on the evening news. He was famous all right and he came with one *big* hitch, he was married.

"Margo, that's a fool's game. Men rarely leave their wives for the other woman. We both know that. I think you are setting yourself up for a hurt."

"It's okay. He told me to be patient and he will work it out. You see his wife is practically an invalid. She's fat, has a heart condition and is seriously diabetic. That's a lethal combination." How prophetic that comment was to be.

"Does his wife know about you?"

"No way! We have to be super careful. He's much too prominent. We simply cannot afford for anyone to suspect us. There's even some rumor that he will be asked to run for president on the Democratic ticket. You can image what a problem it would be for him if it were to get out that he's having an affair."

"Don't affairs and politics go together?" I snorted. "I thought from what I've read that he's a Republican."

"He was, but he switched."

"Okay, back to the issue at hand. Do you love him?"

"I might." She shrugged. That had been well over two years before I met Maurice. Now she and her man were deeply involved and she was hoping to marry him. He had arranged a job for her in New York with a well-known ad agency that was doing business with him for the financial corporation he headed. This gave them an excuse for her to travel in the entourage when he went on speaking engagements and business trips. Margot had moved to a midtown apartment in Manhattan, selling the property in Miami. When I talked with her, I could tell she was very happy and felt that this man was the love of her life. She respected his business acumen, his intelligence and the aura of power he exuded. In some ways, they seemed to have found a complementary other. He was powerful and accomplished. While she could bring nothing of that to the table, she did bring a fun, charismatic personality. Margot made him laugh. He needed her light hearted and youthful exuberance and happiness. I wondered if she needed the adoring father figure who gave her a magic new world of glamour and power, a new stage on which to perform her life dance. The only fly in the ointment appeared to be that Margot harbored growing feelings of unease about his older daughter who had promoted their relationship initially. But now, as the two of them were growing closer, the daughter saw Margot as an unwelcome rival for daddy's affection, just as her mother had been. The dynamics for a disaster were in place, could she have but known the serious implications of this daughter–father relationship. With the new job and new life, she had not seen Maurice since a few weeks after our conversation many long months before.

Maurice was still in pain, raw and fresh and he poured his rage and obsession out to me that night in Rome. His spat the words as though they were laced with the taste of bitter gall, his face a mask of agony. I have never suffered a lack of imagination, so it took little effort for bizarre images to begin forming in my brain. As he continued ranting, I felt a growing fear that he would do something rash, perhaps go to the States and try to kill Tony. For while he was furious with her, it was against her lover that he vented his greatest hatred.

"Maurice, if you love her as much as you say you do, you don't want to hurt her by hurting someone she loves. It wouldn't make her love you. Just the opposite: she would hate you for it. You don't want that."

"Why not? She deserves to be hurt after what she has put me through. Does *she* care that *I* am hurt? You don't know the *deceit*...how she got down on her knees the last time I saw her and kissed my hands and swore she loved me and would be back in two weeks and we'd be married. She *lied* and she *stole* the diamond earrings I was going to give her for a wedding present." He slammed his fist hard into the sofa.

We were sitting in his hotel room at the Jolly overlooking the darkened pines of the Villa Borghese gardens. I was growing seriously frightened by the depth of his fury. I even began to wonder if I were safe or if he would try to hurt me to get back at her. I knew the earrings that he referred to. She had wanted them for over a year...almost three perfect carats in each ear. They were stunning and surely very expensive. Through the time I knew him, the earrings continued to rankle. Later he told me that he hoped that some day, Beth would have the diamonds. It is an ironic twist of fate, that at my death, indeed she will.

According to his version of the gift, it seems he had agreed to buy them for her as a wedding gift but they were to be presented on their honeymoon. He had arranged for a tray of diamonds...loaned by his cousin, a jeweler...to be ready for her to select from when she arrived on her next trip over. According to him, she palmed the earrings she liked from the tray and neither he nor his cousin realized they were missing until later. He had to pay for them of course. Later when I told her what he had said, she vehemently denied the whole scenario, swearing that he had given them to her then and there, no strings attached.

The more he talked the deeper my realization of his despair. He walked over to the desk on the wall opposite the sofa. On the desk was a large, red leather soft-sided suitcase with black leather clasp and bindings. It was obviously not new as the bindings were fraying. Equally obvious was the fact that it was stuffed to bursting. He unzipped and flung back the top of the suitcase exposing the contents. There were no clothes in it...only paper, every line she had ever written him, a copy of every letter he had sent her or any of us in her family, receipts, and photos. As well, he had diaries in which he had written every phone conversation he had had with her and later with me, every thought about her, every *imagined* conversation he had held with her since they had broken up nearly two years previously. The more he pulled from that bag, the more it looked like Pandora's box. He shoved fist after fist full of receipts into my startled face...receipts for every item he had purchased for her, every cent she had cost him in meals, hotels, entertainment, whatever. I was appalled.

I needed air badly. Walking to the window, I opened it and leaned out. A street was directly below, six floors down. Hastily I pulled my head back in and crossed over to sit on the bed. I wished badly to be safely in my own hotel room. I looked at Maurice, and without thinking blurted the first thing that popped into my mind...a failing of mine.

"This is sick!" I was frightened at myself the moment I said it. In his present state of mind, I didn't know what might tip him over the edge into total irrationality or violence.

"*Sick!*" He yelled at me. "Yes, by God! I am sick...sick in my soul from the lies, the treachery. Why wouldn't I be? I have lived for the past two years with this eating my insides like acid on a wound." He waved his hand at the case and then whirling, he stalked to it and slammed it shut. In a low growl, he promised, "She will pay! She is the very *devil*, I tell you. She is *possessed* by demons."

"Put away those papers. Throw them away. They're like a sore that you keep picking the scab from; it only deepens and grows worse. You have to stop this, get over her, and get on with your life or this will kill you."

"I cannot! I am obsessed by her and what she has done to me."

"Yes, I think you *are* obsessed. But in English, the word has negative connotations...an unhealthy sick emotion which is not based on facts or real love at all."

"Jo, I'm not English! I am French and part Corsican. We don't see obsession that way. And we know how to hate and how to avenge!"

"What good are hate and revenge if you only hurt yourself more in the process. You will be the biggest loser if you continue this way. Can't you see that it's stealing your life away from you?"

"This travesty against me cannot go unanswered. You must help me. Tell me what you know of this man."

"I don't know anything, Maurice, except that she's in love with him. You won't get her back by hurting him in someway."

"I don't want her back! I hate her and I pity her. She is beneath my contempt. But she must pay for the pain she has caused. She has killed my soul and left me mad with grief. It is the dishonesty of it that hurts most of all. How do I forget that? How do I forgive that?"

"Please don't do this. You say you love my parents and me. Have we caused you harm? Are we to pay, too? Don't you see that anything that you do to hurt her will also hurt us? Do we deserve to pay for the wrong that you feel she did you? Will any of this anger make it better or bring her back?"

I could read in his eyes that he had not thought of those questions. It seemed to jolt him and I hastened to take advantage of the momentary hesitation. I talked on rapidly, dwelling on how innocent people would be hurt if this rage continued and he acted on it. In the end he was calm, and while he never agreed that he wouldn't cause problems for her, he did agree to wait until I could find a way to help him see her. I promised that to buy time, but I knew it was one promise I would never keep. I felt that I had done the best that I could to help him, help Margot, and to avoid harm to her man. More than that, I couldn't do. I was limp with relief and exhaustion when suddenly he changed tack.

"So, what is going on with you in your marriage? I want you to leave that man. He's no good for you anymore than Margot was for me. Don't stay and let him hurt you the way I have been hurt."

"I want to leave him. I have for a long time, but it's not so simple. On a teacher's salary I can't afford to do a great deal. I have Beth to consider. When I married Tom Crippins, her father refused to continue paying child support and he never was reliable anyway. Moving is expensive. A place to live in a decent neighborhood is expensive. At the moment I feel trapped. We co-exist in the same house like strangers but it's no marriage. I don't think it ever was." I didn't tell him that my husband and I lived in separate bedrooms and had little communication with one another.

"Do you love him? Are you happy? Impossible from what you have told me and are telling me now."

"At one time, I cared for him but I was never truly in love with him. He just wore me down asking and I finally said yes. After that I am not sure he even wanted me anymore. In a way, I suspect he was determined to get me just because I had been so elusive...a challenge that once he conquered he no longer needed. I suppose I was frightened financially, wasn't meeting anyone any better and just gave up...decided to settle."

"Jo, surely you realize that lack of money won't keep you trapped if you want out? I'll help you, gladly. I'll give you the money you need to move and find another place to live. I do not want you and Beth to stay with him."

"I can't ask you to do that. Hasn't my family cost you enough already?"

"You didn't ask. I offered. You're my sister and I love you. I will help you and your child in every way that I can. When you became my family, you became my responsibility. Margot talked so often of Beth that I began to feel that she's my child, too. I have adopted her in my heart. I know that she is the child I will never have. I need that in my life. Please don't deny me that."

Margot had often teased me that Beth was really her daughter. She felt that they looked more alike than Beth and I do. They did. She had no children of her own and that seemed to help assuage her maternal hunger since at thirty-three her biological clock was ticking a reminder. They had shopped for gifts for Beth during the time they dated and Beth had been thrilled to open those surprise packages. I began to surmise that in some way, Maurice was sublimating his thwarted love for my sister to 'their' daughter. He seemed desperate for that last chance at a pure love in his life and someone to whom he could leave his heritage.

When we finally finished talking that night, it was after two in the morning. He drove me to my hotel and kissed me goodnight and goodbye on each check. Then he gave me his big surprise. Beth and I were to come to him for the summer. He would cover all expenses and make all arrangements. I was too drained from the histrionics of the evening to be thrilled then. Later my spirits soared at the prospect and maybe my fantasies too.

The next morning, our group left for two nights in Capri, Pompeii, Sorrento and then on to Greece for the final three nights of the tour. He called the hotel each night to assure me of his devotion, to express gratitude for my friendship and to pledge his determination to be my refuge. I came to depend on him for all of that...maybe too much. He made my life easier, bought me luxuries, gave me wonderful memories, taught me so much and made me greedy for more in my life...more in every way. That brings its own perils.

Chapter 2

A good as his word, he sent me the money, fifteen thousand dollars. By late May, I had rented a townhouse and moved. Maurice called frequently to give his support in what he knew was a difficult time for me. I felt and still feel immense gratitude to him for giving me another chance with my life. He was truly my salvation in a desperate plight. The brightest spot in all of this was my elation at the prospect of spending the summer in Europe. I also suspected it would make the emotional break from the disaster of my short and unhappy marriage easier to bear, as well as bring me all of the pleasures of discovery inherent to visiting so many of the places of my dreams. I spent my time after work in the flurry of the move and once that was done, in research of the areas Maurice had said we would visit. I studied my French dictionaries and grammars, and bought the things we would need for our two months away. It was only when I crawled exhausted into my bed each evening that I felt a hurting in the secret places of my heart. I was alone again. I despised the thought of the superficiality of the dating scene but knew that unless I wanted to remain alone, it was something I would eventually have to face. While I dreamed of a future with Maurice, in the cold light of day, I did not see it happening.

Beth was not elated at the idea of spending an entire summer away from everyone and everything she knew except for me. She was too young to appreciate the magnitude of the gift of a summer in Europe. For her, France was about as vague a concept in terms of place and location as the moon. But at least she had seen the moon and knew where to find it. It was with grumbling and grudging acceptance that she packed her bag and organized the things she wanted with her during her time away. I was afraid that she would hold Maurice responsible for this disruption in her life.

Jaynie was a real lifesaver to me during this time and we were fast becoming the best of friends.   Since she customarily spent every summer abroad visiting a wide circle of acquaintances, when she learned that I would be going to France, she arranged to spend some time with me there.   Maurice had procured an apartment for me in the small Provençal town of St. Remy, famous for the ancient Roman ruins of the town of Glanum and the Van Gogh painting Starry Night, created while he was hospitalized there in the monastery hospital of St. Paul de Mausole.   Maurice told me his business obligations would keep him tied up until after the middle of July when he would be free to travel with Beth and me.   The idea of a month alone in a small town in the south of France was intimidating to me at the time; now it would be heavenly.   When Jaynie offered to spend a week with me to help me acclimate, I was delighted.

Three days prior to my departure, she left for Paris to visit with a friend of hers there, Erica Perez, a doctor.   In the meantime I was waiting in nervous agony for the arrival of the promised tickets that Maurice had arranged for his agent to send me.   They had not arrived by the day of departure, so at the last minute it was arranged that I would pick up the prepaid tickets at the various ticket counters along the way.   I wasn't too happy with the solution, but with no choice, we set out on our journey.   What a hassle it was to sweat at every stop getting tickets from poorly informed ticket agents who resented the computer time and inconvenience it required.   We also had to change carriers three different times.   The hairiest segment was Brussels where we arrived with only fifteen minutes until departure of the flight to Paris.   Grabbing Beth by one hand and my hand luggage by the other, I did a marathon, heart-pumping run down what has to be one of the world's longest moving walkways.   We arrived panting at the ticket counter only to learn that our tickets were being held for us on another floor.   The agent there took pity, called the gate and then sent a runner upstairs to retrieve them.   Otherwise, no doubt I would still be in Brussels, permanently planted in the pauper's cemetery.   We dashed onto the plane, which was rolling down the runway before we reached our last row seats. No matter, I was so relieved at making the flight I would have ridden in baggage. Which our luggage didn't. It had not had time to make the transfer. Feeling I deserved some in flight tranquilizing wine, I stumbled through customs about three sheets in the wind. Jaynie was waiting for us when we walked into the terminal without our luggage.

"You're traveling light for a month in Europe, aren't you?"

I groaned, not sure if it was from hangover or lack of luggage, "It's a long story."

She had a taxi waiting but I had business to conduct before I could go to the hotel where Maurice had reserved rooms for us. Our first stop was the Société du Crédit de Marseilles, where he had wired a thousand dollars to cover our expenses in Paris and the month in St. Rémy. From there we next went to the travel agency, Havas, to pick up the   arranged rail tickets for the TGV, Train Grande Vitesse, for the following Monday that would take us from Paris to Avignon. There I would collect the car from a garage near the station and drive the three of us to the hotel apartment in St. Rémy.

When we finally arrived at the Hotel Royale Monceau, Beth and I were exhausted. Particularly me, since I didn't sleep on the plane...I never have learned how as I can't seem to turn off the adrenalin of excitement. On the way to the room, we had the chance to appreciate the architecture and decor of the grand old hotel. When we reached the room, I was pleased to note the Recamier period antiques. Jaynie did not stay long as we both wanted a shower and a nap, so she returned to her friend Erica's. I suspected that while Beth might nap, I was much too excited to at last be in Paris, city of my dreams, to waste that time napping. Nevertheless, we both showered and changed into the plush terry cloth robes we found hanging in the bathroom. Neither of us could face the prospect of re-donning the clothes we had worn for over twenty-four hours straight.

The phone rang. I was across the room from the twin beds that were pushed together to make a king sized one and for whatever reason I decided to prance across them to answer it. Unfortunately when I stepped down on the far side, there was a protrusive railing waiting for me. My leg hit it forcefully, immediately raising a huge and painful hematoma. Cursing under my breath, I grabbed the phone just as it stopped ringing.

"Hello!"

"*Allo*, Jo. At last you are in Paris. I am so happy to have you back so close to me. How are you? Did you have a good trip?"

Biting my lip to keep from crying with pain, I replied. "Actually, I just hurt my leg on the bed and I have a huge lump where it hit, so right this minute I don't feel too great."

"Is it broken? Do you need a doctor?"

"No. It just hurts and it looks nasty."

"You must go to the pharmacy and get a homeopathic Arnica preparation from them that will reduce the bruising and make it heal more quickly. There is a large pharmacy just up the street from the hotel. If you ask the pharmacist, he will show you what you need. Please go and get that when we hang up."

"I would but we are waiting for our luggage so we can change clothes."

"What happened?"

The plane was late leaving New York so we almost didn't make the Brussels connection to Paris. Unfortunately our bags didn't make it on with us. We still don't have them but I called the airport and they promised to send them by taxi when they arrive. We are sitting here in hotel bathrobes waiting to get some clean clothes."

"They're really excellent about that so try not to worry. I am sure the bags will arrive soon. Did you get to the bank and to the Agence Havas?"

"Yes, we did that before coming to the hotel. Thank you so much for arranging the tickets and the money for us."

"You are welcome, Darling. And remember the hotel should be charged to me. I have stayed there often and the staff knows me so it should not be a problem. The money is for you to use for other expenses in Paris and for you to have in St. Remy." He paused, "Are you tired?"

"Very.   It was so hectic getting moved, giving exams and finalizing grades at school, and then arranging everything so I could be gone for two months. We're just resting this afternoon and hoping that our bags will come so we can find somewhere to eat before so very late. If not, we'll just order room service."

"That's good. You should rest and sleep well so you will feel like exploring tomorrow. There is so much for you to see. You must go to the Louvre, Nôtre Dame, the Tuilleries, the Eiffel Tower, the Orangerie, the Centre Pompidou and the Jue de Paume...all of the tourist things. You should also try the Bateau Mouche. It is really lovely to see Paris from the river and I think Beth would enjoy it a lot. It also saves your feet, darling. While you are near the Seine, cross over to the left bank and see some of the art supply shops, bookstores and galleries. You are going to love it all. Will your friend, Jaynie Grantland, be with you?"

"She was here earlier but she has gone back to her friend's for now. She'll be back later and will be with us tomorrow. As you know, I also asked her to spend the first week in St. Remy with us so we will all go together by train. She picked up a ticket as well while we were at the Agence Havas."

"Good! Is Beth there?"

"Yes. She's right beside me."

"I'd like to speak to her, please. And Jo, I'll call back later to check if your luggage arrived. If not, I will try to pull some strings from here."

"Thanks, Maurice. Here's Beth."

I looked at her and she rolled her eyes. She was not happy about having to talk to him. She was very shy and having never met him, did not know how to carry on a conversation with a stranger. She also had not forgiven him for taking her away from her home and friends for the two long months to come.

I mouthed, "Please." to her and she grudgingly took the phone. Her conversation consisted almost solely of "yes" and "no" or monosyllabic answers and head nods. I mimed to her that silent nods did not communicate over the phone line. She shrugged at me. When they were off the phone, she turned to me with exasperation apparent in her expression.

"Mommy! I didn't know what to say to him. I've never even met him."

"I know, Baby. He just wants to hear your voice. He feels especially close to you because all of the things that Aunt Margot told him about you."

"But I don't feel close to him!"

"I know, Honey. I do understand."

We sat in the window overlooking the Avenue Hoche, one half block from the Champs Elysées and the Arc de Triomphe. I wanted so much to be out there in Paris, but the thought of those same wrinkled and smelly clothes was repugnant. I did not relish the idea of introducing myself to Paris, fashion capitol of the world, in rumpled and tacky attire. Fortunately in late afternoon, the desk called to say that the luggage had arrived and a porter was on the way up with it. We were at the door waiting when he rolled it down the hall. As soon as we closed the door behind him, we tore into the suitcases and assembled fresh clothing for our entrance into the life of the city. Jaynie called as we were dressing to beg off for the evening. Beth and I were on our own. We finished dressing and walked down the street until we found a bistro that captured our attention. I stopped to read the posted menu, and salivating with anticipation, we entered. I was finally in Paris, in a foreign country, knew little of the language, wasn't sure of the money and prices, and had an eleven year old child to keep entertained and happy. Small stuff! By damn, I was in Paris.

The bistro seemed terribly French and therefore heavenly. Since I've now eaten in France in many fine restaurants, I know that while the food was adequate by French standards, it wasn't exceptional. I was hungry, it was Paris, and I didn't care. It was delicious. Besides, by Raleigh standards at the time, it was gourmet fare. I was so impressed with myself when I could say "L'addition, s'il vous plaît" at the end of the meal. Beth giggled at my sally into the world of French. Although it was almost ten in the evening when we left the bistro, there was still enough daylight to see. It took me days to adjust to the much longer length of the summer day in France, which ended much later than that at home. I was just one more thing to add to my list of those that made France unique from North Carolina. By the time we reached our room, we were tired and very ready for bed. Just as I was beginning to drift into sleep, the phone rang. Maurice was calling to wish us good night. I didn't stay on the line long as he could tell from my responses that I was half asleep.

The next morning, I walked to the window and threw it open to a perfect sunny and cool June day. The breakfast we had ordered the night before arrived as I was standing there. I opened the door to the aroma of fresh croissants and cappuchino. Rousing Beth, we quickly devoured the food. She decided on the spot that this first experience with room service would not be the last. As we were munching the delightfully light and flaky croissants, the phone rang. It was Jaynie, again canceling for the day. I suspected she did not want to do the tourist routine with us, so we made plans to meet for dinner instead. No sooner had I returned the phone to the hook, than it rang again. This time Maurice was calling to wish us a good morning and to detail our itinerary for the day. I listened politely, but I knew that our time and energy would not begin to encompass all he envisioned. Furthermore, both Beth and I wanted to see the famous Rue du Faubourg Saint-Honoré and its legendary shops. He had not even considered that worthy of mention.

Shortly after we hung up, Beth and I were dressed and awaiting a taxi. When the doorman handed us in, I requested a detour past the Eiffel Tower on our way to Nôtre Dame. The driver slowed at the tower so we could crane our necks at the famous view. From there we continued down the left bank of the Seine past scores of quay-side stalls, packed with tourist inspired "art" as we approached the landmark cathedral. At the front where he left us, the driver pointed out the star on the pavement from which all distances are measured in France.

I played tour guide to Beth for the next few hours. Although I had never before been in Paris, years of studying and teaching art history, and my love of art and geography, gave me considerable resources to fill the role. From Nôtre Dame, we walked to the Louvre. It was a must for me to see the Venus de Milo, the Nike of Samothrace, the Mona Lisa and the hundreds of masterpieces I had so long craved experiencing first hand. With a full heart, I left the Louvre with Beth in tow. We ambled through the Tuileries past street vendors who vied with the view to take our attention. It was at the Jeu de Paume that I found a long awaited fulfillment of my love affair with the Impressionists. It was apparent that it found a new fan in Beth who exclaimed over the art as we wandered in leisure past a roll call of late nineteenth century artists. At the Orangerie, she was enchanted by Monet's famous Nymphéas series. I was pleased that she was enjoying herself, as I did not want it to be a day that was all about my interests and me.

Leaving the Orangerie, we strolled down to the Rue Montaigne where we found a lovely flower bedecked sidewalk cafe with an enticing menu. I think at that point she was as ready as I to sit and give our feet a rest. When we left the cafe with energy restored, the shop windows of such designers as Dior, Chanel, Gucci, and Hermes awaited us. The Rue du Faubourg St. Honoré was a fairyland of enticing boutiques. Beth, who loves beautiful things as much as I lit up like a Christmas tree. That was the moment she fell in love with Paris. We had had enough culture for the day, next was some material gratification. Fortunately I had scrimped prior to departure so I had a few dollars with which we could treat ourselves. I splurged some of my largesse on a Hermes scarf which was only forty-five dollars at the time, not the nearly four hundred that it costs today, and a pair of Charles Jourdan shoes that were on sale...very high heels, of course. Beth found a colorful yellow, orange and blue shorts and blouse set that were perfect for her.

My feet were on fire from all of the walking...naturally I was in heels. I may have been walking my way into a wheel chair, but I've always said I'll do it in style. At any rate, it was obviously time for a stop. We rounded the corner onto the Rue Castiglione and headed for the bar of the Intercontinental Hotel. The interior was rich in dark woods and wine colored banquettes and small Louis XVI style chairs at little round marble top tables. At that time, you could also buy lunch, light meal items, as well as gorgeous desserts from a rolling cart. It was wine and an empty chair for me so I could slide off my shoes and prop up my feet. Beth opted for a Coca Cola. At five dollars a glass, it was a good thing that it came with chips as well. I was to learn that invariably Coke was more expensive than the house wine. It was interesting to discover over the course of the summer, that waiters constantly and sneeringly referred to it as American Champagne. Apparently California's wine reputation had not yet crossed the Atlantic.

Despite the wine, or maybe because of it, when we left my tail feathers were dragging. Undauntedly brave shopper that I am, I still mustered the energy to cross the street to Catherine's for a bottle of Fracas cologne, a wonderfully Gardenia scented fragrance. We walked the short half block from there to the Rue de Rivoli and made a right turn to begin the walk to the Champs Elysées and the hotel on Avenue Hoche. We made it only as far as the American Embassy, before I called it quits. Beth didn't quibble when I hailed a passing taxi and announced: "We ride!"

Back in the room we quickly plopped on the bed, exhausted from the day's excursions. Jaynie called to make arrangements for us to meet for dinner. When I hung up, Beth begged to be allowed to stay in the hotel and have room service. That and an early bedtime sounded heavenly to her and truth be told, to me as well. When the French onion soup, crusty baguette, and an icy glass of Coke arrived, Beth sealed her infatuation with Paris and her utter devotion to room service. While she ate her supper, I dressed in an elegant pink crepe dress I'd found at my favorite designer shop, the local Saks outlet.

Kissing Beth goodnight and giving her instructions for staying alone, I went down to a waiting taxi. My feet were too sore to walk back to the Intercontinental where we were to meet.

Jaynie was waiting in the atrium lobby, her head swiveling like a swinging door, checking out the passing scenery. I joined her and soon I was eyeing the passing attractions as well. Based on the number of handsome men without women in tow, we decided it was an excellent place for dinner, especially if a couple of those gorgeous men would invite us to join them in doing so. Neither of us was so flush with funds that we could ignore that option. However we were going broke on drinks when we gave up and decided to have dinner in the courtyard restaurant. We ordered sparingly, conscious of our wallets. Almost a hundred dollars later, two gorgeous men found us. I thought they would have looked even better had they found us before dinner. They asked if they could join us and we indicated the two vacant places at the table. I'm tall so the taller of the two, addressed himself to me. Jaynie, a short but stunning redhead with a cuddly look about her, had an instant slave judging by the admiring stare of the shorter man. We chatted for a while over after dinner drinks before agreeing to accompany them to their favorite restaurant.

Dinner again! They were French Moroccans and their favorite hour to dine was late and their favorite restaurant, Arabian, with belly dancers for appetizers. After watching them for a while that night, I figured out which appetite was getting whetted. The belly dancers served one critical need: they eliminated the necessity for heavy conversation. The men spoke broken English, I spoke mangled French, and Jaynie spoke "Oui!" which I figured was about enough to get us into major trouble.

The waiters began to bring the food until dish after dish filled the table. Wine bottles were liberally scattered among the food. The dancers were gyrating. But there was no silverware. I watched the others who plucked what they wanted from the dishes and began eating with their fingers, following suit since our earlier dinner had been sketchy, I discovered that the spicy food was delicious. It was a good thing that American fashion, I was keeping my left hand under the table. Jaynie later told me that the left hand is considered unclean by Arabs for reasons having to do with their ancient toilet habits. As tired as I was, I wasn't in danger of breaking too many rules of etiquette anyway. By two in the morning, I was flagging and my date's increasingly amorous overtures were irritating. Deciding desperate measures were called for, I requested pen and paper from the waiter. My three companions were watching me in puzzlement. Carefully pondering which French words and sentence structures I could write with some degree of accuracy, I penned a note which I will translate: "I am a widow. My husband is dead. I have a daughter who is alone at the hotel. I do not like to leave her so late as she is young. I must go fast to see if she is okay. Please take me there now. Thank you."

I hoped the widow bit would elicit some sympathy and by leaving Beth's age vague, they could imagine her as young as they wished. At any rate, the minute my "date" read the note, he called for the check and Jaynie and I were hustled out to his car. He drove Jaynie and the other man to corners that were mutually convenient for them and then took me to the Royale Monceau. When we arrived, he parked the car just down from the lights of the hotel entry.

He gave me his business card, which showed that he was an attorney for an agency on the Champs Elysées. "I would like to see you tomorrow night for dinner. It is a date, yes?" He was handsome, successful, romantic. I said yes which encouraged him to offer me a late, late night tour of la belle Paris. I declined repeatedly with one foot dangling out the door of the car. He accepted the postponement of his ardor and escorted me to the door where he gave me a goodbye kiss much to the prurient delight of the doorman.

Wearily I went up to my room to find a note propped on my pillow: "Mommy, Maurice called. I missed you. I love you. Mwaa! Baby." Mwaa is her word for love and kisses. I don't know where she picked it up but we still use it even though she is now nearly as old as I was then.

Long before I was ready to awaken the next morning, the phone jangled me into the day. I stumbled around the bed to answer the phone before it stopped ringing.

"Jo, good morning. I trust you had a pleasant evening?" Did I hear a faint tinge of jealousy in his voice, I wondered.

"Yes, I did. Thank you." I wasn't about to elaborate and he was too proud to pry.

He asked about our previous day's sightseeing and our plans for the day. I mumbled what I suppose were reasonably intelligent replies, said *"au revoir"* to his promise to call later and re-sought my interrupted sleep.

At eleven-thirty, Jaynie called and I invited her to the hotel for lunch since they had a Sunday buffet in the dining room. It was a beautifully trellised garden room and I was eager to dine there. Lunch was to prove marvelous but far more expensive than I had expected. I charged it to the tab and hoped Maurice would have neither heart failure nor the urge to kill. After lunch we left to see the Gustave Klimpt and Egon Schiele exhibit which Jaynie and I had both been anticipating.

The exhibit provided to be most interesting to Beth, since all were drawings of adolescent or prepubescent girls and nearly all were very erotic in feeling. Her sex education *á la Paris*, much to my chagrin, was greatly enhanced when we emerged into the sunlight in time to greet the beginning of a parade of France's proud sons and daughters of the gay liberation movement decked out in some of the most bizarre get-ups I have ever seen. I covered Beth's eyes with my hands but gave up when she spread my fingers to peep between them. By then, the Klimpt's seemed tame in the extreme. When the parade had passed, much to my relief, since it appeared that some of the more vigorous and insinuating hip thrusts and jeers had been demonstrated specifically for our edification, we headed for a sidewalk cafe and a supper of croque monsieur sandwiches. While we sat there eating them, I could not help remarking to Jaynie that while it wasn't my life style, and I had no objections to theirs...to each his own...I did not see that parade as a celebration of a diverse way of living so much as a vulgar sexual display that would have been vulgar regardless of who was involved. After the sandwiches, we split up: Jaynie going to Erica's to pretty up for dinner, and Beth and I back to the hotel so I could bathe and dress.

On the way in, I stopped at the concierge's desk to cancel my date for the evening. Giving him the card that had been pressed into my hand the evening before, I asked him to call for me and say that I had to leave Paris a day early and regretted I would be unable to keep our appointment. Palming my tip, he grinned like a close ally and assured me the gentleman was history.

With dinner and a room service Coke to comfort Beth, a phone call from Maurice to comfort him, and a nice long shower to comfort me, I was prepared for another night in Paris. I was looking forward to the fun of playing with a girlfriend and enjoying a light flirtatious evening without any demands on me. It had been a long time since I had enjoyed that kind of fun. Growing up the eldest of the children, I had been expected to be serious, responsible and studious to the point of being cloistered. Such simple fun was something with which I was little experienced. Except for Jaynie, the only other person with whom I could play and be silly was Margot. After the heavy and unpleasant emotions of the past few months, I wanted to spread my wings unencumbered by male expectations and demands and simply *be*.

Jaynie was waiting for me in the hotel bar, where we decided to sip a glass of wine and plan our evening itinerary. When I passed the concierge desk to join her, I noticed the shift had changed and regretted that I had not thanked the earlier concierge for making the call for me. It was unnecessary I was to learn, as the new concierge appeared in the doorway just as we were paying our tab.

"Madame, you have a gentleman caller. Shall I send him in here?"

"Oh, no! Please *don't*. Just tell him that I was called from Paris early and am no longer here." So much for a wasted tip, I thought.

"As you wish, Madame."

"Thank you, Merci." We watched through the drapes until my date left, then dashed out to a taxi.

When we were settled, the driver turned to us expectantly.

"Where are we going, Jaynie?"

"I don't know where to go. How about you?"

"I don't know. I thought you did."

"Well, I don't."

"All right. *Nous voudrions aller á l'Hotel Intercontinental, s'il vous plaît.*" I turned to Jaynie, "Okay?"

"*Oui.*" She grinned.

Since we couldn't afford dinner and the sandwich had taken the edge from our appetites, we opted for the hotel's American Bar where they featured a pianist. We took a table close to the piano and soon had the pianist's attention. The place was nearly empty so it was unlikely we would garner any other. He played several requests, dedicated a few numbers to us, and during his break came over and whispered that he would like to buy us a drink. We whispered back our acceptance, wondering why we were all whispering. At the next break, he introduced himself and began to tell us of the marvels of the hotel, offering to give us a tour of the splendors of the ballroom and meeting rooms.

"That would be lovely." We both cooed in unison. So, with one of us on each arm, and the pianist on his tiptoes between...he was even shorter than Jaynie...off we went. The rooms were exquisitely Baroque, impressive in their gilt encrusted grandeur. He was an informed and pleasant guide, increasingly more friendly and animated, taking turns flirting with Jaynie and then me. It was obvious he couldn't decide on which of us to concentrate his attentions.

In the last room, he switched off the lights just after we entered. Jaynie and I were both stunned and instantly wary. I heard a shuffle and a rustle of fabric and then Jaynie emphatically saying "NO!" He either had the eyes of a cat...or radar, for the next thing I knew his arms were around me and I could feel his breath approaching the protuberant area of my chest. He must have been on tiptoe again. I stepped out of his reach, echoing Jaynie's "NO!" There were some more shuffles and rustles and Jaynie again saying no. Having had enough, I started slapping the wall for the switch. I flipped it on about the same time he grabbed my rump for a squeeze. I leaped up, landing hard on his toes. That seemed to supply the needed discouragement. Totally unruffled, he continued his dialogue on the hotel's attributes as Jaynie and I hastened away. Inch for inch and pound for pound, he may have been the "ballsy-est" little guy I have ever met. As for us, we had had enough of the evening's *nightlife*.

The morning of our last day in Paris arrived much too quickly. Beth and I packed and I called the desk to have them prepare the bill for our checkout. Maurice called to say that he would phone the receptionist to arrange for the bill to be forwarded to him for payment. However when I reached the desk to turn in my key, I was presented with a bill for $758 and a polite but firm request to pay. They regretted to inform me that due to a change of management, they would be unable to accommodate Maurice's request. After paying, I was nearly broke and more than a little upset by the size of the bill. I hated to have to tell Maurice that his thousand dollars were nearly spent.

Jaynie arrived with a taxi and we join her for the trip to the Gare du Lyon to catch the TGV...Train Grande Vitesse...to Avignon. Riding to the station, I watched those charmed streets of Paris slipping past the window like grains of sand through a child's sieve. I promised myself that I would sift through those streets yet again. It was and is the most beautiful city I know. Despite many returns, I don't think my appetite for it can ever be sated.

The train was sleek, modern, clean and very fast. The trip to Avignon went quickly, the passing landscape but a blur. We had time to wander into the dining car for Cokes and sandwiches before it was time to gather our belongings and step off onto the quay in Avignon. Although a couple of other people also left the train at our stop, we were so pre-occupied with the luggage that we failed to notice where they had gone. The train left, the other passengers had left, and we were left not knowing where to go. We could see the station across the three or four sets of tracks but couldn't see how to get there. We didn't dare cross the tracks themselves. We could hear another train blasting down the track and knew we could not begin to move that rapidly, especially with our luggage. In our ignorance we had no way of knowing the peril of the electrified tracks.

"Jaynie, how do we get over there and how do we move this mountain of luggage?"

"Oh Lord, I don't know! What happened to the others?"

"There were only two others and I didn't see where they went. I swear the earth swallowed them." It had. Two men from across the way saw our confusion and came to the rescue, popping up from an unobtrusive underground passageway to indicate we should follow. Neither of them spoke any English, but when we gestured helplessly to our luggage, they realized our predicament and wordlessly shouldered the heaviest portion of the burden. When we reached the station exit, we tried to indicate to our rescuers that we would like to give them a tip but with a bow of exquisite gallantry, they refused.

The next step was to collect the car so we could begin the drive to St. Remy. I fished for the instructions Maurice had carefully dictated to me.

"Jaynie, why don't you and Beth wait here with the luggage and I'll bring the car. The garage I have to find is supposed to be just a block or so from here down on the right."

"Don't worry! I'm not about to truck this junk if I don't have to." Jaynie sank wearily onto a heap of luggage and Beth perched beside her. The tension and confusion of the last few minutes had unnerved us all.

Finding the garage was no problem. Getting a car from them was. Some very nice men, all smiling broadly and speaking rapidly in French, staffed it. I quickly surmised they spoke no English. As best I could, I introduced myself and explained my mission, praying for comprehension. They looked at one another; lifting their shoulders in a Gallic shrug, they shook their heads.   I tried again.   More puzzlement. We were beginning to draw a crowd of chattering and gesticulating Frenchmen. Raising the volume, both sides tried again. One bright fellow among the on-lookers suddenly struck his head. Ah, hah: illumination! A few more gestures, heads nodding...mine and theirs, a few more "s'il vous plaît's", "oui's" and "Merci's" and a few more anxious minutes later, they led me down deep into the tenebrous bowels of the earth. Indicating the car, they began a rapid-fire explanation of its features. At least that's what I think they were doing as they were pointing to various parts of the car. Since we weren't communicating so well topside, I didn't see why they would think this unbroken volley of French was going to sink in. Finishing with a flourish, I was given the keys and a document to sign.

The car was mine. Never before had I driven this type of car, a white, sparkling, undented, new VW Golfe. It was a straight shift, and I was a long spiral upward ramp away from daylight, and I was in a foreign country. Pulling up my figurative bootstraps, I eased myself behind the wheel and just sat. I had the shakes. After several minutes with all those anxious faces peering in, curious as to why I hadn't left, I got it started. So far, so good. With a few grinding attempts, I got it into gear...third, and aimed for the ramp. It stalled in front of my audience of gaping men. Grinding the gears again, with a hop, skip and a jump, I started up the ramp with them trotting anxiously behind. Had they known how worried I was it would stall again and roll backwards, I think they might have exercised greater caution. It was not a graceful ascent, punctuated as it was with fitful jerks, but I arrived at the street only to realize that it was one way going away from the station. I signaled to turn as they gathered to wave me off.

I was not happy. I didn't have a clue where the one way away from the station would take me but I had no choice but to go. Fortunately the street circled the ancient walls of the town, past the Palais du Pape and then returned to the station. I turned in and was crowded by the cars behind me into the wrong lane and promptly belched out onto a side street with no left turn. Several miles later, I was back at the station and this time managed to get into the right lane. I could tell by the expressions on Beth and Jaynie's faces they had fully resigned themselves to permanent abandonment.

The minute I lurched to a stop, Jaynie grabbed the door handle. "What happened??" Obviously she wasn't about to let me go past twice.

"It's a long story." And a longer detour, I might have added. I climbed out, my knees shaking, and headed to the back to open the trunk. Right! After ten minutes of unproductive fumbling and a growing line of horn-honking cars lined up in the rear, the man immediate behind whipped out of his car and stalked up to me. With a glare and a flourish, he jiggled the key, slapped the button and the trunk flew up. He didn't give me time to thank him, merely whirled around and stomped back to his car flicking a cigarette butt disgustedly to the ground. Judging from his expression, tone, and the few less than complimentary and understandable words, I gathered that 'male chauvinist pigs" aren't a species limited to the good old USA. We heaved the luggage in and again I was back on that damned side street which I didn't want as I had no clue where it went. The "pig" honked his horn and blew past as I dithered along. Good riddance. I eventually returned to the main circular street that divides the old walled town from the newer periphery.

"I'm thirsty, Mommy."

Jaynie sighed in a dying voice, "So am I. Let's stop for a Coke." Both she and Beth were avid aficionados of American champagne.

"Fine. I need to collect my wits and figure out how to get out of this town and to St. Rémy." And I needed a calming glass of wine. A block or so past my garage, we pulled up to a cafe, trudged in and collapsed at a table: three damsels distressed!

"*Deux Cokes, s'il vous plaît et un verre du vin blanc.*" The owner brought our order over. I could tell he was both curious and amused at us. We were laughing at our dismal start and bemoaning our woes, when he haltingly interrupted in broken English. With his English and my French and a lot of sign language, he surmised that our greatest immediate problem was finding the road to St. Rémy. He began trying to explain, shook his head ruefully, and called out the door to a friend across the way. When the other man arrived, the owner pulled out his keys, gesturing for us to follow him. With a smile, the Cokes he said were on the house.

With a hasty "Merci" and a silent "thank you, God" we hustled to the car. Some twenty minutes and several miles and turns later, he pulled over to the side of the road, pointing to the sign reading St. Rémy, 15 Km. He grinned, waving us on our way and yelling, *"Bon Voyage!"*

"Merci, merci beaucoup!" We called back. Chivalry was still alive and well, and I still bless that nameless friend.

Chapter 3

Distracted by the passing beauty of the landscape, my nerves began to settle down as I drove past the little town of Chateaurenard with Jaynie and Beth echoing my cries of delight. The road turned south, now flitting through patches of shade created by parallel ranks of colorfully mottled Plantain trees and then flowing like a languid asphalt river through sun-dappled stretches flanked by small fields framed with woven reed fences. It was only with the arrival of Maurice several days later, that we learned the small, carefully fenced plots were a protective device to shield tender vegetation from the barreling force of the Mistral, that howling wolf of a wind that sweeps from the Alps to carry the lavender laden air of Provençe far out over the azure waters of the Mediterranean.

We entered St. Rémy beneath a welcoming canopy of fluttering Plantain leaves. The light filtered down, cool and green, to splash the ancient walls of the town with the pied beauty of sun-warmed ochres and cool, shaded grays. It was a typical town of old Provençe: a walled city, girded by a one-way street dividing the old internal town from the new areas lying beyond the walled center. With craning necks, we circled slowly around the old area of town peering through arches that opened onto narrow, twisting streets designed in Medieval times to baffle and lose the enemy. They are just as effective on me today. We glimpsed the small shops that lined the serpentine streets: *patisseries, boutiques, charcuteries, boulangeries, bijouteries* and all of the other *établissements* necessary to civilized French life. On our right were the small hotels, banks and sidewalk cafes of the newer town.

On the first circle of the town, I discovered that the street we sought, Rue Pasteur, was one way coming into the town. We finally figured out the proper paralleling street and were shortly driving through the towering gates of the Hotel des Antiques. It had been a lovely and elegant estate during a previous century, but the vagaries of time, divided inheritances and the burden of the French tax system had reduced it to a family operated hotel...small but still elegant, and our home for the coming weeks.

We drove into the graveled courtyard, lurching to a stop before the copper hooded entry and making obvious the neophyte status of my gear shifting. We tumbled out into the strong Provençal sunshine to be greeted by Marie Reynard, a gracious, silver-haired lady of about fifty and her blond, Nordic looking, blue-eyed son, Patrick, who spotted Jaynie's crown of fiery red-gold locks and was instantly smitten. We were led into the reception hall to register. The hall was surrounded by formal rooms embellished with *faux marbre* walls and columns, ceiling frescoes, and lovely and fragile antiques, some recovered in a golden cut-velvet of recent vintage, giving the rooms the aura of a once grand dowager reduced to the onerous indignity of being revamped by those of lesser sensibilities. A grand staircase swept upward from the entry hall to two upper stories that had been converted into guest rooms with private baths. The rear of the house opened onto a glazed-tile floored loggia, glassed and awned against the weather and furnished with white, wrought iron chairs and small, pink linen skirted tables. Beyond the windows lay several acres of garden with a pool for swimming and sunning.

Just as I was relishing the prospect of settling in, I was informed we would be accommodated across the courtyard in the former chauffeur's quarters. We crossed the gravel, going from early Nineteenth Century elegance to the spare simplicity of rustic Provençal. The *rez-de-chaussee* or ground level contained the coach house-become-garage that now sheltered an ancient Citroen and cases of dusty bottles of wine, a small toilet containing only a commode, and a small foyer with a narrow wooden stair leading up stark whitewashed walls. Abutting the garage, but without an adjoining door, extended a wing containing a laundry and gardening room.

We entered the small foyer and climbed the winding stuccoed

walled stairs to a second foyer containing a single bed, table, chair and lamp. To the right was a bath and the main salon, furnished with two more daybeds, coffee table of dubious vintage, end table and lamp, writing desk, two dark, straight backed antique wooden chairs and a wooden armoire. The room gave the impression of being furnished in early-attic style, clean but not pretty. At the far end from the entrance door, a huge pair of French windows opened onto a small balcony over-looking the courtyard and entry gate. It was the apartment's best feature. To the immediate left of the foyer lay a kitchen containing a narrow gas stove, miniature fridge and a scarred enamel sink. A table with three chairs was placed before another set of French doors and small balcony overlooking the entry to the main house. Turning back past the stairwell was a corridor leading to a large bed chamber furnished with another armoire...this one less imposing than the other, a double bed, bedside table and small lamp, desk and chair. It had a large pair of French windows but since they were not floor length, there was no balcony.

After the charm and elegance of the main hotel, I felt that Maurice had been a little less than to my taste in putting us in the annex. He would explain that he had chosen it as more suitable for us since it had a kitchen and allowed room for a studio. He intended that I would paint with vigor. I was to badly disappoint him on that score as I completed only two serious paintings, one of which I gave to him and one to his mother, and several smaller quick studies. How could I sit in solitude and paint when I wanted only to savor the thrill of discovering this special little corner of the world? As well, Beth and I were of necessity to become playmates and good friends due to the three weeks of our enforced and intense reliance on one another for companionship and diversion. That left little opportunity for the monkish act of painting.

We three moved in, unpacked, made beds with the linens Maurice had purchase and packed in the trunk of the car before delivering it to the garage, and hung our new, snowy white towels in the bath. When finished, we whipped back the green velvet curtains that were suspended from a wooden pole by large wooden rings, flung open the French doors, and draped ourselves over the balcony railing. Across the entry way we could see beyond to the large public square furnished with benches under the perimeter of trees. A church bell rang a hollow clank to announce the hour. The herbal scented wind swept dust from the room behind us and ushered in a few flies while playfully tossing our hair about our faces. Patrick appeared in the courtyard below.

"Madame Russell, your friend from Marseilles telephones to you. You will come, yes?"

"Thanks, Patrick. I'll be right down." We had no phone in the apartment. I would have to take all of my calls in the hotel's powder room. I dashed down to answer the phone, Patrick leading the way as he reluctantly tore himself from his station beneath the balcony. Beth giggled when Jaynie tossed him a flirtatious wave of *adieu*.

Maurice welcomed me to his Provençe, asked me if we were okay, if I had the papers for the car, the maps on which he had used markers to colorfully delineate itineraries, if the trip was uneventful, and finally, thank goodness, if there had been any problems with our checkout at the Royale Monceau.

"Maurice, it was terrible. I had to pay and it took almost all of the money you gave me." When I told him how much, he didn't quite gulp but I could tell he hadn't anticipated the size of the bill. The room service and lunch I had charged had added to an already expensive room.

"Jo darling, don't worry. It is very simple for me to send money to you there. Tomorrow afternoon walk down to the main street and turn right. About three blocks down is a branch of my bank. I will wire funds there for you, so just introduce yourself and ask for the manager. He will take care of everything."

Relieved, I relaxed and chatted with him about the beauty of the countryside we had driven through. I regaled him with the story of my difficulties at the station, in getting the car and reaching the hotel. He was chuckling and I was much happier as the financial angle had been a worry. I had not only spent his thousand in Paris, but the additional taxis, meals and shopping had dug into my own funds.

"For dinner tonight you must go to Chez Silvio, the Cafe des Beaux Arts. It is just around the corner from the hotel on the right side of the main street. The owner and his wife are expecting you and will see that you are well taken care of. You'll love it, Jo. The walls are filled with paintings that were donated to the father of the present owner's wife when it was first opened and since, by artists who exchanged their paintings for a meal. It's really charming and the food is good...not four stars, but not bad." He enthused some more before bidding me goodbye.

"Wait! Before you hang up, I wanted to ask when you are coming to see us? I want you to meet Jaynie before she leaves for South Africa."

"When is she to leave?"

"This Saturday."

"Let's see." He paused, "I think I can come Wednesday night. I also want to meet Beth at long last. I will make reservations for dinner at Le Beaumanière in Les Baux. It's one of the most elegant restaurants in all of France. The owner and chief, Monsieur Raymond Thuiller is a friend of mine. I want you to meet him as he has said you are welcome to use his pool. Normally it is reserved for his hotel guests, but he will make an exception for you."

"That sounds wonderful. I look forward to seeing you again."

"And I you, *ma cherié*. I'll call you tomorrow. *Bon soir*."

"*Bon soir*, Maurice and *merci*."

I left the cool shade of the hotel and walked into the blinding sunlight. Jaynie and Beth yoohoo-ed down to me.

" Hey, bring my bag and the door key and let's go exploring. I'll wait for you here." They were down in a minute, as eager as I to merge into the life of St. Rémy. We ambled beneath the mottled trees of the circular street, the Boulevard Victor Hugo. Unable to resist, we turned beneath one of the arches to penetrate into the old town...past fountains at corners where citizens once came to fill their jugs, past ancient buildings still wearing their dusty charm as they cant slightly towards their more contemporary neighbors... distinguished by renovated windows, trade signs and fresh paint, past the prefecture, the mairie, the église...whose bells have marked the passing hours, passing sunsets, passing years, and passing centuries with soft melodious notes that end with a long sigh. Past the house of the Marquis de Sade, past the museum housing relics and artifacts of Glanum, the ancient Roman town that lived and died just south of present day St. Rémy, past the town square, the patisserie...closed for the night while the shop-keeping women rest and their men baked the morrow's bread, past butcher. Past all of the little shops that breathe new life into this old, old body. Enchanted and tired, we re-emerged on the main street. We knew by our rumbling tummies that we were as hungry as Ebenezer Scrooge's mice: it was time for Chez Silvio's.

I might as well have been wearing a sign. Obviously Maurice had well apprised them of our anticipated patronage.

"Ah Madame Russell!" Their faces were warm with welcome as they greeted Beth and me by name, and smiled at Jaynie. "It is good to have you. We hope that you will love St. Rémy. We hope to give you a good time. Please to come in to dinner." The wife, who spoke English, did the talking while her husband smiled and nodded, nodded and smiled. We were led past the sidewalk tables into the first room which was obviously a bar and the local gathering spot for the male denizens of the town, their female counterparts staying home according to former Mediterranean custom which apparently was still observed here. Opening the door at the back of the bar, the wife ushered us into the small and fully utilized L-shaped dining room. The walls were indeed covered with the paintings that Maurice had described. The tables were small and simple, the chairs...slat backed rustic Provençal with woven, rush seats. Each of the tables was covered with white linen and centered with a small lamp and a bouquet of fresh flowers. The inner wall of the L was opened by multi-mullioned French windows, which swung open onto a miniscule courtyard punctuated with plants, a small tree and a vat for keeping fish fresh and lively for the pan, and a fly making machine. At least, I think there must have been one as they were buzzing everywhere. It took some adjustment coming from a screened, Grade A, sanitized and Pinesol-ed world. The flies were free to come and go at will unimpeded by screens and swatters. Some of them seemed to even grow fond of us, as they took up residence in our hotel rooms. Perhaps they and their progeny were hoping for a summer of cultural interchange with the foreigners who proved less than hospitable hostesses with their cans of air-impregnating death. Draped with cheesecloth on a small sideboard were platters of cheeses, tarts, and crème caramels. Nearby and undraped were baskets of crusty bread. Each passing waiter's swipe with a white cloth merely raised a dotted cloud, which quickly resettled. The food was wonderful and plentiful...flies not-with-standing, and reasonably priced.

The week that Jaynie was there the local snail population was in peril of extinction. We ate them...twelve to the plate for four bucks...every day that week. The garlic and parsley butter sauce that surrounded each one combined with a crispy baguette for dipping, a crisp salad of baby greens and a cool carafe of the local white wine made for a heavenly meal. After she left, I tapered off a bit but indulged often enough there were no sighs of relief circulating through snaildom. Beth quickly settled on the closest thing to innocuous American food she could find: French fries and ravioli that were to serve her needs *ad nauseum* day in and day out. One of the biggest thrills of the summer for her was the day we discovered a McDonald's in Aix en Provençe. Adventurous and gourmet dining had not yet introduced themselves to my young lady no matter my prompting.

The restaurant would prove to be our best entree into small town life. At lunch the local businessmen would dine, casting flirtatious eyes in our direction as they masticated. Any further overture was circumvented by our mutual language affliction, the food in their mouths and the derision of teasing cohorts. At night some of the other local hotel guests frequented the restaurant.

One of the most delightful evenings of that lonely month occurred when a young pink clad toddler of about four who had made Beth's acquaintance at the hotel pool, showed up with her parents, David and Judith Jenkins, on vacation from the north of England. She was a bubbly little charmer who soon clambered into my lap for a closer interview.

"Where is your daddy?" She looked up at me with a pert look on her face. I could tell from her tone and the glance toward my daughter and then her father, she was concerned that I had no husband.

"I don't have one."

Embarrassed, her parents tried to deflect her, but she continued undaunted by their efforts, "You don't? Why not?"

"I guess I'm just not very good at finding one. Do you think you could help me?"

"Sure. I know just the one for you. Dada is *sooo* nice. You'll like him."

From the Jenkins' comments and chuckles, I gathered Grandma might not approve this generous offer. "Thank you, Honey. That is very sweet of you but I believe I should find someone else so we don't make Grandma angry with us. Don't you think that's a good idea?"

"Well, all right. But you still need a daddy." She slid from my knee and returned to her table where she resumed munching her fries, returning occasionally to pat and feed the family pet that had cozily ensconced himself on my feet. Periodically she would cast an appraising glance in my direction. I could tell she was highly dissatisfied with my single status. Finally, with rounded tummy taunt beneath a ruffled, batiste, pinafore styled sundress, she bounced over to plant a lightly greased little kiss on my cheek. Hugging my neck with plump, dimpled arms, she gave me a last promise to help me in my plight. Unfortunately they left the next morning before she could send any recruits my way. So I was still single and I suppose

Grandma is still safely wed to Dada.

But Jaynie was there that first week, so we had company enough. Our first day in the hotel ended with the dinner at Chez Silvio's as we returned directly to the hotel to sleep the sleep of the exhausted. The next morning it was almost nine before we roused ourselves and went over to the hotel terrace to splurge on one of our few breakfasts there. Following the typical breakfast of croissants, strawberry jam, cafe au lait, and with Coke for Beth, we walked across the square...where local men gathered to while away lazy afternoons playing pétanque...to the grocery where we purchased the essentials: wine, cookies, coffee, jam, toilet tissue, bread, cheese, Coke and some fruit. Thus provisioned with a stocked larder, we decided it was time to venture further afield.

We began with Glanum where we ambled among the ruins, most notable of which was a beautiful arch. From there we drove the short distance to the Monastery of St. Paul de Mausole where Van Gogh was hospitalized following the famous ear episode in Arles. It was here that he went out into the surrounding fields to paint and where he created his famous Starry Night. These attractions were but a short distance from the hotel, a matter of minutes. Now we were ready for the five-mile drive to Les Baux.

Just in case we were lost forever, we had packed a picnic lunch of cheese, baguette, wine and Coke. We anticipated finding a promising site for a pleasant lunch, however, when we climbed into the car to proceed to Les Baux, we discovered we were thirsty and hungry. Not wanting to wait, Jaynie and I nibbled cheese and passed the wine back and forth, drinking from the bottle. Beth opted for the Coke. We had finished the wine, the cheese, the bread and most of the Coke long before the twisting five miles to Les Baux were done. By then, with the added inducement of the wine, I was feeling much more relaxed and attuned to driving the roller coaster of a road that wound over the Alpilles, a calcareous extension of the Lubéron Range. The spiny hills were dotted with sparse and seared grasses and low, stunted and twisted trees that gave an eerie charm to the landscape.

Les Baux, named for bauxite...an aluminum ore that was discovered here...lay just off the main road. Across fields of vines and olives, we could see the sheer cliffs, atop which perched the medieval town, razed by the edict of Louis XIII. By daylight it is a trip back in history to the days of the Troubadours, famous in the Thirteenth Century "as a court of love," and infamous in the next century when Raymond de Turrene used the citadel heights to terrorize and raid the surrounding countryside with fiendish zeal. At night the ruins of its floodlit walls hover above the road leading past.

We entered the town on foot, as the streets are too steep and narrow to be accessible by car, passing through the Magi Gate, so denoted because the lords of the town traced their genealogy to the Magi king, Balthazar. Climbing our way into town we were fascinated by the charm of the rebuilt area and romanced by the ruins of the Castle that loomed from the highest ramparts. Both sides of the street leading up were filled with shops and cafes. Everywhere was the pervasive scent of the herbs of Provençe: basil, thyme, rosemary and lavender.

I suppose for Jaynie and me one of the most remarkable 'tourist sights' of the day was a young man of about twenty, swarthy of complexion and dark of hair and eye. Dressed in white shirt and quite abbreviated shorts, the contrast was vivid; however, the most compelling feature was the excessive prominence of that most male part of his anatomy. To this day, we chuckle at the double take we did when he walked past, seemingly oblivious to the sensation such a notable attribute might generate. Yeah, right: he was strutting it.

Giggling we walked into a shop selling cool cotton dresses in a simple peasant style. I bought a white one and wore it out of the shop, as the clothes I had with me were not suitable for activity under the hot sun. Beth found a toy she liked and Jaynie shopped for packages of lavender to give as gifts back home. We stopped at a cafe for a cool drink. A gorgeous man of about forty approached me and introduced himself. He chatted for several minutes before remarking that he had a vineyard nearby and that he would very much like to show me the caves that night. Uh huh, and I have a palm tree in Alaska he should see. I declined his invitation and the three of us left to climb to the castle ruins.

Beth loved Jaynie, as she was kind and playful with her. It was wonderful for me to have a girlfriend to be silly and have fun with as I had not had one since college. Even then, because I was a scholarship student, I was very serious and responsible and did not have as carefree a time as many of my peers. I was still not carefree but I felt as though a load had been lifted from me when I returned to Europe, as though my soul was blossoming in the warm light of the Mediterranean. In a strange way, it was as though I was at long last beginning to grow into my own skin and it was good to have a free spirit like Jaynie to share this unfurling of my own spirit.

The following evening, Maurice arrived in St. Rémy and at dusk we found ourselves back in Les Baux. As we sat at our table under the stars, the cliffs and ruins were suddenly lit against the glowing night with spotlights that limned the sheer walls in glowing, golden splendor. That has to be one of the most beautifully romantic and stirring sights in Europe, especially when viewed from the terrace restaurant of the L'Ousteau de Beaumaniére. From the terrace, I could see the candle lit tables of the interior dining room, the back wall of which had been carved into the living rock. Replete with wine and the ultimate gourmet cuisine, we sat back in our chairs to talk. Maurice had invited friends of his to join us, Frederica and Piero Garibaldi, lawyers from the nearby town of Fontainvieille. The French was flying thick and fast between them, leaving *Les Americaines* to chat among ourselves much of the time. Piero was a handsome descendant of the famous Garibaldi of Italy and a totally delightful personality. His wife was sexily European, not beautiful but very sultry. Even as they talked among themselves and intermittently to us, Maurice was obviously on two planes: one the socially alert perfect host and the other intensively pensive and analytical, assessing of Beth, Jaynie and me.

Piero laughed loudly, bringing me back to the present. "Eet ees zee season for St. Tropez. Avery one ees zere. Eet ees hell, but zen, I likea hell!" He grinned at us like an impish schoolboy. We liked Piero.

I turned to Maurice, "Will we be going to St. Tropez?" I was ready to leave then and there.

"We must go to Chamonix and then I have reservations for us in St. Moritz and Monte Carlo. It will depend on whether we have the time darling. But I must tell you, I am not so crazy for it." Turning from me, he called for what had to be an astronomical tab. I later learned that it was over six hundred dollars. That was a lot of money in 1984, to spend for dinner and it still is. With chorused goodbyes, we bade his friends goodnight.

I had become increasingly uncomfortable with Maurice's intense and unreadable scrutiny as the night progressed. That coupled with the discomfort Margot had assiduously created by her aspersions and the anxiety engendered by our Easter-time discussion in Rome, had given rise to a substantial paranoia. I had shared my apprehensions with Jaynie and we had decided that I should be honest and discuss my feelings with him, my anxieties, and their sources. Given an artist's imagination supplemented by Jaynie's own artistic temperament, it made for a rich scenario of potential and alternative scripts. We arrived back at the hotel to find the entry gate for the car locked. Maurice left Beth and Jaynie to go through the small door on the side and I rode with him to park the car a short distance down on the Rue Pasteur. We stood by the car, awkward with one another. The comfort we had felt in Rome was displaced by my tension and for him, I suspected, by the long awaited meeting with Beth who reminded him far too much of an idealized and childhood version of Margot. We chatted inconsequentially for several minutes before I could stand the suspense no longer.

Unable to stop myself, I blurted, "Maurice, thank you for the dinner. I really do appreciate all that you have done and are doing for me and for Beth, but I must tell you I feel very uncomfortable. Margot is angry with me for coming here to be with you this summer. She says that she's afraid of you and worried that you might try to hurt her in some way through me. I don't know if she really believes that or if she was saying it just to keep me away, but it's upsetting."

His face was rigid with suppressed anger when he replied, "Surely you see that she is crazy with jealousy. She knows that you and I are far more compatible...have more in common...than she and I ever were. She was merely trying to keep us apart when she told you those things. I think she's afraid I will fall in love with you and forget about her."

"Maurice, I doubt that seriously. She has moved on with her life."

"Come on, Jo. Think about it. You know your sister. What else did she tell you?"

"I'm not sure I should say. It is probably best not to dig into all of that."

"I want to know." He took my elbow and turned me to face him. "Tell me what you are holding back that has you so concerned? I insist you tell me!"

I took a deep breath and prayed I was not making a big mistake. "She said that you would never like me as a woman because you don't want women romantically. She also said your friendship with Rene is not natural and she detests him and says that is why she did not stay in the relationship with you. What your sexual preferences are, or aren't, isn't important to me because I'm your friend regardless. I'm not asking if it is true or not. My concern is that I not be used against Margo to avenge your anger and pain."

He slammed his fist into the trunk of the car. I jumped as though I had been struck. "My God!" He yelled, "She is a vicious, evil woman! My friends would laugh if they could hear this. They all think I'm such a hound after women. Rene is my tennis partner. That's all. I don't know why she would tell you such things unless she is desperately afraid that I will turn to you and finally stop wanting her. She couldn't stand that, you know. I know her well and I know her ego. She still wants me."

"Maurice, you are my friend and you have been more generous and kind to me than anyone I know. I respect you and I admire your intelligence, but I also know the deep rage you have for my sister. You have told me and shown it to me. I don't know why you would spend so much to help me, her sister, or to bring my daughter and me here. No one has ever done anything like this for me before. Maybe it isn't a big deal for you but it is a really big one to me. I just don't want to pay a higher price than I can. I don't want to be used to hurt someone else. What is it that you want from me? I have nothing to give you but my friendship, not my body or romantic love. You don't want that."

"Don't presume what I want," he growled.

"But what do you want? Do you want a last desperate tie to Margot? Or do you want Beth as a replacement...pure and unspoiled for the Margot you dreamed of, a Margot that never was and never could be? I don't want to be a mere conduit for you to achieve some goal. I want to be a better friend to you than that."

"You should not ask me these things. You have no right to say them to me. Surely you must realize than I am deeply offended." He stalked back and forth on the street like an enraged tiger in a flimsy, confining cage. "I think we should say goodnight. I'll call later this week."

"I am so sorry, Maurice. I didn't want to tell you all of this and I don't blame you for being offended. Please forgive me." I wanted honesty between us, but sometimes it is best to accept things without looking too far below the surface. It is a failing of mine that I am too blunt and I look too hard for the motivation behind people.

When his car roared down the street, I leaned against the wall. He was angry and I was furious with myself for telling him the things I had, and for not just letting the truth evolve. I went inside not really knowing if I would ever see him again, not blaming him should I not, and not knowing if I wanted to or should.

"God, what happened? You look like hell." Jaynie was subtle.

"It was so awful. I should have kept my fool mouth shut and not said a word. He was furious, absolutely livid. I would have been too."

"What do you think he will do? What did he say?" I reviewed it, replayed it, rehashed it, and restated it for her. It still sounded ugly and it still does.

For the remainder of Jaynie's time with us, we spent the hours sight-seeing: Arles to see the famous Roman arena and the house that Van Gogh stayed in while there, Nîmes to see the Maison Carrée and other Roman ruins, Avignon to see the Palais du Pape, Aix en Provençe where we had lunch on the Cours Mirabeau, and Ile sur Sorgue where we prowled the shops along the street lined canal. All too soon it was time for Jaynie to leave. I helped her pack and we took her to the station in Avignon, where on leaving I managed to take the same wrong turn. Beth and I were on our own, Jaynie was gone and Maurice had not yet called. We went back to the hotel, slipped into swimsuits and headed for the pool where we spent the afternoon splashing around and sunning ourselves. That evening Maurice called the hotel while we were at dinner. Persistent, he called Chez Silvio's where he at last reached me.

"Jo, Darling, forgive me for being so lax in calling you but I have been swamped at work. I must apologize for having abandoned my angels so long. I would like you to meet some dear friends of mine, so I took the liberty of inviting them to join us for dinner next Thursday. There will be two couples besides us. If that is suitable for you, I will make reservations at the Beaumanière as we all love it." He sounded as though our terrible scene had never occurred. Taking my cue from him, I never again mentioned it.

"I've missed you, Maurice. Dinner with your friends sounds wonderful." He didn't mention coming sooner and I did not ask.

"I hope that you have enjoyed seeing some of the area?" We talked on for several minutes as I described where we had been and what we had done. Due to the difficulty of trying to be heard above the noise, we did not prolong the conversation. Some of our comfort level had been re-established and deep inside I knew no matter the fury he felt towards Margot, he would never harm us...no matter his eccentricities, no matter his irrationalities. I also realized a further problem would be to provide a buffer between Beth, who did not yet feel any affection for him nor sympathy of spirit, and Maurice, who had a desperate yearning for Beth's love and dependency. In some way, I began to feel that I understood and accepted him in all of his complex and puzzling facets better than he could accept himself. I respected him and selfishly, I needed him just as he needed us. He was the strong, nurturing patriarchal figure that I needed in my life at that point. He was generous of spirit and I knew he would see to it that my daughter and I did not go lacking. He needed my companionship and approbation and most of all, he had reached that point in his life when he craved a family of his own, no matter how tenuous the link. His own fantasies would fill the gap. We left it at that and the rest of the summer passed with peace and between Maurice and me, except for one unhappy moment in Marseilles. Beth was to be slow to win over.

When I returned to the table and my dinner, Beth remarked, "Mommy, there's a yucky fly in your wine."

I looked. There floating lazily about was a fly, drowned in the wine I had just raised to my lips. I caught the waiter's eye. He was my nemesis: very stern, very impatient and very brusque. He spoke only "Thank you" and "Hello" in English. And he had intimidated me from day one, I over-tipped, took whatever he brought, and never complained. But I wasn't about to drink that damned fly.

He came over. Holding my glass to the light, I pointed. *"C'est une mouche dans mon vin. Je voudrais un autre verre du vin, s'il vous* plaît.*"*

"Ah, une mouche! C'est libre!" His mouth twitched, his eyes twinkled and then he began to laugh. I'd misjudged him. He was really very pleasant under that stern facade.

"What did he say, Mommy?"

"The fly is free, no charge." So was the second carafe of wine and the dessert he insisted we eat.

For our first full day solo, Beth and I drove to Beaucaire, Tarascon, on past Remoulin to the Pont du Gard. There we gaped at the scale of the aqueduct as it soared high above the river carrying water on its way to *Nîmes*. Over the river and through a tunnel in the mountain, it maintained a constant downward grade. We walked through the water channel at the very top with me ducking my head to accommodate the ceiling stones that capped the length of the course to prevent contamination and evaporation of the precious water. At the gaps where the capstones were missing, I could look over to the road that ran along the lower row of supporting arches. It had carried traffic until a few years previous. I marveled at the engineering of the ancient Romans and madly snapped photos and stored memories to share with my students in the fall.

It was a beautiful day, sunny and not too warm; I was at peace with Maurice and confident in my ability to navigate, reassured by my carload of carefully marked maps *à la Maurice*, and the French system of road directions that is unexcelled in my experience. As long as I could read, I could find. I never got truly lost in France. The only flaw in my restored ebullience developed on the way home as we passed the quarry between Remoulins and Beaucaire. A passing car threw a rock into the windshield of the new, undented, shiny, borrowed car Maurice had provided me on loan from a friend of his, a car dealer. I now had to tell him his new, borrowed car was damaged. I prayed mightily for a miracle that would make the crack go away, but each morning when I checked ...hoping against hope, that damned crack had only grown. I decided the damaged car could still go and I delayed telling him even though he was calling almost daily. My reasoning being that I'd just save it all up and tell him in one big swoop. No sense in chipping away little bits when one big blast would do, nice and clean. Fortunately that ended the car damage for the summer except for the ticket in Avignon.

Beth and I had gone to Avignon when the days sunbathing and socializing with one another began to wear thin. In one of the shops there, we met a nice French woman and her daughter, who appeared to be about Beth's age. She was an English teacher and her daughter was learning the language so they were both happy to have us to practice on. For us, it was a joy to hear our language coming from lips other than our own. Beth and Estelle became pen pals for the summer, helping her feel less lonely. Once her mother brought her to our hotel and the two girls spent the day playing by the pool while the mother and I chatted. We were glad for their diversion.

I had parked the car that day in the only empty place that I could find. The sign with the circle and diagonal slash on it meant nothing at the time so it didn't register on me that I was in a no parking zone. When we returned to the car, the ticket on the windshield did register. There was no way after the cracked windshield that I was going to tell Maurice that I had received a ticket, too. I decided there was no alternative but to persuade the police not to charge me for the ticket.

With my little French and some sign language, I found the local police station and went in. It took some minutes for me to make them understand my mission. It was apparent that they had expected me to pay for the ticket I was clutching in my sweaty palm. They were unprepared to deal with a nonpaying ticket recipient. They conferred as I continued to perspire, making the ticket even more limp. With a shrug, they decided not to deal with me but to send me on. They directed me to another office located down a shaded alley, into another building and up three flights of stairs. The stairway was narrow and sided with walls of cracking plaster and peeling paint, which gleamed dully where it had fallen to litter the poorly lit treads. The building looked seedy and more than a little abandoned. Uneasy, I was about to turn back when we mounted the last stair and the door we sought stood directly ahead.

In the office seated at his desk was a weary looking man in uniform. In even more broken French than normal, Scarlett O'Hara sighs and batting lashes...sign language of the southern belle variety, I pleaded my case: poor dumb little woman, all alone in a foreign land and unknown city, how could I be held responsible for such a picky little thing as a parking ticket. I smiled sadly and wrung my hands. I became increasingly more obtuse as he became more comprehending. Beth even took pity and pitched in to try to translate and she couldn't understand much past "oui" having learned her French from Jaynie's system. In the end, he not only tore up the ticket but also offered to share his lunch, which had sat on the desk untouched since our entry. I declined sweetly and taking my daughter by the hand decamped before he could change his mind. I was also in a panic to move the car before it could collect another ticket. This was one peccadillo that Maurice would not need to know. I could not talk my way out of the windshield crack though and it was still growing.

When he came on Thursday, I met him in the pink crepe dress with my hair in an upsweep and hoped I looked pretty as I had resolved to make my confession. Beth had not wanted to go that night; much to Maurice's disappointment and despite his urgings, she remained adamant. I arranged for Patrick to keep an eye on her and to be available should she need someone. She waved us goodbye from the balcony.

Maurice drove swiftly and skillfully over the tortuously curved road from St. Rémy to Les Baux. That night it appealed to something wild and restless in me. I think it may have been the first time I was relaxed when he was behind the wheel. Perhaps I was becoming comfortable not only with the speed and verve of his driving but also with the local roads, which were narrower, and more dramatically twisting than those I had known at home in a countryside as flat as Twiggy's chest. But then does anyone remember her, the English model who was so skinny she could slide through a soda straw and not touch the sides?

The evening with his friends was a repeat of the previous dinner at Le Beaumanière, except this time I did not have Jaynie and Beth for company, nor Piero to admire. The dinner was superb so I concentrated on the food when I became lost in the rapid-fire conversation. I wasn't sorry for it to end as sitting uncomprehendingly while laughter and camaraderie flow around me isn't something I enjoy. After waving goodnight to his friends, Maurice drove to just below the ramparts where there was an overlook. There he parked and turned on a beautiful and romantic cassette recording of "Anonimo Veniziano" taken from Marcello's "Concert for Oboe in

D Minor." Opening the car door, he reached out to pick me a nosegay of yellow wildflowers. With a full moon hanging above, the glow of the spotlighted ramparts, the music and the impromptu bouquet, I could not bear to spoil the mood with news of the broken windshield. Unlike the last dinner at Les Baux when I had unwisely broached my concerns, this time when he left me at the hotel, he drove away humming. I was glad I had spent the twenty minutes getting the car parked so the gleam of moonlight would illuminate only the uncracked rear window. He was returning for Bastille Day on the weekend of July 13th and 14th. I could tell him them. Besides, if a guillotine was in order, I figured that was appropriate timing.

He arrived that Saturday late for dinner. We had waited most of the afternoon for him and were starving and about bored to death...no radio, no television, and we had both read all of our books at least twice. But not a word of reproach did I utter. I accepted his apologies gracefully and assured him we were happy to see him no matter how late. Besides, it was time for *true confessions*.

"Darling, why are you so concerned? It's quite simple to replace the windshield and it's probably covered by insurance, if not it won't be expensive. When we move you to Marseilles, I'll have it replaced for you."

Fine! I could eat dinner with head intact. We dined at Chez Silvio's and then came back to the apartment that I had decorated with flowers we had found in the country market held every Wednesday morning in the town square. The back bedroom was aired and fresh in preparation for his first overnight visit with us. To pass the time until bedtime, Beth and I taught him to play rummy. He lost badly for several hands until I explained the strategy. After that he began to win steadily for the remainder of the hands, whooping like a boy each time. He had a happy evening and I could feel the gratitude in his eyes when he kissed my cheeks goodnight.

The next morning, Beth and I were up first. We had toasted day old bread from the patisserie, jam and butter. I made a less than wonderful attempt at strong French coffee. Putting it all on a tray with a fresh rose from the hotel garden, we surprised Maurice with breakfast in bed. We found him fully dressed, except for shoes, in his typical outfit: black trousers and black Izod shirt. He was under the cover of his own down filled sleeping bag that he had unzipped and spread over himself. Eventually I would learn that he always slept this way. That sleeping bag traveled with him like a king-sized kid's security blanket. I granted him the eccentricity. Beth just shook her head when we returned the dishes to the kitchen and muttered, "Weird!"

Following breakfast, which he had struggled bravely to down, we cleaned and made our beds while he dressed. We left to walk down to main street which during the night had been flag bedecked and barricaded in preparation for the annual running of the black, fleet-footed Camargue bulls. We browsed in the bookstore beside the Cafe des Artes while we waited for the bulls. Maurice also found time for a cup of coffee, standing at the bar to drink it. All of the sidewalk tables and chairs had been crowded inside leaving little room for patrons. Hearing the excitement level of the waiting throngs increasing, we pushed out to the barricade to view what was happening.

Leading the way were cowboys on horseback who waved proudly at the cheering crowd. Young boys followed them on foot running madly ahead of the bulls. The largest of the bulls suddenly broke free and barreled toward where we stood. In panic we madly scrambled through the bookshop door immediately behind us to peer at the enraged bull as he vaulted over the barricade and furiously smashed a large cement planter, scattering flowers high in the air. I realized then why all of the cafe furniture had been moved inside. That done he turned and pawed in the direction of our refuge before resuming the circular romp around town. Beth and I squealed in terror while Maurice laughed indulgently at our fright.

With the excitement in St. Rémy done, we boarded Battleship to drive to Nîmes where we were invited to lunch with the friends I had met on Thursday night: Jacques Reyes de Nîmes and his wife Nani, Bernard Lepère, a Parisian film producer, and his girlfriend, Christine, as well as another couple from Paris whose names I have forgotten. Jackie and Bernard were both charmers with a delightful sense of humor; the third man had spent some time in Chapel Hill following the war, I assumed the Second, and loved southern women. The three men were very nice to me and spoke English fairly well. The women could not and thus seemed less friendly, particularly Christine who appeared jealous of Bernard's attention to anyone but her.

The Reyes home designed by Jackie, was a large contemporary one that terraced down a beautifully landscaped hillside overlooking the city of Nîmes. On the lowest of the terraces were a huge pool, cabana and the second of the two guesthouses on the estate. Following a lunch of Tuna Niçoise, wine and fresh bread, we all donned swimsuits for a swim. Maurice was the exception. He disappeared for nearly an hour to visit with the Reyes' son, who because of a handicap that Maurice did not specify, stayed cloistered. Just as the others were beginning to ask for him, he reappeared and began snapping photos of Beth and me. Much to Christine's annoyance, Bernard joined him with his own camera wanting me to make poses with my hands as he said they were beautiful. The following summer, Maurice opened his wallet and a picture of me looking like all legs fell out. Unfortunately it also looked as though I was picking my teeth. He liked that picture of me he had taken that day and I think it was the only one of me that he carried.

Shortly after three, everyone loaded into cars for the day's big event located in the area called the Bouche du Rhone. There lies the Camargue, miles of windswept, sun-drenched marshlands drowsing beneath azure blue skies flecked with raucously wheeling sea birds. On the grassy flats roamed once wild horses now herded by gitanos, the gypsies of the Camargue. Dotted about we could see whitewashed huts or small houses with the northeastern ends rounded to withstanding the onslaught of fierce Mistral winds. As we drove, Maurice explained that there are seven named winds. The two most important to the area are the Mistral that originates in the Alps, and the Sirocco that blows from Africa bringing sand and an oppressive sultriness to the air.

Perhaps one of the most dramatic of the Independence Day spectacles held each year in the Camargue is the Andalusian style bullfight in the arena at Mèjane, a small community about twenty miles south of Arles. The Andalusian bullfight is a must for the lover of beautiful and exquisitely trained horseflesh.

"Jo, in this fight, the toreador rides horseback to fight the bull. And such a fight it is. This is like an equestrian ballet virtuoso with a fillip of danger." I could feel Maurice's excitement as he talked and his love for Andalusia where he promised to take us one day.

Once we met the others, we made our way to our arena seats. Maurice was becoming concerned for the sensibilities of his American girls, as he did not want anything to spoil the day for us. He obviously hoped an explanation would prevent us from being too upset by the bloodshed. "The Andalusian"...(he pronounced it *An da loo thi ahn)*..."horses are first cousin to the Lippizaners of Austria, forever separated by the dissolution of the Hapsburg Empire. Even though they are less well known in the States, they are every bit as beautiful and give just as thrilling a performance as their more famous cousins. The horses selected for the fight are trained intensively for years in all of the maneuvers necessary for eluding the bull yet at the same time putting the horseman in striking distance of the vulnerable spot on the bull's shoulder. Usually the horse is trained for one specific stage of the fight with the rider changing to a fresh horse as many as four or five times during the fight. While the horse is changed, the bull is tired by assistants called picadors who approach on foot, cape in hand in the traditional format. The rider dismounts only to deliver the final *coupe de lance*."

Although it was hot and dusty that afternoon and the sun was in our eyes for much of the fight, it was a memorable day despite the discomfort. The excitement of the crowd, the courage, skill and beauty of horse and riders and some indefinable magic in the air made even Beth thrilled and happy. Bernard sat beside her teasing and making her laugh. I was on her other side and Maurice was beside me. I felt his envy that she was responding warmly to Bernard while she retained cool reserve with him. I wanted to tell him to back off a bit as children are often cool and suspicious of those who try to hard, but I hesitated to seem critical.

According to custom, the fight had begun in late afternoon. There was a standing room only crowd, when shortly after four, the five horsemen featured in the program paraded into the arena. We all stood and cheered as the horses side-stepped and prance together in choreographed dressage around the circumference, guided only by the gentle pressure from the rider's knees since their hands were lifted high in salute. The men were busy comparing notes on the merits of the various horses, picking their favorites. Maurice and Jackie, who was also an avid photographer, were busy snapping shots of everything, both in the arena and the stands. One of the horsemen, who Maurice said was French, had to have been one of the absolutely best looking men I had ever seen. I would have been happy just to look at him for the rest of the afternoon.

Both horses and riders were groomed for elegance: the horses sporting ribbon braided manes and the finest tooled leather equipage, and the horsemen sitting in haughty pride and wearing the costumes of Spanish Grandees. The tight knee pants, 'ballet slippers' and gaudy colors were reserved for the terrestrial assistants, the picadors. After the grand salute, the fight was ready to begin. I found the good-looking rider in the front row where he watched the other riders take their turns. I planned to watch him if the bullfight itself did not prove more interesting.

The first bull entered the ring. After being kept in dark seclusion, yanked from his nice pasture and willing concubines, and being shipped all the way from Spain in a narrow crate he charge into the arena as mad as all hell. Skidding to a stunned halt, he looked the situation over. He did not like it at all and the roaring crowd only added to his fury. He wanted out badly. Finding no ready exit, he lowered his head, sized up the waiting horse and rider and went for them, pure murder in his eyes.

Maurice leaned over me and took Beth's hand, "Don't feel sorry for the bull. They are very mean animals, not little house pets." No mistaking that, I thought, as he leaned back and continued...teaching me. "By careful gene selection, the bull has been bred to be especially fierce in the arena. Spanish bulls are used rather than the leaner and faster Camargue bulls which become very mean from feeding on a chemical found naturally in our local grass. To keep the bull from being impossibly dangerous, he has never before been fought. Prior to his selection for the arena, he was given a two or three-minute trial test to see if he would be aggressive enough for an entertaining fight. Any longer and he would have learned how to anticipate the man and horse's moves. When he exits that chute, make no mistake, that bull is a formidable, vicious, and powerful opponent. The lives of the man and the horse depend totally on their own skills in eluding the bull."

The stands around us erupted with cheers of "Ole! Ole!" at a particularly daring maneuver. We watched mesmerized as with breathtaking thrust and parry, narrow escape and exquisite harmony of man and horse, they did battle with the bull. Between the primitive rage and force of the bull and the controlled dignity and cultured beauty of the man and horse, I found an almost symbolic parallel between ancient evil and civilized man. In this case, evil was vanquished. Beth hid her eyes as a team of horses pulled the bull from the arena. I sickened a little as I watched them hide the pool of blood by smoothly raking the sand over it in readiness for the next fight. I was reminded from my study of art history that the word *arena* comes from the ancient word for sand used in Roman amphitheaters for the very same purpose.

Even for one of somewhat delicate sensibilities, the pageantry and beautiful precision of the horse and rider provided relief and enjoyment. Rarely could I hope to see in any exhibition, a performer who exceeded in sheer artistry the then sixty-three year old Perralta, a Spaniard and the most famed of all Andalusian horsemen. Once over the squeamishness, few pageants can compare for heart stopping excitement and vibrant color.

Afterwards in the gathering dusk, the Camargue of the gitanos awaited with more tranquil pleasures. Caravanning, we followed Jackie's lead to the restaurant where we had reservations for dinner. There we were: three cars, eleven hungry and thirsty people, tearing down dusty roads, turning down what looked like cow paths to me, backing up at obvious dead ends and then going some more. It was a sure way to see some more of "La Belle France," but patriotism aside, it was clear Jackie was lost and like the typical male of my experience, he did not believe in stopping to ask directions. I heaved a sigh, sat back and figured to hell with it...it was all new to me and I still had most of the summer ahead. But Maurice was getting upset because he was growing very hungry...the stale bread at breakfast and the salad at lunch were not high on his list of preferred foods.

Just at the moment of mutiny, Jackie came through and we found ourselves pulling into the parking area of the Chateau de Villevieille near Sommières. The building was a marvelous old fortress dating back to the thirteenth century and the cuisine was to prove superb, however for me the most remarkable aspect of the evening was Maurice's ebullience. He laughed, told jokes, and became far livelier than I had seen him at any previous point. It was apparent that he was well liked by his friends and they were happy to have him return to them. From their conversation, I gathered he had not seen much of them for some time. They kept turning curious and speculative eyes to me. I think that they considered both Beth and me good for him and since we seemed to make him happy, they were openly ready to accept us into their circle as well.

All the way back to St. Rémy Maurice sang, "I'm just wild about Harry and Harry's wild about me..." He did it well but Beth rolled her eyes at him suspiciously. I wished he had chosen *Sweet Adeline* or something of that ilk. He had planned to return to Marseilles that night after delivering us to the hotel but he was loathed to end what for him and for us had been a lovely weekend. I don't think he had had too many happy weekends in his life and certainly not recently. So he stayed on in St. Rémy that night. The next morning we all slept late and then had breakfast on the hotel terrace. Maurice had declined my offer to make breakfast.

That afternoon he drove us to Aigues-Mortes, the port where the crusaders under St. Louis in 1248 and again in 1270, set sail for the Holy Land. The trip there through a bird preserve was tranquil and picturesque. For dinner we ate at a gypsy restaurant in the town. The leader of the gypsies, El Tio (the uncle,) and his young kinsmen owned the restaurant, waited the tables, and serenaded the diners. Their guitar music and singing was wild and free, yearning, poignant, and hauntingly beautiful. I wanted to dance and cry and love. It was fabulous. The food was delicious, too, and I say that having eaten my very first octopus. Maurice sang in Spanish along with the gypsies. He had a rich full voice and knew the music and these people well. They knew and liked him, respected him for the respect that he showed them with his appreciation of their music and cuisine. They also liked his more than generous tip.

Tuesday morning after another breakfast on the hotel terrace, Maurice returned to his office in Marseilles. He drove away looking the most rested and happy that I had yet seen him. Some of the deep lines in his face seemed to have softened even. I was glad that I could give him that in return for his generosity to us. He had found peace and joy being with a woman who accepted him and with my child. He told me at breakfast that morning that it was the first time in his life he had felt a part of a warm and loving family. He was the saddest man I ever knew; yet to the world he seemed to have it all: wealth, looks, intelligence, talent, culture and a wide circle of both prominent friends and simple people. Why had happiness so eluded this man? He said he had been misunderstood all of his life. Perhaps that is why he so much appreciated my acceptance and attempts to understand.

Margot also knew his unhappiness and felt that it stemmed from being too proud to face the stigma of his sexual preference for men. He had been twice married and divorced in his younger years, had known many beautiful women and seemed the most male of men.

However, just as Margot wondered so did I, primarily because of the young sycophantic men with whom he surrounded himself. He never gave me any reason to know one way or the other, except maybe once in Paris and even then who knows? I'll get to that in time.

Chapter 4

The following days found me so alone and so lonely. Even though Beth was with me, it was not the same as having another adult with whom I could talk, share ideas, and savor and appreciate all of my new experiences. I missed Jaynie and I missed Maurice. He was returning for us in a few days and we were leaving to take his mother to the mountains for the summer, so I marked time in the interim playing eleven years old again: making doll clothes, playing "Go fish," cavorting in the pool, and trying to be entertaining for Beth who was even more lonely than I. We surreptitiously picked a flower in the garden, a beautiful pink rose for Maurice's mother...hoping she would like us for the gift, and we were all packed and ready to leave on the appointed day. He said to expect him at eleven in the morning.

We did. We shouldn't have. At one he called to tell us to have lunch, as he would not arrive until around three. We walked to Chez Silvio's: ravioli for Beth, escargot for me for one last time. I took photos of the people we had grown to like there, of the paintings and the tables, the waiter who had become a favorite and who would not allow me to pay for this last meal. We walked back to the hotel and sat on our small balcony to resume our watch. The rose wilted and so did we. Three sounded on the un-melodiously clanging village church bells, but no Maurice. Four came and Maurice did not. Five, and still no Maurice. At half past five as the shadows were beginning to lengthen on the gravel courtyard and we had long since grown weary and short on patience, he at last arrived.

With a quick hello wave from the balcony, we tore down the steps grabbing our luggage on the way. Maurice parked the car in the center of the courtyard and walked up to us, saluting French style with a kiss on each cheek.

"Please forgive me for being so late, but problems arose at the office and I could not leave as planned." He took our arms. "Come, meet Maman."

"We're just very glad you're finally here. It's been a long day for us." I thought that was truly an understatement and knowing Beth was ready to explode from annoyance with him, I shot her a rueful smile that silently begged her not to make a scene.

"Maman, this is Jo, my dear friend I have told you so much about. And this is my Beth. I know you will love them as much as I do."

"Hello, Madame de Beaubourg. I am so glad to at last meet you."

Beth shyly offered her the limp rose. "It's for you."

"For me? Thank you very much." Her voice was frail and she was old, perhaps in her mid-eighties. She was obviously hard of hearing but could understand a bit of English if spoken loudly and clearly. Even so, I was glad Maurice had given us advanced warning. Judging from the pleased expression on her face and her tremulous smile, I knew that we were off to a good start thanks to the simple gesture of a rose. She turned to me, "Please, call me Marie."

I left her holding Beth's hand and the two of them smiling tentatively at one another, as I walked to the rear of the car to help load our luggage. In amazement, I saw the trunk was already full: a small bag for Marie who was spending six weeks in Chamonix, two bags for Maurice, his sleeping bag, and mountains of cameras and photography equipment.

Looking at the space and our bags skeptically, I asked, "Do you think this will all fit in here?"

"Don't worry. It's simply a matter of thinking and organizing properly." He loaded and unloaded three different times and three different ways. Three times it just would not all go in. I could tell he was furious that it seemed to be defying him, especially with me watching. Wordlessly he snatched up the three bags remaining after the fourth effort and headed for the back seat where Marie and Beth had installed themselves. He crammed two of the bags between them making a mountainous barrier and grabbed the third to stuff it in as well.

"No, let me have it. I'll put it under my feet." I looked at his mother who already looked weary and I knew Beth would rather have me beside her. "Marie, please allow me to sit in the back. This is much too uncomfortable for you."

"No, no. Please, you must sit with Maurice."

"Oh no, I beg you. I really don't mind." My traditional southern heritage had taught me to extend a deferential respect to my elders, however despite my protestations, she refused to budge and Maurice was no help.

"Don't be silly, Jo. I course you must sit in front with me." At that, I got into the car, feeling terribly rude to be sitting in front in relative comfort while relegating Marie to cramped misery in the back.

Conversation was a bit awkward initially but by the time we reached Valence, where we stopped at La Licorne for dinner, things seemed to be somewhat easier. The restaurant was cozy and charming and the food was *formidable* as the French would say. A bottle of wine further took the edge off. Beth was charmed by the sculpture of the unicorn that stood in the entrance, and Marie was beaming at her in grandmotherly warmth, helping her to relax as well.

I liked his mother. There was a quiet, proud old-world charm about her. She took pride in her appearance. Her hair, although very white and sparse, was carefully and stylishly coiffed. Her clothes were suited to her slender build, flattering in color, and of the best quality. Maurice had told me that her favorite designers were Balenciaga and Celine. When we were installed at their apartment in Marseilles, I learned that while she had only a few clothes in the small closet in her bedroom---which I used while there, they were all superb. She was a cultured lady. Marie loved classical music and could discuss it knowledgeably and in depth. Because of many hours spent alone watching television, she had also developed a tremendous enthusiasm for soccer and would go on endlessly about her favorite teams. She knew the players, as well as she knew musicians and composers. Since neither topic was one of my fortés, I spent the time listening. Her other love, was Maurice. He was all she had. Her husband had widowed her long since and her only other child, a girl, had died at ten years of age. When she looked at Beth, her eyes lit with the fire of rekindled memories banked by the pain still buried in her heart. Maurice seemed impatient and abrupt with her which I suppose isn't unusual or remarkable, since we are often that way with the people with whom we live in proximity day in and day out and come to take for granted. Even so, despite the occasional bark in her direction, it was obvious he appreciated her intellect and stimulating conversations with him.

It was a long ride from Valence to Chamonix. Beth and Marie talked for an hour or so and then I heard gentle snores from Marie's corner and Beth's own slow steady breathing. Maurice smiled, and reaching over, took my hand.

"It means so much to me to have someone I can talk to about the things that matter in my life: art, my photography, the books I am working on. I need to talk about these things, to discuss ideas and to touch the inner recesses of my heart. For so long, I have feared that I was damned to be lonely and alone for all of my life. Now I dream that doesn't have to be."

"You know so many people who all seem to really like you. Surely there must be someone among them that you have been able to talk with about the things that are important to you."

"One might think, but, no. In my entire life, I have been misunderstood. I have never felt part of a warm loving home. That is why I want so much what you and Beth have between you, that warm, simple, open affection. When I was a child two memories stand out. I can picture my mother and the two aunts who lived with us, dressed to go out for the afternoon: hats, gloves, and elegant dresses. I was angry that I couldn't go with them. It was my favorite game to climb on top of the elevator cage, that my father had installed in our house, while they were riding in it. I learned how to make it stall. I would lie there atop the cage and listen to them complain about the unreliability of it. When I started it up again they would always remark at how contrary it was and they would stand there with the feathers on their hats swishing about as they looked in bafflement at one another. They never discovered my game. I always wished that my mother would tell me bedtime stories and tuck me in or play with me. But in the evenings they were always going out and the nanny would hold me so I could kiss her cheek without mussing maman's dress."

"She loves you very much. I know she did then as well, and I'm sure she didn't realize that you felt rejected." I could only pray that she would not awaken and hear his hurtful comments.

"I did though. My other memory is also painful. When I was just a little fellow, I fell in love with an electric train I had seen in a shop window. I wanted it so badly, so for Christmas my father gave it to me. He set it up in a room on the third floor with all of the accessories: platforms, buildings, trees, people, everything. It filled the room. I thought it was a fairyland, but I could only play with it with my father and even then he would not allow me to run it or touch, I could only watch him do all of the things I had dreamed of. He said I would break it. I came to hate that train because it was really my father's, not mine." He continued to talk as I grew tired and started to drowse. Suddenly I felt cold mountain air pouring over me. Beth and Marie stirred in their sleep. "Jo, wake up and talk to me so I won't get sleepy."

"Okay, but please close the window; the air is freezing. Where are we? Are we nearly there?" I could see by the clock on the dash that it was almost one in the morning.

"We're in the Alps of Savoy, the Haute Savoie. Another thirty minutes and we will be in Chamonix. My mother goes for a six weeks-vacation every year since my father died. She has friends who have chalets nearby. Maman loves the mountains and the concerts in Chamonix. Before my father died, they had a chalet in St. Moritz and she would spend summers there. But after his death, it was too depressing for her there so we sold the chalet and she began coming to Chamonix instead. I do want you to see St. Moritz though, so we will go there for a few days after we leave here."

"I'd love to see it. I know it's very famous for winter sports."

"True, but it's busy in summer as well. Chamonix also. You will see lots of Japanese in Chamonix. They come for the mountain climbing and to see Mont Blanc. It is amazing to me to see how popular this area has become for the Japanese. As a people they have a love and reverence for mountains."

Maurice was quiet for a few minutes. "My mother is part Swiss. Did I tell you?"

"I don't think so."

"Her mother was Swiss and her father Corsican. Although she was also born in Corsica, she spent most of her youth in Switzerland. We still have cousins there, some quite prominent. One is very influential in the Swiss government. My mother's uncle was a duke. Another uncle was instrumental in establishing the museum in Winterthur when he donated a substantial art collection containing quite a few Picasso's."

"Will we go to Winterthur? I would love to see the museum and his collection."

"We'll see. I suppose it's possible."

"Was the spice business in your mother's family or your father's?"

"Oh no, it was founded by my father's family. At one time we were the largest import-export spice business in Europe. There were plantations in the Orient, Africa and Provençe where we grew many of our own spices and herbs. They've been sold now and we contract for everything. We get spices from all over but many of the herbs come from Provençe." He continued talking about spices telling me about the different ones, how they are grown, and what is involved in contracting for, packing, shipping and processing them. It was a very complex and risky business. It sounded a lot like playing the futures market since crops were contracted for in advance. I gasped when he told me the mark-up factor and the profit potential. Some spices were more costly than gold. His words were beginning to buzz in the air around me as I grew sleepier. Details slip my memory because of it.

"Jo, this is the Arve River. We're in Chamonix. Two minutes and we will be at the hotel.

The Hotel Mont Blanc was a beautiful sight. Beth, Marie and I followed Maurice in. The desk clerk emerged sleepily from behind his counter warning us to be quiet. It didn't take long to summon a porter and get settled in our rooms. Maurice told us to sleep late and he would call us when he was up. Once the door of our room closed behind us, Beth who had had some sleep was alert and excited to explore the room. We opened the window to the sharp, cold mountain air and adjusted the wooden shutter that could be hooked close to the window to keep out morning light but still give fresh air. We both exclaimed in delight over the fluffy duvets and crisp linens on the beds. While I took a quick shower, Beth found the form to request breakfast, filled it out and hung it on the door. It certainly had not taken her long to cotton to that routine.

I emerged from my bath yawning. "Baby, it is so late and I'm very tired. Let's go to bed now and explore in the morning."

"Mwa, Mommy."

"Mwa, Baby."

I awoke to the sound of bottles clinking. Beth had found the frigo-bar. Rolling over, I found my watch on the bedside table and opened an eye to peek at the time: nine-thirty. I groaned.

"Look, Mommy. They've got Coke and peanuts and everything in here. Can I have some?"

"Beth, we will have breakfast in thirty minutes. Didn't you tell me that you checked ten o'clock on the room service form?"

She dragged out a reluctant, "Yes..."

The room was cool but smelled so clean and fresh. I climbed out of bed and walked over to the window, threw it back and then swung the shutters open to a beautiful sunny morning. The air was bright and sparkling clear. I leaned out to breathe it in, loving the way the mountain air made me feel invigorated.

"Beth, come look. There is a pretty little church just over to the right that looks like it was made for dolls." She crowded into the window with me. I pointed, "Look. Do you like those houses? They're called chalets."

"Ohh. They look just like the ones in my Heidi book."

"I think you're right." I laughed. "If you look up the mountain you can see the *téléferique* carrying people to the top. Maybe Maurice will take us on it."

He must have heard his name, because the shutters of the adjacent room opened and he popped his head out to greet us. "Good morning to you, Beth, and good morning, Jo. The mountain air is wonderful for you. You look nineteen."

"If that's the case, I'm moving here permanently." I laughed with delight, my vanity well pleased. "Did you sleep well?"

"*Pas mal.* I took a dose at bedtime, that always helps me." Indeed he always took pills and usually still complained about not sleeping. He didn't believe in alcohol, drinking only a little wine, never went to doctors, hated drugs, never took medicine...but he believed in sleeping pills. He ended each day with those and began each day with wheat germ...great heaping mouthfuls which he gulped directly from the box. I hated it when they sifted down onto the perpetual black Izod. He never noticed, so eventually when I could stand it no longer, I would point it out to him. His other health maintenance regime was regular potions of tisanes. He carried packets of herbs that he had concocted himself from those he sold in order to brew the various herbal teas that his indispositions required. Maurice believed in homeopathic medicines only. I assumed they worked for him since he appeared, as the expression goes, as healthy as a horse and as strong as an ox.

After lunch with Marie we walked down to the station to take the *chemin de fer* to the *Mer de Glace* so we could see the famous glacier. Marie opted to stay in the hotel and take the sun in the rose garden. The little train we boarded climbed steeply up the slope of the mountain. Looking down we could see the valley containing

Chamonix hazy blue in the distance. Maurice sat in the facing seat with his camera at the ready. I could tell from the way Beth grimaced and squirmed when he lifted it that she felt as scrutinized as a fish in a goldfish bowl. I was a little nonplussed myself knowing how un-photogenic I have always considered myself. I put my arm around Beth to reassure her. I had accepted that Maurice was constantly carrying enough cameras and related equipment to seriously strain the carrying capacity of a pack mule. I watched him write on the film boxes each location he had taken shots and the setting used. On maps he would mark areas where he had taken the photos or wanted to return to take more. Although he was so hyper and impatient in many ways, when it came to his craft he was the patient perfectionist. He took it seriously, whereas we used our cameras just to record memories of the trip. I had tried early on to explain the difference to her without much success.

"Beth, don't move."

She looked at me and grimaced.

"No. Go back the way you were; it was perfect. Jo, just a little more to the left, chin up and move your hand a millimeter to the right. Okay, now hold it."

I heard Beth sigh. She had absolutely no patience for it and felt very self-conscious with him. It didn't bother me the same way it did her, but at times I too grew impatient. Now I treasure those memories he captured so beautifully for us. I also felt it was a small price to pay to see the many places I had longer for and dreamed of. I would have given anything at Beth's age for the opportunity to travel. But my parents were hard working and had neither the time, money, nor interest for international travel. I could only travel in my dreams and books. And that is where I often stayed, as my childhood was unhappy in ways far more serious than those experienced by Maurice.

I had wanted to travel to Europe since the fourth grade when a distant cousin of mine, who was a senior, presented a slide show to the school of his year as an exchange student in Holland. I had been enthralled at the exotic images and yearned with a hunger akin to pain to have been the one that went there. Instantly I developed a schoolgirl crush on Reginald. Even when I went to the university that was only thirty miles from home, I realized he could still make my pulse race just a little. I had just emerged from the library with an armful of books and he was ascending the steps of the library when I spotted him approaching. He recognized me and stopped to chat, explaining that he used the library because it was the best around. I was so flustered I was practically tongue tied and could feel myself blushing. I think that was the last time that I saw him but even now whenever I pass his house on trips home to visit family, I still feel an inner smile.

When the train reached the end of the line, we followed all of the others out onto the platform and then around to the deck that overlooked the Mer de Glace. That close to the glacier it was chilly, so the three of us ordered hot chocolate from the bar in order to warm up.

"Maurice, I'm cold. I think I'll stay inside here while you and Beth go to the glacier."

For added warmth I wrapped my sweater over Beth's own before they left me to board the lift to the glacier. I watched them as they swooped over to the ice field and climbed out onto the hard frozen surface. From the distance it looked gray and dirty and was intricately grooved with gashes and deep convolutions. I watched them walk with the others into one of the areas that tunneled into the glacier. Sometime later I watched all of the others re-emerge and come out to catch the last lift back for the day. When I did not see Maurice and Beth I became uneasy, as the posted signs emphatically warned that the last lift of the day left the glacier at five. I looked at my watch and it was close to the ominous hour. Surely they would not be left behind. They would freeze to death there at night without warm clothes, and the lower the sun sank the colder it was getting. My southern blood was nearly congealed from cold where I was. I wondered how much colder it had to be on the glacier. In near panic,

I started to make my frantic way to the ticket window when I saw them emerge from the tunnel at a dead run. Suddenly he stopped and Beth as well. I watched puzzled for a moment and then realized he was making her pose for him...perfectionistic and ignorant of all beyond his art and as slow as usual. I had nearly despaired of them making it when they again began running. The lift was waiting. When they were back on the deck with me, I could tell Beth was beyond annoyed. Maurice was oblivious. He delightedly showed me the photograph that the photographer inside the glacier had taken of them in the 'house of ice.' His favorite was a shot of Beth seated in a chair carved from the ice. She was so red with fury that I was surprised it hadn't melted.

"These are for you, darling." He handed the photos to her.

"Thank you." Her voice was tight with tension and sounded about as chilly as the ice below.

When we boarded the train to return to Chamonix, Maurice stood just inside the door in what could only be called a pose, a very theatrical and vain one at that: chest out, head up, shoulders back. I noticed that a group of young and very attractive men, apparently mountain climbers, were seated in the benches adjacent to the one that Beth and I shared. I knew Beth was wondering just as I did why he did not take a seat with us. I didn't think it had anything to do with the chill of her thank you, but perhaps I was wrong.

At the hotel we found Marie on the terrace and sat with her in the late afternoon sun. She was well known there among the many other guests who were also regular summer residents. She greeted them in Italian, German, French or English and in an aside would tell me to whom she had spoken. Many of them appeared to be either prominent or titled. I was impressed with the mental acuity she displayed and with her command of the various languages despite her more than eighty years. English she told me was her weakest language as she had used it less often over the years and had forgotten much. As we sat there chatting comfortably with one another, the concierge came out to tell Maurice that the reservations that he had requested for dinner were confirmed.

"Darlings, I have a special treat for you tonight." I could tell he was excited by what he had planned for us. "We must all go up and prepare for dinner. The restaurant is about forty-five minutes from here in Talloires. If we leave soon we will have time for a little drive through some of the countryside around Megève."

Leaving the terrace view of Mont Blanc behind, we repaired to our respective rooms. Maurice would spend the next hour on the phone conducting his business affairs. It became a ritual for us to get ready and wait as morning and evening of every day that we traveled, he called his office, various suppliers or customers to conduct business. Beth had trouble understanding the delays and repeatedly I would try to appease her with an explanation and a request for tolerance and understanding. Sometimes I felt like a hypocrite, as I would grow impatient as well, despite trying to keep it hidden.

We descended to the lobby to find Marie already seated there. "Maurice is always late. I tell him and tell him not to be late. It does not help."

I gave her a wry smile, "So, I'm learning."

Beth walked over to the guest registry book by the piano and was busily occupied there. I joined her to see that she had drawn a unicorn reminiscent of the one in Valance on one of the registry pages. Marie walked over to see what we were doing.

"*Ah, charmant. C'est très charmant. Vous avez le talent.*" Sorry, I say in English. Charming. Very charming. You have talent."

Beth blushed at the attention and at having been caught defacing the registry book. We were so engrossed in the moment that the three of us were surprised when suddenly Maurice spoke, "I see you have all been waiting for me. I am so sorry to be delayed by so many phone calls. What is this?" He asked, pointing to Beth's drawing.

"Why that is wonderful. What an artist you are, darling. You have real talent. I must get you some materials so you can make drawings for me."

I thought "fat chance." I knew she disliked for anyone to be too effusive with her and she was in no mood to accommodate him after the scare on the glacier. In the room as we were dressing, she described for me how frightened she had been that they would be left there to freeze. I told her not to worry as that would never have happened because I would have been so angry I would have melted the glacier and she would have just washed right down to me. She had laughed with me at the image, but she wasn't over the pout.

Leaving Chamonix to drive to Annecy on our way to Talloires, we had a chance to view the mountains rising sharply on either side of the road. It had been too dark for us to see them on the night before. Even though Marie was complaining about her ankle that was still sore from a recent fall, Maurice parked the car on the edge of Annecy and insisted we all get out and walk into the old town. The three of us were walking together, when I noticed that Marie was trailing further and further behind. I tugged on his arm and asked him to check on her. Maurice walked back to her and I could tell by his gestures they were exchanging angry words. He caught up with Beth and me and insisted that we pose for some more shots of the two of us. We complied but I kept turning my head to look at Marie struggling to reach us. It struck me then that she was crying but too proud to allow it to show. Furious with him for his brusqueness and inconsideration of his mother, I left him and his cameras and went to Marie. Beth followed. He continued photographing what truly was a beautiful old town with winding canals lined with flower-boxed railings and pastel Alpine buildings.

"Marie, may I help you?" I put my arm around her to help support her weight as Beth held onto her right arm. Fat tears began to spill slowly down her wrinkled cheeks to hang at the jaw before dropping onto her bodice. She clung to me, gratitude for my compassion shining in her eyes. Maurice gave up and walked back to join us. I could tell from the expression on his face that he was ashamed, embarrassed and angry all at the same time. He knew his three ladies were all unhappy with him and he could not bear it.

Gently I helped Marie get resettled in the backseat and I removed her shoe and propped her foot up as best I could. I didn't wonder that she had trouble with walking. The heels of her shoes were both worn at steep angles on the outside edges. They should long since have been trashed. It wasn't as though she could afford no others.

"Marie, I think these shoes are aggravating your ankle injury as the heels are so worn they change your balance and ankle position. Perhaps you can wear another pair tomorrow."

"Alors, because of the swelling these are all that I can get on my feet. I think..."

Maurice was eager to distract this line of conversation, as he interrupted her, "We have time to drive through Megève on our way to Talloires. It is a beautiful drive and I do want you to see it."

He didn't exaggerate: it was gorgeous. In Mègeve, he pointed to the slopes famous for winter skiing but converted in the summer season for skiing on the grass. I found that amusing. Just outside of town, we parked by a pasture dotted with cows brought there for the summer grazing. He asked me to get out with him. I was not sure what was coming.

"You look lovely this evening, darling. Could I take a shot of you with those mountains behind?" I suspected it was his way of apologizing for upsetting us all but he was either too proud or could not decide on a more direct way to do so.

When we reached the Père Bise restaurant in Talloires, Maurice rushed in ahead of us worried that we had lost our reservation by being over an hour late. As we caught up with him, I saw him slip the Maître'd several bills. Beth and he were quickly escorted to a table while I held onto a limping Marie. I helped her get comfortably settled and then took my own seat to look at the view of the lake of Annecy. It was beautiful; the restaurant and auberge were famous for that view and for the superb cuisine. Maurice

explained with French pride, that people come there from all over the world to dine in the celebrated restaurant. He and his mother conducted a passionate discussion about the food; replete with comparisons of meals they had eaten there relative to other memorable meals. As an American, it was a novelty to listen to such a detailed and succinct discussion of every minutia of the various dishes they had eaten right down to the decoration on the plate. I had noticed the same thing when we had eaten with his friends and they too had talked at length about food. I came to realize that good food and dining are a large part of French life, and as such, merit serious discussion. No doubt this attitude towards their cuisine is responsible for the generally excellent quality of French restaurants that we encountered. I decided that Americans could take some pointers there as our restaurants are often disappointing, making up for lack of taste and appeal by serving overly large portions as though that could improve quality. But then, perhaps there lies the difference: sadly, as a people we seem to predominately prefer quantity to quality.

A lot of my memorable and not so memorable moments were spent in restaurants that summer. My typical day consisted of a continental breakfast of croissants and hot tea around ten and lunch at two. In France lunch is a serious meal with the menu the same as that for dinner, and it often lasts until four or so. Our dinner was usually late, after nine, and unless it was a special occasion, not as heavy as lunch. Even so it generally lasted a couple of hours. I have found that in Europe in general, service and dining are at a more leisurely pace allowing time for conversation and appreciation of the chef's efforts. Europeans tend to dine out more and spend more of their income for food than Americans. Maurice also pointed out that the French are more reluctant to entertain at home unless very intimate with their guests. I decided I could understand, as who would not be reluctant to compete with professional French chefs.

As we sat there discussing the comparative dining habits of French and Americans, Beth tired of our conversation and was wandering along the edges of the lake, keeping a wary eye on the hissing swans that had claimed the shore for themselves. She was wearing the very feminine pink and white batiste dress with flowing skirt that I had bought her for our trip. With the setting sun lighting the lake and sky with warm hues and silhouetting her dancing form, she made a charming picture of childhood innocence and joy. We were all struck with the animation and poetry she brought to an already beautiful view. Maurice snatched his camera and ran after her where he began furiously to snap shots before the light could change or she would tire. Those photographs became our all-time favorites of her from that summer. His artistry and sensitivity as a photographer had created a special mood and ambience that captured the very qualities that had mesmerized us as we sat at the table watching her.

While the two of them were beside the lake, Marie and I conducted a conversation in French. I wasn't entirely sure what she was saying as my comprehension and vocabulary were not nearly as profound as she assumed it to be. Her diction was beautiful, her vocabulary more than a challenge for me, and the pace of delivery far beyond my speed to translate. After two summers there, I would begin to comprehend without first translating and it would become far easier to keep pace with conversations. Despite my difficulties with the language, that was an enjoyable moment with Marie as I could sense her growing attachment to me, perhaps due to my earlier compassion for her.

The next day we all went by *télépherique* to lunch at a restaurant on the edge of the glacial field. Marie was relaxed, as the swelling in her ankle had subsided some. I noted that she was wearing different shoes so she could walk without as much stress. After an amble through Chamonix and a rest on the terrace of the hotel, we had a quiet dinner and retired early. We were leaving the next day and I could feel Marie's growing pangs of coming loneliness. She had grown fond of me and I of her. She was totally enamored of Beth who reminded her so much of the daughter she had lost at that age. She walked into the town with Beth and bought her a simple keepsake while Maurice was occupied loading the car. When he had finished with the car, Beth showed him her gift and he decided that he would give her one as well. He then walked with her to purchase a beautiful stone, a geode with green rhodolite crystals embedded within. He warned me to assure that she would treat it carefully as it had been quite dear to buy.

As we drove away, Marie stood on the steps of the Mont Blanc waving to us. There was an expression of ineffable sadness on her face, as she knew she would not see us again that summer since we were returning home before her vacation ended. I felt tears well in my eyes at the forlorn picture she made standing there...so old and so alone, and prayed that my years would not end that way.

We stopped in Geneva for lunch and a quick tour. Maurice had promised Beth that he would buy her a watch. Shopping for a watch was almost overwhelming as there were so many from which to choose, however we finally found one she loved at the Piaget store...with gold case and lizard band. She was thrilled and made it a point to look often at her watch and announce the time. For several days after that, she made no objection to posing and made it a point to be friendlier with Maurice. After Geneva, we drove along the shores of the lake with its famous fountain and on to Lausanne and Montreux. It was a beautiful drive and it was with reluctance that I saw it slide by as we turned north to drive to Fribourg, where we left the autobahn to detour through the picturesque town of Murten nestled on the shores of its own lake. We walked through the gates of the town beneath a huge clock tower to emerge onto a large square filled with sidewalk cafes, boxes spilling a riot of colorful flowers, sparkling and splashing fountains, and beautiful buildings of the vernacular Swiss architectural style. Beth and I loved it and would have been happy to spend the night in Murten, but Maurice was intent on spending the night in Basel. He was eager to show me the museum there and its superb collection of Holbein's and Klee's.

In the morning, we strolled past Basel's grand old cathedral and ambled along the banks of the river where we were amused to see nude men bathing in the alpine fed water. When we entered the museum and found ourselves standing before the stunning Van

Gogh's, I felt my eyes well with tears. Beth was amused at my emotion, but not Maurice, as he felt it too. We walked through the collection with quiet reverence pausing longer before the Impressionists that Beth loved and the Holbein's, Klee's, Picasso's and Cranach's that Maurice favored. For me, it was all heavenly and each work so special in its own way. We talked softly sharing our joy and the information we knew about the artists and these works. He was far more knowledgeable than I at that point and could hold forth for hours with scholarly and succinct analysis. I was intimidated, impressed, and increasingly respectful of his intellect. In turn he appreciated having a receptive and attentive audience in me. The landscape and charm of Switzerland are legendary but so should be that museum. It is a gem of rare quality and equally an asset to the country.

I would have loved to spend more time there, but we had reservations in St. Moritz for the night. Taking the autobahn again, we sped past Zurich, too late to detour by Winterthur and the museum there. From there we turned south to Chur and the drive into St. Moritz. The route runs through the Lenzerheide Pass and what was to me some of the most beautiful scenery in Switzerland. We stopped in a beautiful mountain meadow between the towns of Lenzerheide and Tiefencastel and stretched our legs. Maurice took more photographs.

"Jo, we will shortly reach the Julier Pass. It is the highest pass in Europe and is closed much of the winter due to the heavy snows. This season of the year, the pastures on both sides of the road are filled with Alpine cows that are brought to the high meadows for grazing. You can see the huts the herders live in during the summer months while they tend their animals here on the roof of Europe. It is one of my most treasured places: so free of crowds, so serene, and so beautiful." When we reached the pass, I knew what he meant. The sky was startlingly blue and the white fluffy clouds looked close enough to touch. The rock-strewn meadows were lush with flowers, lichen and grass, made green by the glacier fed springs that bubbled up everywhere adding the soft murmur of flowing water to the sound of the contented cows lowing in appreciation of their own version of bovine heaven.

Maurice stopped beside the road and Beth and I dashed off to pet a beautiful cow that exuded the very essence of friendly tolerance of these strange humans. She was the color of amber, softened and grayed; her eyes were large and luminous. In all, she was a marvelous cow and we gloried in stroking her forehead and talking to her. It was a world apart: so high there were no trees, just dark outcroppings of rocks that lifted this high meadow into the clear, crisp, invigorating air; no crowds, pushing and noisy; the sounds only those of the softly moaning wind, the gurgling of little brooks that danced playfully away from their mother springs to amble among the lichen and wildflowers, and the tinkling music of the bells that adorned the softly mooing cows. If Paradise ever needs renovation, I think it would do well to emulate the Julier Pass in summer.

We descended from there to the Inn River which is born in the lakes of Segl and Silvaplauna, carves the valley of the Engadin and then flows north to Innsbruck and on to the Danube. Our hotel, the Chesa Gaurdalej, was just outside St. Moritz in the village of Silvaplauna, but before stopping for the evening, Maurice gave us a quick tour of St. Moritz Bad and St. Moritz. Passing a shop window filled with plush toys, he stopped to buy Beth a soft, cuddly-plush Alpine cow of just the right color. It even had a little tinkly cowbell around its neck. That night he took us to the famous grand old hotel, Badrutt's Palace, where we had a marvelous dinner finished with a creamy Swiss chocolate dessert. After that chocolate, I knew Beth was going to like it there.

St. Moritz was a lovely interlude that summer. Although Maurice was spending more time on the phone with his office, we still had time for long walks along the shore of Silvaplauna Lake and in the village of Sils Maria where we passed the house where Nietzche had lived. When he could not join us, Beth and I took our own walks to a pasture by the lake where beautiful Alpine cows grazed the lush grass. We were charmed by a small chapel on the edge of the lake and by the colorful small boats anchored nearby. Our last night there, Maurice came into our room and tossed a pillow at Beth. Immediately a pillow fight commenced with the girls on one side and him on the other. He played with an almost hysterical zeal and was laughing like a boy.

The morning we were to leave, Beth woke me and excitedly pulled me to the window. It was snowing, big beautiful flakes that piled up several inches and I wondered if we would be able to leave. Although by noon it had melted, it had provided one more visual treat for our stay, a beautiful summer snow that was a bizarre event for two girls from the sunny south.

All of us were reluctant to leave the peaceful tranquility of St. Moritz but we had been promised a stay at the Hotel de Paris in Monte Carlo following a detour through Milan. Maurice had told us enough about it to soften our sorrow at leaving. It sounded like the ultimate in grand hotels and I'd heard about Monte Carlo all of my life. I especially remembered recent television shows that had been filmed there with stars like Perry Como, Suzanne Somers, etc. They had made it look like a luxurious version of Heaven. I also wanted to visit Milan to see the Galleria Vittorio Emanuele, the first covered shopping "mall" and the gathering spot for the Milanese, and the imposing and ornate Gothic cathedral. I knew we would not have time for a visit to the Chapel of Santa Maria della Grazie to see Leonardo's *Last Supper* nor the Brera Museum. It would be another seventeen years before I finally achieved that goal, and I am still waiting to see the Poldi Pezzoli Museum and Leonardo da Vinci's museum of science and technology. Perhaps, before I exit stage right...or left.

We spent the night in Verona where we ate at a wonderful restaurant overlooking the river. We had parked our car near the ancient Roman amphitheatre where *Romeo and Juliet* are performed each summer, catching a glimpse of that on the way to dinner. The next morning we took the autostrade to Milan. Although we enjoyed our brief visit to Milan, it was miserably hot and by the time we regained the car we were all wet and grumpy. A cool air-conditioned lunch prior to resuming our trip to Monte Carlo helped to restore our good humor despite the hassle of traffic to come.

The drive from Genoa along the shore to the Haut Corniche highway that runs high above the Mediterranean is a beautiful one with mountains plunging steeply into the dazzling blue of the sea. Oleanders paint the cliffs with splashes of color, and cypresses provide exclamation points for the view. Breathtaking vistas are interspersed with small dark tunnels called *gallerias* making me almost hold my breath in anticipation of what would come at the end of the brief darkness. The music of the cicadas, the smell of the rosemary, thyme and lavender laden air, and the touch of the sun on our faces brought all of our senses into play.

When we pulled up in front of the Hotel de Paris, a porter skirted around a group of people clustered on the stairs to reach the car. He told us they were in the process of filming a movie starring Marcello Mastroianni. Camera crew, stars, directors and extras were all milling around adding an air of excitement to our arrival. The porter motioned us to the side door to enter so we were deprived of making our grand entrance through a movie set. I thought it was just as well as I was wind-blown and bedraggled from a long day in the car.

The main square in front of the hotel was jammed with tourists gawking at those entering and leaving. Each time we descended the steps, we felt like celebrities. You could tell from the way the onlookers stared and whispered, they were trying to decide whether or not we were and if so, who. In my big black hat, over-sized shades and strapless black dress, I might have looked the role enough to fool a few; however not enough that anyone asked for my autograph. Beth gained a new career aspiration there: she decided she wanted to be a movie star. For someone who had always been rather shy, I thought she had made a brave choice

Maurice was well known at the hotel. The valet parking men, the concierge, and the porters all greeted him like a long lost friend. We were led to an exquisite suite of rooms: a huge pink marble foyer, a large main salon with a balcony overlooking the sparkling Mediterranean, a basket of treats and a cooler of chilled champagne at the ready on a sideboard, and a bouquet of flowers taller than I standing on the table by the sofa. The room was so grand that a smaller bouquet would have been lost. On either side of the salon, doors led into a bedroom each with its own bathroom complex consisting of a large main space with sink, vanity and tub, a shower in its own glass fronted room and two smaller closeted areas containing a toilet and a bidet respectively. Pink marble covered the floor and more covered the walls between large beautifully gilt framed mirrors. The bath alone was like a palace. The bedrooms had walls of padded silk exquisitely detailed with white molding and deep cornices. The ceilings were centered with beautiful chandeliers in ornate plaster medallions. Maurice gave us our choice of the two bedrooms. Since the one on the left was done in pink and the other in blue, we chose the pink. One look at that suite and Beth and I were ready to take up residence for life. Each afternoon a maid appeared to take our clothes for the evening and give them a fresh pressing. In the mornings room service arrived on a yellow linen draped cart with heavy silver, gorgeous china and crystal, and a basket of delicious pastries and croissants accompanied by rich butter, really fruity preserves, freshly squeezed juice and hot tea with lemon. After our stay, Beth decided that her two favorite places in the world were Paris and Monte Carlo. I could hardly find fault with her choices.

We had dinner that night at the most celebrated little restaurant in Monaco, Rompole. Maurice made it a point to tell us that there was a pecking order to the seating with the less desired tables in the rear. He wanted us to know the significance of our prime table. The food was so good I would have been happy to eat in the kitchen.

It wasn't late when we returned to our rooms. I settled Beth for the night and then put on my robe. Restless and not yet sleepy, I wandered into the salon and out to the balcony to stare at the moon shining on the water. Lights of big yachts twinkled where they lay at their harbor moorings and up on the hill to my right I could see the royal palace. It was so romantic that I longed for a man to hold me, make love to me, and share the magic of the moment. Beth was in bed, Maurice was taking his nightly ritual of a cold tub bath, and I was on my balcony looking for my Romeo to emerge from somewhere in the mellow night spread before me.

"It is a beautiful view, isn't it?" I jumped a little not having heard him come up behind me.

"It has to be one of the loveliest and most romantic places in the world." I laughed a little ironically, "It's a place for long walks in the moonlight listening to the distant melody of some old song, a place for dancing under the stars to just the rhythm in your hearts, of lovers embracing as the morning sun begins to pink the sky."

"You are such a romantic." He changed the subject and began to talk of the art collection in Basel and of the one he was taking us to in St. Paul de Vence. Maurice was so nervous I wondered if he thought I planned to launch myself at him. I could see the headline: *'sex starved woman rapes man on public balcony'*. It is not my style to be aggressive with men, but I didn't know how to tell him he was quite safe. When he said goodnight leaving me to my nocturnal musings, he hugged me to him and kissed me on the mouth. I knew he felt that it was the expected thing and I hated that it was forced. I told myself then and there to forget any romantic fantasies with him, and to *remember to forget*. If the ambiance of the evening and the presence of a desirable and desiring woman elicited no inspiration, nothing would.

The next day, Maurice was all charm. He took us to the hotel's beach and settled us in chairs by the water. Beth was annoyed by all of the bare breasted women as she found them totally lacking in modesty. As her own breasts were just beginning to bud, she was very self-conscious about that particular anatomical part. She had nearly died when on the last visit home, my mother with noticeable lack of tact, had commented on her 'Sunday bumps'. That was the local expression for young girls, who dressed in their Sunday finery, would wear padded bras beneath to enhance nature's progress or lack thereof.

Maurice spotted Helmut Newton on the beach, sunning like us. I commented to him that I found some of Newton's photographs a bit misogynous. That set Maurice off on a galloping defense on his idol's behalf. He said that he had met him and I could see that he was itching for Newton to notice and recognize him. Giving up, he finally went over and spoke to him.

When he returned to us, he suggested we have lunch in the beachside cafe. While sitting there, he held my hand and took great pains to be attentive to me. Afterwards he had me pose by a palm tree that made a pattern of sun and shade across my body. Beth got off lightly that day. I suspected he was trying to make up to me for the lack of romance the previous evening. We were treated to a gourmet dinner at the Hotel de Paris's dining room with the roof that slides back for dining under the stars. Beth was thrilled with his choice and I knew she ached to get her hands on the control button for that roof. After dinner, we walked Beth back to the hotel and tucked her in for the evening. Maurice was taking me to 'Jimmy'z', the elegant disco that sits right on the water's edge. I was shocked when he told me our after dinner drinks, champagne for me and water for him, both cost a flat thirty bucks a glass. I enjoyed dancing with him, as he was a good dancer with an excellent sense of rhythm. It was good too, to have some grown-up fun as so many of our activities were geared to the interests of an eleven-year old. Back at the hotel, I turned to him in the foyer of our suite and kissed him on the cheek and thanked him for a delightful evening. Was it with relief, that he thanked me as well before turning to his room? I went into my own where Beth was quietly sleeping, satisfied that by taking the initiative I had averted an awkward goodnight scene.

We left in the morning driving through Beaulieu and Nice before turning north to St. Paul de Vence. Maurice was again annoying Beth with his photographs of her that required frequent stops. She was not obvious about it despite her heavy complaints to me afterward. I began to feel tremendous pressure trying to keep things pleasant between the two of them and I also felt a growing frustration that a man I found attractive, who professed to love and admire me, could so ignore me as a woman. Again I reminded myself to just forget it. However, the most exhausting factor that summer was the intensity of his personality. My brain constantly grew weary from the pressure to be ever profound. I would have loved a few more of the days like the carefree ones that Jaynie and I had enjoyed before she left. Even so the thing that kept me captive and eager for more was my greed for Europe and all of the places I had dreamed of, read about and longed for since childhood.

My childhood fantasy world was an escape from a martyred, overworked mother and a physically abusive, philandering father. I as the oldest child I was expected to be responsible and serious. No matter what I did it wasn't enough. If I came home with a 99 on a test, the immediate demand was to know why it hadn't been a 100. Challenged once too often when my 99 was the only passing grade in the class, I remarked that just because I was intelligent there was no guarantee of eternal perfection. I became a surrogate mother to my siblings and a confidant to my mother in her marital woes. I was also my father's whipping post when he needed to vent his frustrations. After years of being beaten with a belt so that summer would often find me in skirts instead of shorts to hide the dark purple welts striping my legs, I finally had had enough when in the ninth grade he threw another of his tirades. By the following evening I had determined that even if it killed me, I was going to tell him just how his anger and abuse affected our family. Although I was quaking in my shoes I did not let him see it, and proceeded to lay out my case in calm and dispassionate statements of fact. When I was finished he was oddly quiet. He shocked me then by saying he was sorry. He never hit me again nor any of the others in my presence.

With a start I brought myself back to the moment, "I'm sorry I didn't hear what you were saying."

"I was just pointing out the town of Vence. You can just see it there on the crown of that hill on the right side of the car. Like many medieval towns, it was built on a hill for protection. There is an excellent inn and restaurant there called Le Colombe D'Or or the 'golden dove' on a street leading up to the town. We have reservations for dinner and to spend the night. It is one of my favorite places and the art collection on display in the restaurant, around the terrace pool, and in the hotel is superb. Before we check in, we're going to visit the Foundation Maeght. Have you heard of it?"

"Yes. Remember you sent me a book on it several years ago?"

"Ah, that's right."

"I've studied it cover to cover. I want very much to see the Giacometti's."

"The Matisse Chapel is marvelous too. I want to see your reaction to that. Did you tell Kiki that Matisse donated the funds to build it in honor of the nuns who nursed him during his later years when he was debilitated by an intestinal condition that destroyed the connective fibers supporting his intestines so that it was intensively painful for him to stand or even sit?"

"Sorry, I don't think I did."

"The book store is very well stocked. I hope that I will be able to find several books that I have been wanting. Perhaps, you will find the Bonnard book that you want. Beth will like the gift shop and the beautiful posters for sale there." Turning to her, he asked, "Would you like that, Kiki?"

"Yes." She was abrupt with annoyance and I knew it was because he insisted on calling her by this new nickname. Although he explained that in France it was a very nice nickname, she wanted no part of it. That had not deterred him. He continued to use it as his own special term of endearment for her. From time to time, she would point out that *Beth* not *Kiki* was her name, but he continued ignoring it. Counter opinions never quite registered.

The grounds of Fondation Maeght were a lush green from sprinklers that were working in concert to banish the dryness of the Mediterranean summer. Large trees shaded sculptures scattered about the lawn, created by some of the most renowned names in contemporary art.

"Jo, there is a Calder. It's one I like very much. But I think my favorite here are the Miro's. They have a light-hearted *caractère capricieux*...ah, that is to say whimsicality which I find very sophisticated in their simplicity." Turning to Beth and pointing, he asked, "Do you like that Miro there?"

"It looks weird to me." She pointed, "I like that dog better." It was a delightful Giacometti and I think I agreed with her.

I did not find the Bonnard book I had wanted, but Maurice purchased one that he had sought, a book of photography by Stieglitz. Beth discovered a surprise for me for my approaching birthday: a bright yellow canvas tote bag with a Matisse design in vivid red and blue. Maurice also insisted that he treat us to posters. I bought two Braque's and one Matisse to take to my friends at home and Beth selected a delightful Matisse. Maurice opted for two Picasso's and one of the Braque's that I had chosen.

As we were leaving the small Matisse chapel that was located on the foundation grounds, Maurice explained that the museum itself had been built as a memorial by a wealthy man as a memorial to his son who had been killed in a traffic accident. Walking in the middle, he took my hand and Beth's as we returned to the car.

"My cousin and his wife live in Nice. I would like to call and invite them to join us for dinner if you have no objections. My cousin, Christian---not the one called Christian that I don't like...is the one who used to deal in diamonds."

I hastened to agree as I did not want him to dwell overly long on that subject considering the rancor he held about those diamonds of Margot's. They joined us that night on the terrace of the Colombe D'Or. To my relief the subject of the notorious earrings never arose. They were a pleasant couple, I guessed to be in the seventies, and both spoke broken English and delighted in trying to describe their travel experiences in the States, however most of the conversation was in French. The talk of the other three was incomprehensible to Beth most of the time and only semi-lucid to me. I translated as best I could for her. But his cousins, despite the language limitations, were very friendly to us and seemed delighted to be invited to join us for dinner. I puzzled that had Maurice's story about the diamond been true, would they have been so friendly?

Our table was under one of the many large white canvas umbrellas that protected the tables from debris falling from the trees that spread leafy branches above our heads. The yellow linen covered table was by a low wall that provided protection from the steep drop along the edge of the cliff. Candlelight flickered and reflected in the crystal glasses on the tables like hundreds of little captured fireflies lighting the dark of the evening. Beneath those trees and stars, the owner, an elderly woman dressed in black so severe it resembled a nun's habit, had assembled one of the best private collections in France. There was a Calder by the pool, a huge Braque ceramic mural on the dining terrace, as well as numerous other significant pieces. In the interior were several Picasso's as well as paintings by other luminaries of the contemporary art world.

With the final adieus finished, Beth and I wasted no time in returning to our room in the Colombe D'Or's annex. It was decorated with five superb paintings and although I didn't recognize the names, their quality was unmistakable. Maurice phoned to bid us a final goodnight.

"Darlings, sleep well. Christian and his wife loved you both. They told me that they are so happy I have you in my life. I hope you liked them and enjoyed the evening. I know you sometimes felt left out of the conversation, and I am sorry. Really, you must both learn French."

"They were very nice and the dinner was wonderful. Thank you for a special evening." I silently agreed that I needed to learn more French and resolved to take classes when I returned home. "By the way, we love our room. It's huge and has wonderful paintings, a great view, and a bathtub as large as a small swimming pool."

"Mine, too. *Bon nuit, mes chéries. Dormez bien.*"

"*Dors bien, aussi. A matin.*"

We would be late leaving the next day as Maurice spent several hours on the phone. He called about ten as we were munching our quotidian croissants to tell us to be ready to leave around noon. We used the time for a quick dip in the pool, to relax and to catch up on some grooming. I did my nails and we both washed our hair. The phone rang again about one-thirty.

"I'm ready, darlings. I have been on the phone to Maman. She sends you her love. She says you are very natural and charming, Jo. And she thinks Beth is a little love. *Une petite ange*, a little angel."

"I'm so glad she liked us. We liked her too, very much. Is her ankle better?"

"I didn't ask. Since she didn't mention it, I assume so." I could tell by his tone that he didn't want to get into that line of conversation. "I also called the Hotel Concorde in Marseille. You will be staying there for a week or so until I have the apartment ready for you."

"I hope that will not be a lot of trouble for you."

"Oh no, it's nothing. I just have to move another bed into Maman's room and pack up some of her things so there's room for you. You'll like the Concorde Palm Beach. It's right on the water, the pool is nice, and the restaurant is quite good.'

"That sounds fine."

"Are you ready to leave?"

"Yes, all packed."

"Good. I'll be there in two minutes." It was twenty.

We left with tummies ready for lunch. My stomach growled and I guessed he heard as he remarked, "There is a very nice restaurant near here, Les Oliviers. We'll have lunch there before going on to St. Rémy. I have reservations at the Hotel des Antiques for us tonight. Tomorrow you will drive your car and follow me to Marseille."

The whole idea was daunting to me as I was not sure I was up to the challenge of driving in the second largest city in France. I also knew I could never keep up with him at the speeds he drove. I drive fast but he seemed to think the speed of sound was a realistic goal for a car.

Although the waiters were annoyed at our late arrival at Les Oliviers, they did not refuse to seat us when Maurice surreptiously slipped them a bit of happy-money. No matter how late we arrived in a restaurant, he always managed to get us seats and a nice meal. Two other couples were having lunch as we arrived, both American. Listening to their conversation, I gathered they vacationed there every year. I had so fallen for La Belle France, I could understand what kept bringing them back.

Beth was silent as Maurice and I conducted an exhaustive and exhausting discourse on art, history and philosophy. To occupy herself, she began idly arranging breadcrumbs, flower petals and bits of garnish from her plate to create a lady on the tablecloth. Maurice was thrilled at this evidence of her creativity and took several photographs, all the while lavishing on praise. She wiped it off the table to fall on the tiles beneath our feet and wordlessly began building another. Although she was still put off by his effusiveness, I suspected she was secretly pleased at the praise. The remainder of the summer we were to see numerous breadcrumb ladies left on restaurant tables following almost every meal. I was delighted she had found some amusement that didn't depend on me. Maurice decided that she exhibited a talent for design and was busy planning her future: finishing school in Lucerne, and then to the Sorbonne in Paris. After that he said he would arrange an apprenticeship in one of the leading fashion houses in Paris and then launch her on her own. Kiki was to be his own answer to Madame Coco Chanel. Beth listened. In private she vented her adamant objections to being sent away to school. I didn't force the issue. When plans are made so far in advance, time becomes either ally or enemy. Besides, I would miss her too much and there was no way I would let her spend tender years on one side of the Atlantic and me on the other.

Chapter 5

St. Rémy left behind, we were on our way to Marseille, Maurice in the lead and Beth and I bravely following. We were 'flying low' when I noticed that the car was becoming increasingly difficult to steer. I blinked my lights frantically to signal Maurice and pulled onto the shoulder of the autoroute. We were about twenty kilometers from Marseilles in a long stretch of highway without houses or exits and certainly miles from any service station. The tire on my rear passenger side was flat and so hot from the speed at which we were driving that it was a miracle it had not caught fire.

At Maurice's instructions, I dumped on a liter of Coke to cool it, nearly breaking Beth's heart in the process, and he began the changing process: unload the car which was packed, fish out the spare, find the jack, twenty minutes to figure out how to make the jack work, and then the task of avoiding the on-rushing cars that zipped by at such speed the backwash of air was like a physical blow. The singing *cigales* (cicadas) made the lull between cars loud with their noise. Wild herbs growing beside the road spilled their aromatic perfume into the dry summer air. I would have enjoyed the austere beauty of it had I not been kept busy handing tools to Maurice and reading instructions to him from the manual. I had two choices: German or French. I read the French and hoped that my accent wasn't too atrocious. He raised a wicked eyebrow several times but he made no comment and didn't die of horror, which I took to be some small accomplishment on my part. The French are terrible snobs when it comes to French.

He managed to get totally filthy from the tire change and his white duck cloth slacks were beyond salvage. The Coke had dried to a sticky sheen wherever it had touched making the dirt even dirtier. We fished in the car for water and found only one empty bottle with maybe four drops left in the bottom. He poured or rather, dripped, those onto his handkerchief and scrubbed it black, shrugged in disgust with his efforts and tossed it into the maquis where it fluttered like a sooty flag.

By the time we reached Marseille, I was shaking with nerves at driving in so much fast moving traffic and terrified that he would be lost from view because of the cars that kept passing or pulling in front of me. He decided to take advantage of the first exit into Marseille to see some of the sights. I would have loved to stop the car and say to hell with it or maybe wring his neck, but caught as I was, all I could do was drive like crazy to stay behind him. The sights I was to see were a blur on either side that I could not afford to notice and Beth was so busy trying to help with her backseat driving she saw nothing. A magnum of wine might have relaxed me and she kept reminding me she was thirsty because we had taken her Coke. All in all, I decided it was not my favorite day of the summer. Finally he pulled to a stop at the docks, and I drew up behind him, grateful for the breather.

He walked back to us to explain, "This is the commercial port and one of the largest in Europe. Look at the size of those ships, Beth. I thought you girls would like to see this since we were going to pass so close. I also need to run over to that warehouse...one of mine. I need to check a shipment of spices before they are loaded. The foreman is concerned about the quality and asked me to inspect them on my way into town. You two just enjoy a look around. It will only take me a moment."

"Okay," I agreed with resignation. It was too industrial and dirty to appeal to our decidedly feminine tastes but we had little choice so we looked around carefully avoiding the little engines that ran around with prongs extending wickedly from the front.

Beth kicked the pavement with disgust. "I'm tired of riding, tired of Maurice, tired of being here, Mommy. Let's just go home."

"Let's wait until you see if you like Marseilles. If you are still so unhappy, I'll see what I can do."

"I'm just bored. I miss my friends. There aren't any children for me to play with here."

"I know, honey. I don't make such a good kid, huh?"

"It's not you, Mommy. You know what I mean."

I heard Maurice helloing and turn to wave to him, surprised it had taken so little time. He caught up to us smiling as though his problem had been favorably resolved.

"Everything okay?"

"Yes, fine. Let's have lunch. It's late and I'm famished. I want to take you to the old port, *le Vieux Port*, to try a local specialty. It's on our way, which makes it easy."

I nearly choked on that one. Resigned to the continuing behind the wheel ordeal, we followed him without raising more than five or six shaken fists and maybe ten furious horn-honks, managed to park the car near his, and got my shaky legs under me so I could climb out.

"This restaurant makes a terrific fish soup called bourride and I prefer it to bouillabaisse," he remarked once we were seated.

"I was not impressed with bouillabaisse when I had it at Chez Silvio's: too many bones and heads. I wonder if the soup is like fish stew? We had that at home when I was growing up." I explained to him that when I was a child if one of the neighbors had a lot of fish or my father had been fishing and caught enough, everyone would gather and the big black iron wash pot, that women had used to do laundry in the days before rural electrification, would be put on an outdoor fire. Bacon would be rendered crisp in the bottom before adding layers of diced potatoes, sliced onions and fish. When the pot was two-thirds full, canned tomatoes, salt, black pepper and some red cayenne pepper flakes would be tossed in and it would all boil until done and the bones had settled to the bottom. At that point, eggs would be cracked into the top where they would coddle. It was ladled out into our waiting bowls and accompanied by soda crackers. It really was a fun outdoor party where the men talked fishing or crops and the women about their children or gardens. We kids ran around shrieking and playing tag until time for the homemade ice cream that the men hand cranked in big wooden, salt and ice cooled churns. It would be strawberry, peach or vanilla depending on the season and the availability of fresh fruit and none has ever tasted as good.

He enjoyed my explanation and responded, "Just trust me. You always like what I order." And he was right, I nearly always did. He grinned charmingly, in top form and at his best. I loved how handsome he was when he smiled and laughed so easily with us. It took away the all too frequent stern sadness.

The restaurant was small and filled with paintings of the Alps and chalets. I found that rather bizarre for a Marseilles fish restaurant.

Laughing at my intrigue with the walls, Maurice explained, "The owner is from the Haute Savoie very near to Switzerland. He only gets to go there once a year on his August vacation so these paintings help him to keep from missing his home too much. Except for that anomaly, this restaurant is very typical of those in the Vieux Port. I really think it is the best."

"The port is beautiful. I love the way the sunlight glints on all of those hundreds of ships. How can they possibly anchor so many in such a small space?"

"That is a puzzle. It's a very old port. You will see the gates and walls that protect it as we leave. The ancient Greeks and before them the Phoceans used this spot. It's a great natural harbor, protected by arms of stone and sheltered from the wind by surrounding cliffs. Did you notice the golden statue atop the church that sits high above the harbor on that mountain?"

"Oh, yes! It's neat," Beth piped up. "What is it?" She was interested and definitely sounded less cantankerous, thank God.

"She's the patron saint of the harbor, Kiki. She is standing on top of the church of Notre Dame de la Garde. She is it's protector; that's what the name means."

"Could we go there sometime, Maurice?"

"Of course, Darling."

"I'd just as soon go when we are all in one car," I interjected.

"Tired of Marseilles traffic so soon, Jo?" He was laughing at me but kindly.

"That I am, but I'll never tire of this soup. It's wonderful." As far as I was concerned, it was a far superior choice to bouillabaisse and fish stew. It had all of the flavor, but without the mess since the bones and heads had been removed. I took a particular liking to the two sauces served on toasty rounds of French bread that floated like rafts on the soup. One was a piquant sauce called *rouille*, made of garlic and red pepper. The other, *aioli*, was a garlic mayonnaise. Following lunch, Beth who had eschewed the bourride in favor of a simple poached lotte, studiously kept her distance from my garlic-laden breath. My skin seeped it for days after but it was worth every odiferous whiff that enveloped me. Beth might not have agreed.

Maurice enjoyed teasing me that day, further evidence of his good humor. He commented, "This soup is made from boiling a sea rock to give a taste of the sea to the soup."

"Rocks! I thought you said this is fish soup?"

He laughed, "Seriously, the chef puts rocks in the bottom of the stock pot when cooking the broth because the flavor of the sea is in the rocks and it adds taste to the soup. Fish are used too, by the way."

"I'm glad of that. I'd hate to go back to Raleigh raving about the rock soup I ate. They would all ascribe it to a new lunacy on the part of the eccentric art teacher."

That really set him off. "Eccentric! Ha, artists are nearly always misunderstood. It was the bane of my life as a student. Although I was excellent in school due to a certain facility for memory, I frequently felt alienated from my professors and nearly always from my peers by a different way of thinking, feeling, and viewing life and the world around me. Yet that is called eccentric because it doesn't conform."

"Maybe that is because you said your favorite soup is made from rocks." I wanted to keep it light. He became morose too easily and if not morose, so introspective and intensely philosophical I felt drained. The energy required by the prolonged concentration such a conversation demands is considerable, especially if you do more than nod like a complacent idiot. I enjoy conversations with some meat, but not a constant diet of it.

Grinning, I cocked an eyebrow at him and stated, "I need a strong rope, Maurice. I need it badly and soon."

"A rope??" He looked at me in bafflement.

"Yes, a rope, really strong."

"Well, I suppose we could find you one tomorrow."

"Tomorrow is not when I need it. I need it now."

"But, Darling, I thought you wanted to go to the hotel. Are you sure it won't wait?

"Nope, I can't get to the hotel without it."

"Did you say *rope* or *nope*?" I could tell by the light in his eye that he was beginning to see the direction I was going. A smile played about the corners of his mouth that turned into a roar, when he caught Beth's puzzled expression. She was convinced I had taken leave of my senses.

"Ah, I see. Shall we leave the cars here and walk to a ship chandlers? I think there's one not too far from here where I can get you some rope."

"I think we must. I cannot drive in that mess again. You will have to rope our cars together and tow me to the hotel."

"Oh, no, no, no. You told me you'd driven all over Provençe the last month so you've had plenty of practice."

"Not at following you, I don't"

"How do you get practice if not by doing?"

"Some things I don't need to get experienced at, like racing freight trains to crossings or following you in crazy traffic down narrow streets I don't know."

"Surely, it isn't as hazardous as all that?"

"Worse." I grimaced and assumed a doleful expression. I was teasing, yes...but 'many a truth hath been spoken in jest.'

"Ah, Jo, I thought your sense of humor had deserted you. I'm glad it's back.   You get much too serious sometime."   I nearly strangled on the sip of wine I had just taken.

I'll give him credit: he tried to go slower but with narrow streets in an ancient city crammed with swarming cars manned by impatient, crowding, flamboyantly rude and pushy drivers who had little but derisive hoots and angry honks for my stateside style driving, he could do little to ameliorate the situation.   We reached the hotel and except for perspiration, I had managed not to wet myself.   Beth looked ready to swear off cars forever.   I knew she was debating whether I deserved commiseration or censure.

The hotel valued Maurice's patronage judging by the alacrity of the service his appearance inspired: luggage was whisked in, cars were wheeled off, and the concierge bustled from behind the reception desk, both hands outstretched.

"Ah, Monsieur de Beaubourg.   Your American friends have arrived.   Madame Russell we are so pleased to welcome you and your daughter to the Hotel Concorde Palm Beach."

Maurice took his arm and began spelling out instructions for our pampering as the luggage was sent up to our room.   We were in the city of his birth and he meant for us to love it.   "I will show you some of the hotel to help orient you and then I am going to the office and after that to my club for a game of tennis."

Beth had spotted something she liked in the entry area that was lined with a row of over priced boutiques and I had noticed the hairdresser's salon located there.   After several weeks of intense sun and my sole efforts at coiffing my hair, my tresses were in desperate need of some specialized attention to avoid being mistaken for old straw.   Maurice didn't take us back by the boutiques; we did that later on our own.   He took us to the pool.   The swimming terrace overlooking the sea was well staffed to provide refreshments, umbrellas, mats, etc. for the bathers.   We were introduced to the attendants who promised we would be well cared for on their turf. On to the bar we went, which after that drive, I could have used then and there had he slowed down a bit; and then around to the restaurant, where the stiffly proper maître'd unbent enough to show Maurice his eagerness to nourish us, and back to the lobby where we completed our tour.

Maurice pointed, "The rocks you see on that wall of the lobby are the actual cliff into which the hotel is built. The same springs that you see bubbling up there are the ones the ancient Phoceans used for water when Marseille was first settled about five hundred years B.C. You can see some pottery chards of pots similar to the ones they must have used to collect their water. Actually I think I remember that they are authentic chards. I am not so sure about the unbroken pots you see."

"This is marvelous. I just love it here." I smiled happily and Beth did as well. "Thank you so much for arranging it for us."

A large skylight high above our heads lighted the area where we were standing. Water gurgled from the pebbles that lined the springs just inches below the marble flooring of the lobby. When the dancing bubbles swirled aside, the pebbles were sharply limned by the clearest of water. The pottery looked as old as the cliffs and of much the same color, like ashes on biscuits. With my love of history and my imagination, I was instantly enthralled. This particular destination had more than offset the perils of our arrival.

Our room opened onto a view of the dazzling blue gulf of Marseilles and on to the envisioned shores of Africa. Looking straight down from the window, we could see waves dashing on the rocks below. Colorful sails dotted a frolicking sea flecked with whitecaps. The light was so dazzling as to be almost blinding. I could see to the pool area, built hard into the rocks on my left, where colorful flags from a dozen or more countries snapped smartly in the breeze. Bronzed bodies of every degree of pulchritude or lack thereof, lolled around the pool. Judging from some of the female forms so casually bared of all but the most minimal cover of the pubis, a bit more modesty for some of them would have enhanced the view. It was obvious the French are far more comfortable with their bodies than most Americans, good-looking or otherwise. The men I scanned with something akin to the hunger of a penniless child at a candy counter. Those Speedo's were pretty spectacular. I had been months without a male interest in my life and as my mother used to say, I was feeling "wolfy." Although I felt a little unease due to the lack of appeasement of certain appetites, Beth was in "little pig heaven." She had a pool in which to play, a beautiful view, interesting shops right in the hotel, and another week of room service before we would move to Maurice's apartment. She was purely addicted to room service by this time and wasted no time picking up the phone to request a Coke and a snack.

Maurice had left us to return at dinner with his slim, mid-twenties friend, Rene, in tow. His tennis buddy seemed cool to us and although he could speak perfect English, he determinedly chattered at breakneck speed in circuitous French. Judging from his surly demeanor, I would have preferred he had been left on the tennis court maybe wearing a racket for a necklace. I don't think he took a shine to me either. Unfortunately for the next few days, Maurice invited him to join us frequently. Beth and I were both so sufficiently excluded from their male comradery that we spent our time building crumb ladies or talking of whatever we found of sufficient interest at the moment. I knew and was concerned that Beth, who was cognizant of Margot's suspicions without really understanding the full import, watched them as intently as I for some sign of aberrant behavior.

The final straw occurred the night Maurice showed up with Rene and his friend Bruno in tow. Bruno had formerly done some kind of photography work in Paris and Maurice had met him there and offered him a job. He was as docile and servile, and as droolingly pleasant as Rene was surly and obnoxious. While Rene dressed like a bandy cock, Bruno was a ramshackle slob. None of them were dressed for dinner at the hotel restaurant including Maurice who had begun alternating the habitual black trousers for white duck ones, heavy and un-ironed. When we walked down to the lobby expecting to join Maurice for dinner and found the unsavory threesome, I decided I could do without dinner with them for the evening, especially since Maurice had specifically said to dress for dinner and it would be only we three.

"Maurice, how good to see you. Beth and I were just on our way out. I see it is just as well that we have other plans since you have your friends to keep you company for the evening. Do enjoy yourselves and please excuse us. It's good to see you again, Rene. It was a pleasure to meet you, Bruno."

Shock registered on his face: so, the lady has claws in those velvet gloves. I smiled pleasantly and continued on my way to the exit. It was a new me, as far as he was concerned, and he was unsure how to deal with the challenge. While he puzzled, we left.

Leaving the Concorde, we walked up to the sidewalk along the Corniche and turned left taking us past the Chateau D'If anchored to its barren rocks, stark and forbidding, its stern profile looming against the glow of the dying sun, surrounded by a leaden sea. It suited my mood. The swelling, demanding bubble of pain within could be suppressed no longer. Tears of desolation slipped tentatively down my cheeks to be followed by a cleansing deluge. I cried silently as I walked doggedly into the gathering gloom. I was both repelled by and attracted to a man who answered so many of my needs and dreams and yet frustrated me with the puzzles of his personality. I was torn by my love of Europe, the excitement and thrill of so many long dreamed goals at last attained, and burdened by the chore of keeping my child happy in an alien environment. It would have been far easier for me had I traveled without her, yet each day, I saw her growing more adventurous, more out-going, more assertive and more knowledgeable of the world. I knew some positive gain had accrued to us both despite the loneliness and frustrations that Maurice brought us along with so many good and wonderful things.

"It's all right, Mommy. I love you and I am sorry you're sad."

"I know, honey. I don't mean to upset you or make you share my sadness. I just couldn't hold it in any longer. It has been such a difficult year for me in so many ways that sometimes I need a few tears just to wash away a little of the troubles."

"Maurice really is a nice man and he is so good to us. He tries so hard to make us happy that it makes me feel guilty that I don't love him the way he wants me to. I don't like his friends either. I don't mean Nani, Jackie and Bernard...those friends; I mean nasty old Rene and Bruno. Yuk! They are just plain weird!"

"I'm sure I wouldn't choose them for friends either, but I don't have the right to select his friends for him. However, I would prefer that he not keep including that pair with us."

If at times my reaction seems overdone, I can only explain it by way of my genes. I was conceived of, born to, and nurtured by a genuine group of southern female hysterical personalities. Many Sunday afternoons of my childhood were spent on the wraparound porch of my Grandmother Lena's where the women would generally pull up slat backed-chairs on the shady side of the porch. The men would usually scuff around in the brush-broom swept, hard packed dirt yard or sit on the sunny side of the porch. And the Sunday dinner sated, Sunday-school bored mob of cousins would stake out our own territory when we tired of pestering one another. My spot was the porch swing if I was fast. There I could gain enough momentum to propel myself into the branches of the crepe myrtle that grew at the end of the porch directly behind the swing, aggravating the bumblebees that considered the tree their turf. From the swing, it was easy to monitor the adults in case one or the other group's conversation warranted closer attention.

The men could usually be discounted since they generally yammered on about hunting, fishing or crops, all of which were mighty dull to my tastes. The women's conversation was often another matter. Loud volume meant they were laughing at the antics of their 'young'uns' or the equally childish notions of their men. Medium meant they were discussing the recent neighborhood deaths or those of cousins twice removed complete with all of the gruesome details, parting words and final sighs, or they had moved on to recipes. Ear straining meant I wasn't supposed to hear. That was my cue to leave the swing for one of the cousins or a sister who had given up begging for it. I would move to the corner, careful not to round it, for that would have warned them to go back to recipes.

At that corner, with crepe myrtle blossoms dusting the top of my head in pink benediction, I got my woman's education: childbirth...which meant labor, and if that didn't kill you, you were lucky if the brat didn't worry you to death later. Female trouble...every one of them had it in some form, or if they hadn't were honor bound to invent something to keep from being outdone. Then there was the listing of whose husbands were running around, often mama's, which was explained by saying that men were like dogs and just couldn't help themselves; and finally there was sickness. That meant if you so much as stumped your toe, you might just as well go ahead and shoot yourself to avoid the indignity of a slow and nasty death. The scenario would run: "You know how they are just real slow healing in that family. Why there's no tellin', they are just as likely as not, to not heal at all, diabetes running in the family and all. Well, when it doesn't heal, it just has to be whacked off. Don't ya'll remember hearing about Luther down the road yonder who died in the house fire 'cause he couldn't exactly run out, being one legged and all. Yes indeed, he hurt his leg and it wouldn't heal so it had to be chopped smack off." The moral seemed to be: don't stub your toe because you'll get diabetes, lose a leg, burn your house down and get killed in the bargain. I kept my shoes on hoping my fate would not prove to be Sunday afternoon fodder. Of course, that left open the possibility that both feet would plain rot off from some kind of fungus due to the lack of air.

Thus, as we walked back to the hotel, I wondered if my childhood 'lessons' were causing me to over-react or if I were allowing my summer to be ruined by Margot's suspicions, which regardless of whether they were fact or fiction, did not change the fact that Maurice was a genuinely kind and interesting man. A car drove past, slowed, and the handsome man behind the wheel stuck his head our and whistled. If I had ever learned how to whistle, I might have returned the compliment.

"He thinks you're pretty, Mommy."

"It's not me. It's you. You're getting so grown up and gorgeous this summer."

She giggled, well pleased with the compliment. "I'm still your 'mwa' baby."

"That you are. Even when you're really grown up, you'll still be my special, wonderful little girl."

With my resolve firm, my inner pain fenced, and my chin up, I left my tears and the Chateau D'If behind.

"Madame, we have a message for you." The concierge beckoned me over to the walnut reception desk. "Monsieur de Beaubourg called to say that he will return shortly and would like to have you join him for dinner. He has made reservations in our restaurant for nine-thirty."

"I see. Thank you."

We walked to the elevator. Beth pushed the button and while we waited, asked,

"Please, can't I just have room service?"

I glanced at my watch. It was already nearly nine. "It's late and if you're tired and want to go ahead and eat, I can understand. I'm really not hungry anyway."

"Does that mean you're not going to have dinner with Maurice when he comes?"

"I honestly don't know."

When we reached the room, Beth ordered her dinner and I climbed into the tub for a therapeutic bubble bath. The phone rang as I was soaking and I heard her answer. I knew that I really didn't want to see him that night. I needed some distance to regroup.

"Mommy, Maurice wants to talk to you. He says he's waiting downstairs."

"Please tell him I don't feel well and that I'm going to bed as soon as I finish my bath."

I had just donned my robe and finished brushing my hair, when the doorbell rang. I opened the door to find Maurice, dressed in an unaccustomed suit and tie and bracketed by his two friends who were similarly attired.

"Maurice, I was just going to bed." I was embarrassed because I knew he could look at my eyes and tell I had been crying. I was also annoyed to see the ever snarling Rene and the cloying Bruno, Ying and Yang.

He turned to them, excused himself and shut the door behind him. I turned from him then with tears of frustration and embarrassment filling my already swollen eyes. As I sank onto the bed with face studiously averted, I felt his arms encircle me.

"My poor, Jo. It has been so difficult for you this year. I wondered how long it would take for the pain to catch you. You can only reject it for so long, you know?"

As I cried anew, he held me and stroked me like he would have soothed a child. "It's all right, Darling. I'm here now. Don't you know I will never let anyone hurt you again?"

'If only I could tell you that you hurt me too,' I cried inside.

I felt like a heel: ungrateful and rude.

Chapter 6

We were packed and ready to leave the next day when he came for us. Beth had bid room service and the pool a final farewell and was resigned to moving on. I felt some trepidation at the close proximity in which we would all now live, knowing that it could exacerbate any areas of friction.

The apartment he and his mother were sharing at the Prado Parc was in a nice wooded area on a hill sufficiently distant from the traffic of the city that it was a quiet location. The living area and his mother's room overlooked a beautifully manicured private park at tree top level. The furnishings were museum quality antiques from the home they had sold and that had since been razed to make room for a high-rise construction. I gasped when he remarked that a chest I admired had been in his family since the fifteen hundreds. It was an exquisitely carved, grand and imposing piece that surely belonged in a castle, not a modern apartment flat. I began to comprehend how wrenching it must have been for them to sell their former home and move into such an incongruous space. His mother's room was centered with a fabulous crystal chandelier that cast a sparkling glow over the gilded Louis XVI furniture. In the center of the far wall was a beautifully carved sleigh bed covered with an embroidered silk coverlet. The day bed that he had moved in for Beth made a jarring note in the perfection of the room.

"I hope you will both be comfortable here?" he asked anxiously.

"I'm sure we will. It really is very lovely. Are you sure your mother doesn't object to us using her room?"

"Oh, don't be silly. She is delighted that you're here with me."

As Beth and I unpacked, we could hear him speaking rapidly on his office phone in beautiful Castilian Spanish. When he was finished, he went into his room that he had to first unlock. Never in the three weeks we were there did he leave his bedroom door unlocked. When we inquired as to why he always kept it locked, he explained only that it was a habit and he had always done so. That was the only explanation we ever had from him so naturally our imaginations ran wild with speculation as to what was so secretive behind that ever locked door. It never occurred to me that he might not trust us not to pry, as that is not my nature to do something so invasive of another's privacy, although I later conceded that possibility. I could see when he opened the door that the bed was covered with his sleeping bag. I thought sleeping on the same covers night after night was singularly unsanitary but it must not have bother him as I never saw it being washed or cleaned. The room also had the messy look of one that had never benefited from a cleaning.

He emerged from his room in clean pants and shirt and remarked, "Tonight I'm taking you to Bonnieux and then on to Lourmarin for dinner. The drive through the Lubéron Mountains is wonderfully scenic and the restaurant there is a favorite of mine. I hope my ladies will love it too."

It would have been impossible not to have. *Pâté de fois gras chaud*, champagne, and an exceptional dinner by candlelight in a romantic, picturesque town featuring a fifteenth century chateau overlooking a valley, sprinkled with olive trees and lavender fields glowing golden, purple and silvery green in the setting sun. Maurice held my hand and was kind, gentle and entertaining. Afterwards we walked along the main street, skirted by a low stone wall overlooking the valley below. Along one section the distance between street and wall was widened enough to allow for the playing of Boules. Beneath the streetlight and with a full moon as a backdrop, players were studiously tossing their steel balls and calling encouragements or derision at one another. Both Maurice and I took photographs of the players with the shadows of the Plantain trees dappling the playing field a deep black.

When we returned to Battleship for our drive back to Marseilles, Maurice took my hand and kissed it. "Thank you, Jo, for a wonderful evening."

"No, I am the one who thanks you. It was truly special to me and I so much appreciate you making it possible for us." Sleepily Beth chorused her thank you from the backseat.

He held my hand as we drove, the music of our special tape, 'Anonimo Veniziano', washing over us. With the trees forming a leafy tunnel over us, the flickering light from the ripe moon, the soft lavender scented air welling through the sunroof and my hand in his, I felt his promise of comfort and security and an immense joy that I had experienced such beauty.

"Jo, you give me a peace I have never know with another woman. You cannot begin to know how very much it means to me to be able to share this summer with you and this child I so adore. Can you imagine the awe I feel when I look at her and see those little dimpled hands and listen to her as she discovers a little more of the world each day. I have never known a child before and now I shall never have one of my own. But, she *is* my child. That is a treasure beyond compare. And you. You cannot know what comfort, what love it brings my heart to have a woman like you with me. You are beautiful to me inside and out. I especially admire your mind; and the talent and sensitivity you carry within are so very precious. Share that with me, Jo. We can build a studio like that one you said you dream about, with terrazzo floors, big glass doors, and a view of the sea. Two studios: one for you and one for me and we'll spend our days painting and be so good for one another. We will watch Beth grow up and we will nurture her and help her to be the most she can be, the best of finishing schools, and the right people to meet. Everything. It would be so ideal. I can't think of a more wonderful way to spend the years left to me."

"It's like a beautiful dream, Maurice. In the harsh light of day, I would have to wonder if Beth would allow us to move her here so far from family, friends and all she knows. I don't think she's ready for that."

"She loves you so much. I've watched her with you. The bond

you share is so special that if you asked, she would do it to make you happy."

"If it didn't make her happy as well, I couldn't be happy." He had not asked me to marry him, only to live with him and yet he seemed to need that so desperately.

"You're good for me, Jo. Don't say no. Think about it. You bring me a comfort and companionship I have needed so long and never hoped to find with a woman. You're my best friend. I love the two of you more than anyone else in the world. Just think about it. I know it can't be now, but maybe in a year or two."

"Maurice, I love you too. I respect and admire you so much and I am so very grateful for all you have done for us. Even though I don't always understand you, I'm still your friend and I always will be. Nothing will ever change that nor the importance of you in my life."

"I know. You have great loyalty of spirit and I can always trust you. That is a rare thing. Don't you see how compatible we are, how perfect together? With our art we share so much; think so much alike. I have enough money that we can live and paint and not worry about work. Just think what that would be like. You would never have to worry again about finances and a job. I would take care of you and your child. I know you love France and it's my home, but we could live anywhere: Spain, the Riviera, Rome, London, or Switzerland. You name it. I can do my photography anywhere."

The following morning arrived fresh and bright. The mistral was blowing, making the curtains billow into the room and bringing the magic air of herbs in from the mountains to the north. I knew that some people disliked the strong mistral wind. Maurice had told me that there are more suicides when it's blowing. But I loved the vigor and excitement it brought me. That, combined with the residue of warm memories from the previous evening, made me wonderfully happy. I climbed from bed eager for the day and conscious of just how quickly this precious time was fleeting.

Following a late breakfast at a nearby cafe-tabac shop, Maurice kissed our cheeks and left for his office promising to return in late afternoon. Beth and I walked from the tabac on the Rue du Prado to the Sudim supermarket, a boulangerie and patisserie gathering the items I needed to make dinner. I had decided during our last coffee at the tabac that I wanted to surprise him with a dinner party as a way of saying 'thank you' for all he was doing for us. He had essentially suspended the ongoing demands of his daily life to make a special summer for us, showing us the places and things he held so dear, knowing that I would treasure them as well. My recent frustrations seemed silly and too much the pique of vanity that he had made no attempt to appreciate my feminine charms.

I had never cooked for him before and the very thought gave me cold sweats. Even though I had belonged to a gourmet-cooking club in Raleigh and I'd been told I am an excellent cook, this was a different league. Maurice was accustomed to a lifetime of the best restaurants in the world staffed by the best of the Cordon Bleu. I made no claims to that status then or now, but I was going to tackle a dinner for him anyway.

On our walk back through the apartment grounds, Beth gathered a few blossoms from the more inconspicuous rose bushes, using them to make a small nosegay for our table. In the massive antique chest I found linen tablecloth, napkins, china and crystal and prepared the table. Maurice arrived home to be intercepted at the door by a determined Beth who was assigned to barricade him from the kitchen where I was busy trying to decipher the workings of the gas stove...not the electric I had always used, strange utensils and novel implements. Judging by their paucity and condition, there were no cooks, gourmet or otherwise, to outdo me in that particular apartment.

He could not help but see the table on his way in and I could tell from his joyously shouted hello that he was as pleased as a kid with his surprise party. Beth was playing bossy hostess judging from her directions to make himself scarce and stay out of the way while she put the finishing touches on her place cards. He laughed in delight, pleased to humor her. He worked in his office no doubt filling his journal with the day's activities where three columns, neatly divided into-fifteen minute segments awaited completion. One column was for the office, one for his personal life, and one for photography. The journal was far more than a time schedule as I had seen all to clearly in Rome. He filled it with notes on his plans, his thoughts, his dreams, his frustrations as well as the mundane activities of daily life. Anything that crossed his mind became fodder for the journal. He had stacks of those spiral bound notebooks covering every day, every moment of his life. Such documentation takes time and discipline, but it was an invaluable aid to his memory. With his many business affairs, the added obligation of keeping two American visitors happy, and a myriad of other obligations, I wondered where he found the time and suspected it was often in lieu of sleep which came so hard for him.

At last the candles were lit, the chilled champagne poured and dinner served: a veal piccatta with capers, fettucini Alfredo, a simple salad, fresh rounds of crusty baguette, a chèvre cheese and for dessert a tarte tatin. It was a simple meal to cook but I thought it good and Maurice ate heartily while Mozart played softly from his office stereo. Beth had been friendly and relaxed with Maurice for the first time that summer. With the final sip of wine and the last sputtering of the candle, Maurice reached for my hand and pulled me into his lap.

"Thank you, Jo. This was the most perfect evening I could imagine. I feel so content with my little family."

"You're welcome. I'm just so relieved you liked the dinner. I was *terrified* to cook for you."

"But why would you be afraid?" He asked in bafflement.

"Because you're French and you've known the best food from the best chefs anywhere."

"But they weren't lovely ladies and wonderful friends."

Smiling happily, I cleared the tables and cleaned the kitchen while Beth helped by gathering the linens and returning things to their proper places. While we worked, Maurice slipped quietly into his office. As I finished the last of the dishes, he reappeared at the kitchen door.

"Jo, this is for you."

I turned to take the extended paper, warmed by the glow in his eyes. I read, slowly translating for Beth: "Thank you for a wonderful dinner, the champagne, and our three delicate place cards that were the first nuances of an evening which surpassed in animation all of the flutes of Mozart." I have that note still and the memory of that evening lies as lightly in my heart as the paper in my hand.

Each day for the remainder of our summer with him, Maurice planned special treats for us. We made trips to Cassis to walk along the quay, crowned by the looming violet hued mass of Cap Canaille and warmed by the ochre glow from the walls of a thirteenth century chateau nestled at its base. We often dined at Chez Nino's where we fell in love with *spaghetti au pistou* and their fish. We took midnight swims in the Bestouan, the shingle beach just past the port of Cassis where Maurice pointed out the house made famous in the filming of the "French Connection." With a towel wrapped around his middle, he would change into his swim trunks on the beach. Beth and I draped towels over the car windows and wiggled into our suits as best we could. I was game to try the towel caper on the beach, but that set up such a shocked outcry of offended modesty from my young lady, that I reluctantly abandoned that idea and continued the seated contortions. Even in the dark, lit only by the moonlight gleaming on the water and the mellow glow of lights from the house on the cliffs, I could tell Maurice had the body of a young man, firm and slim. It was astonishing to me that he could be sixty or so years old.

"Damn, Maurice! How can you *walk* on these blasted rocks? This is torture to my feet." At that point I resorted to doing "fanny boosts" to struggle my way to the water. Since my feet were too tender for the rocks, I figured I had no recourse but to sit and lift myself down to the water using my hands braced on the rocks behind me. Beth also had seen the wisdom of this efficacious but ungainly, crablike approach.

"My poor tender-footed darlings!" He roared in laughter at our novel but effective maneuvering. "Don't worry, your feet will become accustomed to it. Come on in; the water's great."

"And cold!" I gasped with shock.

"Come here with me. There are thermal springs beneath the rocks that bubble up much warmer water." He reached for me. "Here...just here. See, isn't that warmer?"

"Wow! It really is, thank goodness."

Beth swam around in happy little circles, splashing water on us.

"It is good to see her so happy and relaxed here at last."

"Yes, it is. I have been so worried for her because she was so lonely. She has really missed being with other children."

"Perhaps I can arrange something with some friends of mine who have children." He looked over at her and waved. "Beth, darling, look at your skin. It looks silver in the moonlight, doesn't it?"

She looked down and asked in amazement, "Yes, what is it?"

"Those are microscopic plankton in the water that glow silver in the moonlight. It's magical looking, don't you think?"

"Neat! Can we come here again, Maurice?" She pleaded.

"Of course, Kiki."

Just then a swell from a passing boat unbalanced me and I reached out to brace myself. My left hand touched Maurice's chest and he instantly recoiled, but not before I felt the huge scab, perhaps the size of a silver dollar, located just to the right of center and several inches below his collar bone.

"What's wrong with your chest? Have you hurt yourself?"

"It's nothing. Just eczema."

"Can't you have it treated or something? You really should see a doctor."

"No. I just need to come swimming more. The salt water is good for it. If I could swim daily, it would disappear."

Obviously he was as reluctant to discuss his chest as the place beneath his eye that he kept covered with a band-aid. Once when the bandage fell off, I asked him about what looked like a clear blister area about the size of a pea, some kind of wart or mole I assumed. He had been evasive then too, quickly replacing the bandage and the opaquely dark sunglasses that he wore both day and night to hide it. He explained that lesion had developed following Bell's Palsy, a facial stroke that is viral in nature and supposedly triggered by drafts. He had suffered that about six weeks prior to Margot breaking it off with him, and he blamed the unsightly although temporary effect on his face for causing her to be repulsed. I knew she would be the last person to do that as she had suffered from the same affliction at sixteen and remembering her own disfigurement, was very sympathetic for those who had to endure it. He was paranoid of drafts the entire time I knew him. He would never sit in one, no matter to what lengths he or anyone else had to go to prevent it. Many a waiter or maître'd had been sent scurrying to adjust windows, doors or air conditioning to accommodate his paranoia. He was so emphatic about it, that I too began to avoid drafts and do so to this day.

As well as Cassis, Maurice took us again to our favorite places: Les Baux, Lourmarin, Aigues-Mortes, and Aix-en-Provençe, where we had wonderful dinners. Several times business acquaintances of his would join us for dinner, usually accompanied by their wives. Except for infrequent tennis games, Maurice no longer saw Rene; and Bruno he left at the office. I knew from what he had told me that he had been a major contributor to Rene's education at the University of Marseilles where he was studying pharmacology. He had also helped Rene's father by financing a golf course. Bruno he had rescued when he was down and out from alcoholism and a broken marriage. Beth and I were happy to restrict our socializing to friends we found more amiable.

Jean-Marie and Martine Sciadoux were our favorites. They lived in a contemporary home on the hills above La Ciotat, a small town located on the sea not far from Marseilles. From their poolside terrace, I could glimpse the blue of the Mediterranean above the cascading Oleander blossoms. The silvery green of the olive trees and rosemary made a beautiful contrast with the fuchsia of the flowers and the azure sea, all punctuated with the dark green of cypress trees that poked into the sky like steeples. Beth and I had driven there in the afternoon at Martine's invitation. Maurice and Jean-Marie were to join us after their day at their offices. I knew Maurice had maneuvered for the invitation by inviting them to join us for a couple of expensive dinners. His first motivation was their son who was the same age as Beth and was studying English. The second: he wanted Jean-Marie who worked for a bank to work for him as he admired his management skills and needed them badly.

Martine, her son, Beth and I spent the afternoon visiting the nearby town of La Castellet, a picturesque hill-top medieval treasure. Beth was charmed when the son presented her with a small crystal heart-shaped box he found in one of the numerous antique shops that we visited near the ancient Romanesque church in the main square. Back at the house again, the children swam as I assisted Martine in the kitchen. She spoke English to me and I spoke French to her. Even though neither of us was fluent, it seemed to work and we laughed companionably at our arrangement.

The men arrived to join us for drinks on the terrace. Since I knew Maurice hoped to lure the husband, I watched him with the Sciadoux's. His cordiality and charm should have been bottled. I knew he could be hard to resist, but Jean-Marie, while obviously flattered by his interest, was unready to leave his position at the bank. Other than that, the evening was a great success: superb wine, lamb chops barbecued on rosemary branches harvested from their garden, Martine's own *Spaghetti au Pistou* (the Provençal dialect word for pesto,) courgettes, baguettes, a platter of artisanal cheeses and a fresh fruit tart for dessert.

Our last weekend there had arrived and Maurice treated us with a trip to Juan-les-Pines and Antibes where we visited the Picasso museum. The summer was ending for us the day after my birthday. Rounding a corner suddenly, I would catch Maurice and Beth in joyful collusion and know they were planning for my birthday. I pretended elaborate innocence and allowed them their fun. On my birthday the two of them were madly signaling one another across the breakfast table while I bustled about making the coffee the way he liked and plating his favorite Biscotins (a toast,) jam and butter.

"Jo, I have to run an errand and Beth wants to come with me. I need to find a notebook for her to use to study French this fall."

Making it easy for them, I remarked, "I have some errands to run myself before Beth and I leave. You two go along and don't worry about me."

They went one way in Battleship and I took my car and went the other. I needed a bag to carry the excess from our suitcases. The gifts Maurice had given us that summer far exceeded our capacity to pack them. I also wanted a gift to present him on our last day. When I spotted the beautiful paperweight, I knew it would be perfect for his desk where he would use and see it daily. They returned not long after I did, carrying packages that they hid unsuccessfully behind their backs as they sidled through the door.

Taking the cue that I needed to make myself scare, I went to our bedroom, closed the door and busied myself packing shoes in the new vinyl bag that I found cheaply at the local Sudim.

"Mommy! Come to the kitchen, please." Her voice was charged with excitement. I walked through the kitchen door to find streamers taped from wall to wall and a rose from the garden standing next to a *very* pink cake on the cloth-draped table. From their spot on the chair seat, several packages peeped from beneath the cloth.

"Surprise!" They chorused in unison.

"We're having birthday cake for lunch, Mommy."

She was happy with that arrangement. No better than Maurice liked sweets, giving up his hearty mid-day meal was a special concession to his Kiki. He lit the candle as she prepared to slice the cake. As she placed each huge slice on a plate, he handed me my gifts. There was a Sony Walkman stereo with mini-speakers and ear- plugs and pair of Charles Jourdan heels with matching handbag from him. Beth presented me with the canvas bag that she had bought in St. Paul de Vence and some Rogier de Gallet soap that she knew I loved.

"Don't you like your presents, Mommy? You look like you're going to cry."

"Of course she likes them. She has tears because we have made her so happy."

"Yes, you have, both of you. Thank you so much for my gifts. I love them all."

"I have a copy of *Anonimo Veniziano* for you, too. I know how much you like it and it will keep you near me and Provençe when you are back in Raleigh."

"Wonderful. I really do love it and was going to miss it. Now I can play it on my new Walkman, and believe me, it will make me ache with longing to be here when I do."

Despite all of the gorgeous and fabulous desserts in Marseilles, that pink cake was truly awful. I ate every bite though, grinning as though it were wonderful. Maurice was struggling bravely with his huge slab and I knew he considered it a sacrifice. That afternoon he worked in his office preparing what he said were his goodbye notes for his journal.

Finally hunger brought him forth for an early dinner just as I thought I would have to plead starvation. Dinner was Bourride at Chez Fon Fon just off the Corniche John F. Kennedy. The restaurant was in the tiny Vallon des Auffes, the picturesque fishing village that had been engulfed by the expansion of Marseilles. Throughout dinner Maurice was as brittle as glass and progressively more withdrawn. I felt and identified with much of his sadness as a special time in my life was drawing to a close. Despite the occasional tensions and frustrations, in so many ways it had been magical. Too, I did not know what the future might hold for any of us.

"Jo, we need to talk tonight. There are things we need to discuss after Beth goes to bed." We were walking along the shore of the small harbor and Beth had wandered off to peruse a particularly colorful local fishing boat.

"That's fine. But, please try not to sound so sad. I want our last night here to be happy. The day has been wonderful for me."

"It has been a happy day for me too."

"Kiki!" He called her back to us. "I want to take you and Mommy to a special place before night comes. We need to leave now."

We drove to Les Goudes, scenic fishing village on a rocky, barren spit of land as stark as the moon and as remote in feeling as Siberia and yet it was only moments from the Rue du Prado. Secluded smugglers' coves, wind-swept promontories, and the persistent cry of the singing Cigales floating to us on a dry wind brought a mysterious, exhilarating and yet peaceful ambiance to Les Goudes. Maurice wanted photographs of Beth leaping on the rocks and silhouetted against the pastel glow of the sky. She complied after a bit of discrete prodding on my part. Posing for his photos had become increasingly irksome for her and she had repeatedly vented her ire to me. However, any pique quickly vanished when he handed her his camera and allowed her to take numerous shots of the rocky landscape.

That was her second opportunity to use his camera. Maurice secretly hoped she would grow to love photograph...another legacy to bequeath her, and to that end, lavishly praised her efforts. She did seem to be increasingly interested.

Her first occasion was one of my favorite days of the summer. He had left work early and come for us. Driving the winding craggy road into Cassis, we stopped at the little market on the quay to shop for the makings of a picnic supper: wine for us, coke for Beth, saucissons, fresh raspberries, cheese and crusty, fresh baguettes. Maurice had reserved a charter boat for us from his friend, Monsieur Paul, the captain and owner. Paul had been in the navy and sailed to numerous American ports, thus priding himself on the bit of English he used with us.

He and Maurice were obviously old friends. So when asked to extend his day and forego his evening dinner with his wife, he had complied willingly. He was one of several captains who earned their living taking tourists to the Calanques to see the small ports and anchorages hidden in the sheer cliffs of rock festooned with audacious tuffs of rugged little pines. We anchored in En-Vau, the most beautiful of the Calanques, or fjords, and there in the twilight Maurice and Beth swam in the cold water, so clear their shadows dappled the rocks forty feet below. As there were no warm springs to entice me and since my swimming skills are on a par with a rock, I stayed onboard to chat with Monsieur Paul and laid out the food for our picnic supper. Maurice and Beth climbed aboard, toweled off and redressed, eager for dinner.

"Ah, that was so cold. It makes me ravenous."

"I think everything makes you ravenous. I never cease to be amazed at how slim you stay despite all that you eat."

"It's because I swim in cold water. Here, don't you want to try? I'll help you overboard." He made a playful swoop at me, and the three of them laughed at my shriek as I hastened to elude him.

Before the light had faded, Beth had photographed every inch of the cliffs, the boats, the small sandy beach at the end of the cove, and us. She was a happy girl.

It was a magic moment that I hugged to myself as I sat in the darkening night, watching the glow of the men's cigars as we chatted after dinner. I'm enriched to have it in my store of precious moment even if I feel an ache of loss when I think of my friend who made it and so many others possible. The moments of minor irritations seem petty when viewed from the perspective of today and I know that my own actions and those of Beth must at times have rankled him, too. Yet he was ever a gentleman, patient and tolerant of us, trying to please.

I dreaded the coming talk with Maurice, dreaded the moment of departure, and dreaded the prospect of the coming year of humdrum existence after our sojourn in Paradise. Too, I worried that again I might be faced with his rage over my sister.

Beth was sleeping peacefully and it was time to talk. "I know you must be ready to reclaim your life and time for yourself. We've been a lot of trouble for you this summer and I know at times you have sacrificed yourself to serve our pleasures when it would have been far easier for you to have done differently. I am so very grateful to you for all you have done for us. Words are so inadequate for me to express to you how wonderful this summer has been...to be with you, to be in France and to see so many of the fabulous places that I have hungered for all of my life."

"You know that you are welcome, Jo, and also know that you have given me even more than I you. It is the first time in my life that I have had my own little family, that I've had the joy of sharing my life with ones I love and watching them grow. Jo, my darling, wait for me, come back to me again."

"You know I will if you want us."

"If I *want* you!? If you only knew the pain I feel when I think of you leaving me just when I feel we are beginning to accomplish so much between us. Beth is growing and learning. I've watched her and marveled at her and want to go on watching her become all she is capable of. There is so much magic, so much potential in that child. How could I not love her? She is my daughter. She is the child I will never have and I need to see her, be with her, and help her. You must allow me, Jo. Will you let me do more?"

"You have already done so very much, Maurice."

"No, no. I want you to move here. Not now. I know it is too soon and she wouldn't accept it, but you could talk to her about it...get her to accept the idea. We could build a house wherever you would like. Just imagine you would never have to work again. You are wasting yourself, your talent. You shouldn't have to spend your time on students. You shouldn't have to work, cook and clean at home. You need to use your talent. You must. You must believe in it. You should spend your days painting. Art is your life! Art! Believe it. I know it. I can give you that freedom."

"But what freedom would I lose? You are a very powerful man. You are accustomed to controlling, of everyone waiting for you, planning his or her time around yours. I'm not used to that and sometimes it can be frustrating for me."

"But, darling, I never asked you to do that. I want you to paint, to do what you want. That's why I have the car for you, gave you the money to spend. You didn't have to wait for me."

"I felt I did." I smiled at him. "Maurice, you're the kind of man I've dreamed of in so many ways. There is no one else in my life. If I thought we could be happy together here, I would come...I will come. But I need time to think about it."

"I know, Jo. I want you, but you know how busy I am now. I don't have enough time for you and that would make you resentful. I've also noticed that Beth is careful to remind me that she has a father. I know she thinks I'm trying to replace him in her affections. I'm not. I would never try to take her love for her father away from her. I ask only to share your lives with you as best we can for now. I love you both so much. . You're all in my life that has any meaning except for my art. I love you my friend."

"And I love you. And I am your friend and I always will be no matter what the future may bring us."

At the airport the following morning, the guard must have had a romantic Gallic soul as he allowed Maurice to sit beyond the security gate so that we could prolong our last moments together. Maurice couldn't talk for the tears lodged in his throat. When the announcement came to board, we were all crying.

"Au revoir, Maurice. Je t'aime beaucoup."

"I love you too, Maurice. Thank you for all you did for me this summer." Beth too was sad to leave him.

"Je t'aime, je t'aime. Oh, Jo, how can I live without you? I'll call to see if you arrive home safely and I'll call tonight when you get to Brussels." He kissed my tear-streaked cheeks, then choking, he turned to Beth. *"Ma petite enfant, ma chérie, au revoir. Je t'aime tellement."*

Chapter 7

We took a quick tour of Brussels in the late afternoon on the way to our hotel. Actually it was a detour as the hotel was near the airport, but I hated for us to be so near and miss the Grand Plaza, the main square of Brussels. It is there that you feel the heart throb of this old city. The taxi driver let us out on the edge of the square so that we could walk about for a few minutes to see the sights. He promised to wait. Since he had our luggage, I could only trust that he would. He seemed nice enough so we set out to gaze at the architecture, representing centuries of stylistic diversity, the flowers in boxes adding color, and the sidewalk cafes humming with activity, while I kept a wary eye on the taxi. Beth's favorite sight was the Mannequin Pis fountain where the sight of the little bronze boy peeing had her giggling with delight. We didn't take long since the taxi was waiting. The driver was quite affable and spoke excellent English, and with pride in his city and considerable knowledge of its history and monuments, he took it upon himself to give us a tour of the city on the way to the hotel. It was one of the best twenty dollars I have ever spent. I knew he must have given us a break on that fare even so.

Maurice called shortly after we checked into the hotel to see how his girls were doing on the first leg of their journey home. It seemed strange to know that our summer had ended and we would not see him again for many months. The pain of loneliness for us was in his voice as he talked and I knew even before he said it, that he was counting the months before the arrival of another summer with us. Maurice was so afraid Beth would grow up too fast, grow up without him to watch the process and guide her in the direction he envisioned for her. He was afraid that the progress he had made with her would be lost in the long months ahead. As for me, he trusted in my loyalty and friendship just as I knew I could rely on his. It was a comfort to me to know that when I arrived home to a world without a man in it to love and care for me, that Maurice was there waiting...not in a romantic way perhaps, but at least as someone who valued me as a person, who respected and needed me. In a way that was even more special, more romantic to me to know that a man could like beyond the surface, could appreciate and want to delve the depths of me that I had kept so carefully hidden from the world all of my life. He understood me as perhaps no other ever has and never censored or condemned, but rather encouraged me to grow, to be more, to be as much as I have it in me to be.

At times the summer had been so difficult: living with one another, working out a mutually tolerable rhythm to daily life had been so arduous, as between any two people and especially two from such disparate worlds. By summer's end we had achieved equilibrium and had cemented our deep rapport; but the frustration of an undirected sexual energy had been difficult for me and left me knowing that I also needed a more physical relationship with a special man. I never hoped to rival the platonic one that I shared with Maurice, but it needed augmentation on an earthly level. When we talked that last night, Maurice asked me to wait for him. I knew he didn't mean sexually, even though he didn't use precise language. He also knew the potential for losing me inherent in my fulfilling my needs for companionship and intimacy with a man. He had asked me for no promises and he had given none, except to vow that he would always be there for me in friendship and love. And I pledged the same devotion in return knowing that what we shared surpassed the needs of the human animal within me, that it would survive the change of circumstances and other relationships. There is such value and rarity in such a friendship between a man and a woman.

He called our first night home. It was nine in the evening for us, three in the morning for him, but he had stayed up wanting to know that we were safely home. I could picture him sitting at his desk writing in his journal, waiting for the hours to tick by. It was a week before I heard from him again, this time a telegram:

"One week without you two. I miss you terribly. You are with me, I see and hear you around here everywhere I go, everywhere I am. Normal has gone crazy; at the office work has closed up on me again. At least I fight for my little family. I still have the rose Beth picked for me and a splendid Mozart symphony is playing as your paintings sit before me, both escorting me in memories of you. The last two rolls of film are fine and I am busy duplicating them for you. I have been linking elements of our time together for the diary I am doing for Beth. I will send it later. Tried to call you twice, shall call again. Of course you must call me too, and collect. I am with you in your days and struggles. Oh, do come back quickly. Let us soon bring back our time together.

Love,

Your Maurice"

Life began to settle into its normal routine for Beth and me. One Saturday not long following our return, Jaynie called.

"Jo, what are you doing tonight?" She sounded breathless and I could tell from the tone of her voice that she had been up to something. I knew she was afraid that I would become lonely and depressed and she thought a man in my life would be a preventive for that. Finding me a date had become an obsession for her.

I answered warily, "Well, I'm not sure. What did you have in mind?"

"Have you made dinner yet?"

"No. Beth is visiting her dad until school starts. He's furious with me for keeping her away all summer. I don't see cooking a lot just for me. I could meet you somewhere if you'd like to go out for something."

"Nope. I'm coming to your house for dinner with a friend of mine and someone else that I know. You don't have to do anything because we're bringing everything."

"Who are you trying to fix me up with?" I was not enthused at the prospect.

"Just *trust* me. You're going to like him. I promise. Besides you really do need to get on with things."

"Getting on with things and getting it on are two different matters."

"Yeah, I *know*." I could almost see the suggestive waggle of her eyebrows.

"Jaynie, you are impossible."

"Just shut up. We're already on our way. I told you to trust me. Okay?"

"Okay," I reluctantly agreed.

His name was Bill Rutledge. He walked in like a strutting bantam rooster...western variety: expensive crocodile boots, a three hundred dollar Stetson, Levi's, and a tailored, monogrammed shirt. He was colorful and with a personality to match. Bill was one hundred percent proud, entertaining, full of himself male and damned good looking. Jaynie caught my eye and winked, "Well?"

It was apparent that he liked me too in much the same way that I liked him. Our personalities meshed due to their differences and there was undeniable electricity between us. He was obviously accustomed to being the life of the party but escaped being an overbearing, loud-mouthed bore due to his out right, engaging, bad-boy charm. If he enjoyed his charade, who was to mind when it was obvious that we all enjoyed it too. There was an air of tremendous virility about him that reminded me of Maurice but with a fillip of danger. I decided it was the absolute force of their dominant strong wills. Maurice was the product of the strongly patriarchal society of Mediterranean Europe and Bill of the equally patriarchal society of the American South where the 'Big Daddy" figure still existed in my youth. Maurice was the ultimate cultured, art oriented Frenchman. Bill was the brash, unpolished, new-money American who could discuss horse breeding and poker but didn't know an original oil from a reproduction and didn't pretend he did. Nor did he care.

The powerful male is a strong aphrodisiac for me, and Jaynie was right: it had been far to long since I had enjoyed the romantic attention of an appealing man. I eyed Bill appraisingly and caught him returning the compliment as we sipped our after-dinner drinks.

As Jaynie and Ken left, she gave me a knowing look and whispered in my ear, "Go for it, girl."

Bill was regaling me with some of his exploits when suddenly he diabolically cocked one eyebrow at me and demanded, "Woman come over here."

It was not with any great reluctance that I left my corner of the sofa to join him in the other. He knew how to kiss. He came up for air asking, "Well, do I have to spend the night on the sofa or are you going to invite me to bed?"

"You certainly don't beat around the bush, do you?" Oh no, I thought. That was a poor choice of words and I prayed he would not follow with a dirty pun.

"You didn't answer my question."

"No, I didn't."

"Well...?"

"Well what?" I asked evasively.

"You know you want me and I want you. So let's do it."

"Don't you think you're just a bit premature?"

"Nope. Let's go to bed." He reached for me and swept me into his arm, making like a homing pigeon straight to my bedroom.

"Do you have sonar or something?" I couldn't help but laugh at him.

"I plan to show you what I have." He leered comically.

"That sounds awfully salacious to me."

"You talk too much."

He laid me on the bed and lowered himself onto me, kissing and caressing all the while. After so long alone, it was wonderful to feel his male body against mine, to smell his masculine aroma, to feel the slight stubble of his beard, and to feel his growing hardness pressing into my belly. I wanted him badly, but I was not ready for the rush into intimacy.

"Bill, why don't you just hold me? It's been a long time for me and I don't feel right doing it this way." The compunction of a strict southern Baptist upbringing was kicking in.

"What way?" He looked up genuinely puzzled.

"Surely you know what I mean? I don't even know you."

"What do you want to know? I'll talk fast."

"No. Talk slowly." I looked into his eyes and smiled. "I may hate myself later, but could we make it another time, please?"

He raised himself on one elbow, surprise etched on his face. "You mean it. You really want me to leave?"

"Yes, I do."

"I like you lady, so don't think you've heard the last of me."

At the door, he kissed me lightly on the lips. "I'll call you." He smiled and was gone, leaving me with my back pressed against the door wondering if a cold shower would help. I settled for a book on life in ancient Greece. It was the driest and most soporific one I could find. But sleep would not come. I missed Maurice, I missed Europe, and I missed having the arms of a man around me, cuddling me to sleep. I even felt some regret for sending Bill on his way.

Jaynie called the following morning to see how the evening had gone, but the call I wanted didn't come. I wrote Maurice a long letter detailing all of the trivialities of my day. After another week with no letter and no call from him, I telegrammed with mild irritation to see why I was being ignored. His telegram to me crossed mine somewhere over the ocean:

"My darling, hope you got our card from Chamonix. Mother and I just back from Milano. Sent you more slides and four recordings of Marcello's concert. Am working fourteen hours a day. Hired seven new people. These days are especially hard and my only escape is when my thoughts turn back to you two in that sudden quicksilver, forever time. My eyes see your grace and glee and the outstanding natural similarities and harmonies between us. I hear Kiki's voice all the time. Tell her I hold her shoulders when she studies and would love to swim, tennis ball fight and play madly with her. Is she really starting French? I hope you paint with strength. If only we could all drive and glide on our long beautiful Provencal roads lined with the Plantain trees, and the pines and cypresses. Your, Maurice."

I was chagrined that I had sent him a telegram chiding him for his silence. I was especially abashed when the following day, I received a second telegram, this one in response:

"My Jo. I got your telegram. Don't you know my thoughts are with you? My protection and total tenderness go to you. I cannot wait for your return, your being here. Don't you feel it? Shall call tonight. Your, Maurice."

That night found me sitting by the phone when it rang. No one said anything; there was only the beautifully lilting and hauntingly melancholy strain of our song, *"Anonimo Veniziano."*

"Maurice! You surely know how to announce yourself."

"Hello, darling." I thrilled to the sound of his deep, warm voice.

"It is so good to hear you. I have missed you so terribly and France, too."

"Ah, Jo, it's been crazy for me here. I've had to be constantly away on business and when I return to the office the work is piled and waiting. I can't seem to catch up no matter how I try. But at least business is good. I have just signed an agent in New York who will handle a lot of new business for me there."

"I must apologize to you for scolding you for not writing or calling. I really didn't realize just how busy you've been. I suppose all the time you took for us this summer is putting you even further behind."

"That's time I could never regret spending. It was the most wonderful summer of my life."

"For me too."

"Do you know I live through each day dreaming of next summer when we can be together? Everything I do here now is for the two of you."

He made up for the time of silence by talking for over an hour and even when we had finally said goodnight, he called back five minutes later.

"I have missed you so much I wanted to hear your voice once more before I go to bed."

"Maurice, it is so very late for you. I love and miss you, too. I'll write you another long letter tomorrow and so will Beth. And let me hear from you more often if possible."

"I'll do better, I promise. Kiss my Kiki goodnight for me. It's almost two here so I should try to sleep now. *Je t'aime*."

"Je t'aime aussi. Bon nuit."

How I wished I were back in France. I dug out all of my memorabilia and my slides from summer. While I played our song I looked back through it all and reread his telegrams to me. It seemed like some fantastic dream compared to the reality of my daily life: up at six, at work by seven, classes at eight, lunch at my desk...a diet bar not *sole meunier*, home at three, a shower, a glass of wine while reading the day's mail, dinner to cook, clothes laid out for the next day, a little reading and bedtime by eleven, five days a week, week after week. And time to be lonesome. Bill called but I knew he wasn't for me, especially when I learned that he was still in a long-term relationship. Jaynie called or I called her nearly every day and one night a week we would go out, usually Tuesday night.

About the only place to go was the Marriott. It had a good bar with live music and one of the best restaurants in town, The Scotch Bonnet. An added advantage was the location, midway for both of us. We would usually have dinner in the restaurant and then go into the bar to listen to the music. We often ran into people we knew and would spend an hour or so talking to them before going home. On occasion we would meet someone interesting from out of town. Those times were more fun because we would flirt and laugh, maybe dance, and pretend we were tour guides just back from Europe. Or we would come up with some other unlikely story. We always gave ourselves other names. If I felt really upbeat, I used Charlie and for my most negative moments, which fortunately were rare, I became Gertrude. The shallowness of it, the tedium of daily routine were enough to drive me mad had it not been for the magic world I could escape to in my painting, books or daydreams of Maurice and Europe. Knowing I would return in the summer was a lifeline to the future that lifted me above the sea of daily frustrations.

It wasn't so much that I did not like my job, as in many ways I felt passionate about the importance of it. Rather I had begun to despair of the profession and the process that we were about. I think teachers are a bit like missionaries taking religion to the infidels. We take knowledge to the ignorant. However to convert them and make them want to buy into the message, we must also convince our students that if they follow in the path we lead, their lives will in some way be better. And maybe we are also a little like insurance salesmen. We provide an intangible product that is supposed to provide future benefits. However to convince someone to buy, we must assure them that without what we are selling they risk dire straits. Teachers are among the most important, under-appreciated and underpaid people in society...past, present, but hopefully not in the future. The world has changed from the day when the teacher was a parsimonious master with a cane who was determined to beat the beacon of light into the recalcitrant brains of his pupils. The world has changed from the day when the teacher was a persnickety old maid with a ruler who was determined to march her pupils, single file and orderly, and stereotypically formed into the sunset of her dry vision. The world has changed.

In times past, mostly women entered the profession, expectant of the patriarchal structure of education and anticipating working only as a fall back in the event of the reversal of family fortune, stopping to raise children, and if needed, able to teach and still be home with their children in the afternoon. Yet the world that my generation of women was raised to expect had left us even as we were entering it. Now there are other reasons for the ones who come into education. I am not sure they are any more right than those of my own generation. Some, like me, just always loved learning and teaching is a way to stay in those ivied halls of our youth. Unfortunately, now too few bright and capable students see education as a viable career option. They are turned off by the status of teachers in society, unexcited by the rigidly structured division of time and process in those cloistered chambers, and not attracted by a pay structure that is traditionally among the poorest relative to educational requirements. There are far more options for women today than ever before in history and they are choosing career paths more like their male counterparts. So a profession that has long been sustained by women is no longer going to be "manned" in the same way. The short-term consequences of this dynamic shift in societal structure are coinciding with an even greater shift in world dynamics and culture.

I tried to explain the implications of this to Maurice when he asked me why I continued teaching. I told him, "We are now in an era when the brightest and most prepared will flourish and the rest will experience disenfranchisement from prosperity and self-actualization unless we find a way to drastically alter the current patterns. Ditch digging is no longer a back and shovel proposition. The age of technology requires a whole new set of skills for survival. If we do not find ways to employ and utilize the minds and energies of most of our population, the 'lost' majority will rise against the established order. Will we then go back to a Dark Ages and a painful restructuring of political and cultural systems? It may not happen tomorrow but we cannot house the disenfranchised in ever-larger prisons. We cannot live within a society where no lock is strong enough to protect us. We cannot flourish in a system where the few work and the masses languish on the fruits of others. We cannot survive on a mountain of fomenting alienation. Louis XIV said it, 'apres moi, le deluge' unless we find a way to change the current order. The schools have a tremendous burden in this effort to turn our nation and the world around. And the existing school structure is not working. I have seen it go from a 'bell curve' to a ditch, a valley of despair. Too many have slid from the middle to a lower level of performance and expectation. We have lowered the standards on such measures as the Scholastic Aptitude Test. I see too many students graduating without the needed skills and knowledge to function in a new world order. Too many will find tomorrow colder and more inhospitable. Maybe the schools cannot do it all and certainly they cannot do it alone, but we must mightily try. I try not just for my students but also for my child and her children who must inherit the world we leave them."

"That frightens me for Kiki, too. I have seen some of what you are talking about here but because I am not in the schools, I don't see the same things you do. One of the biggest problems for France and for much of Europe is the influx of poor and uneducated people from Africa and elsewhere who set up shops on blankets laid in the street and sell shoddy, fake designer merchandise to tourist and others foolish enough to buy. There was a riot last year in Florence when the shopkeepers tired of these people blocking the sidewalks, living off the system and contributing nothing back. In France they are straining the national budget because of the welfare demands they make on us. Plus, they are alien to our culture and norms."

I remarked, "I know what you mean. We have a growing problem here with workers from the Latin American countries similar to what you are dealing with there. While I sympathize with their plight in their homeland and with the destitution and needs of those they have left behind, we cannot continue to have such a drain of funds from our own country. While we were and are a nation of people who came here for opportunity and freedom, in the past the immigrants came here, learned the language and melded into our society. By and large this is not happening with this current influx of immigrants who see themselves as working transients, forcing government and business to become bilingual to accommodate them and creating an isolationist inner structure. We see an increase in gangs, enslavement for prostitution, and crime. It's frightening."

"Frightening it is!" He sighed, "I must go now Jo, but I promise to do better about calling. And remember, come summer we will have a wonderful time and forget about all of the world's problems."

From then on Maurice was as good as his word. At least once a week he either telegrammed or phoned. When he called he would talk to us for over an hour. And most of the time, he would call back shortly afterwards, sometimes two or three times. His phone bill must have been astronomical and his telegram expenses as well, but it was reassuring to me to know that I was missed, that somewhere someone really cared. I consoled myself with impossible dreams.

His telegram read: *"October 27. Have raised my working hours to fifteen and sixteen a day. There is no other alternative for now, however things are moving slowly but strongly in the right direction. Darlings, in my thoughts I am with you two all the time. I will be calling you tomorrow. Your, Maurice."*

I wrote him a long chatty letter telling him about our days, my classes, the paintings I was working on, ideas for others, and Beth's efforts to learn French with the tutor he had me hire for her. It was all written in French requiring hours with a dictionary to compose and I was tremendously proud of it. When his reply arrived it was in an interesting mixture of English and French, the English garbled by the French operator and the French mutilated by the American operator. All in all, making sense of his telegrams was often a challenge and sometimes a total frustration.

"November 6. Jo, chérie, ta lettre en Français premier morceau de bravure, je dis tendrement, fierement: bravo. Beth must be removed from the mediocre tutor that you have for her now and given to a person with charm and good methods. Business is a constant race against time but things are progressing. I endure it with the palpable feeling that you two are in it with me. More words and plenty of photographs are coming. Love, Maurice."

"November 20. My efforts to free myself of this business are consuming. Truly my Jo and my Beth, every day is an agony without you. And the evenings are so lonely. There is no joy in my life without the ones who should be with me all of the days of my life. Le soir je rentre les nerfs vides mais devant mes forces comme ci encore plus décuplees et inventant de rage des echos pour ma course je les cherche fixement ces échos ceux que mon coeur et mon âme. In a few short weeks, I should be able to write some real letters to you regularly. I hope that the coming Thanksgiving holiday will be a happy one for you Jo, Kiki and your parents. I would love to be able to spend this special day with my little family. But I must be apart that my course be victorious. Maurice."

I missed him and sometimes these telegrams would make me sad with longing to be back in France. I was grateful that I had good classes and students I liked so that the days provided some moments of levity. One student, Douglas, had developed a big crush on me and constantly pestered me to kiss him. I of course refused and told him to behave himself. One day as I was standing by his desk helping him with his painting, I felt his hand start sliding up my leg. Shocked I jumped back and asked him what on earth he thought he was up to and warned that I would call his father if he ever tried that stunt again. His response, "If you do, he'll just say 'congratulations, son.' " That was such an audacious response that I could not help but privately be amused. At the end of the school year, I gave him the long awaited kiss, a very chaste one on his cheek. He beamed at me and remarked that it was better than nothing. My students and I had a good rapport and I was very proud of the quality of their work. It was rewarding to see them grow and it kept me from dwelling on my inner desire to escape to more exotic places.

The days slipped past and it was Christmas. I had mailed Maurice and his mother gifts in early December hoping that they would arrive in time. Beth and I, finished with school and holiday shopping, left for Greenville to be with my parents. On Christmas Day following dinner, I returned to Raleigh alone, Beth having been picked up by her father to spend the remainder of the holiday with him. It was tough being alone. To assuage my loneliness, I decided to call Maurice but never got through due to constantly busy circuits. The next day brought me a long telegram from him.

"*December 24. I have just tried to call you two dozen times for Christmas Eve. In desperation, tried calling your parents but got no answer. Merry Christmas, my darling Jo and Beth. For me the only merry thought is that half the time until I see you once again in Rome is gone. I leave on January 2nd to go to Milano but will be back in time to call Beth for her birthday on the 6th. I would give so much to hear her play 'White Christmas' on her violin. Please let me have your pardon for not really having begun to write to you. Can you feel my sense of achievement and accomplishment? Behind the timelessness of the Plantain trees I face constant loneliness. No matter now agonizing and costly, it has not been for naught. One day we shall look back on this and see that it was worthwhile. Tonight while trying so hard to reach you, I tell myself it has been incredibly difficult in retrospect surviving since you left me last August. Have I walked past the worst of this time of separation? Did Beth receive her Christmas gifts from Marie and me? As for you my darling, your gift is a Sony television. I will wire you two thousand 'pine trees' for the very nicest you can find. I suppose it will be responsible for many lost hours for our young lady. Please give my holiday greetings to all of your family. Love, Maurice."*

New Year's brought a card from him fronted by a Monet painting, "The Poppy field." It is a lovely scene of a field of poppies beneath an azure sky. A woman and child pause there in a moment of eternal peace.

"For Jo and Beth, the fields of France await you...because surely it is you there in Monet's painting and it is you who must appear there without ceasing. The crickets of Provençe seem to be singing as they bid you gracious welcome and they watch over you for me in vigilant protection. Thus when you have returned to Provençe and to me, 1985 will at last be beautiful. Maurice."

The wire of funds, the 'pinetrees,' to my bank was completed by the fourth and I hastened to buy the television Maurice wanted for us in order to be able to tell him about it when he called for Beth's birthday. His package for Beth also came bringing her some moments of great excitement as she burrowed into the packing material to unearth her goodies: two Cacharel skirts, a blouse, a sweater and a pale blue Dior dress. Miraculously they were all a perfect fit. Maurice's discerning eye was once again accurate. One of the loveliest parts of the gift was the two perfect Plantain leaves nestled atop the tissue, one of heavy gold foil and the other in silver. Beside them was a card dedicated to Beth for her special day depicting a foal peering from blades of tall Camargue marsh grasses, above the foal its parent bends low in tender protection.

"1 January, 1985. Mon enfant chérie, (I'll translate what I can of his note to her) it is the first time that I have wished you Happy Birthday and I

send you my wish that God will bless you. God has given so much to you and such grace, thus much is expected of you. In order that the stars that shine over you should reflect your most splendid passions...those which are the highest and most exacting, and that your wishes, greatest desires and purest joys be realized to the fullest extent possible, you must endeavor always to hold onto that which is the highest you can attain. Thus an irrepressible fountain of joy, of deep satisfaction will always dominate your life. Prepare for it. Earn it. And know that I will shield you and be beside you in spirit ('cotoverai'...will be close to without touching, reaching.) Keep this card. Read it now, read it later and later in the coming years. Always, Maurice."

The package had arrived only a couple of hours prior to his call.

"Jo, my darling. Happy New Year!"

"Happy New Year to you too! It's so good to hear you! It feels like ages since I last heard you or saw you."

"I know. I've been so busy and when I have tried to call I got no answer. Did you get my cables?"

"Yes. The telegrams, cards and gifts have all come. The wire of the 'pine trees' came too and I bought the Sony. Thank you so much."

"Wonderful! I'm so glad that you got everything. Did the clothes fit?"

"As though they had been tailored for her."

"Perfect. She liked them?"

"Very much. When we finish talking, I'll put her on so she can tell you herself."

"Good, good. Oh, Jo, it has been so long since summer and so very, very hard. I miss you, my friend."

"And I miss you. I hope my letters help. I try to make them long and interesting and full of the things we do so you will feel closer to us."

"The letters help a lot. I especially enjoyed the one in which you told me about things from your childhood. It does make me feel closer to you. I very much enjoyed the mental picture you painted me of your great aunt. Ah...Aunt Alcy."

Aunt Alcy was as imperturbable as a biscuit filled hound on a fly-buzzingly lazy summer afternoon when the dappled light sifted through the green canopy of Black Jack Oak and Pecan trees spreading ragged parasols of shade over the swept-dirt yard of my grandparents. Maybe that very unflappability is what led her to survive the rigors of this life for ninety-six years. The last forty or so years of her life, following the death of her husband, Uncle Dumpie, she spent on a continuous round of those extended visits common to indigent female relatives in the Old South. At that time, my grandparents still had at home two of their eight children who had survived childhood. Two more had died as infants and a third, Mary, was killed by lightening at the age of ten. The six who had left the parental nest were frequently back with a swarm of grandchildren of all ages. I was one of the noisy, joyful swarm. These moments with my mother's family provided some of the happiest of my childhood. Often these Sunday visits gave me the chance to study Aunt Alcy at some leisure, all be it with little appreciation at the time of what I suppose you would call, the "color" of the experience.

We grandchildren in the sometimes-unkind way of children, often found her an object of amusement. Perhaps in a way the amusement was mingled with a certain confusion as to how to react to her. In height, she seemed much as we...just wrinkled with age. She couldn't have been more than four feet nine or so inches tall and was as round as any dumpling in the Sunday chicken stew. She was what you might call comfortable looking, not fat. Her hair, long and severely bunned, never grayed, just faded from black into a non-color, neither black, brown, nor gray. Her dresses were long and prim of color and cut, just clearing the tops of her sensible black lace-up shoes by a mere few inches, the exposed bit of leg covered with opaque flesh-colored stockings that had a propensity to sag at the ankles. A snowy-bibbed apron was always tied at her waist and often would be festooned with a needle somewhere in the vicinity of the neck strap. She had never worn glasses and could still thread that needle unaided when she died. However the thing that stood out about her to me, my sisters and cousins, and what caused us to dart around the back corner of the house and imitate her before an audience of disinterested, dirt scratching, grit pecking chickens was her drawl. I have never seen anyone who could drag out words more slowly. That alone, sufficient to insure our deprecating humor, was yet further exacerbated by her use of old southern homilies and expressions most others had long forgotten but we as children found new and novel.

I remember well that early spring day with the dogwood's fresh green leaves gleaming in tender newness just beyond the kitchen window that my grandmother kept propped up with a stick, the cord long since having broken. While a newly arrived bumblebee announced it would soon be time to shed our shoes...we had to spot three first, Aunt Alcy launched into a monologue on the evils of dancing. I don't think she was talking to anyone so much as she was just talking, certainly she was not talking to the suddenly attentive cluster of children. At the time in youthful innocence, her statement on the sinfulness of dancing and how it did little but trigger carnal appetites in men had little meaning to me or my peers as we snickered solely at the delivery. As she put it, "Iiittt juuuusst giiivees meenn haarrrd feeelliiinns." Years later when dancing and occasionally feeling my partners arousal, I have enjoyed an inward chuckle when her drawling words came to mind. I have truly relished wondering what that round, wrinkled little doll of an old lady was like when young and courting. I can only hope she could talk faster than when I knew her or she would never have gotten a 'no' out before the dirty deed would have been done.

Following the marriage of my very slim Uncle Jake to a woman of more than robust proportions, she commented that she supposed, "He had to take the whole thing to get the piece he wanted." The family is still laughing over that one.

Now years later with wrinkles beginning to etch the story of life on my own living canvas, I find a warm joy in holding those comfortable, secure days of youth close, enriched by the circle of family that will always live inside me now that many of them have long since found eternal refuge in the weed choked cemetery just beyond the back pasture where mules once mulled the day's drudgery. Something of that passing of the color of the south is like the gotterdamerung Margaret Mitchell described in her own lament of the homogenizing of this our homeland.

"You must write me more about your family, Jo. I love getting to know about you and them." We chuckled together in memory of that particular letter. "Did you and your mother receive the gifts we sent you? You haven't mentioned them, so I don't know if you never got them or if you just didn't like them."

"No, I'm afraid they've not arrived yet. But then the mails are so slow for the holidays and here we have many strikes, who knows? Maybe they will be here soon, so don't worry. When did you mail them? Did you send them to the office or here?"

"I mailed them to your home address just after Thanksgiving."

"Umm...that is rather long but not terribly so. We shall see."

"Will I see you in Rome again this year, Maurice?" Jaynie and I were again taking our students on the same tour as the one of the previous spring and I had written early in October to tell Maurice of my plans and my hope of seeing him once again in Rome. He had only alluded to the invitation in one earlier telegram so I felt compelled to hear him say that he would meet me.

"But of course! I'm counting the days. You must write or call as soon as you know which hotel so we can plan where to meet."

I knew had he said "No," no matter how good the reason, I would have been crushed. I smiled at his response and hugged myself in silent relief.

"I'll call you as soon as I know which hotel the tour company will put us in. It will be no more than a couple of weeks prior to departure before they can tell me anything. If I don't get through to you on the phone, I'll cable as the mail is too slow."

"That would be good darling because I'm traveling quite a bit on business."

"Maurice, I have a problem calling you. Often your line is busy for hours, even days at the time. Are you having a problem with it?"

"No, no. I take it off the hook when I go to bed so it doesn't disturb my sleep or my mother's. Also when we are gone, I take it off the hook so if people are watching and call to see if we are gone, they won't be able to tell. There is a real problem with robbery in Marseille now with the influx of immigrants from North Africa and as you know we have some valuable things."

"I see. I didn't think you were talking all of that time." I laughed. He didn't know just how aggravating it had been to call as he had so often encouraged me to do and to be greeted only by a perpetual busy signal. I did know about the crime increase as he had told me that summer and also about his mother's robbery. It seems they were stopped at a traffic light when someone reached in her window and snatched her purse and the jewelry she was wearing. Her purse had also contained jewelry. When they told me about it in Chamonix, I could tell she was still very upset about it, particularly the loss of the large diamond engagement ring she had been wearing.

"Well, darling, tell me about the television you bought?"

"It's gorgeous, 32" screen, great color. We love it. I'll send you a photo of it. *And thank you again. You are so generous to us.*"

"Good. Now, darling, I'll say goodnight to you and talk with Beth. *Je t'aime et bon soir.*"

"*Je t'aime aussi et bon soir à toi*. Here's Beth."

Beth caught my eye as I handed her the phone. I knew she still felt shy and uncomfortable with him, and that she was torn by feelings of gratitude for all he did and guilt that she did not feel greater affection. She was also more than a little afraid that we would marry and she would have to move to France.

I must confess Maurice's talks with me and my newly found romance with Europe had me thinking somewhat along those very lines. Beth, sensitive to my moods and expressions had picked up on that secret yearning for a kind of life that I had only read about, seen in movies and dreamed of until Maurice gave me entree into his world. I would spin daydreams in idle moments picturing myself living in Provençe, in a house on a cliff overlooking the Mediterranean. There would be a studio filled with light from huge glass doors opening onto a terrace made of cool and sleek stone from the Bebemas quarry near Aix en Provençe. Maurice would be in the other end of the house in his own studio working on his books of photographic essays. As the wind wafted into the room, billowing the sheer white draperies, it would bring in all of the special aromas and sounds of the south of France and I would hear Beth's voice singing as she played happily among the Laurier bushes in the garden or by the azure pool.

Maybe to understand the intensity of my longing, it is necessary to have lived the kind of childhood that I had. It hurt so much for I was too sensitive, too shy and much too aware of the imperfections of life. My grandparents and aunts and uncles made much of me, as I was the first grandchild on both sides, so I was happy when I stayed with them and it was their love and delight in me that kept my childhood from being much sadder, as at home, I watched the pain of the unhappy union between my parents. Often I was the scapegoat for my father's angers and frustrations and with little provocation he would loosen the belt from his trousers and beat me until huge purple welts covered both my legs and buttocks. In shame, I would wear dresses rather than shorts even on the hottest days so no one could see my degradation. In silent rage, my mother would hear my cries of terror fearing his temper too much to provoke it by defending me. And she talked to me. She told me of her woman's resentment that her husband had become her best friend's lover. I was just five when my eyes were opened to the ugliness of a world that I often found hostile and cruel. As I grew up, I turned increasingly to a world of books, bringing me distant places, happy times and loving people. I learned to concentrate until I could feel myself transported from that little speck of dirt I was on to whatever locale I was reading of. Often I concentrated too well and would not hear my father calling me until it was too late and I once again was the object of his vengeance. Looking back I can forgive and try to understand the frustrations and unfulfilled dreams that led my parents to the misery they acted out day after day. I can try to understand and forgive but I cannot forget. Perhaps that is why my art became so important to me. It was another way to escape into happy and perfect little worlds of my own creation. With so much ugliness already in the world I'll never understand the artists who feel the need to create more.

Chapter 8

The winter was cold and gray, but the prospect of seeing Maurice and Europe in a few short weeks kept me warm and sunny inside. Maurice continued to call sporadically and to telegram frequently.

"March 6: Your Christmas gifts just arrived with the wonderful messages. The sweater fits me like a glove. Beautiful. Just great. And my mother loves the scarf. Shall answer Beth's letter apart. Am rather exhausted from work. Never have I missed you so much. Rome seems like some kind of vaguely unreachable, but surely coming and certain, spring heaven. I made my reservations in Rome this morning. I hope I have you two on the phone Friday. More coming tomorrow. Love, Maurice."

The seventh of March was his birthday...he hadn't told me which one...so, we called to wish him happiness and to tell him that I would take his presents with me to Rome. It seemed safer and surer in light of the time it had taken them to receive our Christmas gifts. Maurice was thrilled by our call. I got the impression it was the only moment of celebration in his day. We talked for about ten minutes before he insisted I hang up so he could call back at his expense. When he rang back, not only he, but also Marie talked. She seemed humbly and inordinately pleased with our gifts to her. I knew what we could afford to send was modest compared to what they could buy, but just knowing that we cared enough to give her a present was what really mattered to her. Being from a large and close family, their loneliness and isolation struck me anew. I felt that Beth and I truly had become their family and the part that brought love, laughter, youth and the joy of living back into their hearts. Maurice talked for over an hour after she was off the line, reliving the past summer together, planning for the one to come and arranging to meet me again at the Casa Valadier. He told me of his struggle to find time free of the demands of his business to work on his photography. I was admonished that I must paint, work, produce as an artist for he would brook nothing less from me. When we hung up I felt guilty that I produced so little since summer and vowed to do better. The next day brought another telegram from him obviously sent the moment we hung up.

"My Darlings, your call was the nicest present. A wave of happiness invades me to hear your love. We must stop being apart. I do and shall do everything possible for that. Your, Maurice."

Shortly on the heels of the telegram a terrible bout of flu arrived to keep me trapped at home. I spent my time writing Maurice long letters in French that were dictionary correct, but no doubt, far from the proper idiom. Nonetheless, I was proud of my effort. I had begun to find that thoughts in French would pop into my mind and I often would subconsciously translate into French things that I heard. I was finally learning to communicate with Maurice in his own tongue.

"March 13. Just a quick message before loosening Battleship. The mailman climbed the hill with a letter telling me that you have been much more ill than previously said. We need ateliers forever in a warm country with the Laurier and Lilacs endlessly perfuming the air. Jo, I want it so much. Be with me; think of me this coming weekend as I drive to Rome to await you. You will be my companion every mile of the road. Love, Maurice."

Jaynie and I decided to get together at the Marriott that last Tuesday night before our Saturday departure. We needed to discuss some details for the trip and we both just needed to get out, I suppose. She was good for me, kept me from taking myself to seriously and forced me to leave my cocoon. As we sat in the bar talking, at the same moment we both fastened our eyes on one of the best looking men I had ever seen. There was something about him that made me feel as though he had been created by the blueprint of my dreams.

Jaynie tugged at my arm. "Hey, do you see what I see?"

"I do and he's gorgeous."

"So, why don't you go talk to him?"

"No way! If he wants to talk to me, he can come over here. Besides, just in case you haven't noticed, it is obvious that he knows we're talking about him."

"Yeah!" Jaynie grinned at me. "Go on, don't be such a chicken." She was still determined to fix me up because she had begun dating Roger Smithson steadily and was becoming serious about him. It worried her that without her company I tended to hole up at home. When I made no move to get up, she persisted, "He looks like he has a great body. If you don't go talk to him, I'm going to go over there and tell him that you want to."

"Do that and I'll murder you!" I groaned, knowing that she wouldn't hesitate for a moment unless I was really emphatic.

"I know; we'll send him a note." Her eyes lit up with delight at the inspiration.

"No!"

"Yes? And if we don't do that, I'm going over there."

"So, what are you going to say in the note?" I asked sarcastically..."You're the one I'd most like to see naked?"

"Yeah, that's great!" She said it with a wicked gleam in her eyes.

"You are absolutely out of your mind!" Ignoring me, she was busy searching for a pen in her purse.

"Jaynie, don't!"

"You write or I will!" She ordered me, slapping the pen and cocktail napkin in front of me on the counter.

"All right." I heaved a sigh of resignation, knowing she was determined.

"Write: you've been voted the man most likely to look good with his clothes off."

"No doubt he would, but I'm not writing it."

"Yes, you are!"

"Jaynie, I must be as crazy as you are." I gave her a wry grin and wrote the note as she dictated. That done she grabbed the note from me and called the bartender over.

"You see that man over there on the corner?"

"Yes."

"Well, put this in an empty glass and take it to him, please."

"Yes, ma'am."

I couldn't look up and I was flaming red with embarrassment.

Jaynie grabbed my arm. "Look he's coming over here. I knew it would work."

"I'm leaving." I muttered, my nose nearly on the counter.

"No, you're not!"

It was too late anyway. He stopped in front of me and I could feel him looking at me and waiting. I was mortified but pleased also that it was me, and not Jaynie that he approached. With a warm voice he announce himself. "Hello."

Blushing furiously, I looked up into twinkling blue eyes, both amusement and kindness were there. I could only croak, "Hi."

We talked and the hours flew past and suddenly it was closing time. He told me his name, Ed Branson. He worked for GE and traveled constantly all over the world and was a specialist in quality control. He said he was divorced and his ex-wife and son lived in Montgomery, Alabama. The music in my heart almost drowned the words spoken with a tidal wash of feeling that left me overwhelmed with it suddenness and intensity. He excited me the way no man ever had.

"Would you allow me to walk you to your car?" He patiently awaited my reply.

I hesitated. I have always felt it looks cheap for a woman who enters a bar without a man to leave accompanied by one she's just met. But Jaynie had long since departed and I was hesitant to walk through a darkly shadowed parking lot at 12:30 in the morning. And most of all, I was reluctant for the evening to end. I felt as though I'd found a puzzle piece that had been missing from the picture of my life and I wanted to turn it over and over in my mind until I found its place.

"Would you please?" I finally responded.

Putting his arm around my shoulders, he walked me to my car. I turned to say goodnight and knew by his nearness that he was going to kiss me. It seemed so right. We kissed, holding one another and thrilling to our mutual discovery of the other. His birthday was the same as mine, only one year earlier. If I believed in astrology, fate, predestination, I would have said that it was fated that at that time and in that place our paths would cross, our hearts would join. I felt as though I had known him forever, a separate person and yet in some mysterious way, an extension of myself.

"May I call you? I want to see you again. In fact, I don't even want to leave."

"Please do. I'd like to see you again too." I gave him my number, praying that he would use it and soon, that he felt the same chemistry and soul-bond that I felt.

It was almost one in the morning. With an alarm set for six, I knew I had to get home and get some sleep before I could face that day's classes.

We laughed and kissed one final goodbye. Sighing I pulled myself from the sweet paradise of his arms and drove away into the night.

He called the next day. "Hello, I'm in Pittsburgh and plotting to be back in Raleigh."

"Well, do you think you'll plot successfully?"

"I'm sure of it. How about two weeks from tonight, Tuesday night at seven."

"I'd love it. I return from the tour of Italy and Greece on that Sunday, so I should be rested enough by Tuesday to go out."

"You are a bad influence," He teased. "I couldn't keep my mind on business for thinking about you and I found myself nodding off in my afternoon meeting."

"You're a worse influence. I could barely teach my classes for yawning and almost fell asleep at my desk during lunch. Fortunately I had no soup to fall into or I'd have drowned."

He laughed, "I'll call from my hotel when I arrive just to confirm.

I don't know Raleigh too well, so do you think you could meet me at my hotel?"

"No problem. I'll just meet you in the lobby whenever you say."

The next few days flew by and then it was Saturday and time to leave for Rome: Jaynie, our thirty people, Bill and me. He loved to travel and had decided to go with us...as my date, apparently. That was just *wonderful* since Maurice would be awaiting my arrival in Rome. Here I was without a date for months and months and suddenly I had three men in my life. Rome was going to be busy. In the idiom of the single woman, it is always either a case of 'feast or famine.'

Bill and I sat together on the plane and I made it clear that I had plans in Rome that would not include him. Nevertheless, he was good company, loved to talk and kept me regaled with tales of his adventures. He is one of those people who seem to serve as a catalyst for creating *events*. We finally tried to nap. Since sleep and planes seem mutually exclusive to me, I arrived in Rome red-eyed and weary. Bill looked as disgustingly fresh as the proverbial daisy.

When we checked into the hotel, The Metropole, I had a message from Maurice waiting at the desk. As soon as I reached my room, I called him.

"Jo, you're here at last! Did you have a good flight?"

"Yes, but very tiring. How about you? When did you arrive?"

He laughed, "As usual I was late leaving so I ended up driving all night. It was five this morning when I reached the Jolly, so I'm in bed trying to sleep. What time is it, darling?"

"It's noon."

"Hmm. You must be exhausted. Why don't you take a nap and we'll meet at four at the Casa Valadier. I think that would be the appropriate place, don't you?"

"That's fine. I'll see you there."

I was keyed up from the adrenalin of jet lag so there was no way I was going to sleep. I called Joy's room. "Jaynie, I don't meet Maurice until four. What are y'all doing?"

"We're hungry. We're going out to get some lunch. Want to go?"

"Yes. I'll meet you downstairs. Who's going?"

"Crystal, Mrs. Markham, and me."

"And Bill?"

"Nah. He said he was going to sleep."

"O.K. I'll see you in a minute."

We walked across the street to the *Est, Est, Est Tratoria* where we had a wonderful meal. Mrs. Markham, a ninety-year-old charmer who still spoke with the strong Russian accent of her homeland, entertained us with her lively wit and stories of the family's escape in 1918. Crystal, Jaynie's vivacious and impish sister had obviously attracted the interest of the restaurant owner who buzzed near our table like a mustachioed fly. By the end of the meal, he had invited us out for the evening...after he closed, which would be around midnight. He made plans for our group to meet him at the Brown Derby nightclub, the 'in' place for live music and dancing. Crystal and Jayne accepted immediately, Mrs. Markham for obvious reasons declined.

Following lunch, I repeated my inaugural ride to the Casa Valadier. The passage of a year had done little to ameliorate the experience of a Roman taxi ride. And again I awaited Maurice on the balcony of the Casa Valadier. The shadows began to lengthen and the day to cool as the sun began to slip nearer the dome of St. Peter's and still I waited. It was nearly six when he arrived and I had just opened the door of the taxi I had summoned when exasperation and weariness had triumphed over patience.

"Jo, WAIT, darling!" He shouted to me.

I turned to watch him walk to me. "What happened? I had given up."

"I'm sorry, darling." He smiled ruefully, "I had to buy gasoline for the car and traffic was terrible...*terrible, tellement! Je regret, mon amour!*" Pulling me into his arms, he closed the taxi door behind me, waving the disappointed driver on to other fares. Kissing me on both cheeks in the traditional French greeting, he sighed, "I've missed you so much. I thought this time together would never come."

"It has been a long time, hasn't it...much too long? How have you been?"

"It has been mad, mad, I can tell you. Never have I worked so hard. But at last it is beginning to happen. I can feel the end of this ahead. Then I will be free, free for my little family and for my art. I want it so much."

Arm in arm we strolled over to the outdoor cafe where the waiter beckoned us to a newly vacated spot. Maurice ordered espresso for us both before facing into the sinking sun and leaning back, eyes closed to bask in its weakening warmth.

"You're tired." I couldn't help but notice, trying to keep the shock from my voice, that his year had been unkind. The lines of his face were more deeply etched. Beneath his tan an ashen tone invaded his skin. His stomach seemed tight, almost swollen beneath the customary black Izod shirt. His exposed arms seemed less muscular than before, giving him a new and almost vulnerable quality. I tried but could not keep my anxiety for him from creeping in when I inquired, "Are you not well, Maurice?"

He gave an impatient and proud flicker of his hand and the muscles of his face tightened, plowing the furrows even deeper. "But of course I'm well! Just very tired. This year has been difficult beyond imagination. You cannot begin to know the problems." He was silent so long, I thought he had forgotten me in his retreat within himself. "And Beth, how is my Kiki, *mon ange*?"

"She's fine and she asked me to tell you that she has missed you." I slipped from my purse the small drawing she had given me as I packed. "She made this for you."

He sat forward and gently cupped the drawing. His eyes moistened with tenderness and I knew that small and honest token of childish affection and gratitude had moved him deeply. His voice roughened with emotion when he asked me to help him find a special gift for her.

"How I long to have our magic summer days again, the three of us together. The joy of that child!" He paused reflectively and a wistful note entered his voice, "She hasn't grown up too much has she?"

I hastened to reassure him that, while she was a little taller, she was not yet beyond the gates of childhood. He desperately felt her slipping past him in her inexorable journey into young adulthood. Sitting in companionable silence, we listened to the singing of the early evening birds as the gentle wind coaxed the glowing sun into a nest beyond the feathered pines.

"I made dinner reservations at the *Girrarosto Toscano*. I thought you'd like that, Jo. Am I right?"

"That sounds fabulous. You know that's one of my favorites."

"And mine." He held my hand as we walked to his car. "Tell me, as well as Florence, would you like to go to Ostia or perhaps to the Villa d'Este at Tivoli or Hadrian's Villa? We actually could do all of them, if you'd like? I want you to see some of the things that we didn't see last year." He looked down at me and grinned, "I also intend to buy you another pair of heels to show off those legs of yours. D'accord?"

"Yes! One: I'd love to see those things; two: I want to see some of the other things I didn't get to do last year such as Florence and Siena; and three: I'd love a gorgeous new pair of shoes."

"Good. It's yours. All of it."

The evening was fun and easy. There was no heavy session of Margot questions. In fact, he seemed much calmer about her when I casually and deliberately introduced her name into our conversation.

"You know, she is a part of the past, a very unhappy part. I'd much rather be here with her sister. Let's not spoil our evening talking of her. It's our time now."

That was fine with me, as I never wanted a repeat like the one of the previous spring. It grew late. The dinner, the wine, the jet lag conspired to make me droop my head on his shoulder as we still sat at the table. "It's late, Maurice. Let's call it a day so we will be rested for all of the things you've planned for tomorrow."

"Of course, darling. I'm tired as well." It was almost 11:30 when we reached my hotel where he pulled over to the curb and stopped the engine. He turned to me and smiled, "I'm so happy to be with you again. You bring me peace."

Before I could respond, he leaned forward and kissed me sweetly and lingeringly on the lips. Suddenly he wrapped me tightly in his arms and began kissing with increasing ardor. I pulled back, surprised and confused. "I think I should go in now. Thank you so much for a lovely evening."

"*Bon nuit, mon coeur.* I'll phone you in the morning just as I leave the hotel."

When I entered the lobby ready for my bed, I found Crystal, Jaynie and Bill waiting for me in the bar there. They spotted me and sprinted forward to surround me. "Hey, come on! What kept you so long? We're going partying and since we've waited just for you, you're going too." They chorused and I groaned. Bill grabbed one arm and Jaynie the other and we were out the door and in a taxi before Maurice had gone a block.

The Brown Derby had a wonderful pianist and singer performing when we arrived. It also had the owner of the restaurant where we had eaten lunch and a friend of his. I could feel Bill bristle. He hadn't anticipated any competition for my attention and it was soon obvious that the friend was zeroing in on me.

"Let's dance." Without waiting for a reply, he had me on the dance floor moving to the romantic melody of '*Never, Never, Never,*' in Italian '*Grande, Grande, Grande.*'

We danced several songs before Bill felt the call of his beer, apparently confident that he had secured my interest with his skillful and *close* dancing. I remembered Aunt Alcy. The moment Bill returned and settled himself to reach for his beer, the owner's friend, Guiseppi, asked me to dance.

"Would you excuse me, Bill?"

"Sure, no problem." I chuckled inwardly at his attempt at nonchalance; but accurately surmised that at the rate he was downing beer, he would soon be too inebriated to care. Guiseppe was an even better dancer than Bill and we enjoyed the tease of our moving bodies, in unison, but not quite making contact. When we finally returned to our table, Bill was immersed in conversation with the restaurateur and continued to studiously ignore me. Guiseppe didn't and soon we were dancing again, closer. When next we returned to the table, Jaynie and Crystal were both engrossed by the solicitous attention of two gorgeous men, the restaurateur was still talking to Bill, and Guiseppi was beginning to annoy me with his increasingly amorous intentions. I glanced at my watch and was appalled to see that it was nearly three in the morning. Suddenly I was exhausted.

I leaned into Bill's ear and told him I had to go. He was obviously irritated with me and equally obvious. had drunk too much. Not wanting to wait until Jaynie and Crystal returned from the dance floor, I slipped from the table and asked the doorman to hail a taxi for me. By this time, Guiseppi had caught on to what I was about and arrived just as the taxi pulled up. Waving to him, I hopped in, instructing the driver to get me to my hotel pronto: Roman-crazy-fast was just fine. Guiseppi was certainly not one to refuse a challenge as he followed in his car at break-neck speed all the way to my hotel. Screeching to a halt, he was out of his car by the time I had paid my driver and climbed from the taxi.

"Why are you leaving? The evening is still young."

"It may well be, but at the moment, I don't think I am."

"Then we have a drink, yes?"

"No. I'm going to bed.

"This is good too. I come to bed with you."

"NO."

"You like. I promise."

"NO!"

"Then we have a drink."

"NO!!" I turned and stalked off.

Soon I was undressed and in my bed. I had barely fallen asleep when the buzz of the phone jerked me back to consciousness. I groaned, wondering who could be calling at four in the morning. "Hello?"

"Hey, Jo. This is Bill."

"I know this is Bill!" I snapped at him.

"Listen, I need your help."

"What do you mean?" I wearily asked.

"I'm in jail." He said it softly, apologetically.

"You're *what*??"

"Well, this guy made a comment about you and I punched him. I had to defend your honor, didn't I? So the police came, and arrested me and here I am."

"Here you are where?"

"You know, where the guide pointed out today: the police station around the corner from the hotel."

"Super! Just wonderful." I exclaimed angrily. "Just what am I supposed to do about it?"

"Come bail me out?" Pleading like a bad little boy this time.

"Oh, my God!" I could have murdered him with relish. "I'm on my way. Don't go anywhere now." I said bitingly. Groggily I struggled into my clothes that were on the floor where I'd dropped them. I managed to get my contacts into my protesting eyes, ran my hands through witchy hair and lurched through the door trying to decide if I knew enough Italian to even find him once I reached the station. Head down and hustling, I charged into someone. Arms were instantly around me and I looked up into two dancing eyes. Bill!! With both fists I beat him on the chest, furious and relieved at the same time.

"You turkey! What do you mean pulling a stunt like that at this time of the night?"

Tears were making tracks down his cheeks he was laughing so hard. Still holding me, he began edging me to my door. Realizing the intention, I pushed him back. "Goodnight!"

"Nope! Not yet."

"Yes!"

"Come on, it'll do us good."

"At the moment I'm so tired I'd have to rest up to die. You like it with corpses?"

"I can think of a few ways to put some life into you." He leaned forward to kiss me but I blocked him with both elbows firmly jabbed into his chest.

"Back off. I'm going to sleep...alone, and if you pull another stunt like this one, you're going to sleep too...permanently!"

"I love it when you're mad."

"Don't push your luck." Despite myself, I grinned. He *had* pulled a smooth stunt with his jail caper and I had fallen for it all the way. "Goodnight."

"Tomorrow night." He grinned and whistling walked down the hall to his room.

I fell across the bed exhausted, having paused only to remove my contacts, and quickly slipped into oblivion."Oh, God. What is it?" I groaned into the phone long before the sun could pry its way through the crack in the crooked drape.

"Madame, you wished a wake-up call at six, si?"

"Si, si. D'accordo. Grazie." I stammered. Time to get up, shower and see the group for breakfast then hope that Maurice would be on time. He was to be at the hotel sharply at seven to take me to Florence. Last year I had missed out on that in order to spend the day with him in Rome. This was to be my day for Florence if only I could get both eyes open and a weary body moving.

I managed somehow. The group left the hotel at 6:30 and I trudged back to my room to look longingly at my bed. I knew if I stayed there I would only collapse into its waiting warmth for at least the next month. I regretfully returned to the lobby to await Maurice there. A miracle! He was actually on time. It may well have been the only time in all of the days I ever spent with him. The drive to Siena, our first stop, was relatively quiet. Maurice talked, the tape played Bach, and I slept.

"Close your eyes, darling." I chuckled wryly to myself: if he had only known just how very closed they had been. I kept them peacefully closed as he described our approach into Siena, warning me not to open my eyes until that most precious of moments when he would so instruct me. I allowed him to play tour guide to the blind, grateful for the information and yet glad I did not yet have to open my eyes and begin another long day.

"Well, darling, how do you like it?"

Siena looked like a picture from my *'History of Art'* by Jansen. Somehow it had survived the Middle Ages intact. The drama of his method of introduction had served its purpose, as I was indeed enchanted. "I feel as though I've entered a movie set. Can't you just see the medieval townsmen bustling about, prosperous, secure in their proud city as the bell tower casts its long shadow of protection over them. I love it."

"Let me tell you about the Palio." He smiled down at me as he helped me from the car onto the cobbled paving of the central piazza. "We are forbidden to stop here but I want you to see the place where the most famous and oldest horse race in Europe is held each summer." He regaled me with stories of the race as we ambled about the piazza.

"Let me get my cameras. Wouldn't you like to take photos too?"

"Yes I would. What a tower. You know it's the tallest in all Tuscany. I've read how tall but I can never remember. I teach about the tower when I do Romanesque and Gothic architecture. Having slides not only of it but the piazza will help me give a much better sense of its size and setting. That loggia is gorgeous, too." I was excited and the nap had thankfully proven refreshing enough that I could enjoy the setting. Maurice smiled indulgently, rewarded by my enthusiasm, as he helped me to find just the right angles from which to shoot.

"We're parked here illegally. In fact, we shouldn't even have driven into the plaza but I wanted you to open your eyes to the sight of it. However, if we don't move quickly, the police are going to strongly suggest that we do." I looked to where he gestured to see a policeman marching furiously towards the car.

"Let's run for it!" I saucily flung over my shoulder at him while racing for the car.

"Made it!" He laughed like a naughty boy, as gunning the engine, we leaped forward and into the haven of a twisting side street leaving a thwarted policeman shaking his fist in our direction and colorfully describing our parentage.

"Wait! We can't leave Siena without seeing the cathedral. It's so beautiful in the slides I have of it." We stopped there for more photos, lingering as Maurice struggled tediously for just the right effects and angles. I went inside and took some shots of the interior and then back out to study the unfinished walls that were to have been a huge extension to the present cathedral, which had been begun in 1288. Unfortunately the Bubonic plague of 1348 swept Europe killing nearly half the population, hitting particularly hard in Siena where two thirds of the population died, effectively stopping the remodeling of the cathedral. Today only those ancient perimeter nave walls of what was to have been the new cathedral bear silent reminder of the tragedy the town endured. As he took his last shots, I dashed to the lower level of the cathedral reached from a side street, in order to see the famous baptismal font designed by Donatello.

Leaving Siena, I realized that it must have taken much more time than we thought. "Oh, no! We were supposed to meet Jaynie at the Ponte Vecchio at noon. Remember, we promised to take her to lunch with us? Do we have time to get there?"

"It's only twelve now and Florence is only twenty minutes or so away. Surely she'll wait."

"Hopefully. If we aren't too late..." However, by the time we reached Florence it was nearly one. Maurice had stopped for gas and I began to suspect him of stalling deliberately as he then drove far more slowly than was his habit and made several circuitous turns in Florence consuming even more valuable minutes for scenic side excursions and stops to savor the view. Furthermore the drive is much longer than twenty minutes even at his breakneck speed.

Finally, "Maurice, there's the Ponte Vecchio. Please put me out here while you look for a parking place and I'll see if I can find her."

"But, darling, she'll wait for you and if she hasn't you don't want to wait alone here. It will only take a minute to park."

"Good. That means I'll only have a couple of minutes to wait for you. Please let me out."

"If you insist. But it really is quite foolish of you."

"Hurry back for us." I closed the door and began searching anxiously for her. She wasn't at the appointed spot and I could see her nowhere in the crowds of tourists. I walked a short distance onto the famous bridge looking into the glittering shops lining either side with their seductive array of gold jewelry. That certainly was an improvement, I thought, over the butcher shops that had conducted business there in medieval times. Not finding her in any of the shops, I walked back and crossed the street to the Uffizi but still no Jaynie. Maurice walked up to find me sitting dejectedly on the wall leading to the bridge.

"Jaynie gave up I suspect. I just hope her feelings aren't hurt."

"Darling, I'm taking you to such a wonderful place for lunch, that you will forget to be sad. So, let's not spoil our day with futile worry."

"Where's that?"

"Fiesole. The Villa San Michele. It's a marvelous hotel and restaurant in a former monastery on a mountain high above Florence. You can see all of the city from there and the cuisine is superb." He turned to flag a passing taxi, commenting: "He probably won't stop because we're not at the stand. Hey! We're in luck. This is easier than trying to find my way there, besides I found a good parking place for the car and I don't want to lose it since after lunch we must come back to buy you those heels I promised."

"More importantly, I want to see the Duomo and Ghiberti's doors on the baptistery and the Uffizzi."

"But of course, Jo."

Lunch was superb. The Renaissance period monastery had been

transformed into the most quaintly elegant of hotels. The black tie and stiff white-shirted wait staff exuded the confidence garnered from catering to scores of satisfied diners. The thing that most struck me, that almost seemed to seep from the mellow, golden stone walls, was a sense of pervasive serenity, as though all of those decades of prayers and meditations had left an indelible aura of peace and tranquility. Afterwards we sat sipping espresso on the terrace and looking through the lacy screen of tender new almond blossoms to the roofs of Florence divided by the silver ribbon of the Arno river, all lying in a luminous mist far below.

By the time the taxi had us back in Florence and at the doors of the Uffizi, It was four o'clock in the afternoon and I knew the treasures of Florence were in for a cursory inspection. No nuns, no Sistine Chapel, but elbows out and moving we made a similar charge through the crowded rooms of the museum. Botticelli's 'La Primavera,' Uccello's 'Battle of San Romano' and a dazzling array of tightly packed jewels of art lovingly acquired by the Medici family and cherished and supplemented through the years filled the ancient walls.

"It would take years...maybe a lifetime of quiet contemplation to absorb all of this and to do it honor," I remarked wistfully.

"You're right but I think we'd better wait for another time to give it that much attention." I could tell by the tone of his voice that the crowds were annoying him. He hated to be caught in any kind of crowd but most especially one of tourists. I think his aristocratic French pride bristled at the enforced familiarity of the swarming masses and he could not bear that he might be thought one of them. He would have been happy strolling with 'Il Magnifico,' Lorenzo de Medici, along the upper corridor of the Uffizi that had allowed him to move from office to palace without mingling with the people in the street.

"Now the heels, darling." He breathed an audible sigh of relief, as we broke free into the relative emptiness of the piazza.

Fearful that he would forget the things I wanted to see, I implored, "Could we go by the 'Gates of Paradise' on the way. I want to see them so much."

He seemed not to have heard me as he sat off at a brisk pace towing me flapping from his elbow. After blocks of shops that we breezed into and out of before the revolving doors could stop turning, after miles of hard streets and tired feet confined to too high heels, after nights of little sleep and three days with no rest, after a day which had been dedicated to Florence and I still had not seen the most significant monuments, I finally reached my threshold of frustration.

"Darling, what's wrong?" Maurice turned back to where I had stopped, tears trickling from my eyes.

"I'm so tired. Could we please see the 'Gates of Paradise' and then go?"

'But of course, Jo. I told you I would take you wherever you want. But let's go in here first. This is Beltrami's and they have fabulous shoes. Once you sit for a moment and rest you'll feel better. On the way to the car, we'll go by the Duomo for you." He took my elbow and led me gently but firmly into the shop as I surreptitiously blotted my eyes and dabbed at my nose. I sat docilely while he perused the shoes, making his selections. I knew I had to provide only the feet and of course the legs if they would hold me up for the trying on ritual. They did and Maurice happily made his choice. The shoes were beautiful and ultra-stylish, also wonderfully made and expensive. His taste was impeccable and he was obviously thrilled with his selection.

"You have nice legs. You should never wear anything but heels."

"Right now I'm not sure my feet agree with you. Both soles feel like two big blisters."

"Are you sure you feel like walking to the Duomo?"

"I certainly do. Even if you have to carry me." He laughed as he guided me back onto the hard stone street.

"Slowly, please." I begged, as I gingerly trudged my way to that long awaited destination. Through sheer determination I managed to at last find myself standing at the legendary baptistery doors, annoyed to find they had been marred by plywood inserted where sections had been removed for restoration.

"Wouldn't you just know it? I'm surprised they didn't pick the whole thing up and replace it with a cardboard replica." Since then, they have indeed removed the original doors to a museum and a bronze replica stands in their place.

Maurice wryly agreed. "Wait over there for me and I'll bring the car. Here, let me carry those shoes for you." He paused a moment to study me. "Are you sure you were able to get to bed right away last night? You seem to be terribly tired."

"I'm just exhausted. It would be great if you would bring the car for me." I had not intentions of telling him about last night's escapades.

He settled me into a chair at a sidewalk cafe, ordered an espresso to revive me and then went for the car. I sat sipping the rich, fortifying coffee and searching the passing throngs for a glimpse of Jaynie, Crystal and Bill. Despite my constant searching that afternoon, I had spotted only two members of our group but never them.

On the drive back to Rome, I sensed a growing tension in Maurice and knew intuitively that Margot was going to be a topic of discussion before we reached those pined crowned hills, despite his early remark that she was a thing of the past. Abruptly he began, "I've decided I must confront this Tony guy. I know who he is. I know where she is and I'm going to New York."

"How do you know all of this?"

"Never mind how. I have ways of finding out."

"But why would you want to see him? She chose him; it was her choice and also her right to make that choice."

"No! Not when she told me she would be back in two weeks and we were to be married. Not when she took my diamond earrings, my wedding present to her. How can you say she has the right to be with him when we had that understanding between us?"

"It was wrong of her to take your gift if she knew she would not return. But Maurice, you cannot force her to love you. You cannot demand love. Love doesn't go by rights to the one who deserves it, you know."

"I could cheerfully kill him. She should have to hurt, suffer for the pain she has caused me. I tell you, she has killed my soul. You can't know the pain I feel, my sense of betrayal."

"No, perhaps not." I agreed. "But, I do know that you feel that way. I also know it would help nothing to harm either him or her. All it would do is hurt innocent people who love them and those of us who love you too." The battle raged over the same scarred and rutted ground we had covered before but I knew I must find the words to dissuade him from his determined course of revenge.

"She doesn't deserve your loyalty, darling. She is a demon, a thing of evil. I know her and I tell you she is truly possessed." He sighed and took my hand.

"Maurice, she's not a demon. I love her and I love you. I think perhaps the two of you were never meant for one another. You are too different."

"Of course you're right. Perhaps, I was meant to be with you. We have far more in common, and more importantly; I'm at peace when I'm with you. That is so important, Jo." But even while he said it, I knew the rage was just barely suppressed.

Dinner was low key that evening and we didn't tarry. It had been a long day for us both and I wasted no time crawling into my bed where I slept like the dead. The next day he took me to Ostia Antica and then to Tivoli to see the Villa d'Este's famous thousand fountains and then to Hadrian's Villa. I posed for him in both places and he later sent me the slides. The day was peaceful between us and the dinner a bit sad, as it was our last together until the coming summer. I left for Sorrento the next morning while I knew Maurice still slept. I was weary, Bill elated, as we rode south seated side by side.

Chapter 9

Ed called just as I was settling into bed following the long flight home. "Welcome home. Did you have a good trip to Italy and Greece?"

"Very, but it was so exhausting. I can't seem to sleep well when I'm jet lagged." I chuckled to myself at the understatements. We talked a few more minutes about what he had done while I was away.

"I won't keep you then. See you Tuesday night around six. I'll call when I get to my hotel."

"That would be great. I look forward to seeing you again. Goodnight."

"Goodnight to you, too. And I hope you'll sleep now you're back to your own bed."

If he could have seen my smile, he wouldn't have had to guess at how elated I was at the prospect of seeing him again. By Tuesday I was giddy with anticipation. I tried on at least a dozen dresses and not one was perfect enough. I did and then redid my hair until it was a wonder it didn't fall out. Suddenly my nails looked all wrong. By the time the phone rang at 6:30, I was a nervous wreck from all of the what ifs: what if he wasn't coming, what if the plane had crashed, what if he fell for the stewardess and asked her out instead.

"Hello!" I was nearly panting from my dash to grab the phone.

"Hi." I prayed he couldn't tell how nervous I was. "I just got to the hotel. Would you be able to meet me in the lobby at 7:00? I have dinner reservations at the Angus Barn for 7:15. Does that suit you?"

The Barn was the best steakhouse in the area and was known by businessmen from all over the country, so I was not surprised when he knew of it. When he saw me walking up to the hotel, he came out, a huge smile lighting his face. Wordlessly he took my hand and led me to his car. I smiled back and found myself caressing his profile with my eyes as he maneuvered through the heavy traffic on the street in front of the hotel.

Catching my rapt gaze from the corner of his eye, he teased, "What are you doing? I'm beginning to wonder if I've grown a sudden wart on the end of my nose."

I laughed a bit nervously and blushed at having been caught. "I was just drawing your profile in my mind."

"That's right, you're an artist. Tell me, what other weird things do artists do?"

"Since it's me doing them, I don't think they're weird." We laughed together. I wanted to tell him that I ached with the wanting of him. I wanted to tell him just how perfect he was to me. I wanted to tell him how long I had waited to feel such passion and joy at being with a man. I wanted to tell him, but I didn't.

We walked into the restaurant still holding hands. The Barn was an institution in Raleigh and had earned considerable acclaim for its quality. It was a great place to take a date for a special evening, a bit rustic but with a sophisticated edge, upscale without being stuffy. Our waitress, Delores Aikens, knew me. I had taught her son Brian, a marijuana addict and petty criminal who had brains, talent and a sweetness about him, all wasted by the drugs. Ed smiled indulgently as we chatted. She remarked how much her son had liked and respected me as a teacher. Then she looked from Ed to me and grinned.

"You two make an absolutely beautiful couple. Just perfect!"

"I think so too. This is our twentieth anniversary celebration and I tell you, this woman is as gorgeous now as the day I met her."

"What a nice thing to say. I'll give you time to look over your menus and I'll be back in a moment with your wine."

"Ed...the twentieth? Really now," I teased.

"It is about twenty days, you know." He grinned, pleased with himself.

The evening was light, fun and warm and the food and wine delicious. I felt like a cat basking before a fire. I wanted to stretch, to purr, to rub against this man who smiled into my eyes, who made me feel so special and beautiful, who kindled such ardor within me.

"I hope you like my choice of restaurants. It's one of the few that I know here. You'll have to choose next time."

"How about room service?" Would he think me forward and be turned off. I waited with bated breath, furious with myself for saying it and anxious at how he would receive it. It was not at all typical of me to be so forward and I felt my heart pounding at my temerity.

Slowly a grin began in his eyes, crinkling them at the corners as it spread across his face lighting it with joy. "We could always order dessert. Let's go."

"I always did have a sweet-tooth." We grinned like two kids who have just been given a cake-icing bowl for licking.

In his room we turned into each other's arms and slowly as if to soft music only we could hear, undressed one another, caressing with hands that flowed as softly as delicate silk gossamer, eyes locked to eyes.

He swept me into his arms and carried me to the bed where he gently lowered me to the pillows. "I want you so much. I not only think you're beautiful, but you're also sweet, warm, fun and wonderful. I have never wanted anyone the way I want you right now."

Words faded into the nightglow of the room and we communicated in that age-old language, with our kisses, with the warmth of thirsty body pressed to body and with the glow of joy in our eyes. With a frenzy of longing, I struggled to get him to take me, to plunge deep into that lonely depth that craved his filling. Slowly it dawned on me that he had a problem. He wanted me with a savage intensity, but his body was failing to sustain his desire.

"I want you too much." There was a world of agony and embarrassment in his voice.

"Don't try so hard. It's still early and we have lots of time."

"I know." He kissed me with smoldering passion on mouth, shoulders, and taunt breasts, lifting me to a burning peak of desire. Gently he spread my legs and lowered his weight onto me. As I gasp, he took me and I closed around him, stroking him, moving against him and pulling him deeper into me. Exploding with wild delight, I came and we laughed joyfully together. Caressing me he pulled away, smiling into my eyes and teasing the corners of my mouth and lids with light feathered kisses. "We'll rest a minute and then I'm coming back for more."

I knew that he had not climaxed and had softened even before I came. He tried again three more times that night and each time was like the first. I was worried that he had not liked me after all or that I was doing something wrong. As I dressed to leave, he pulled me to him kissing me tenderly and lovingly...and with sadness. "Will you see me next week?"

"Of course, I will. I would love to. Do you have 'business' here again?" I wanted to sound pert to bring the lightness back to the evening.

"Yes, unfinished business." He smiled ruefully and I knew it was all right.

Five days later he was back. We had talked at least once a day since he left. On Saturday night he called to tell me he had special reservations for dinner, however no matter my entreaties he refused to satisfy my curiosity as to the restaurant he had chosen. When Sunday arrived, he rented a car at the airport and called for directions to my house. I waited eagerly for him to make the thirty-minute drive to my house. I heard his car door close and had my hand on the doorknob when he rang the bell.

Saying nothing, he pulled me tightly forward and kissed me slowly and lingeringly. "I've missed you."

"And I you." Oh, so very much, I added to myself.

"Let's go."

"Okay. Can you tell me where now?"

"Nope. It's a surprise."

As we walked into his hotel room, I realized I had selected the restaurant after all: room service.

"This is the restaurant you chose last time, remember?"

"Absolutely."

He had arranged a beautiful dinner of champagne, filet mignon, salad, twice baked potato, cheesecake for dessert and a bouquet of fresh flowers on the table. We ate slowly, my feet pressed between his at the small table. Lifting his flute, he leaned forward. "I want to make a toast."

I lifted my glass to his. "Please do."

"To the woman I have dreamed of and finally met. To being together tonight and many more to come."

"I'll gladly drink to that."

Taking my glass from me, he pulled me into his lap where we kissed lightly and tenderly. Slowly our passion deepened but I could feel him holding back. I sensed that he was fearful of failure once again. Teasing him with my lips, caressing his face and hair, I lightly licked his lips with my tongue. His hand moved from my waist to cup my breast. Lazily he stroked my nipple as his eyes held mine. Releasing my breasts from the dress I wore, he unhooked my bra and lifted throbbing nipples into his mouth.

"You're so beautiful." He mumbled through lips thickened with passion.

Again he carried me to the bed where he gently undressed me. I watched as he removed his own clothes, never taking his eyes from mine. He was a handsome man, slim but well built. His chest was deep with soft fur in which I came to love to bury my face. When he lowered himself next to me to caress my heated flesh, I reached for his manhood and felt it hard and hot in my grasp as I stroked him to greater arousal. Then he was inside me, moving slowly as he pushed deeper, filling me with his desire. And this time it was right. Together we climbed the heights of wild ecstasy and together we reached that ultimate goal.

"God, you're fabulous."

"So are you, Ed." And I meant it.

Twice more that night we made love. Our passion seemed insatiable and we left still hungry for one another's embrace. As we walked to his car, he pulled me to him and we move arm in arm looking more at one another than where we were going.

"You don't know what you have done for me and how very much you mean to me."

"How do you mean?"

"I'll tell you sometime."   He sounded embarrassed and I suspected he would never explain, and he never did. I couldn't help but wonder if he were perhaps thinking of his previous failure with me and I surmised it had been a continuing problem with him. He had seemed too desperate and somehow resigned that first night for it to have been a unique thing. The next day a dozen red roses arrived at my door with a card attached saying simply: "Thank you...Ed"

He called that day to ask if he could see me again.

"You know the answer to that...when and where?"

"I can't get back for a couple of weeks but I'm working on something. I'll let you know as soon as I can put something together."

He called me every day between then and his return. Again we made love and again he had problems even though he eventually was successful. We would make love as he furiously, almost frantically moved within me. He would tire and hold me until he rested and could enter me again. He was so warm and loving, so romantic and tender that I came repeatedly, feeling guilty that it was not so easy for him. It became a pattern for us but he seemed not to mind and to want me ever more passionately. And for me, even though I was left sore and a little unsure, I ached to protect him from that special hurt, to reassure him how very much I needed, wanted, and cared for him. Indeed in some way it made my feelings for him even more tender. Soon we were in love. We both knew it, could feel it, but we were reluctant to put it into words, perhaps thinking the magic would go, snatched away by gods jealous of that happiness that was too great for mere mortals to know.

As summer inexorably neared, I became more and more agitated, knowing that I had committed to spending the summer in France with Maurice. I feared the loss of my new and precious love. How could I tell this man of fragile manhood that I would be with another man for two months? Would he or anyone believe me if I said that Maurice and I had a platonic relationship? My commonsense suggested otherwise. I wanted very much to see Maurice and to recapture those magic moments we had shared, moments that were as precious to me in their own way, as those I shared with Ed. Yet, I could not bear the thought of risking my new relationship. I knew also that not to go could well destroy the one that I had developed with Maurice. Until I knew where the relationship with Ed was going, I was unwilling to risk the one I had committed to long before meeting him. Maurice called frequently and our plans for the summer were made. He sent tickets for Beth and me well in advance of departure this time, and even better we were to meet him in Paris for two weeks there first. I wanted the summer in Europe very much and Beth seemed to be much more receptive to this trip than the one previous. But each time I saw Ed, I hesitated to tell him of my plans. And then it was almost time to leave and I had no choice. He had not been able to get back to Raleigh for a couple of weeks and I knew with departure eminent I could delay no longer.

"Where are you going to be? Give me your hotel numbers and I'll call you. Will you be gone all summer?" He didn't come out and say it, but I could tell he didn't like it and was suspicious. I tried to reassure him, gave him the name of the hotel in Paris, actually the Grand Trianon Hotel in Versailles, and promised to write him often and to tell him of my other hotels. What I would do when I stayed at Maurice's apartment in Marseille, I didn't know.

I called Margot before leaving to touch base with her. She was progressively more preoccupied with Tony and less often calling than had been her previous wont. I could tell that although she loved him, there were areas of real concern. Whereas his older daughter had previously promoted the match, with her mother dead and the mourning period nearly over, she knew it was more than a brief fling. Now she seemed to be increasingly antagonistic and jealous of Margot. Since Andrea was the favorite of his two daughters, that made it difficult for him as well. I knew Margot was unhappy that she had not been able to gain the acceptance she wanted from Andrea.

"Hi, Babe! I just wanted to give you a call before I leave to go to Europe. Are you doing okay?"

"Great except for some shit to deal with from the daughter department, but other than that no problem. I was going to call you, too. Tony has arranged for us to be married in New York, maybe early next fall. We aren't having any big deal, just a quiet wedding in the priest's study. I guess my patience has finally paid off." She laughed lightly but I also heard her sigh.

"Oh Margot, I am so happy for you. I do so hope that you'll have a wonderful life together. Have you decided where you will live, New York I guess?"

"No. We're going to live in his family home in Boston for a while. I'm definitely not thrilled about that since it's practically a shrine to his dead wife. But what can I do, except wait for him to get around to buying something of our own. We're keeping the apartment at the Waldorf Towers so I intend to spend most of my time there. I cannot deal with having to sleep in the maid's quarters to keep from contaminating their bedroom with my presence. For God's sake, her clothes and stuff are still in the master bedroom right down to the stub of her last cigarette in the ashtray."

"Boy, that sounds grim to me. I don't think this is going to be easy for you. Surely there will be times when you have to be in the home. What about the younger daughter, Nina? Is she okay with the upcoming marriage?"

"Oh, she's terrific. We get along fine and the household staff like me. It's only Andrea that's driving me nuts. I am beginning to think she has an unhealthy obsession for her father. An Electra Complex, I think they call it."

"Is Tony aware of how you feel?"

"Well, he knows that things are rocky between Andrea and me because he hears the snippy things she says. I get ticked off with him because he does nothing to defend me or to get her to back off." I could feel her shrug on the other end of the line. She pause and them made a small bitter laugh, "And that's not the only problem. Let's change the subject. When are you leaving?"

Something sounded terribly wrong with her and the situation she was in but respecting her privacy, I obliging changed the subject despite my deep reservations. "We leave the day after tomorrow. I'm trying to get bills paid in advance and the last minute packing done. I had to make a list as I thought of things and now I'm checking them off. Two months is a long time to be away and plan for."

"Well, be safe and have a good time. Is Beth there? I'd like to talk to her too before you leave."

"Sure, I'll put her on. Take care of yourself and I'll call you when we get back. I love you." I sensed there was something more that she wanted to tell me but could not bring herself to say it.

"I Love you, too, Kitty Puss." Margot often used her own nicknames for people, sometimes sentimentally sweet and at others pejorative, but done in such a loving way that you knew it wasn't meant as an insult.

I gave the phone to Beth and continued with my packing, wondering as I did so how Margot was going to cope. With the note of distraction and lack of enthusiasm in our conversation, I could only hope that she would be able to win Andrea over. As the baby of the family, we had always catered to her and made much of her. For Katerina and me, she had been our real live doll given by our parents as a special toy for us to play with and pamper. My parents were smitten with her as a baby, melted by her big blue eyes and sunny disposition. She was a beautiful baby, a pretty child, a lovely teenager and now a stunningly beautiful woman of warmth, and an exuberance and joy that were magnetic. Her friends ran the gamut from the poorest and least educated to some of the richest and most famous in the world, and they all liked her and sought her company. She so hated it when the people around her did not love her and enjoy being with her. I knew Andrea's animosity was going to rankle her far more than it would most people.

Margot called me a couple of hours before our taxi arrived to take us to the airport. Her voice was shaky and from the nasal tone, I could tell she had been crying. I asked, "Are you all right, baby?"

At that, the sobs began. I listened, making soothing noises until she could talk enough to tell me the problem. "Oh Jo, I'm four months pregnant and I want this baby so much but Tony is making me get an abortion. He says he'll get me a puppy and after we are married we can get pregnant again. I don't want a puppy, I want my baby." She moaned in agony. "What am I going to do? He says it's all off unless I do as he says. I don't want to lose him and I don't want to give up my baby."

"Honey, have the baby. I'll raise him for you until you can claim him as your own. Don't do this if it is hurting you so much. You know I will help you through this any way I can. If he loves you enough, maybe he won't go through with the threat."

"Oh yes, he will. He's made that very clear. I think he feels it will hurt his political ambitions."

"Screw his ambitions! What about you and what you need and want? Besides, you're engaged and planning to marry. Just move up the wedding and keep the baby."

"The timing doesn't suit him. He wants to wait longer so it doesn't look like we were having an affair and married soon after his wife died."

"Don't act rashly, Margot. Think about it. Think about it hard and try to work something out with him. Please. Tell him I can keep the baby for you until later if that will help. You can always say it was mine and you are adopting it."

"I don't know..." stifling another sob she continued. "Call me from Paris please. I need someone to talk to and I can't tell mama and daddy."

"Tell Kat. She will understand and help you."

"Okay. But still call."

"I will, I promise. Please, please take good care of you. I love you." We hung up with my heart nearly as heavy as hers.

The packing was finished; all arrangements made, my parents called, and the taxi had arrived. Fortunately the trip to Paris was uneventful and we arrived to find Maurice waiting for us at gate with a beam on his face bright enough to light the entire terminal.

"Jo! Beth! Oh, how much I have wanted this moment: to see you two again and to have another summer with you. We'll get this luggage into my new car and then I'll take you to the hotel in Versailles. It is a wonderful hotel in the grand tradition and backs up to the gardens of the Palace. In fact the dining room there is where they signed the Treaty of Versailles ending the First World War. After we check in, I thought we would have lunch in the village and explore a bit of the area and tomorrow, when you are not so tired, we'll do the tour of the Palace and its grounds."

Beth and I settled into our room overlooking the gardens and unpacked, showered and were ready for lunch when Maurice called. Meeting him in the lobby, we walked together in the cool dappled light cast by the arching trees that lined the road leading into the village. Lunch was in a little cafe where I fell in love with their Frissee au Lardon salad...frissee lettuce topped with crisply sautéed pancetta. Maurice told me that it is typically served *au cheval* or with a raw egg cracked on top. Detesting even cooked eggs, I knew that was one version I would not be tempted to try. Beth happily cut into the chopped entrecote...the closest thing to hamburger she could find...with fries, while Maurice plied her with questions about her school year. While we ate, I studied him. He seemed even more tired and drawn than when I had seen him in the spring and his color beneath the perpetual tan did not seem as robust. I became even more convince that it was not just tiredness but some underlying health problem that was contributing to his apparent decline.

Turning to me, he took my hand. "Jo, I have some wonderful things planned for the summer. First of all, we will be here for two weeks so I will have time to show you some of the things that I love in Paris. Then we are going to a wedding in the Loire of the daughter of friends of mine. They have a chateau there and a townhouse in Orleans where I thought we would stop so you could meet them before the wedding. You two girls will need to go shopping while we are in Paris and buy something wonderful to wear for the wedding. After that, we will go to Marseilles for two weeks and you will be again at the Concorde Palm Beach, as I have not had time to move Maman's things to make room for you. I have already taken Maman to Chamonix, so you may not see her this trip. We'll see if there's time. From Marseilles we will drive to Buchloe in Germany to the Alpina factory. I want to have my new BMW reconfigured to racing standards so they will retool the engine and install special brakes to accommodate the increased speed potential. I think you will enjoy the drive through the Alps, as there are some wonderful places to visit on the way. I thought we might come back through Monte Carlo since I know how much my girls love it. Then we'll return to Marseilles for the balance of the summer but it will not be as much time as we spent there last year as I have arranged my schedule so I can be away and spend more time with you. I have missed you two unbearably. I don't want to spend a moment of this time we have away from you unless I cannot avoid it. Since you will be flying back from Paris, I return with you and see you off from here that way we lose none of our time together."

"My word, Maurice! You have really been busy organizing all of this. It sounds terrific and I can tell from Beth's smile that she likes the itinerary too. Right, baby?"

"Yes! I really want to go back to Monte Carlo and stay at the Hotel de Paris again."

"That you shall, Kiki!" Maurice laughed indulgently and gently squeezed her hand. "What do you say, shall we take a walk around the village and look at some of the little boutiques? I think it's time for me to buy you a surprise!"

He found her a beautiful stuffed dog that she promptly placed on her pillow when we returned to our room following the leisurely amble about the village of Versailles. I had hoped to have a message that Ed had called waiting for me at the desk, but inquired to no avail. After an early dinner in the hotel, I called Margot and listened with a sinking heart as she told me that she had gone ahead with the abortion and was now mother to a Yorkie. She seemed totally obsessed by the dog, almost as though it were the baby she had lost. Despite my sadness and worry for her, I went to bed that night, anticipating a wonderful summer but wondering if Ed would be waiting when I returned. The die having been cast, I could only hope that he would and I would try not to spoil the summer ahead by worrying about it.

The next day, following a leisurely room service breakfast, we spent touring the palace and gardens of Versailles. Knowing it only through slides and art history books, I was eager for a firsthand introduction. We entered the Palace through the imposing gilded gates of the main entry leading into a vast courtyard. In the time of the Sun King, Louis XIV, thousands of people lived there: gardeners, stable hands, household servants, army officers and staff and the royal retinue composed of the noble families of France. During construction and renovations, of which there were many, often as many as 35,000 workers were on the grounds. In the famous Hall of Mirrors, just one of the many square mirrors, that filled the arched spans on the wall opposite corresponding arched windows, was reputed to have cost as much as the annual income of a family of four. This fabulously extravagant palace would set the standard for decades of palaces throughout Europe and particularly those of Mad King Lugwig in Bavaria. We walked through fantastically ornate and beautiful rooms, many furnished with exquisite draperies, paintings, and other elegant accoutrements.

It was a shocking contrast to walk from the elaborately embellished palace through the gardens to the Petit Hammeau with its thatched cottage and simple pastoral buildings. It was designed to be a rustic escape for Marie Antoinette when she tired of the exaggerated elegance of court life and wished to play as a simple peasant, although one dressed in silks and jewels. We visited the smaller palace buildings Petit Trianon and the Grand Trianon, the conservatory which could supply as many as 2,000,000 potted plants capable of changing the gardens to renewed glory with each of the seasons, the parterre, the fountains requiring a million gallons of water a day and which could jet as high as 75 feet without the aid of electricity, and the artificial lakes that stretched into the distance like a grand canal provided an entrancing view from the rear of the palace. It was overwhelmingly beautiful in its Baroque grandeur and Beth and I loved it. Maurice, exuding pride in his heritage, happily educated us on all that we were seeing. I could gladly have spent days there, wandering about and appreciating the many wonders.

After a day touring through and about the Palace, we were all tired and ready for an early evening following dinner in the hotel dining room. Again I asked at the desk if there had been any messages for me and again was disappointed to learn there were none. I resigned myself to having been forgotten by Ed or written off by him due to his dislike of my long absence. Feeling abandoned by Ed and overwhelmingly sad for Margot, I did cry a few tears in the still darkness of that night while Beth slept beside me in peaceful oblivion to my pain. The busy pace of the summer would allow few moments for grieving and I was glad. I would learn later that Ed had called the hotel repeatedly only to be told that I was not registered there. Maurice had registered us under his name and although they had taken Beth's and my passports for registry at check-in, supposedly they had not associated our names with our room. Or had Maurice blocked my calls? I sent postcards to Ed at least once a week all that summer, mailing them to his office as he had told me he would be traveling out of town much of the time that I was away.

The next morning at the crack of noon, Maurice's idea of an early start, we left to spend the day in Paris. Following lunch at the Intercontinental, Beth and I were on our own to explore and shop while Maurice conducted business and consulted with a photographer about the book of photographs he wanted to publish. We headed to the Palais de Justice for a much anticipated visit to the small chapel of St. Chapelle, where I stood in thrall of the magnificent stained glass windows sparkling like vast walls of twinkling jewels. I explained to Beth that of all the Gothic buildings, this one had the greatest ratio of windows to wall of any of them. The arched windows were separated by thin springing arches that supported the soaring ceiling of the upper level, whereas the much shorter and more intimate lower level was saturated by red, blue and gold paint on walls and ceiling, giving the impression of standing inside a colorful royal playhouse. This strangely devised and magnificent little building came into being to house relics brought from the holy lands by Louis IX following the ill-advised sixth crusade.

From there we ambled along the quay pausing to watch passing house barges and tourists gaily waving from the decks of the Bateaux Mouches. We passed the Orangerie and on impulse turned back to visit the misty beauty of Monet's water lily series. Although Beth liked the things we were seeing, I suspected she was nearing the day's limit for cultural saturation.

"Okay, Baby. What would you like to do now?"

"Let's go shopping and then we can have a coke while we wait for Maurice."

"That's a deal. I wonder if we could fine a pretty toy store or maybe a children's shop that has cute clothes. You could use another shorts outfit I think. Which would you prefer?"

"Great, let's do the clothing store." She bounced off ahead of me leaving me two-stepping to catch up. We found her a bright red, yellow and turquoise plaid shirt with matching yellow shorts and she was thrilled at the purchase.

At that point, it was after 5 and I was beginning to tire and I knew that she was too, so it seemed time for her coke. We were to meet him in the bar of the Hotel Crillon at 5:30, which suited me fine as it gave me time for a quick glass of wine. We were sitting there at 7 still waiting and the wine was doing little to dispel my fatigue and impatience. Even the obnoxious chatter of two English ladies trying to out-snob one another by dropping the names of aristocrats with whom they claimed familiarity, did little to distract us from the tedium. Finally he arrived two hours late to find us both a little less than warm in our reception.

"Darlings, I am so sorry. I was involved in a lengthy discussion with a photographer friend of mine and did not realize how late it had become. Please forgive me."

"It's okay. We're just getting a bit tired and hungry, so we feel a little impatient to leave."

"Of course. We'll just dash around the corner to Fleurette. It's not fancy, but nice enough, and the food is pretty good and then we'll go back to the hotel. I have to return tomorrow for another meeting so perhaps it will be a good time for you to shop for the things you will need for the wedding at the Chateau. Outfits for both of you, *d'accord*?"

"*D'accord.*" Okay, I responded. I knew we needed something more suitable than anything in our suitcases as we had not anticipated any formal functions when we packed for the trip. Besides it would be fun to really explore the designer boutiques with the possibility of doing something besides window-shopping. The next afternoon, found us eagerly perusing the wares in some of Paris's best shops. We found a beautiful blue and white dress for Beth at the Christian Dior shop for children and a matching hat. Asking them to reserve them for us, as Maurice would return with us later to pay, we then shopped for her pair of shoes. She insisted that we make it heels for this her first major party with adults. The two inch ones we found were perfect, although I did tease her about getting training wheels so she wouldn't fall off them. Unfortunately she would wear them only twice as she decided they were too uncomfortable. When we returned home they ended up being a present to Jaynie for whom they were a perfect fit.

At Fragonard I found an elegant royal blue dress of their own design styled with a diagonal peplum trimmed in black. It fitted beautifully and enhanced my figure, making me look slim and curvy at the same time. Maurice took one look at me in the dress and smiled. When the sales lady, knowing a sure sale when she saw it, remarked "Trés Mignon!" (very pretty), I knew it was mine. I still have that dress and still love it despite the fact it is over thirty years old and fits much more snuggly now.

The most special evening of our time there was the dinner at the Pres Catalan Restaurant in the Bois de Boulogne Park. Gourmet gained new meaning for me that night with a wonderful pâté de foie gras chaud, followed by sole Meunier and a perfect bottle of Condrieu Viognier wine. We could hear a wedding party underway in the private dining area, and when they started shooting off fireworks in sync with the finish of our meal, it was the absolute icing on the cake. After the last sparkles of dying light dripped from the sky, we drove into the shopping area around the Faubourg du St. Honore where we parked to window-shop the spectacularly staged displays. Maurice was fascinated by the artistry of them and loved to take snapshots of those he found especially well done. On the sidewalk by the Hermes store, an old and shabbily dressed man was peering into the window at the array of fashionable and expensive goods. There was a poignancy about his face and posture that moved Maurice to reach into his pocket withdrawing a handful of bills that I knew was hundreds of francs and press them into the old man's hands. He looked up with an utterly dazed expression on his face that slowly turned into a smile that spread from his mouth to his eyes. "Merci, Monsieur, merci!" Maurice smiled happily and ushered his girls back to the car.

His spontaneous generosity was always amazing, but sometimes I knew he was being gulled. Once while stopped at a traffic light by the Madeleine church we were approached by a young woman who explained that her purse had been stolen and would Maurice please give her twenty francs so she could take the train home. He handed her fifty. I watched in the side view mirror as she made her way to the car behind us to repeat the performance. Being young and pretty obviously did nothing to hurt the routine. I suspected that by the time she made it home to her little village in Normandy, it would be driving her own new car and not riding in a train.

One evening we took the Bateau Mouche or "fly boat" for the night tour of the Seine. It gave an entirely different perspective of Paris to see the monuments and quays glowing in the boat's spotlights as they slipped past in the balmy night air. The next day Maurice took us to the suburbs of Paris to visit a friend, a duke, whose large rambling home was surrounded by an expansive and lush garden planted in the English manner. I knew the title was impressive to him by the tone in his voice when he introduced the elderly man. Maurice also took time to go with us to visit the Louvre, Notre Dame, the Jardin des Plantes, the Eiffel Tower, the Pompidou Center, Les Invalides and other sites that he loved. A couple of times he took us to his favorite left- bank restaurants La Closerie de Lilas that he said Hemingway frequented and Le Dome, famous for its oysters. The two weeks in Paris went quickly and we were soon on the road.

In Orleans, hometown of Joan of Arc, we would meet Alexander de Muratel and his wife for a late lunch in a restaurant where the outdoor seating area was bisected by a pilgrimage path. Alex explained that it was forbidden to block the pilgrimage route that ran to the church of Notre-Dame-le-Grand in Poitiers and on to Santiago de Compostella in Spain, one of the three great pilgrimage destinations of the Middle Ages. Alex and his wife Yvette were very friendly and both spoke English well. They were obviously excited by their daughter's coming marriage and gave Maurice painstaking instructions on how to find their chateau in the country. Alex remarked that he was struggling with writing an English advertisement for his new perfume line and asked us to come back to their apartment where I rewrote the ad for him. Maurice explained later that Alex's family had munitions factories that were vital during the previous wars and also detergent and soap manufacturing facilities. The perfume industry was a new venture for Alex. He gave me bottles of his different perfumes as a way of thanking me. One of them I treasured. It was the perfect floral scent and I used it sparingly for years until it finally went bad. Even then I kept it sitting on my vanity tray for at least ten years more, unable to bring myself to throw out the bottle.

We spent the night in a small hotel near Chinon, the Chateau D'Anzay. Beth was charmed when we arrived at our room to find that our bath was in the turret of the castle.

"Mommy, I feel just like a princess. I'm going to sleep in a real castle."

"Just don't be a broken princess. Those stone stairs are little bit tricky where they are badly worn, so be sure to watch your step as we go up and down." I should have told her I felt a bit like a princess myself amid the beautiful antique furnishings.

The next day we visited the famous chateaux Azey de la Rideau, Chambord, Chennonceaux and the famous gardens of Villandry. We had time for a wonderful lunch at Le Cheval Blanc restaurant, a serendipitous find located on the road between Chambord and Chennonceaux. Lunch the next day was at Chateau Marçay, another chateau turned hotel, as we continued our tour of the various famous castles of the area.

We spent that night at a grand hotel in Tours, Hotel de l'Univers. It was a late arrival and we were tired, however the hotel restaurant was too good to miss. While we ate our dinner, Maurice arranged for our clothes to be pressed and neatly laid out for the wedding the next day.   We lingered at the table idly chatting and making the breadcrumb-flower petal ladies that Beth had discovered for herself the previous summer. She seemed much more tolerant of Maurice and happier on this trip. I suppose it did not seem quiet as foreign to her anymore and she was enjoying the excursion through the countryside to see the various chateaux.

We had a late brunch in our room the next morning, before carefully dressing ourselves and arranging our hair. Maurice met us downstairs in the lobby, looking resplendent in an impeccably tailored custom-made tuxedo. He looked the nicest that we had ever seen him and seemed genuinely excited and happy about the coming celebration. Beth and I modeled our outfits for him and the three of us took turns admiring one another before leaving to drive to the Mairie, or mayor's office, where the wedding party awaited the exodus of the bride and groom from the civil ceremony. From there we all caravanned to the church for the formal religious wedding. Maurice explained that the civil ceremony is a necessity in France to legitimize the marriage; the religious ceremony is the bigger symbolic event and the one where guests are invited. We spotted Bernard, Jackie and his wife whom we had met the previous summer, and some friends of Maurice's that we had met in Paris and walked over to stand with them in the church. The absence of pews was typical of the churches of the Romanesque period and although most have long since added them, this one had not.

Maurice craned his neck looking about the small church for faces he recognized. He spotted the Duke that we had visited in Paris and nodded in greeting. He pointed out three women who he said were hired celebrants. Beth and I found it a curiosity that the old custom of officially paid mourners for funerals and celebrants for weddings and christenings was still observed in that church. And I was happy to note that my French was enough improved that I could follow the wedding ceremony, but then it was mostly "oui."

From the church, we drove to Alex's country estate where the marriage would be celebrated with a formal dinner and dance followed by fireworks. We were given a quick tour of the twelfth century chateau before Alex disappeared to attend to other guests. I admired the beautifully preserved and tastefully modernized structure, the large swimming pool that sparkled in the late afternoon sun and the meticulously landscaped gardens that flowed down to a huge pink and white striped tent and parquet dance floor set up near the river.

Beth and I were thrilled to actually be attending such a party in such a magnificent location. As we made our way to our places, I noticed her mincing her steps as she practice the new art of walking in her heels. She was conscious and proud of her unaccustomed adult shod feet and the designer dress and hat. I was proud of not just how nice she looked but by the grace with which she met the new experiences and so many new people.

The dinner was a culinary delight consisting of an array of artistically arranged dishes accompanied by an unending river of perfectly chilled champagne. The heirloom linens, china and crystal, the profusion of flowers and the infusion of romantic music made for a heady evening without the champagne. With it, the crowd soon unlimbered to some serious partying. When Bernard threw a bit of bread that he had rolled into a pellet striking Maurice on the cheek, the battle was on. Beth joined in gleefully but I hung back not sure how to react to this informality at such an elaborate celebration. However no one else had any similar compunction, so I decided to pitch in with my own dough balls. One of the men that Maurice introduced me to in Paris interrupted my participation by asking me to dance.

On the dance floor, he pulled me close and we flowed to the rhythm of the music. When the song ended, he immediately led me into the next one.

"You look really lovely to night. I admire your body very much and would like to get to know you later in a much more private way. Is it possible for you to arrange to meet me somewhere." His English was obviously limited but he had learned enough to make a pitch.

I was shocked and totally unprepared for the solicitation, so much so that I tripped and he caught me, holding me closer and longer than was warranted. I caught his wife's eye on us, and thought 'uh-huh, she knows what he's up to.' Pulling back, I looked him in the eye and coolly thanked him for the compliment and invitation, *regretfully* informing him that I was of necessity declining the offer. I saw Maurice give us a speculative glance and begin making his way to us where he smoothly cut in. It was a relief to dance with him steadily for the remainder of the night, interrupted only by the dances that he coaxed Beth to try with him.

Chapter 10

We left the next morning to drive to Marseilles passing the town of Carcassone on the way. Although I wanted to stop and see the restored fortified medieval town, Maurice drove past barely slowing in his determination to reach home before nightfall. He seemed unusually quiet, however I didn't mind as it gave me time to relive with Beth the things that she had enjoyed so far. Normally Maurice would have interjected comments when she responded so positively, however none were forthcoming so we chatted happily on. I was relieved that so far she seemed to be suffering none of the angst of the previous summer and was excited by her first pair of heels, sleeping in a real castle and exploring countless others, the things we had done in Paris and most thrilling of all, the wedding of the previous evening. Eventually she tired and began to slumber and I retreated into a fantasy of drowsy daydreams. Moments like those of these first weeks of our summer are so rare in a life that so often is consumed by the humdrum world of daily existence. Only his wealth and our summer freedom allowed us entree into this whirlwind of exciting new experiences. What a long distance I had come from a rural childhood in eastern North Carolina, the progeny of generations of tobacco farmers who'd never been much more than a few hundred miles from home at best. What a long way I felt from the classroom that defined my diurnal parameters for ten long months each year. What a glorious escape into fantasies-made-real this summer gift was. I felt myself make a humming sigh of feline satisfaction, not realizing I had made a noise.

"Ah, Jo. I thought perhaps you were sleeping. It's only another hour or so and I confess, I'm getting tired and ready to be there." He chuckled, "I'm not accustomed to quite as much liquid celebration as that last night.

"I fear I haven't been such good company as my mind has been consumed by all of the things I must do in Marseilles to prepare to be gone for so long from my office. The next two weeks are going to be quite busy for me, so you and Beth must entertain yourselves during the day. I hope that you will not mind this sacrifice since it is a necessity for me. I would much rather spend my time having fun with the two of you than dealing with the frustrations of my business that seem to be increasingly problematic. I suppose some of the difficulties arise from my own lack of a real passion for it. *Alors,* without passion for what we do, we cannot do our best, can we? I should be working on my books, taking photographs and playing with my ladies. One day, I swear it, we shall. I want so much to be done with all of this, and just spend the rest of my days with the two of you. If I do not make it happen soon, Beth will be grown and gone before I can really know her."

I responded, "You know, for the first time this summer I get a glimpse of her growing from childhood into a young woman. She's just twelve yet she seems suspended between twelve and eternity, not a child and not an adult but a continuum of evolution into the person she will become. It makes me pleased to see that she is happier in this environment than she was last year. I think being here last year was a big transition for her and of course the instability and turmoil of my personal life last year had to affect her too. I feel guilty that I have not given her greater security in a family unity." I paused, looking out the window and continued. "...Guilty, but I don't know how to have done differently. I have been so stupid with my personal life. Sure, I'm smart in books, I suppose, but dumb in life."

"Don't be so hard on yourself. You married too young and unwisely, but then had you anything to compare to, to use for a marker? You married the second time from fear of the unknown future, one in which you didn't know whether or not you could manage alone. No, they were not smart choices but then, how many people really analyze such emotional choices with a clinical dispassion? I cannot any more than you. So I will not censure you for them. After all, I married and divorced twice: both Christian Dior models I married for their looks, not their empty heads."

I looked at him in surprise. Somehow, I had never really thought about him as married despite Margot telling me that he had been and he had never mentioned his marriages before. He saw me looking in amazement and shrugged, "They were both brief and miserable. They married for position and money and I married to have a beautiful woman tied to my name and my arm. Stupid, no? I never had a child of my own and now it is too late for me, so Kiki has become the child of my life. Now I'd rather make wiser choices and seize life's new directions. My biggest crime is that as a young man with so many paths to choose, I chose to be safe, to live the life that my father had created for me instead of taking the route that my heart dictated. I've paid the price for that ever since."

"Will you sell the business then and do something else?"

"If I can. But first I must organize it better and make it more profitable. The last few years have not been good ones and I find myself digging into my personal resources to keep things going. That cannot continue." He flexed his jaw saying this. I knew he was bitterly ruminating the past few years and its hurts, both professional and personal. Too, I could understand the difficulties for him in business. Not necessarily in terms of the daily logistics but in terms of his own unsuitability for commerce. He did not have the inherent qualities needed to deal with the minutia of commercial transactions, projected sales, marketing trends, etc. And when I considered how many times he had frantically sought his lost wallet...kept in a shoulder bag he carried and that I had seen him leave on top of the car, beside a cafe table, or in the floor of a shop, I could see he lacked the basic organization and focus it requires to be really successful in any commercial enterprise.

"No, Maurice, it doesn't make sense to continue a losing proposition. But I know it must be difficult when it has been in your family for so many years, however if your heart isn't in it and you hate it, how can you make it successful again? Also, without your own extensive plantations as your family had initially, I suspect you are more at the mercy of the marketplace. That has to add to the cost factor for each item you sell."

"You understand that well. It does indeed and of course that does exacerbate the problem. Nevertheless, I suspect I'm the biggest problem. I just do not control business, money, and staff the way my father did. It is just all so alien to me. You know I'm an artist. I'm not a business man."

"That's tough. I don't know the answers for you and of course you aren't asking. I just hope that somehow you will be able to resolve it all so you can be happier and spend your life doing something you *do* enjoy." I gave an ironic chuckle, "Despite hating the regimentation and bureaucracy, I do enjoy teaching. I enjoy the kids and the subject and that is the only thing that sustains me. If it were not for that, I could not endure it, much less get pleasure from it."

"Yes, of course that is the point. I must sell this business so I can begin to live my life while I still have it. I cannot bear to think that it will escape me before I can truly have the things in life that I most need."

He turned on the radio bringing the conversation to an end. The remainder of the trip was silent as he mulled the problem in his mind. I was content just to lose myself in the music and the beauty of the countryside as it slid past my window. We arrived at the Hotel Concorde in time for a late dinner. In the restaurant, the feature for the evening was turkey. Maurice was excited, as he loved the dish. When I spurned the featured entree, he looked at me in question.

"Maurice, if you only knew about *turkey*. My mother used to buy it because it wasn't expensive and you could get a lot of meals from it. We would have it roasted, then the next day would be cold cuts, then turkey sandwiches, then the day after turkey salad, then the next day or so it would be turkey hash, and then turkey soup. By the fourth day we kids were all so sick of turkey, that when mama put it on the table we would arrive with our hands tucked in our armpits, flapping our arms and gobbling like a turkey. She would be furious with us but that did nothing to impede the progressive consumption until nothing was left but the stale odor of turkey in the air. No thank you. I've had enough turkey."

He howled with laughter at my adamant refusal. Beth was too groggy to care what she ate, so after a quick meal we said goodnight to Maurice and went to our room. I was happy to collapse into the bed and really looked forward to a couple of weeks at leisure to relax by the pool or make excursions to Cassis in the VW Golfe that he had arranged for a second summer. As I drifted into sleep, I relished the anticipation of Jaynie's arrival in a couple of weeks to spend two or three days with us before we left to go to Germany for the conversion of his BMW into an Alpina.

The next morning, we both headed for the pool where the staff remembered us from the previous summer. The wind was blowing smartly, snapping the many national flags that surrounded the pool and making whitecaps in the azure expanse of sea. Although I thought I had the umbrella securely anchored, it suddenly took flight, the metal end nearly stabbing a nearby bather who glared at me. The attendant rushed over and helped me get it secured.

"Wow, Mom. I thought he was going to get killed." She gestured to the man who had subsided on his deck chair, too relaxed to stay upset for long.

"So did I, shish-ka-bobbed style, huh?"

Beth giggled and pulled me to the pool where we spent the morning playing with one another. It was a fun respite from the constant touring although that had been fun too. We returned to our room around noon to shower and dress as Maurice was joining us at 1:30 for lunch. At two he arrived and we joined him in the restaurant overlooking the hotel pool. The Loupe de Mer was one of my favorite fish and I was delighted to find it on the menu for the day. The crisp Hermitage wine Maurice ordered was the perfect accompaniment. He left at three and we returned to our room, Beth to nap and I to work on my Sunday New York Times crossword puzzle book, two hundred real brainteasers. My favorites were the clever ones by Eugene Maleska. When I became stuck on the puzzle, I switched to reading one of the novels I had tucked into my suitcase, knowing that getting away from it would allow me to return with a new perspective and solve it.

Jaynie came for three days at the end of that first week. On that Saturday, Maurice took us to a hotel on the beach in La Ciotat. He checked himself into a room on the second floor overlooking the pool to work on business. We went to the pool where we spent the afternoon playing in the pool with Beth. Maurice came down only once. A Speedo clad, handsome Frenchman had been eyeing me amorously for over an hour when he finally mustered the courage to come over and sit beside me on an adjacent deckchair. He had talked only a few minutes when Maurice suddenly appeared and made a beeline for me. He stayed there until the man was sufficiently discouraged and made his way to less obstacle-ridden conquests. Maurice then returned to his room, only to emerge several hours later to find three tired, irritable and sunburned ladies, all long past ready to leave.

I was sufficiently aggravated with him for keeping us stuck there for so long that I snapped at him, leading to our only real spat of the summer. We went to Chez Fon Fon for dinner, one of my favorites, as I loved their Bourride. I was over my snit and enjoying the meal, yet when I went to the ladies room Maurice remarked to Jaynie that he was annoyed with me. Naturally she told me the minute she could, thereby making me even more remote with him for the remainder of the evening. Back at the hotel, Jaynie and I had a good time telling stories and reminiscing about our spring trip to Italy. She was leaving the following day much to our sorrow as both Beth and I enjoyed her company. Being with her was often far easier for us than the daily fare of Maurice's intensity and quirks. We relaxed with her; with Maurice it was very difficult to relax, as he demanded response, constant mental presence and interaction.

I took her to the train station the next morning and we sadly waved her off to Paris, before returning to the hotel to begin packing. Maurice was to pick us up at 5 to begin our journey to Germany and the Alpina factory. He came up to our room promptly at five, which was enough to astonish me, however when he tossed a large paper bag completely filled with dollars on the bed, I was truly astounded.

"Good Lord, Maurice! What are you doing carrying so much money?"

"I have to pay the $21,000 conversion charge in cash at the Alpina plant and they want it in American dollars. I just came from the bank where I picked it up. I was afraid they would not be able to get me that much in time for us to leave today. Fortunately, it arrived to them around 3 o'clock so they called me to come. I stopped there and got the money and then ran home to pick up my bags." He paused and picked up the sack of money. "I need you to carry this. It is not allowed for French citizens to take so much money from the country. Can you hide it in something?"

I unzipped my luggage. "Some of it will fit into this fake hairspray can that I bought to travel with. It unscrews and the inside is hollow, but you can see it won't hold all of this. Hmm." Studying the contents, I then pulled out some panty hose packages. Some of the hundred dollar bills I neatly sandwiched inside the packages where they were concealed from casual inspection. Others, I stuffed in the side pocket inside my suitcase and the rest I rolled up in the paper bag and shoved in my handbag. "That does it. Unless the customs guys want to wear my panty hose or use my hairspray, this should do. Is it okay with you? Do you think it will be any problem with customs?"

"That should be fine, darling. Just remember to look very innocent and give them your best smile. Besides as an American, I doubt that they would bother to check you for currency, so we should be fine." He smiled and said, "I would be very pleased if you don't lose it."

"Unless you lose me and the luggage, you'll still have your money. I surely hope you don't have to make a choice between the money-stuffed luggage and me.   As badly as you want that conversion, I think I would lose." I grinned wryly at him.

He grinned back, "I suppose I will have to be careful with both you and my money, as Kiki would murder me if I lost you and I would murder myself if I lost the money."

Despite our precautions, I glanced at Maurice as we neared customs to find that he had broken into a cold sweat. I suggested he wipe his face and relax or they would think we were hauling dead bodies, a ton of drugs, or something equally awful. Fortunately by the time we reached the barrier, we looked innocent enough to warrant not even a second glance as they waved us through.

It was late when we arrived in Chamonix so it was not until the next day at lunch that we saw Marie. We spent a delightful lunch renewing our acquaintance.   She made much of Beth's gained maturity and growth since the previous summer and was regretful that Maurice had allowed only that small visit with her. I saw her glance at my left hand and knew she was hoping to see an engagement ring there. She tried to catch my eye but I studiously avoided it.   Maurice had also noticed her curiosity and seemed discomfited. Again we left her standing on the hotel steps, waving wistfully in our wake.

We arrived in Bern just before nightfall, had an early dinner and checked into a hotel. The following morning, Maurice delayed our journey north long enough to make a visit to the bear pits. They were not nearly as appealing to Beth and me as the architecture of the town. We were fascinated by the timbered facades, the painted decor of the walls, the totally 'Heidi' look of the place. From there we drove through Switzerland, across Lake Constance into Germany. We spent that night in Ottobeuren near the small hamlet of Buchloe where we would visit the Alpina factory.

We arrived at the factory around ten the next morning and were greeted by a charming employee who gave us a brief tour of the reception area and the wine cellar that has a family affiliation with Chianti. He asked if it would be possible to switch from French to

English, with which he was more comfortable. Beth and I happily nodded agreement. As he chatted with us and we responded, he became increasingly more animated and excited to be talking with us.

Finally he paused, and looking directly at Beth and me, commented, "I must commend you all; your English is exceptional. Even the child is fluent. This is most amazing. Did you study in France, England or America? I ask because your accent seems American and not the English."

I cut my eye at Maurice to find him nearly suffocating with laughter. "Thank you for the compliment but it's not so exceptional since my daughter and I are indeed American, not French. In fact, we should be complimenting you on your own English. Ours is merely the accident of birth."

His interest in us dwindled steadily with that clarification, so the two of us left Maurice to deal with the Alpina conversion logistics and walked into the surrounding countryside. It was only a small distance from the factory down a narrow country lane that we discovered a charming small chapel surrounded by wheat fields sprinkled with peregrinated blossoms of red poppy. The whitewashed building had a rounded apse opposite the entry door and split down the middle by an aisle, it was only three or so rows deep. It was just large enough for four chairs across, like a child's version of a playhouse church, and was obviously meant for the worship of only a small congregation. Since we couldn't decipher the German, I have never known if it was a small private chapel or a community church. We sat there quietly and absorbed the charm of the place before opting for some photos of the church and the surrounding field. An hour or so later, we made our way back to the factory where we met Maurice who had been given a car for us to use for a couple of days.

The next day we visited the nearby palaces of mad King Ludwig II, Schloss Neuschwanstein (prototype for the castle in Disney World) and the smaller and more delightful Linderhof Palace, inspired by Versailles. In late afternoon we made our way to Munich were

Maurice gave us a tour of the town beginning with the famous beer hall, the Hofbrauhaus. Beth and I gave him looks of round-eyed amazement when he described the hollow canes that previous customers used to eliminate the need to leave the table to visit the sanitary facilities. He told us the floor was covered in sawdust to absorb the 'processed' beer.

"Dear God, that must have reeked! I hope it's not still the custom." I never found out the truth of his comment since we continued on to our hotel, the Bayerischer Hof where we had dinner. The hotel was not only beautiful and comfortably luxurious but also located in the center of the town. The next morning found us touring the Maximilianstrasse's designer shops where Maurice was captivated by a pair of Charles Jourdan deep cherry red pumps that he spotted in a shop window. He ended up buying me both the shoes and the matching bag, which I loved and wore for the next fifteen years. Finally the shoes were worn out and out of style, so I discarded them but I still carry that bag. After lunch we toured the royal palace where the fantastic collection of elaborate clocks had both Beth and me enthralled. The next day we were back in Buchloe to collect the newly altered BMW, now a BMW Alpina. With instructions for driving the car to properly break in the highly calibrated engine, instructions on speed, braking, etc, we left to begin the drive south. Since Maurice had to drive a certain number of kilometers at each of the ten kilometer demarked speeds before progressing to a higher one, the remainder of the trip was to be much slower. We stopped for lunch in Garmisch-Partenkirchen, a famous Alpine resort town, before continuing into Austria where we would spend the night in Innsbruck.

The following day, we drove only as far as St Moritz, where we arrived quite late at our hotel, the Hotel Margna, located in the outskirts near the village of Sils-Baselgia. Built in 1817, the hotel, which had once been home to the Badrutt family, still retained some of it old world charm despite modernizations. We tumbled into bed and slept until late the following morning. Following breakfast in our room, we went exploring the hotel and the park that surrounded its majestic presence. I knew it would be lunch time before Maurice emerged so we had time to walk into a near by pasture where an old man in faded coveralls tossed big fluffy bunches of fragrant smelling dried hay into a cart pulled by a patiently grazing old nag. He smiled in greeting but continued industriously with his work. We smiled and waved but wasted no time in approaching a nearby amber colored cow that was munching with satisfaction on the stubble left in the field. She seemed quite content with the bounty that surrounded her and that which was on its way to winter storage for the cold snowy months when fresh grass would be but a distant memory.

"Mommy, do you think it would be okay if I petted her." Beth asked, warily eyeing the long pointed horns.

"Let's move very slowly and talk extra gently to her. If she doesn't move away, it means she isn't frightened by us, so it should be okay to pet her." The cow withstood our ministrations, pausing in her munching long enough to give Beth's hand a long affectionate lick.

"Yuk! It's all rough and wet." That ended the petting session. The large, limpid dark eyes mournfully followed us as we turned to walk back to the hotel taking pictures as we went.

When we walked up to the terrace, Maurice was waiting for us with a large hamper in his arms and a big grin on his face. "Let's have a picnic!"

"Great! Give us a minute to run back to the room to powder our noses, and we'll be right back."

We drove from the hotel to the nearby Sils Lake. Parking on the shore, we walked down to the lake past a stand of beautiful fir trees that framed the sparkling blue of the water with a looping fringe of dark resinous branches. The air was fresh, the temperature perfect, and the light soft as satin. In the middle of the lake windsurfers painted colorful moving patterns. Along the edge of the shore, gaily-colored boats bobbed gently against the sandy bank. We spread the blanket the hotel had provided and then unpacked the treasure trove of delicious surprises: a marvelous pâté with fresh crusty peasant bread, fresh and perfectly ripened fruit, dried sausages covered in herbs, a selection of cheeses from the Engadin region, home fried potato chips, small fruit and cheese tartlets in beautifully sculpted crusts, coke for Beth, and a bottle of fine champagne for us. Beth's eyes grew as large as two Harvest Moons when she saw the beautiful and bountiful array. The only thing missing was an orchestra to play background music.   However the lapping of the water and the whisper of the wind through the trees made a more than adequate substitute. The three of us were thoroughly sated by the time we had finished but that didn't stop us from licking our fingers and looking for any stray crumbs. It was heavenly to sit there and just be peaceful. Maurice and I chatted desultorily while Beth chased errant butterflies. I could have stayed for days and been content but the lowering sun and the wind flowing over the glacier-fed water were bringing a chill to the air that demanded warmer attire.

We drove into St. Moritz the next morning and had lunch at the reigning queen of hotels, Badrutt's Palace, and afterwards went back to our hotel where we left the car to walk down into the village of Sils-Baselgia where we visited Nietzsche's summer house, now converted into a small museum.

For our final day there, Maurice decided a hike up one of the nearby mountains was just the thing. Beth had tennis shoes, Maurice insisted his street shoes were fine, but I was a problem. Since none of my shoes were fit for that kind of excursion, the first order of business was to find a pair of tennis shoes I could wear for the coming exertions.   That was the first mistake.   The second was even attempting it. The third was attempting it with Maurice who decided to tour free style. Instead of following the marked trail for beginners, he decided to shorten it up by an overland trail we would blaze ourselves. After hours of struggling through shrubs, climbing over rocks, breaking nails, pulling twigs from snarling hair, blossoming blisters on both heels thanks to the untried shoes, eyeing seasoned climbers with sturdy lace up hiking boots, wooden staffs and incredulous expressions as we crossed them on the marked trails, I had about enjoyed as much of that business as I could stand, not that I was in danger of that for much longer. Beth was beginning to whine and Maurice was studiously ignoring us. But I knew he had bitten off more than he could chew and he knew I knew. Finally we reached a village, centered by a cool fountain surrounded by a low wall. Making a beeline for it, I sat on the wall, discarded my shoes and climbed in. It was heaven and the stares of nearby strangers were not sufficiently withering to haul my carcass out. I don't know how he did it, but somehow he got back down the mountain to the car and came back for us. I think there was probably a happy taxi driver in that little village that night. I recovered my humor on the way back to the hotel and was able to laugh with Beth and Maurice as they recounted the expressions of people who did a double take when spotting me ensconced in the fountain with leaves and twigs sticking out of my hair.

Despite the less than successful mountain climbing expedition, the respite in Sils had been a wonderful one so it was with some reluctance that we climbed once more into the car for the next leg of our journey. The scenery continued to be spectacular as we drove south following the river valleys through towering Alps. I was glad that the speed had slowed as it gave more time for appreciating the beauty of the snow-capped peaks, lush fir trees, rugged escarpments and occasional small villages, so picturesquely perfect they could have been manufactured Hollywood sets. We crossed Lake Como and drove south around the shores of Lake Lugano, the town of Lugano and on into Campione D'Italia where our hotel for the night awaited us.

Beth and I emerged in late morning to find the absolute perfect day. We had been told to occupy ourselves, as Maurice needed to take care of some banking business. He explained, "The tax burden in France is tremendous for someone in my income group. Even though it isn't permitted, many of my fellow citizens have moved their money out of the country to avoid some of the taxes. I brought mine here since Campione has a bank that my family has done business with for some time through my mother's Swiss family connections. Campione is a little piece of Italy that is surrounded by Switzerland, because of its unique structure, gambling laws here also are much less restrictive than in either Italy or Switzerland. There is a very famous casino that I will take you to tonight, Jo. I am not much for gambling but I think it is interesting to see." He turned to her and smiled, "Unfortunately, I cannot take you, Kiki."

We ambled about the small enclave ending up back at the hotel for a late lunch. We then returned to our room for a rest. Maurice called us around six and arranged that we would meet him in the lobby. We drove into Lugano for dinner at what was an early hour for him. Back in Campione, with Beth safely tucked into bed, Maurice took me to the casino. I had donned a colorful dress and taken pains with my hair so I would look nice for the evening. Little did I realize how very distinct my sex and that dress would make me. We walked into a sea of men dressed in somber black suits. I couldn't decide if it looked like an undertakers' convention or a meeting of the mafia. Not that there aren't some interesting connections there. As for women, there were almost none. Accustomed to images of Atlantic City and Las Vegas, this was a far cry from what I had expected. Obviously gambling was serious business in Campione...no showgirls that I could see, no ringing bells from slot machines, no honky-tonk music, no flashing lights, and none of the garishness and glitz. We didn't stay long since neither of us was a gambler. Back at the hotel, he stopped me at my door and turning me to him, gave me a soft passionless kiss on my lips. It was the first time that summer that he had kissed my lips and it left me a bit shaken. I tried not to read anything into it. Later in bed, I found it difficult to fall asleep as I kept remembering the tenderness in his face when he kissed me. Was there a romantic future with him? What about Ed? Would I stop seeing him in favor of a future with Maurice?

The morning found Beth eager to be on our way as the night's stop was to be in Monte Carlo, her promised treat. We left just before lunch, stopping in Cernobbio at the fabulous nineteen-century villa, now grand hotel, the Villa D'Este. Beth and I went to the ladies room while Maurice arranged a table for us. I can still see that room: gold fixtures, beautiful antique furniture, lovely linens and a marvelously designed bidet, a new fixture for me of which I had grown quite fond. Refreshed and hair combed, we returned to the lobby to find Maurice and the Maître d'Hote waiting for us. We were led to a table in front of a low wall with a lush array of flower-boxed blooms just on the outside. The whole room was like an open-air terrace in the summer thanks to large windows that slid completely out of sight. To the left, just beyond the window where we were seated, I could see a beautifully designed garden that Maurice told me had been the setting for many fashion photography shoots. On the right, floating serenely in the lake but anchored to the shore, was a large pool. As I sat there, eating the Bresaola that Maurice had insisted I try, a woman of gargantuan proportions waddled past the window dressed in what was called at the time, a Sundowner bathing suit...something of a bikini like affair with a lot of connecting strings. Unfortunately most of the strings were lost somewhere in that mass of undulating flesh only exaggerating the nudity. The three of us stared in gaped-mouth astonishment. Finally, Maurice shook his head, "You know the French have no sense of shame."

"I must say that takes nerve or total obliviousness, but how do you know she's French?" He didn't answer, just continued to stare in mute horror.

We drove to Monte Carlo that day, going through the many tunnels that line the corniche at a much slower speed than the previous summer. Maurice was still pampering his car and constantly asking me to refer to the manual to make sure that he was following the mandates for breaking it in. I still had time to enjoy the beauty of the oleander draped mountainsides that dropped precipitously into the azure sea. It was late when we arrived at the Hotel de Paris, so after a quick bite at the Cafe de Paris, we were happy to tumble into bed. This time, we did not have a suite with two bedrooms and a common living area, but two separate rooms albeit on the same floor. Beth awoke the next morning to espy the mountainous gift basket sitting on the chest across from her bed. That and a room service breakfast kept her happily occupied until I had completed my ablutions, rearranged an increasingly messy suitcase and painstakingly prepared myself to emerge into this most cosmopolitan of hotels and cities.

In the future Margot and I visited Monaco many times. I grew to love the luxury and beauty of the place and to feel more comfortable and less awed by the grandeur of it. It helped I suppose that Margot and I played like two kids on holiday whenever we were together. Under those conditions, the setting, no matter how elegant and grand, or austerely simple, becomes merely a backdrop for the fun.

To date Maurice had been far too serious to be a lot of lighthearted fun. I suspected he was far more worried about his business affairs that he revealed. That afternoon we went back to the Beach Club and spent lazy hours by the sea following our lunch there.

We returned in late afternoon to the hotel, where Maurice turned to us and remarked, "Kiki, I think we need to have mommy disappear as you and I need to do some special shopping. There's a birthday coming up that we need to find something wonderful for." He looked at me, "Okay, Jo. It's time for you to do something on your own for an hour or two while Kiki and I find a birthday gift." I obligingly disappeared in the direction of the Hermes and Escada stores where I window-shopped but didn't buy as the goods were beyond my remaining funds. When they returned to the hotel, I was already contentedly ensconced in the window with a book. I could see that Beth was bursting with excitement and badly wanted to tell me what they had found, however, she was doing her best to hint without actually disclosing the sworn secret. Maurice was nearly as bad.

We left the following day for the long drive back to Marseilles. Things were uneventful until we were about two hours away. Suddenly Maurice decided the car was not performing properly and he became more and more anxious that something was awry. We exited the autoroute to find ourselves in a small village with a sole garage. The lone mechanic looked at the Alpina like it was something that had descended from outer space. I watched Maurice grow more and more frantic as he waved his arms in the air to punctuate his explanations of what he thought was wrong. The mechanic backed up a pace to gain more than two inches nose space from Maurice's intimidating nearness, and scratched his grizzled chin in puzzlement. Beth and I took the opportunity to stretch our legs and amble about the village as they gestured furiously at one another and the car. We returned after about twenty minutes to find them both under the car and the battle still raging. Finding nothing, and with no illumination from Maurice's phone call to the Alpina factory as to what the symptoms might denote, we returned to the car. I never had noticed a problem and it seemed to be running fine, but Maurice continued to mutter about it for the remainder of the trip. Beth and I just wanted to get to Marseilles and out of the car.

His new spacious, light-washed apartment in the Parc du Cadenelle featured sliding doors and windows opening onto cantilevered terraces. This one was larger by a bedroom and an office than the one of the previous summer and much newer. With views of the surrounding area, gardens and distant sea, we much preferred it to his previous apartment. Maurice led me to his mother's room where I recognized her furniture and the delicate crystal chandelier. Beth's room was smaller but attractively decorated and featured an unusual frosted white and pink bedside lamp that looked like a lady's hat on a small stand. She loved it immediately and despite being in a separate room from me, happily began to unpack her things into the drawers. Maurice and I both left our unpacking for the moment when we were less exhausted from travel.

The remainder of the summer was similar to the one of the previous year with evening trips to the restaurants in Aix, Lourmarin, Les Baux and Cassis that we had enjoyed then. During the day, Beth and I were left to our own devices. We spent our time on mini excursions to Cassis and various nearby points in Marseilles. I was still sufficiently intimidated by the traffic and the size of the city not to be too adventurous. The only additional trip we made that summer was a weekend visit to Cannes and Antibes where Maurice took us along while he conducted business. He studiously kept things light and pleasant for the remainder of our time and never mentioned Margot.

His favorite pastime was playing hide and seek with Beth. Insisting I join the games, we would all soon be popping in and out of the doors and windows and shrieking at one another in the chase. He went at it with a gusto that exceeded mere zeal. Just as with the pillow fight of the previous summer, there was an air of desperation in his play that left me feeling unsettled. Too, I wondered if the neighbors thought madmen had taken up residence. Fortunately it was a duplex and the neighbors on the other side appeared to be away for vacation and the other residences were at a bit of a distance. The bread fights in restaurants were another favorite game and the one that bother me the most as I found it disrespectful to the establishment. While Beth participated with relish, once we were home she never displayed that behavior. Whether from knowing that I disapproved, whether from her own misgivings, or whether it was just a "Maurice game" for her, I never knew.

For my birthday and the presentation of that long hidden present, Maurice took us to the Beaumanière in Les Baux. The evening was balmy and the air soft with the scent of maquis as we sat on the terrace watching the spotlights turn the cliffs beyond the pool into a golden wall crowned with those picturesque ruins we loved. Following a fabulous meal, the owner and chef, Monsieur Thuillier, came to our table and chatted with us. When I complimented him on the menu cover that showed a reproduction of one of his paintings, he autographed it and presented it to me with a flourish. He had written Happy Birthday on it above his name. I realized then that Maurice had told him in advance that it was a birthday celebration for me. Monsieur Thuillier nodded to a nearby waiter who immediately appeared with a small but beautifully decorated cake surmounted with candles and a dewy epergne centered with a bottle of Dom Perignon.

Maurice reached under the table where he fumbled in his leather bag, emerging with a beautifully wrapped gift. "This is something that I hope you will always treasure and look at it with memories of me and this evening together. Kiki and I both love it and think it is perfect for you. We hope that you will too."

I took the gift into my hands and trembling with anticipation, opened it to find a beautiful red leather Cartier box inside. Releasing my bated breath when I saw it was a jewelry box but too large to be a ring, I slowly raised the lid, catching the glimmer of candlelight reflecting on the face of the gold Panther watch he had purchased for me.

"Oh, Maurice!! It's gorgeous. I love it! I have never owned anything so nice and so beautiful. How did you know that I never liked the watch I have and that's why I never wear one?"

He and Beth exchanged satisfied smiles, "I told him, Mommy."

"That's right, Kiki." He patted her hand and then took mine. "That's how we knew which gift to find for you, Jo."

Maurice lifted the bottle of champagne and filled our glasses, including a half pour for the one that the waiter had brought for Beth. "To your birthday, and many more to come. May they all be wonderful and spent with me. I am writing a letter of dedication for you to go with the watch but it isn't finished yet."

Beth toasted with us. "The champagne tickles my nose but I like it. Is it okay if I drink it, Mommy?"

"It's a very special evening, so I think it will be okay." She giggled at me and then at Maurice. I was happy that she seemed to be so much more at ease with him and genuinely affectionate. The frequent animosity of the previous summer had vanished, making the summer a more pleasant one for all of us.

I watched our summer ending with both dread at its passing and anticipation at returning home and finding out what had happened with Ed, as I had not heard from him during my time away. Maurice booked passage for the three of us on an express train to Paris, not the TGV that we had used to come south the previous summer. When he returned with the tickets, he looked at us and with tears welling in his eyes, rushed to his office where he remained for several minutes.

He emerged to give me a sad smile, saying "Only a few days more now. I have tickets for the day after tomorrow for Paris. I thought we might stay at the Lennox, which I like a lot and the location is good. We will have two days together in Paris before you leave. I don't know how I can bear this, but somehow I must."

"I feel sad too, Maurice. And I know Beth does as well. This summer has been so wonderful, even more so than last year which I loved so much. I suspect however when we are gone you will have more time to deal with the business affairs that are causing you so much stress right now."

"More time is not the same as better time. My time with you two is so much better than any other time I spend. The business is drudgery, purely and simply. I do it because I must in order to make a future for us.

"I do have to pick up Maman, next week. She's actually good company and we have been together so long, it's easy, but it's not the same. My girls bring laughter and youth into my life. I need that so much."

"We will have to write good letters and talk often by phone. I know that isn't the same, believe me, but that is our only choice."

"For now..." Looking grim, he added, "We need to talk some when we get to Paris." I could only hope it would not be a tirade against Margot. So far, that subject had been left in peace and the summer had been far easier for it.

Beth had her suitcase packed early on the day we left and it was only with great reluctance that she agreed to leave her special hat lamp as we could find no way for us to get it home. Maurice assured her that her room and lamp would be waiting for her. She didn't dwell on it overly long as I knew she was eager to return to her friends, my parents (particularly Grandpa whom she adored,) and a normal routine. Wisely I had brought fewer things for the summer so I was able to pack our gifts and purchases without racing around at the last minute for another piece of luggage to cart the excess.

On the train to Paris, we played rummy with Maurice, and much to his delight, he won almost every game. The time passed quickly and once again we were in one of my very favorite cities. This time we stayed on the left bank in the Lenox Montparnasse on Rue Delambre. It was a quiet neighborhood and close to the Jardin des Plantes, and some of our favorite restaurants. Maurice was quiet and preoccupied much of the time, so our stay was calm and uneventful. Mentally, Beth and I were already focused on our return. The last night we dined at the Closerie de Lilas and I could tell by Maurice's expression and body language that he was mentally composing a departure speech for us and particularly for me. Reaching in his pocket, he removed a letter that he handed me to read. Despite my improved French it was a challenge and he had to help me, admitting that it was written in a very poetic and difficult to translate formal style. It was the promised dedication for my watch.

The Gift of a Watch

August 12, 1985

For Jo

It was beautiful to our eyes, Beth's and mine, and we quickly reserved it for you.

These lines that I write are a gesture of solidarity and the protection of loving friendship.

It is life that surges through the wrist. Delicate blue veins mark its main course at skin level, like a great long hourglass. The wrist bears a tide of so many things upon its inner bed, where we see life's slow beating, almost at soul's level. In our quiet moments, I did not fail to appreciate its endurance and exulted in the efforts it conveyed.

The wrist is crossed by creases where so many times it has submitted to the wishes of clenched fists or with hands opened at night in longing, in sorrow. Those hands have extended in joy when they clasped their beloved.

Then, then they gave the pulse of life...carrying triumph and ardent gratitude...and flowing and descending within, that life force bears other gifts.   In battle, it is like a bunch of brisk and fibered forces, as it strives onward. In signatures, it commands with its flourishes. In pride it seeks certain things to tame. It bends as it supports for nothing has been short or easy, nor without consequences. Just as it has given of itself, has hesitated and obviated, it has locked itself in steel and wanted that which it sought but did not find. Life is inflicted on it, yet it holds its own so well. The wrist... receptacle, reforming, transforming, inspired...here are carried all of the passions, virtues, and elegances. And all of these things, which I have said, lie there under the watch's little bull's eye, surging and ever present, the everlasting, spouting spring of your life. Until the end, the river that runs here is ruler of life and it is here that one looks to see one's self. And we look here a lot and these perceptions are touchingly our own.

Never see in this watch on your wrist, the monotony of time. May its hands ever caper like nice, friendly horses, may they be an inspiration and a power. For it is in the deep satisfaction of yourself, that this present will find its significance, this present which is valued for its own identity forever.

Always I tell you, I believe in you. This watch will enclose your wrist with the strong grasp of the friend to whom you have brought joy, trust and the blessing of the most beautiful present imaginable...a child to love. And while it is there, there also is my grasp no matter where I may be.

With all my love,

Maurice

With tears in my eyes, I gripped his hand in mine. "Thank you so much for the watch, for this letter and for being in my life. You have given me so much and I treasure it so greatly. Thank you for this summer and for making it such a happy, special one. I will so miss you, Maurice."

"And I you, my darling. Just remember that all of my efforts are for the day when we can be together without the pain of this parting." He smiled sadly, "I don't even want to think about tomorrow when I will see the two of you fly away from me. I don't want to think about the lonely hours and days ahead until we can be together again. I don't want to think about the many struggles that face me in trying to create a future for us."

At the airport the next morning, tears blurred my vision as we walked away from him to begin the long journey home. He watched until he could no longer see us or we him. As I walked onto the plane, it occurred to me that Maurice had not mentioned Margot for weeks, nor had we had that 'serious' talk that he promised. It was just as well for I was torn with images of a future with Ed. How could I plan for one with Maurice when the other man had claimed the passionate side of my nature?

Chapter 11

When we arrived in Raleigh, we were both exhausted and it was late so we merely collapsed into our beds leaving luggage and all the rest for the next morning. My first order of business on waking was to check through the mail and the telephone messages to see if Ed had called or written. There was nothing but he called the following day and told me how much he missed me and that he was coming to Raleigh the following weekend and would spend it with me at my home. I arranged for Beth to visit her father so we would have the privacy we both wanted. The weekend was a renewal of our passion and I found myself even more in love. It was a lighthearted and joyful visit that contrasted in so many ways to the time that I spent with Maurice.

The coming months stretched ahead, long and lonely except for the visits from Ed who tried to come to Raleigh at least once a month, and the calls and letters from Maurice. Jaynie and Roger Smithson had married, so I saw her only infrequently. Christmas was spent in Greenville with my parents and family except for Margot, whose company Tony seemed to keep selfishly for himself. I talked with her frequently and all too often she seemed sad and frustrated with their relationship.

I returned to Europe in April and for the first time was taking a small group of other teachers with me rather than students. On arrival, we were taken to a seedy little hotel in the Montmartre section of Paris. My heart sank when I saw it. The outside was drab and unprepossessing and the miniscule lobby with a bare carpeted stairway to the left of the tiny concierge window provided no hopeful prospect for the accommodations awaiting me. I could do nothing but anticipate the complaints of my fellow teachers who I feared would hold me personally responsible. Fortunately they were so happy to be in Paris that they immediately set off exploring without remarking on the hotel condition.   As for me, I was awaiting Maurice's call to tell me he had arrived so I went to my room and prepared for a bath and a nap.   The first order of business was a trip to the toilet, where I discovered that to sit it was necessary to keep the door ajar with my knees in order to have the space necessary to do so.   As I sat doing my business, I suddenly felt a splash of wetness atop my head.   Looking up I saw a nasty amber stain on the ceiling above and judging from the water dripping from it, could only surmise that the toilet on the next level was leaking down on me.   Totally repulsed and feeling worse than polluted, I climbed in the shower and had a tepid bath as the water refused to get hot.   Shivering, I climbed out, used the towel that resembled nothing so much as cheesecloth, and given the chill in the room hastened to climb beneath the sheets.   I quickly discovered that the sheets were first cousins of the towel and allowed the rough prickly wool of the blanket to stick through the barren threads and walk on my skin like hundreds of creepy caterpillars.   Enough!   My tolerance exhausted and with no phone in the room, I threw on my cloths and marched down to the front desk.

As I walked up, the phone rang.   The concierge answered, *"Oui,"* paused to listen and gave another, *"Oui, oui,"* glanced at me and smiling, remarked *"Vous avez bon gout, Monsieur!"*

Noting her compliment with a lukewarm smile, I took the phone she handed me and responded to a cheery Maurice who had just arrived at his hotel on the other side of the city.   Telling me that he would arrive within the hour to take me to a late lunch, I hung up and immediately launched into my unhappiness with the condition of the room I had been given.   The concierge showed me two others that were if anything worse than the one I had.   In resignation, I walked up to my room to get my coat and returned to the lobby to await Maurice.

When he walked in and saw my downcast face, he knew immediately something was awry.   I regaled him with the story of my trip to the bathroom, the necessary shower and the creepy, crawly bed. Although he laughed, he too was appalled. "Don't worry, Jo. There really isn't a problem. You will simply move to my hotel. There are two beds in my room so it isn't an inconvenience to share."

Stunned by the unprecedented offer and unsure what to say, I stammered a thank you for his thoughtfulness but did not commit myself to the invitation. Ensconced in his car we chatted about my school year, Beth, our parents and his efforts to disentangle himself from the frustrations of his business. I constantly found my gaze wandering to the passing scenery and the tiny green leaves that were just beginning to appear on the knobby-pruned and mottled Plantain trees that lined the Boulevard Saint Germain. He took me to the Closerie De Lilas and found a warm corner booth where we could talk quietly.

"Jo, when we leave, I am going to take you back to your hotel so you can tell your group that you are changing hotels as your room is unacceptable and they have no other for you. Since they are all adults this should not be a problem. But, just to be on the safe side, I will invite them for a lovely lunch at Le Dome tomorrow as my guests. That should soothe things over and I promise to charm them for you. After that we will collect your things, have a bit of a tour and dinner then return to my hotel and get you settled in. *D'accord?"*

Reluctant to spend a night in my own hotel, I agreed. I could not help but wonder what my group would think and figured protestations of innocent friendship would not pass the cynicism test.

We drove across to the right bank to pick up my things and let my group know where I would be and to arrange the lunch for the following day. Afterwards we drove rather aimlessly around sightseeing from the car window and finally stopped for dinner at a small bistro near Maurice's hotel, the Hotel Lenox. The decor of the Alsatian restaurant was rustic and unpretentious and the menu the same. Over a comforting meal of a hearty potage and crusty bread, followed by cheeses and more of the burgundy we both liked, Maurice and I caught up on the months past. I left the hotel, sated with food, wine and conversation and ready for nothing more than a good night's sleep.

His room was tastefully and comfortably appointed and with the separate twin beds, I saw no problem with the accommodations, especially compared to the hotel I had abandoned. Taking my night things from the bag, I decamped to the bathroom to brush my teeth, remove make-up, brush my hair and change into my gown. I returned to the room to put items I had worn into my bag. As I leaned over to fold and arrange them, Maurice came up behind me. Cupping my breasts in his hands, he pressed against me letting me feel his erection. Shocked, I could only wonder if he had been arousing himself while I was busy in the bath.

Turning to him, I smiled wryly before cradling his face in my hands. "Maurice, you are a wonderful friend and I love you, but I must tell you that my friends have lasted far longer than lovers. I wouldn't want to lose you from my life so let's just be friends for now. Besides, until you have fully healed from the wounds of the relationship with Margot, I am not sure you are ready for another romantic liaison."

"Perhaps, you're right, Jo." He smiled at me, and I could not tell if it was with relief or sadness or perhaps a bit of both. Leaving me, he went to the bathroom to make his own ablutions for the night. When he returned from the bath, he placed his worn black sleeping bag on the opposite twin bed and still fully clothed, slid in and turned out the light. I nestled into my pillow, fully prepared for a much-needed sleep, only to be thwarted when he began talking about his business difficulties. And he continued to talk, and talk, and talk. Finally around daybreak, he fell asleep. I was too tired to sleep at that point and inured myself to the idea of just resting. At seven or so, I was startled from semi-sleep.

"Jo, are you sleeping?"

"No, I'm afraid not."

From then until ten, he continued to talk with only an occasional comment from me. He seemed sad, morose even, and I wasn't sure how to respond to offer him the most comfort. It occurred to me that it wasn't my response he needed so much as having someone to listen and as tired as I was, that was about all I could do anyway. I knew from what he said that his business affairs were in far worse condition than he had previously indicated, and I felt guilty that there was so little that I could do for him when he had done so much for us.

Finally I blurted out, "Oh, Maurice. I am sad that things are so difficult for you just now. You really shouldn't have been so generous with Beth and me when you are having so many problems with your business. I cannot offer much, but if I really budget, I can start repaying you for some of the money you have spent on us. Please, let me if you think that would help. It's the least I can do."

"Ah, I wish it were so simple. No, darling. I do thank you and it means more to me that you have offered than I could ever tell you, but I don't need your money and I still have enough for us. However, it would be great if I could finally sell this business and have the funds to do the all of the things that I want to do for us in the life remaining." He sighed and continued, "You know, I think sometimes that I was never meant to have a normal and happy life and yet I have wanted it so much. I want a family to love and be loved by. Why has it so eluded me all of these years? I who have so much have yet had so little of what I really wanted in life. Not just a family but also the career in painting or photography which I also find always just beyond my reach." He inhaled deeply, "Ah well, it will soon be time to meet the ladies at the restaurant for the promised lunch, so enough of this sad chatter.

The rest of the day he proved to be charming company. His looks, class, and command of English and the generosity of the luncheon treat more than impressed the ladies. I knew they were all hearing wedding bells dinging in their heads. When luncheon was concluded in late afternoon, the two of us did a leisurely round of sightseeing before stopping for a light dinner at a small bistro near the L'Etoile. That night was a repeat of the lengthy bedtime monologue of the night before. The next day we spent idly walking about and stopping in quaint sidewalk cafes. For our final dinner together, he took me to a nice restaurant just off the Rue du Rivoli before returning to our hotel and another long night. Fortunately for me, he stopped talking around two in the morning and I was able to snatch a short sleep before departing to join my group for the departure from Paris. I planned on catching up on my sleep in Spain, the last part of the tour. I said goodbye, sad to see Maurice so depressed, but nonetheless happy that we had been together for those few brief days.

When I arrived back in Raleigh, exhausted and ready to sleep for at least a week, the phone rang. Ed was calling to welcome me back and to tell me that he was coming to Raleigh at the end of the week for an overnight trip, again he was staying with me and I arranged for Beth to stay with Jaynie's sister who lived fairly nearby.

Friday arrived and I waited hours past the time he had said he would be there. I spent the time rearranging the pink roses I had placed on the cocktail table in the living room, aligning and then realigning the sterling flatware on the dining table, picking non-existent lint from the tablecloth and stirring and re-stirring the thickening sauce for my chicken. Considering the distance he had to drive, I excused the tardiness when he finally rang my doorbell. Greetings done, I did my best to salvage the overcooked dinner I had made. With a bottle of wine and a dinner that was still good despite the long wait, we relaxed and chatted about various things. Suddenly he smiled and reaching across the table took my hand, "Jo, I have a trip to England in June and I want you to go with me. I have to go to a plant near Telford but first we could stay in London and after Telford we have time to visit Bath and Salisbury before staying a couple of nights in Windsor prior to leaving. Would you like to do that?"

I gasped, "I'd love to." What an embarrassment of riches for someone who had never been much of anywhere two years ago, to now have two offers for trips to Europe. Unfortunately I knew if I accepted Ed's invitation, I would have to forego the summer with Maurice. The remainder of the weekend we spent joyously planning the trip to England. I mentally counted the weeks until departure and worried how I would tell Maurice that we would not be coming to spend the summer with him.

Disgusted with my dishonesty, even as I said it, when Maurice phoned I told him that I had some health problems and did not think that we would be unable to join him for the summer as he wanted. He was distraught at the thought of the summer without us and I was miserable that I was being so dishonestly unkind to someone who had been so good to us, but Ed's magnetic draw was stronger than my remorse.

I was to meet Ed in London where he would be waiting when I arrived. The flights connected through Atlanta and on arrival there a terrific thunderstorm was in progress, making landing a dicey proposition. Thoroughly unnerved by the pyrotechnics, I was glad to disembark in one piece and wait for the storm to pass before boarding the next leg of the trip, the flight to London itself. I boarded the plane, grateful that Ed had purchased a business class ticket. My seatmate proved to be an entertaining British gentleman in his mid thirties with an engaging grin and a naughty twinkle in his eye that contrasted with the innocent schoolboy look imparted by his cow-licked hair and a scattering of freckles across his nose. He had me involved in a witty conversation before the doors to the plane even closed. We had been sitting in anticipation of departure for over an hour, when the pilot came on the speaker to announce that due to lightening striking one of the runways, all planes were forced to take off from the one remaining runway, thus delaying our departure for at least another hour. While that hour came and went, the stewardess kept us well plied with drinks. With the wine and an entertaining conversationalist, time was not dragging for me despite the fact that in the end, we were almost four hours late leaving Atlanta. Because of the length time on the tarmac the pilot was back on the speaker shortly after take off to advise us that we would be stopping in Newfoundland for refueling prior to continuing across the Atlantic to England. Unfortunately, when we arrived in Newfoundland one of our fellow passengers decided that the delay was a sign from God that he was not meant to make the trip and demanded that he be allowed to disembark. This meant that his luggage had to be removed as well. Two hours and uncounted drinks later, we were once again on our way.

By this time, I most decidedly was feeling the effects of the wine I had consumed and my conversational sallies were becoming even freer. When my companion asked me what sightseeing I planned for England, thinking of Ed, I remarked "Ceilings. Lots of ceilings."

At that point, he burst into laughter. "I'm sorry I'm married for I would have loved to take you on that sightseeing expedition." Needless to say with the constant banter between us, I slept little on the flight over.

We arrived over six hours past due and I found Ed waiting patiently in the terminal when I exited customs. It wasn't long before I was admiring the ceiling in his hotel at the terminal and could not help but chuckle at my previous conversation. Ed laughed when I told him what was amusing me. "Okay," he said, "I can take the hint. Let's go look at London and check into our downtown hotel."

Since I had never been to England that was something I had anticipated almost as much as the time that I would spend with him. "Great. You've been here often, so please show me all of the things I should see." Smiling as I looked upward, I continued, "Besides ceilings that is."

We picked up the rental car and I was treated to the novelty of riding in the *driver's* seat with no steering wheel in front of me, and all of the traffic on the wrong side of the road. He seemed comfortable with the English system and I was happy to just ride. The Park Hotel was indeed well located as he had said and since the afternoon shadows were lengthening, we opted for an early dinner at a nearby French restaurant. The next morning we left early for my promised tour of London.

Suddenly while admiring the beautifully ornate fan vaulting in Westminster Cathedral, Ed excused himself and scurried from sight. I continued admiring the architecture and steeped myself in the remembered history of this famous building while I awaited his return.

"Sorry," he remarked when he reappeared. "I just saw some neighbors of mine and wanted to say hello. I hope you don't mind."

"No, that's fine." But inwardly I was a little piqued that he had not wanted to introduce me. For the remainder of the afternoon he seemed distracted and uneasy but dutifully led me to Buckingham Palace for the changing of the guard; to St. Paul's Cathedral, Harrods's, the British Museum, and to tea at the Ritz, before dinner at Bones, the oldest restaurant in London. And yes, I continued to enjoy the ceilings, making for a late morning the final day in London, so we opted for lunch in Mayfair before driving north to Telford. Telford was a small new industrial town built following World War II to house the people displaced from bombed out homes. I didn't find the appallingly repetitive and boring fifties style buildings very appealing visually, and therefore was pleased to find that he had booked a rustic hotel on the edge of town with beautiful views of the surrounding countryside and the nearby Severn River. The hotel restaurant was superb and Ed was again relaxed and romantic so the evening was a pleasant one. The following day he left me to attend a business meeting in Telford. I took the time to do my hair and lose myself in a good novel so his time away from me passed quickly. The following morning we left for Bath, and then the day after that, we drove to Salisbury to see the famous Gothic cathedral and have lunch before going to Windsor where we would spend a final two days before returning to London and home. The time passed all to quickly and it seemed that we had only left, when I was telling him goodbye in the Atlanta airport as we parted to fly to our separate destinations. I found myself even more in love with him than before after our first real extended time together.

Although I waited three days, I did not hear from Ed. Provoked and terribly disappointed that he had not called me after the intensity of the days we had spent together, for the first time I decided to call him. I knew the company he worked for and the city. I called directory assistance got the number and dialed. The main switchboard answered and despite my insistent inquiries, there was no record of Ed ever having worked for the company. In frustration, I called back and asked for a friend in his department whose name he had mentioned in one of our conversations. This time there was no problem and I was immediately connected. His friend listened carefully to my explanation of why I had called him. He stammered with embarrassment when I was finished, and I knew immediately that Ed had duped me. He had given me a false last name, similar but not his real one. The obvious reason: he was married and covering his tracks. Heartbroken, I thanked his friend and hung up. Five minutes later my phone rang. It was Ed. I had suspected it would be.

"Hi." I was wary and he knew it.

"Welcome back, honey. I have missed you so much."

"No doubt you could find company without looking too far."

"I'm sorry. I should have told you but I was afraid you wouldn't give me a chance if I did."

"That's right."

"Are you angry with me?"

"Now why would you think that? I'm not angry except with myself for being so stupid. You did tell me you were separated. I just didn't realize you meant only since breakfast." I paused, "Don't call again. There is no future in this for either of us."

I quietly replaced the phone and then went to the shower, climbed in, ignored the persistent ringing of the phone, and had a good cry while I figuratively tried to wash the disappointments from my body and soul. When I dried off, I walked back to the phone and called Margot. Her cheery voice was a much-needed tonic to me at that moment.

"Hey, Douche Bag, when did you get back?"

I got back last Sunday and I haven't done much except crash since then. I still need to call mama and daddy and let them know I'm home so I can go pick up Beth."

"You sound down, Kitty Puss. Are you okay?"

"No." I proceeded to tell her about the fiasco with Ed and how stupid, hurt and disappointed I felt. "You know, he put in just enough truth to make his lies believable.

But then the best lies are always those that have lots of truth as well, aren't they?"

"Ah, the truth in lies...the challenge is always to try to figure out which is which. Don't beat yourself up. You trusted him. He's the asshole not you. I can't tell you how many of my girlfriends have had the same thing happen to them. Your problem is you were married too young and too long, so you don't know the games that go on out there." She laughed, "Hey, Babe, he's not the only fish in the sea, you know. Besides, it's his loss, right?"

"Right!" I tried to sound as positive as Margot, but I knew it was going to take some time to heal. "So, what's happening with you? Any big plans yet?"

"As a matter of fact there are. We are going to have a quiet little ceremony like I told you. It's already set up for next month. I have to get a dress that's dressy but not too much like a wedding dress. I've seen one I like, a soft blue, street length dress and conservative enough to be appropriate for the occasion. I just need to go get it before someone else buys it."

"The blue should be great. It always makes your eyes look even bluer. So, where is the honeymoon going to be?"

"He doesn't have much time right now...too much going on. I think we will probably just go to a house one of his friends has in Palm Springs. Don't tell the folks. I've still got to do that and I haven't told them we are not going to have any family there. I suspect that's not going to go over too well."

"I suspect not too. I know I would like to be there but if that is the way y'all want it, I'll just deal with it and they will have to as well. The main thing is for you to be happy together. I know he is much, much older...what, two years younger than mama? That could be a problem for some people. But if it works for the two of you, go for it."

"You know, it's okay. Sure it would be nice if he weren't so much older. But I do love him and that's what matters." She paused, "By the way, is Maurice still ranting and raving about me?"

"Actually he seems to be getting over it and I for sure don't bring it up."

"Good."

We talked for almost two hours just catching up with all that had been happening in our lives and with family news. She did not mention the lost baby, so I left it alone as well. It was good to laugh and be silly with one another as I had really missed her while away and her witty and wicked comments kept me from morose tears of self-pity for allowing myself to fall for a man who was unavailable. She was good for me with her blithe spirit and cheerful irreverence.

It was only a matter of days before the school year and its routine again took over my daily life. I occasionally did the Tuesday night date with Jaynie, went to see my parents frequently on weekends as Beth loved it there and they enjoyed pampering her. Since it was only an hour and a half drive that wasn't a problem. Maurice called regularly and sent telegrams and cards as well. He seemed more and more frustrated by his business problems and lonely for us and I more and more regretted not spending the summer with him instead of that fateful trip with Ed.

Late in October on a rainy and chilly Saturday that matched my inner gloom with the outer gloom, the phone rang. I walked over to pick it up despite being in the mood just to read my book and forget the outside world existed.

"Hello?"

"Ah Jo," Maurice sighed. "I needed to hear your voice. I am so desperately lonely here. Please tell me my girls will come spend Christmas with me."

"Seriously, you want us to come for Christmas?" I was shocked, as I had not expected to see him before what was becoming my annual spring tour.

"I do, very much. If you will tell me the dates that you're on vacation, I'll start arranging for tickets. I thought perhaps we could meet in Rome. I will pick you up from the airport and arrange a hotel for us."

"I see you've already been thinking and planning. I will tentatively say okay, because I would love to come but I'm going to have to see how Beth reacts to the idea of being away at Christmas."

"Let me talk with her. Maybe I can convince her to come."

I called her to the phone and listened to her initially guarded responses that became warmer and warmer, culminating in a note of excitement that we were invited for Christmas. I knew then it would be okay and wondered what he had promised to elicit her acquiescence to the trip. Even though she no longer believed in Santa Claus, I still would have to arrange her gifts and figure out whether to take them or present them before-hand. I would have to check the calendar to see what the exam schedule would be and whether or not I would need to take additional time for the trip. As it worked out, the way vacation and teacher workdays fell I had almost three weeks available.

For Thanksgiving we went to Greenville to spend it with my parents and various other family members who could come. Unfortunately Margot could not be there as Tony had committed them to festivities with his family. Still we had talked by phone and she told me about her wedding which had occurred in mid-month.

"I am so happy for you, Baby!" I had exclaimed when she told me.

"Me, too. But I was a bundle of nerves. Actually I'm glad Kat crashed the party and just showed up. It helped to have someone in my family there."

"I can imagine. When Katerina told me she was going, I started to go myself, but I had some things going on at school that I couldn't just ditch at the last minute."

"That's okay, besides you know Tony didn't want any family."

"Yes, I know." I also knew that had not made my family very happy with him. "So, how was the honeymoon?"

"Pppphhh! We fought most of the time. Because of some

business engagements he couldn't or wouldn't get out of, it was only a weekend and since it wasn't very pleasant, I guess that was long enough."

"Oh, dear. That's too bad. Hopefully things will smooth out soon."

"Maybe if his bitch of a daughter would just get over it, it might. As it is, she's making life miserable for him because of me and naturally, if he's miserable, I get to reap the consequences. Screw it! It's done now, so she can just cope with it!"

"Wow, that sounds grim. I just hope the good side out-weighs the bad so you don't get hurt."

"I'm just going to deal with it. Besides, I'm trying to get pregnant. If I give him the son he's always wanted, that'll really pull the rug out from under the bitch. I want a baby so much, just for me. I've wanted a baby for so long. I really mourn for the one I had to give up. You know that. And with the old clock ticking, I need to make it happen soon."

"Honey, he is so much younger than you are. Do you think he still wants to father a child at his age?" I did know how desperately she wanted a child to love and it worried me for her. And I knew she felt terrible remorse that she had allowed him to talk her into the abortion.

"We've talked about it. He says he still would like to have a son to carry on his name." She sighed, "I just hope it will happen soon."

"So what are you up to now, besides trying to get pregnant?"

"I'm going to New York next week to pack up my apartment and get the things I want moved and taking the other things that I want in New York to the corporate apartment at the Waldorf. I really don't plan on keeping the furniture so I'll have Goodwill or someone pick it up."

I didn't talk to her again until the following week when she called me from New York in hysterics. Listening carefully to the coherent words that interspersed the sobs, I realized she was telling me that Tony had been to his doctor to be sterilized while she was in New

York. She had not known that he had even been considering it, but Andrea's power over her father was stronger than Margot realized. Perhaps she had feared that Margot would cement the marriage with a child.

"He betrayed me! He knew how much I wanted a baby and he let that bitch stop it for me. He told me he's always wanted a son. Yeah, and the child he made me abort was a son! And what do I have in place of my baby? A Yorkie. I love Perky, but it's not the same for Christ's sake. How could he think that would compensate? I don't know how he can tell me how much he loves me and still do this to me. I'm just so hurt and so mad, I can't think straight. He wants me to go home to take care of him as it hurts where he had the surgery. Can you believe the gall it takes to ask me that after telling me he will give me a baby? The asshole now wants me to go play nursemaid while he gripes about his sore balls."

I remembered her words about the truth in lies. "Oh, Margot, I'm so very sorry. I know how sad you must be and how angry. I wish I knew what to say to make it better for you, but this time, I don't know how I can. If you love him, somehow you will have to forgive him for this and try to make it work anyway." I paused, "He's old, honey. Maybe he just didn't think he could cope with a child at his age."

"Screw that! It was that bitch that put the kibosh on it and caused this whole mess. She is so jealous and possessive of him you would not believe... jealous that her dad might love me more than her. I think she's also afraid she would have to share his estate with another child as well. Split three ways is not as good as two apparently, despite the fact he has already given her a trust fund worth millions. She's just a mean, ugly, selfish hag. I despise her!"

"Frankly, I think I may as well."

When we finally rang off, she sounded calmer if not much happier. I knew what a blow this was for her as she had counted on a child and now there would not be one unless she left Tony. She said she loved him and apparently he loved her, but they were both strongly dominant personalities, both accustomed to the limelight, albeit in different ways. Maybe the abrasiveness between them produced sparks but it could also create a painful burn. I was sad for her because despite the surface glamour and glitz of her life, she was basically domestic: she wanted to cook, take care of a husband and be the mother to his children. Yet, she was married to a man who had servants to cater to his every need and children by the wife of his youth. Did he see her more as his 'arm candy,' the beautiful vibrant woman who assuaged his aging ego by his possession of her?

Preoccupied by my thoughts of Margot, I began to sort through the clothes that Beth and I would need for our upcoming trip to Rome for Christmas. I was curious as to why Maurice wanted us to meet him in Rome rather than in Marseilles where we could spend it with Marie as well. He never did explain, but I had suspected it was because he did not want to share us with her. I told myself that, anyway. I decided that in some way we were the fantasy life that he had never had and thus it was not to be shared with anyone, in the same way that certain dreams that deeply affect us because of their inner message are not shared but are held close. I worried too that Beth would find it upsetting to be away from the traditional Christmas celebration and the gathering of family. Determined to at least keep Santa Claus in the program, I careful packed the small portable items I had found for her and that I knew she would like.

When we arrived in Rome he was waiting for us in the airport terminal. His face lit up like the proverbial Christmas tree when he spied us emerging from customs pushing our luggage cart towards him. Quickly he closed the distance and taking our carry-on bags from us and placing them on the floor at his feet, he swept us both into his arms.

"My darlings, having you with me again makes me so happy. I have missed you so very much! Let's get these things in the car and we'll go to the hotel and unpack. On the way we can catch up on what has happened since summer." We followed him as he pushed our bags to his car and got them loaded. During the drive to the hotel, we chatted about the previous months and he teased Beth about school and her brief French lessons of the previous year. Despite the tutor he had arranged and the beautiful accent she had acquired, she was much too shy to attempt to speak and the tutoring had ended too early for her to gain any comforting level of proficiency. To relieve her embarrassment, I diverted his attention to ask about his arrangements for our time in Rome.

"I have booked us into the Jolly. Perhaps you will recall from your first visit here that is where I always stay." I did indeed remember the first visit to the Jolly and the awful tirade I had endured. I merely nodded my head in recognition. "I am sure you remember that it's beautifully situated near the Via Veneto and not that far from the center. Besides it's near our favorite restaurant, the Girarrosto Toscano. I have reservations for us there tonight." He happily described his trip to Rome and all of the plans he had for us as we relaxed from the long and tiring journey, offering comments only as needed.

The next few days were a whirlwind of activities as Maurice energetically swept us from one attraction to another. Beth particularly loved the visit to the black beach at Antica Ostia despite the chill of the air. I would have liked to spend my time there looking at the ancient ruins of this former seaport of the Romans, however I knew that was not her program and Maurice and I wanted her to be happy since she was to experience her first Christmas away from the traditional family celebration. We frequently walked the crowded streets at the foot of the Spanish Steps, where Maurice bought her a sapphire and diamond ring, a beautiful pastel paillette-embroidered designer sweater, the inevitable stuffed animal and various other small gifts...all of which he had beautifully wrapped for his Kiki's Santa Claus. At Ungaro, he founded a smartly tailored tweed suit for me. He and the alterations woman took turns pinching this bit of fabric here and that one there until both were satisfied that it was the perfect fit. We would pick it up on Christmas Eve. Despite the cold, we walked for hours, lunching at Nino's, eating bags of roasted chestnuts plucked hot from the coals by busy vendors, and browsing the shops brimming with a sea of temptations. Dinner found us at our favorite restaurants: the Girarrosto, the Antica Paisano, and the Caesarina, as well as some new ones. Each evening when we returned to the hotel, I amused Beth by sitting on the toilet lid while I soaked my feet in the bidet. With heels and stockings, rather than her sensible shoes and socks, I was paying a painful price for my vanity while walking those cold cobbled streets. Those few hours following our perambulations were spent quietly in our room prior to dinner as Maurice said that he needed time to work, conducting business by phone.

On Christmas Eve, following dinner we made our way to the Vatican where we joined the joyous crowds making their way into the Basilica for the midnight mass. Although he had been unable to procure seats, we stood by one of the massive piers at the crossing and listened as the Pope addressed the world in dozens of languages. It was a transcendent moment that moved us with its majesty as we stood there in that ancient place listening as thousands of voices filled the resounding dome with the hymns of the season. I savored the magic of this space made beautiful by the sculptured figures, Bernini's throne of Saint Peter and his majestic Baldachino, and the golden, coffered ceiling. All to soon it was finished and we turned to join the exiting throngs who recessed remarkably quieter than on entry. Like me, the pilgrims to this mass seemed to have been filled with a peaceful reverence that rendered them subdued and thoughtful.

We had only been in our room about ten minutes when he phoned. "Jo, you and Kiki have been visited by Saint Nicolas. I think I saw him leaving things just at your door. Maybe you should check and see what's there."

We opened our door to find the wrapped gifts that he had purchased for us, and a plate of beautiful cookies and beverages, obviously arranged through room service. He leaned against the wall watching as we gathered our gifts and moved them inside. Coming into our room he smiled as we opened the packages exclaiming in feigned surprise, shared our snacks with us, and then once more retired to his room for the night. On Christmas Morning Maurice had a huge breakfast delivered to our room with service for three. He joined us for the opening of the gifts that I had brought for Beth and him. For the first time ever, there were no gifts for me on Christmas Day itself and I found myself suffering from a small and childish twinge of self-pity. That afternoon we spent in the hotel, Maurice in his room and us in ours where I read and Beth played with the Christmas toys I had given her. Dinner was at the nearby Caesarina. There Beth and I gawked at the stylishly dressed beau monde, however in our own new finery we did not feel too outdone. Beth made it a point to keep her ring finger proudly in view much to the silent amusement of Maurice and me.

The next few days, found us exploring the museums and other attractions of Rome. I particularly loved the Villa Borghese's collection of Bernini sculptures whereas Beth was more excited by the visit to Castel Sant'Angelo. Maurice quietly enjoyed our company with none of the serious conversations of our previous visits as he played the ever willing and informative tour guide. Margot was unmentioned and I left it thus. The only serious note came late one evening as he and I were sitting quietly talking to keep from waking Beth.

"Jo, if something should happen to me, I want you and Beth to be taken care of. For that purpose, you must contact my attorney in Marseilles. He knows that you are to receive my estate and he will help you. I hope that I am around for many years, but in this life, one never knows."

"Goodness, Maurice, I'm really surprised and of course so very grateful. But what of your mother or family, want they be upset if you do that?"

"My mother is old and doesn't need it. As for family, there is only my cousin Christian, son of my mother's sister, and I detest him. I do not intend should I die first, that he should inherit anything from me."

"Let's pray that we don't either need to deal with this for a very long time to come."

"Nevertheless, when you are at home, I will send you a letter with all of the details so you can contact the attorney and will know what to do should it happen that I die."

"Maurice, if that will alleviate your worries to know that your cousin does not receive anything from you, then by all means, do so." Smiling, I took his hand. "It is so wonderfully kind and generous of you to want to do this for us. You really are an angel in my life in so many ways."

For New Year's Eve he arranged dinner for us at an intimate and very Roman restaurant full of Italians celebrating the season. I was surprised at the arrival at our table of two friends of his from Marseilles, both young men in their twenties that had apparently ridden down with Maurice unbeknownst to me, and were to accompany him back on the second of January following our departure. Their arrival explained the two previously empty seats at our table, but was an impediment to Beth and me enjoying the remainder of the evening as Maurice's attention and theirs was focused on a rapid-fire conversation in French among the three of them effectively excluding us. Near midnight, one of them at Maurice's instigation asked me to join him on the dance floor for a fast tango whose steps I faked, but Maurice to my disappointment, never asked me to dance. When the midnight toasts were done, Beth and I were happy that it was time to leave. I had thought Maurice might elaborate on why he had asked them along for the holiday but his only comment was that they had helped him drive.

Our departure from Fiumicino was a sad one. Maurice looked so haggard and downcast that I could not help feeling a great sympathy despite my annoyance over the New Year's Eve dinner. Even so I told myself, he had given us a wonderful and memorable holiday, lovely gifts and had been so thoughtful and generous to us in so many ways. I would be returning to Europe with students in the spring and would see Maurice then. As we walked through the boarding gate, I felt his eyes watching us and turned and mouthed over the heads of fellow passengers, "I'll see you in April!" He beamed at me and waved a final time before we were lost from view.

Just before Christmas I had called Margot to see if things were any better. It was quickly apparent from her conversation that he was listening and she did not feel free to talk but I knew from the tone of voice that if anything things had gone from bad to worse. She hung up with a promise to call me later. When she did I could tell that she was mightily provoked.

"I'm sorry I couldn't really talk before but I had to get away from Tony. You will not believe the latest," she began. "This man who has so much money gives me nothing. I have to account for every penny I spend and if I need something I have to essentially requisition it like in a business with supporting documentation as to why I need it. I am literally reduced to borrowing from the maid to buy makeup. On top of that, I have found a really fabulous house I really want so we can move out of this mausoleum, and his bitch daughter is kicking up a storm that he would sell her dead mother's home. I believe she really thinks we should keep sleeping in the maid's room and leaving mama's room just like it was the day she died. Even so, the good news is I think he'll probably get the one I want just because it used to belong to this guy he doesn't like. It will be like an 'ah-ha, I can live here too'. It is a gorgeous house and much larger and nicer than this one. I want to throw out all of this old junk and furnish it the way Tony's home should be furnished for a man with his money and position."

We talked off and on over the next few weeks and it was obvious that the house deal would not happen. Margot was increasingly unhappy and had begun to talk of divorcing him unless things changed and soon.

Chapter 12

The phone was ringing when I walked in the door. Dropping my bags I dashed to reach it before the ringing stopped noting as I ran how musty the house seemed after being shut up for three weeks. I sneezed just as I lifted the receiver.

"Jo, what a way to answer your phone," Margot laughed. "I'm so glad you're back. I've really missed talking to you."

"What's up?" I could tell from her voice that she was very upset. I settled into a kitchen chair and propped my swollen feet on the adjacent one.

Without responding to my question she let out a long breath and asked, "So how was the trip to Rome for Christmas?"

"You know, I think I am still a kid: I missed the whole Christmas hoopla. Somehow it just wasn't the same, even though Beth did far better than I expected she would. Don't get me wrong. I loved the whole thing in some ways. It was an experience to be in Rome for Christmas and to go to midnight mass at the Vatican. You know I'd never before been in Europe for Christmas, so I enjoyed seeing the differences in the way they celebrate. It's just that I suppose I'm very traditional about holiday traditions. I wanted turkey, a Christmas tree, presents to open, and family all around."

"Boy, can I identify with that. I wanted to be home too instead of stuck here. I called on Christmas and Mama and Daddy seemed so sad that neither one of us were there this year. And you know they missed Beth since she's like another daughter to them."

"I know. I've got to call them and I thought maybe I would go see them this weekend and celebrate a late Christmas. Why don't you hop a plane and come down too? You could fly in here since our connections are so much better and we can drive down together."

"I wish I could, but there is too much going on here. Just wish me luck, Jo. This is not easy!"

"Ah, babe. You know I do." I paused to see if she would continue and when she didn't I asked, "So what's making you so unhappy sounding? It's not like you to sound down so much."

"I know." Hesitating and with a sigh, she continued, "I guess part of it is my own fault as I'm having a hard time forgiving him for the vasectomy and that makes me bitchy. Plus Andrea is still a pain and now he even resents my popularity with his friends. Or at least he acts like it."

"He's probably just jealous. After all, you're much younger, better looking and more fun. Plus you're witty. People can't help but responding to your warmth and genuine liking for them. Just think, everyone whether rich or poor, famous or not, you enjoy and are nice to. He's not a people person like you and he doesn't have your charisma. And I suppose his daughter is jealous too and for many of the same reasons, plus she sees you as the interloper in her relationship with him. That being the case, she has a bigger problem than you do and so does he."

"Thanks, Jo. I really needed some encouragement, since I don't get much around here. I'm beginning to think I can do no right."

We talked on a few more minutes and then I hung up to begin the process of unpacking and getting ready for the coming workweek. Walking around I could see that dusting was badly needed, the plants had all drooped and there was a stack of mail to get through and bills to be paid. So much for the exotic holiday, now it was time to return to routine. The drab chilly January weather didn't do much to allay my despondency that I had nothing and since Ed, no one, to look forward to until spring break, all those long months away. And now I had Margot to worry about as well. This was a double whammy for her, to not only lose the baby she had wanted so much, but also the increasing difficulty of a relationship with the man who caused her to abort it to keep his love.

Maurice called the following evening to make sure we had arrived home safely and to tell me how much he looked forwarding to seeing me in the Spring and having us both come for summer vacation. I still felt badly about my deception the previous summer and deeply regretted that I had gone with Ed to England rather than spending the summer with Maurice. What a poor exchange that had proven to be.

Margot also called often keeping me updated on the lack of any real change in the quality of her marriage. She was obviously growing more and more frustrated and pained by the unhappiness of her situation. Because I too had lived through the misery of an unhappy marriage, she found me a comfort for the empathy I could offer. I knew what scars it could bring and what true aloneness could be. The loneliness of being with someone who is not there for you, or even really with you, is the worst kind. Add to that the vitriolic retorts that result from the day-to-day friction of living with another in a loveless and unloving state, and you have the makings of a very despondent life. She was much more ill equipped than I to deal with the situation as she had always been babied, admired and catered to. Not that she was weak. She wasn't. In many ways I felt she was very strong, confident and secure within herself. This was a new experience for her and being the admired baby of the family had not prepared her for it. *That* she was not getting with Tony who expected to be the one catered to and admired without giving anything in return. Rather than taking her with him on business trips he was now frequently leaving her at home without the financial resources to do anything or go anywhere in his absence. She spent her time escaping into books and telephone calls. I found myself more and more furious with him for the pain he was causing her, although I tried not to interpose my own feelings but to simply be a good listener as she talked about her own perceptions and pains.

Despite the long and unusually cold winter, buds began to appear on the trees, daffodils were pushing up and the annual student trip was just a week away. I held the final meeting with parents and students to go over expectations, arranged for Beth's father to pick her up for the holiday, and sorted through the things I was taking on the trip with me. Beth and I went shopping. She found a small green glass figurine of a horse to give Maurice and then drew him a card to go with the gift. It wasn't much, but I knew that he would be thrilled she had thought of him. I was bemused when I remembered that difficult first summer in Europe and how antagonistic she had been to him then. The time since had seen her begin to change from child to teen bringing a greater appreciation for all that he had done for us. I found myself regretting that I was not taking her with me. All too soon she would be an independent teen and then an even more independent adult. I looked forward to the transmogrification into adulthood but knew I was going to miss my 'baby.'

Margot called the night before I left and for the first time in months seemed her old, vibrant and happy self. Tony had given her a beautiful yellow sapphire, diamond and pearl necklace and matching earrings and sent her shopping for some new gowns for events they were attending. He had also given her a more generous allowance so that she could buy make-up and other items for herself without having to appeal to him for money every time she needed something. Apparently they were both making an attempt to mend their marriage and find a happy medium in the relationship. I hung up feeling much more optimistic for her.

I landed in Rome on a chilly gray April morning with thirty-two students, four adults and an assistant chaperone in tow, Meg Graham, a friend of mine who worked with me. I knew between us we would have our hands full with so many teenagers, however she had promised to cover for me in Florence as Maurice was driving from Marseilles to meet me there. Since it would be only for one day, I didn't feel badly about taking time away from the group and if she needed more help the four adults would pitch in. I spent my time in Rome going to the places I had discovered and loved with Maurice and seeing him with me in my mind. Sorrento with the day trip to Capri was one of my favorite parts of the tour. Apart from the stop in Pompeii, it was a chance to enjoy the scenery and casual life of the coast without the heavy emphasis on history of the other excursions provided by the tour.

However with increasing distress in my digestive tract, I knew that before leaving Rome I needed to find some medication. Fortunately I found a pharmacy just down the street from our hotel, the Palatino, my preferred one for our group because of its location close to the Coliseum and an easy walk to the Spanish Steps. The shop was as small as my closet at home and so dimly lit I almost missed the elderly woman hunched behind the counter.

Walking up to her, I realized my knowledge of Italian didn't extend to describing physical complaints. I began, *"Scusi Signora,* I need a laxative please."

She looked up at me over the tops of scratched reading glasses held together at the temple with scotch tape. *"Non capisco."* Followed up by a volley of rapid fire Italian that left me standing there dazed.

I tried louder and higher, *"Laxativo, per favore."* I didn't know if the word existed in Italian. For what I hoped would be added clarity, I gripped my hands over my stomach and grunted.

Making an elaborate shrug, she threw her hands in the air and disappeared behind a curtain of clicking pea green plastic beads that waved like new wheat in a spring storm. Immediately she re-emerged with a man I took to be the pharmacist trailing in her wake. He came up to me and smiled, *"Si, Signora?"*

"Laxativo?"

"Ah, mi dispiace. Non capisco." He gave a massive shrug hunching his shoulders until his neck disappeared and raised his hands palm upward.

What to do? I was determined not to leave without what I had come for. In desperation I stood there reviewing all of the possible words that might get the idea across and then it hit me: purgative. *"Purgativo, per favore?"*

"Ah, si, si!" Ducking under the counter he arose with a baby blue cardboard container held aloft. He handed it to me and smiled wickedly. *"Ecco purgativo. Uno è tranquillo."* He held his right hand flat and waved it side to side. I nodded in understanding. *"Due, molto forte."* This time he raised his right arm bent at the elbow and

with his left hand on his bicep gave a couple of pumping motions. I got the message: very strong.

"*Si, due è molto forte.*" I paid and made an escape with the two of them grinning at me. As I closed the door, I caught the little gnome of a woman pantomiming my hands-on-tummy grunt while the pharmacist shook with suppressed laughter. Just before bed I struggled to swallow one pill, "*tranquillo,*" which resembled nothing so much as a small, perfectly dimpled golf ball, relaxed on my pillow and dreamed of morning relief.

In order to allow time for the expected results, I arose long before Meg and began my ablutions. Unfortunately, nothing was forthcoming so I took a second pill hoping that by night I would achieve the desired results. Resigned I climbed aboard the bus at seven and we began the drive to Naples where we were to catch the eleven o'clock ferry to Capri for the afternoon. When we arrived at the quay I began to feel the first rumblings of coming trouble and rued the stupidity of that second "*molto forte*" pill. But there was no time now to visit a facility as we had to rush to catch the boat. My heart sank when I saw what the tour director had booked. It was a rusty old tub of a boat that I knew would crawl at a snail's pace consuming valuable time from our visit in Capri. We all climbed aboard and settled ourselves on rusty benches along the sides of the groaning boat. As we left the harbor, sleek hydrofoils zippered across the water leaving us to wallow drunkenly in their wakes. They would be in Capri when we were still mid way. Unfortunately by mid way I knew I had no alternative but to find the nearest toilet.

Just inside the rocking doorway to the interior I found the ladies WC. Inside was dimly lit, minus any paper and the only facility was an ordure-incrusted hole in the floor with a foot slot on either side, the infamous Turkish toilet. Dear Jesus, not this I prayed, but I had no choice. Carefully I removed my underwear as a precaution and hung them with my purse on the door after carefully fishing out two mangled and well used Kleenex. Judging by the rolling of the boat in the troughs and swells, this was going to be one mean balancing act if

I was two emerge with two un-spattered ankles. I think that moment stands as one of my nadirs in the area of sanitation. Finally I was purged and blotted as best I could. I staggered back to Meg who was waiting at the rail.

"Success?" She asked. I just rolled my eyes. How was I to tell her about the particulars of achieving it?

I enjoyed showing Meg and the others the places that I loved in Capri and Sorrento. I had called from home to make reservations for the entire group at L'Antica Trattoria on a small side street just inland from the Gulf of Sorrento. It is one of my favorite restaurants in all of Italy and my favorite stop in Sorrento. Making our way to the door through the courtyard, we passed a sea of colorful Cyclamens bursting rampantly from flower boxes. The small and intimate interior was divided into three or so rooms, one more formal than the others. I could hear the melodious notes of a mandolin wafting from an inner room as we were seated. Soon the musician arrived at our tables and sang the ubiquitous O Sole Mio for us. With wine circulating freely, the beautifully presented and delicious food, and that magic Italian ambiance that has to be experienced to know, it was a memorable last evening in Sorrento. For many the stay in Sorrento was their favorite part of the tour and after taking more than a dozen groups on this same tour, I found it to be true for them all.

Except for the normal friction of so many people living and traveling for the first time in such proximity, the tour was going well. We arrived in Florence at nine in the evening after a day's drive from Sorrento with a stop in Assisi to see the Basilica of Saint Francis with the famous frescos by Giotto and Cimabue. After dropping our luggage in our rooms we went down to the hotel restaurant for a late dinner. Maurice called while I was in the restaurant picking at less than tantalizing pasta. The concierge of the Hotel Mediterraneo, who knew me from previous trips, came for me.

"Hi, Maurice. Are you in Florence yet?"

"No, unfortunately I am delayed in leaving so it will be late tomorrow before I arrive. I will take you to dinner and then the following day we will spend together. I am so tired I think it will do me good to escape for a few days despite the long journey."

"Drive carefully then and I'll look forward to seeing you tomorrow night. As for me, it has been a long and exhausting day and except for having to chaperone the kids to a disco, I would be very happy to go to bed and just sleep. Unfortunately the disco is always included in the tour and is a big hit with the kids. It's a chance for them to dress up, meet teens from all over the world and just enjoy being kids. For me, its noise and chaos when I just want some peace and quiet. Oh, well. That's part of the price that I pay to get the trip for free."

"Poor, Jo." He laughed, "Have a glass of wine, find a quiet corner and escape into dreams and wait for the music to stop so you can find your bed. I'll see you tomorrow, darling. Goodnight."

I hung up and returned to the restaurant to finish dinner before the jaunt to the disco. Afterwards I collapsed into bed and was asleep by the time my head hit the pillow.

The following morning I accompanied the group on the tour of the Academia, the iconic Cathedral of Santa Maria dei Fiori that dominates the skyline, the bell tower of Giotto and on to Santa Croce and the tomb of Michelangelo. I pointed out the monument tomb of Dante who had been expelled from Florence for being on the wrong side of the political fence. However at his death the city fathers were quick to claim their famous poet despite the fact that his body was buried in Ravenna in 1321 and there it adamantly remains. The group dispersed in the piazza to explore the leather and gold outlets before standing in line for the Uffizzi. I was free to make a long awaited visit to the Cathedral museum to see Brunelleschi's drawings, models and devices used for construction of the vast dome; the Mary Magdalene sculpture by Donatello, and the Cantoria by Andrea della Robbia among many of the art treasures housed there. Thrilled by the visit and awed at the accomplishments of the Renaissance artists of Florence, I returned to the hotel to rest and dress prior to the awaited call from Maurice. The others had returned and gone to dinner by the time he phoned at almost eight. He sounded exhausted but arrived at nine to take me to dinner. We were both starving and much to our disappointment had a terrible struggle to find a restaurant that was still serving. I didn't know if it was because it was the off-season or if Florentines just dined early, however after nearly thirty minutes of searching we found one that would seat us. I ran in to hold the table while he then looked for a parking space, in a city where they are what we in the south describe as scarce as hens' teeth. I saw him ask for a phone when he entered the restaurant and make a call prior to coming to the table.

"Excuse me, Jo. I didn't get a chance to tell you that I have invited two young friends of mine, who came with me to help drive, to join us for dinner. I hope you don't mind?" Actually I did very much as I wanted the evening for just the two of us, however he looked so haggard I hadn't the heart to say so.

"That's fine, Maurice, but I would like very much if tomorrow we could have for just us. I would hope that your friends would understand?"

"Of course. That's fine and I would like that too. I want to take you into Chianti to see some of the countryside and I want to take you shopping. After that, I have made reservations for us at the San Michele in Fiesole for dinner. I remember how much you loved it the day I took you for lunch, remember?"

"I do, very much so. It is fabulous and so very beautiful. The views from there are pretty spectacular as well." Reaching beside my chair I gave him the package Beth had so carefully wrapped. I wanted this done before his friends arrived.

"For me? From Kiki?" He looked at me with pleased surprise and carefully unwrapped the little green horse. His eyes met mine and I could see they were brimming with unshed tears. "She is such a love. How I have missed that child. Please thank her for me."

"I will." Reaching back beside my chair I handed him my own gift. Mine was a painting of a cherry tree with a dedicatory poem that I wrote to go with it. I wanted it to be something personal and special and I desperately hoped that he would treasure and appreciate them. I held my breath when I gave them to him and waited for his reaction. I felt as though I were standing before him nude to the core of my soul. He looked up and smiled into my eyes when he opened the painting and saw the poem, and wordlessly picked it up and began to read:

The Cherry Tree

Where once gray December chill

Scourged be-nuded branch and heart at will,

Be-petaled pink robe now flung high in air

Holds pellucid sunlight willing captive there.

Birded branches lift aloft their songs

---songs of nature's renewing,

---songs of skies a blueing,

As hopeful would be lover calls to ever-hopeful mate,

Little nests lie waiting high o'er the garden gate.

As with men on aging, the fading into white,

When weary little petals on some windy night,

Drift in downy blanket all about its girth,

Resting lightly, lightly on warming, greening earth.

"Why it's beautiful. I am so amazed. I had no idea that you write poetry. It is absolutely the perfect accompaniment to the painting which is just spectacular. They are wonderful, Jo. I'm going to hang the painting in my office and have the poem framed to hang beside it. Whenever I look at them, I will think of you and in my heart it will be springtime in that moment." He took my hand and kissed it. "Thank you so much. I will treasure them forever."

"I am so glad you like them. I wasn't sure if you would."

"Of course I do. How could you doubt for even a moment. Even if they weren't good, which of course they are, I would still love them because you did them for me."

We had ordered our meal and begun the first course by the time his two friends arrived. I found them totally non-descript and exceedingly quiet. Maurice and I continued to catch up on the months apart while they devoted their attention and ravenous appetites to the surprisingly good food. At the end of the meal, Maurice dropped me off at the Mediterraneo before returning to his own hotel with his two friends. I was glad to be finished with them for the remainder of our time together.

The next morning Maurice picked me up at the hotel and we crossed the Arno to drive into Tuscany by narrow country roads far from the autostrada. That was the day I fell in love with the Italian countryside. Every mellowed and shuttered villa I passed became the repository of a dream of me living there. The small hill top villages were like beads strung together by winding cedar-lined roads. Before the crest of every hill I found myself breathless in anticipation of the view beyond: the azure sky, the budding green of the spring verdure, ancient red tile-capped buildings and the gentle undulating hills bearing a blanket of vines and olives. I felt as though my soul had returned to the place of its ancient birth and I have never lost that sense of homecoming when I am there. Maurice seemed quieter and more introspective than ever before and for much of the drive, he left me in silent awe of my new found spiritual home. Lunch was in a small trattoria in Greve in Chianti where he order a ribollito served with crusty coarse peasant style bread, a simple salad of dressed arugula and a robust Montepulciano wine. Afterwards we wound our way back to Florence where he parked the car to take me shopping.

"I want to buy you a nice piece of luggage, Jo, as I noticed at Christmas that yours is becoming very worn." I knew that was an understatement.

"I know I can use it. Obviously in Florence with all of the leather stores we should be able to find something we like. I take the group to the piazza of Santa Croce where there are lots of leather outlets. We could go there."

"No, darling. I want to get you something really nice that you will keep and treasure and that will last you for many, many years. We're going to the Gucci store. My Gucci luggage is forty years old and it's till superb. Quality is worth the price."

He bought me a beautiful bag that is still handsome these many years later. When we left the store he took it from me to carry it to the car we had per force left some distance away. Much to my surprise, we had walked only a couple of blocks when he turned to hail a passing cab. I turned to look at him and could see that his face was almost gray with fatigue. It was a shock, as I had never seen him in such physical distress.

"Maurice, are you all right?"

He shrugged dismissively, "I'll be fine. I just need to take a nap before we go to dinner. I'll have the cab drop you off at your hotel and then I'll get my car. I'll come back for you at eight if that's suitable for you?"

"That's fine but if you don't feel well, we won't do it."

He patted my hand. "You're leaving tomorrow and our time together has been so short. It would break my heart to waste these last few hours. Just let me rest and I'll be fine. I've been too busy and stressed and the trip here was so long. I'm just really tired."

I walked into the hotel to find several members of my group in the lobby. I sank into a sofa beside Meg and ordered a glass of wine.

While I sipped, she filled me in on the day's events and their trip to Siena and San Gimigniano.

Wearing a beautifully tailored suit, yellow shirt and red and yellow tie, Maurice looked as handsome as I had ever seen him, and he had actually arrived on time to pick me up for the trip to Fiesole and the Villa San Michele. I was flattered that he had gone to the trouble to dress for this our last dinner together until summer. He had made reservations and we were immediately seated and soon enjoying a fabulous gourmet dinner. Afterwards we seated ourselves on a tawny leather sofa in the former refectory where a pianist was playing softly at the baby grand piano situated by the double French doors leading onto to the terrace. Maurice leaned back and closed his eyes while I soaked in the beauty of the room: the faded frescoes dating to the Renaissance, the tapestries and oriental carpets which gave richness, the cozy fire in the grating, and huge vases of artfully sprayed and draped flowers. When the pianist swung into a dance tune, I turned to Maurice with my feet already keeping time, "Do you think we could dance to this one?"

"I'm so sorry, Jo. I simply have no energy tonight. I really hate to end the evening early since it's months before we can be together again, but I simply must get to bed and rest before beginning the long trip back. I know you're leaving in the morning for your final day's excursion in Venice. That isn't much out of the way at all as I'm driving up to Campione D'Italia on the way home to take care of some business. I will try to join you tomorrow for lunch there. Do you think that's possible for you?"

"I'll make sure it is." When he returned me to the hotel, we arranged meeting in Venice at Florian's at noon the next day.

When the tour group arrived in Venice the following morning, the bus dropped us in the car park where we caught a water taxi for the vaporetto station near San Marco. I stood at the railing with my excited students pointing out the Ca D'Oro, Santa Maria Della Salute, the customs building, and the domes of San Marco. My art history students were proudly playing tour guide for those of the group who had not studied the history of the city as they had. I filled in gaps and made corrections absentmindedly while just basking in the early spring sun and the soft vaporous air of Venice. We landed at the quay and quickly made our way over the Bridge of Sighs to the Cathedral for the beginning of our tour with the local guide. Since I had some time to spare, I walked with them into the cathedral. As always, walking across the tiled floor I felt as though I walked on a sea of frozen waves due to the uneven subsiding into the underlying mud of the support piers on which the building, like all others in Venice, rested. I pointed out the beautiful ceiling mosaics to my group and admonished them to listen closely to the guide before making my way to Florian's.

It was just a short walk under the portico that surrounds the main pigeon and tourist jammed square to arrive at the famous bar. Since the day was cool, I eschewed the outdoor tables by the bandstand and decided to wait for Maurice at one of the small marble topped pedestal tables feeling as though I had stepped back a century in time. The waiter left me in peace when I explained that I was waiting for a gentleman to join me. After thirty minutes, I saw him walking purposefully toward me. "Signora, you have a telephone call at the desk from a gentleman named Maurice. I think it is you that he wishes?"

Surprised, I gasped, "Oh, yes. Thank you."

I picked up the phone and asked, "Maurice is that you? Where are you?"

"I am so sorry, Jo, darling. I am not going to be able to join you in Venice. Please forgive me and I will see you in June when you and Beth return for the summer."

He still sounded exhausted and I did not pry, as I knew it offended his pride not to be youthfully energetic. I thanked the waiter for his patience and apologized for not ordering. Maurice had promised me lunch at the Danieli's rooftop restaurant and I was simply going to have it by myself. I walked around the corner to the famous old hotel, created from a former palace, and took the small paneled elevator to the top floor. Emerging into a hall vestibule, I followed the beautiful runner to the glass doors of the restaurant and through them to the maitre d'.

"May I have a table for one please?"

"Of course, signora. Would you like inside or on the terrace? It's cool but the flowers in the boxes are very nice and you can see the water below."

"I think the one here by the open doorway is fine as it's a little cool for me outside."

I sat in an elegant French rococo style chair facing the terrace and admired the snowy white linen tablecloth covering a crisp yellow underlying one. Matching yellow napkins nestled in sparkling crystal goblets, a white and gold charger plate, heavy sterling place service, and a beautiful small bouquet of yellow roses in a vase made the table an elegant setting for the lunch I salivated for. I began with a simple light tomato soup followed by a beautiful shrimp salad. Determined to make it an occasion, I ordered tiramisu as well. As I sat waiting for dessert, I sipped the remaining soave that I had enjoyed with lunch. Suddenly a small bird flew in and perch on the chair beside me where Maurice should have been, and burst into song. I felt as though he had sent an emissary to keep me company as I sat there in the pellucid, liquid air of Venice watching light reflections dancing on the ceiling in echo of the water swirling in the famous watery main avenue below of this floating, jewel of a city. Despite the waiter's arrival with my dessert, the little bird did not abandon me, but merely hopped to a nearby chair to continue his serenade. I stayed until my wee friend flew away signaling an end to my lunchtime interlude and leaving me suddenly melancholy.

The group left very early in the morning after having hurriedly packed, grabbed a bag breakfast and trooped onto the bus only to sleep until the stop for coffee about two hours into the trip. I dashed in the AGIP and grabbed a cappucino for a much needed jolt of sugar and caffeine. It was another two hours to Malpensa where we bid the tour director goodbye, tipped both him and the superbly adroit bus driver who had constantly awed us with his skillful maneuvers, and trucked our baggage into check-in. When we arrived at security control the lines were long. I got all 38 of us in line and prepared to wait. By the time we reached the harried official it had become apparent to me that I had an ardent admirer in line behind my group. He was tall, maybe mid-fifties or so, and handsome with the chiseled Italian features I so admired. I smiled coquettishly at him and invited him, "Please, I have a large group. Would you like to go ahead of us?"

"Ah, no. This is fine. I will wait." He crossed his arms and smiled.

"If you're sure?" I smiled at him and continued checking in our group. I could feel his eyes on my back. The group was finally done and we proceeded to the gate where my Italian seated himself facing me. I caught him glancing at me constantly. I decided to browse the duty free shops while we were waiting. He followed me there too, and I laughed inwardly when back at the departure gate, they had to page him to return to the shop for the purchase he had forgotten. Once on the plane, I noticed that he was seated in the bulkhead two rows ahead of me on the far right of the plane, opposite my own seat about three rows back on the left. There were only two seats where he sat and the companion aisle seat was vacant. He kept turning to look at me but made no overtures.

The meal was served and he kept turning. Duty free shopping was completed and he kept turning. The movie came on and he kept turning. Finally I decided to take matters into my own hands. I stood up and crossed over to him.

"Excuse me, Signore. I am having difficulty viewing the movie from my seat. Would it be okay if I sat here?"

He turned on a two hundred watt smile and hastened to remove his book from the vacant seat. "Please, I would be so happy to have you join me."

I introduced myself and he asked about the group and why I was leading so many people. Explaining that I teach art history and painting and that I had taken my students and several adults on a tour of Italy, I asked him in return why he was going to the States.

Alessandro Mancini explained that he owned a capacitor manufacturing company in Bologna and was on his way to a trade show in Chicago. The preliminaries out of the way, we proceeded to talk non-stop for the remainder of the flight. He told me about his late wife who had died of Lou Gehrig's disease and how horrible it was to be trapped inside a body that no longer responded to the brain's commands. I had never really heard much about the disease and was fascinated by his explanation of the complications inherent to those who contract it. It wasn't all seriousness however, and I found myself more and more charmed by him. Alessandro was tall, handsome, fluent in several languages, well-traveled, and although fifteen or more years older than I, definitely still very appealing. He helped me with my Italian and when I thanked him for an enjoyable trip, corrected my pronunciation of 'grazie.' In typical American fashion, I was not pronouncing the final 'e' so essentially instead of saying "thanks," I was saying "thank." Exiting the plane in New York, I found to my chagrin that I had a colossal crick in my neck from constantly keeping my head turned to the left. I wondered if Alessandro had a corresponding one on the right side of his own neck. We parted just before immigration so I could collect my group, exchanging addresses and phone numbers when we did so. I thought to myself that I would probably never see him again but I gave him my number anyway.

I had barely entered the door and dropped my luggage in my bedroom, when the phone rang. Tired and not interested in talking to anyone, I let it ring. In an hour, just as I had tucked my weary body into bed, much to my annoyance, it rang again and persisted until in exasperation, I finally answered. "Hello." I knew I did not sound very pleasant.

"Ouch. That was a nasty hello. What's wrong with you?"

"Oh, Margot, it's you. Sorry, I didn't mean to snap your head off but I am so tired I just want to crash."

"I'm sorry, Jo. I'll know it's been a long trip and I won't talk long."

"I don't mean to be ungracious, but that'd be good. Besides we can always talk tomorrow. I'm going to take the day off. There is no way I can teach all day and then sit through the hour-or-more-long Monday faculty meeting. Plus I have to drive to Greenville tomorrow afternoon to get Beth so she only misses one day of school. Even though it was a good trip, keeping up with and keeping happy thirty-six tour participants is a big job, not to mention the lack of sleep and the long trip home...with a delay in New York of three hours."

"God. No wonder you're beat. Listen, just go to sleep and call me in the morning. Call me at the New York number, okay?"

"I'll do it." I fell back on my pillow and was asleep instantly.

When I stirred myself from bed at nine, I called Margot to see what was going on with her. From the tone of voice the night before, I knew she was unhappy about something and could only surmise that once again the situation with Tony had deteriorated.

"What's up?" I could tell from the tremble in her voice when she answered that the response would be grim.

"Well, we tried the marriage counselor or at least I did. That's not going to help since he refuses to go. I also think that his bitch daughter has been up to some shenanigans to further break us up." She paused and with a sigh continued, "I think she has promoted him to have an affair with her girlfriend's mother."

"Oh, no. Surely you can't believe that?"

"Oh, but I do. And I have proof. Someone told me that they saw them together being very cozy in this restaurant in San Francisco while he was supposed to be there on business. I asked him about it and I could tell he was lying. He didn't even bother to make up a good lie, just brushed me off with a lame excuse. I give up. I can't live this way. I stay so upset and he treats me like a child. Hell, I even get an allowance, a very tiny one and if I need more I have to justify it like making a business proposal. You'd think he was a pauper instead of a mega millionaire. I told you before that I have to borrow spending money from the maid, for Christ-sake. His brief generosity didn't last. He stays gone a lot and when he is home, we just fight."

"So, where do you go from here? Have you thought about it?"

"You'd better believe. I went to an attorney in New York and told him about what's going on and he agreed to represent me. It's no surprise to Tony since he told me he wants out." She laughed bitterly, "He did ask me to stay until after this big party he's planning for his daughter, Nina. He wants me to do the organizing and put on a nice hostess front. I suppose I will since I have nothing else to do, and maybe that gives me a bargaining chip with him."

I wondered how she would cope with a return to a non-celebrity life divested of the dreams and hopes of years. I knew she had enjoyed the glamour of the jet set life style, meeting famous people, living the life of the fabulously wealthy, and enjoying the perks: staying at the Ritz in Paris, a corporate jet stocked with Cristal Champagne and caviar, and a villa in Italy.

"I don't think that's going to be really pleasant considering that you will be co-existing under the same roof yet effectively considering yourselves separated. I don't know how you do that. All I can say is be careful, think about it long and hard, and if you can't be happy with this man, then get the hell out."

"My thinking precisely." Margot heaved a sigh. "It just makes me so sad, Jo. I really have loved him and I wanted so much to be happy with him. I don't know why we can't make it work if we both try. But then I know I've tried and I just can't see it happening. I dread being divorced and alone."

"Believe me I know about that. But being alone is not the same as being lonely. You don't need to be lonely, Margot. You've got Kat and me, you've got your friends, and you will meet new people as you make a new life for yourself. Actually being alone can be a positive thing as it gives you the chance to define who you are and what you want on your own terms, rather than building around the expectations of someone else. Yeah, you'll be lonely sometimes in the night when you want someone's arms around you, when you reach out for someone to share the joy of loving with you. But there will be others and maybe that special someone. Just believe in it and when you're down, call me. Come see me. I'm single too so I understand what it's like to be on your own. Besides we have fun, Babe."

"That's right, Kitty."

Chapter 13

Two weeks after my return from Italy, I arrived home from school to find a telegram stuck in the edge of my front door. Hastening inside I dropped my things on the

kitchen table and sank into a chair where I ripped it open, expecting a note from Maurice who hadn't called me since shortly after I had returned. He had phoned then to tell me that he had put my name on his bank account in Campione D'Italia so that if something should happen to him it would be there for us. I was totally unprepared to see that it was a message from his company informing me of his unexpected death from a massive heart attack. In stunned disbelief, I sat without moving.

Beth came in from school, took one look at my face and gasped, "Mommy, what's wrong?"

I looked up at her to speak but not a sound came from my open mouth. I just shook my head. She reached for the telegram and read it, not at first understanding the import. Then her eyes widened. "Oh, no. I am so sad. He was such a nice man and so good to us. I can't believe he's dead."

Finally it registered in my brain that it must be true. "I can't believe it either but it has to be. I have to call Marie. She must be out of her mind with grief."

"Poor old lady, he was all she had left."

I called Marie hoping that she had not yet gone to bed. I need not have worried as she hastened to assure me that she had been unable to sleep since his death. She sounded so distraught and fragile that I wondered if she would be able to survive for long without him. It was a difficult conversation as her English was much worse than previously and my French seemed to have left my head. However it also brought consolation for us both to share our loss with another who had loved him. I knew after hearing Marie describe how she heard him fall and went in to find him dead that there was no way the telegram was some strange hoax. Even so, for years afterward I dreamed that he was alive and had pretended to be dead for some reason that the dream kept hidden from me. I would search and search for the friend I had lost but not find him. It seemed so real that I would awaken momentarily confused until I could again compartmentalize in my mind, dream from reality. I still miss him.

We hung up and needing a cry, I walked out the back living room door and sat on the step leading from the deck to the ground. I wanted to cry and scream but I could do neither. So I just sat, repeating 'no, no, no' endlessly in my mind. The little bird at the Danieli restaurant kept flashing on the screen of my mind as though it had been Maurice telling me goodbye then, and now was repeating it a final time.

When I returned to the house, Beth was watching television and half-heartedly working on homework. We talked quietly and I offered my consolation, as I knew she regretted not always being nice to him. I suspected he had never realized that she had initially held such animosity, as she was generally too polite to express her negative feelings. It seemed to reassure her and relieve the remorse. I knew I should call Margot as well and let her know what had happened, but I couldn't do it then so I waited until the following day. She too was shocked but did not seem overly upset. But then their relationship had long since ended. I also called the office of the attorney in Marseilles that Maurice had told me to contact if he should die. Although he seemed very efficient and organized and well on his way to finalizing things for the estate, I did not trust him. Something in his voice told me that he would be no friend to me.

Margot called often in the coming weeks and her mood swung between optimistic about her coming divorce, to frustration with the daily struggle of continuing to live in the same house with a husband who had mentally moved on from their marriage. I commiserated, encouraged, and often laughed with her over the absurdity of her situation. She frequently expressed her gratitude for me being there for her. We were daily growing even closer and with her divorce would become even more so, as we once again shared many of the same struggles.

Tony's daughter's party went well, as Margot worked hard to coordinate and assist in the myriad of details that it entailed. At the same time it was a bittersweet triumph for her as it brought to finality the marriage to Tony that had by then already officially ended. She had seemed almost frightened at times but I couldn't persuade her to tell me why. Her only telling remark was that he had *high friends in low places*. However with her things already packed and shipping arranged, she made the move back to Miami several days after the wedding. With a portion of the proceeds from what had been a surprisingly generous settlement considering his parsimony during the marriage, Margot bought a lovely cottage on Sunset Island in Biscayne Bay. The next couple of months were spent in a flurry of renovation and decoration. As her first act of defiance she bought a new cream-colored Mercedes 560SL convertible. She laughed when she told me that when she was married to Tony he refused to drive, or have her drive, anything but American cars. Her second was to begin dating Xavier, a gorgeous younger man. With Tony's sensitivity about his age, I knew she would not resist calling him for a chat and letting that tidbit drop. When the house was finished she called me to come for a visit.

Since school was finished for the term and we would not be going to Europe, we loaded our things into my car at three in the morning and began the long drive to Miami Beach. What a hellacious trip that was. The fog became thick enough to slice and spread like jam by the time we reached Raleigh city limits. For the next three hours I drove in a cold sweat with my nose pressed on the windshield. Rather than instantly going back to sleep, Beth was perched on the edge of her seat helping me creep our way through the murk. When it finally cleared, I pulled into a neon-glaring diner and ordered coffee and a light breakfast. We were both already exhausted from the hours of nervous tension but with Miami many hours away, we couldn't linger. Things went fairly well after that until we hit nightmare traffic in a construction zone just before the bridge in Jacksonville. I nearly missed my turn, managing to dart over just in time, creating a cacophony of horns in my wake. Once past Jacksonville, things smoothed out again until we reached the northern perimeter of the Palm Beach area. Again construction snarls that reached nearly to the Interstate 195 turn to Miami Beach had me cursing 95 and regretting that I had not taken the Turnpike at Stuart.

"Shit. The assholes won't let me over." I raged at the cars that kept crowding me on all sides. Instantly I was chagrined at the less than exemplary vocabulary I had just used in front of my daughter. "I'm sorry, baby. I shouldn't talk that way I know, but I am just about out of patience and totally exhausted. It's been a long day, hasn't it?"

"I know, mommy. I'm tired too and these drivers are so rude it makes me mad just like you."

With an aggressive I'll-show-you swing into the turn lane and Beth cheering me on with a "Go, Mommy!" we made the interstate over to the beach. Just over the causeway, I veered right onto Alton Road and was shortly at the entry gate to the first two Sunset Islands. I drove slowly so we could appreciate the grand houses, lush tropical trees and colorful flowers that graced the beautiful estates lining both sides of the street. Crossing the bridge to Sunset II, I pointed to the contemporary white house on the right that Margot had told me to watch for. It was being used in the filming of Miami Vice. Beth squealed with excitement as she craned her head in hopes of spotting Don Johnson. I could tell she was going to love our mini vacation on Aunt Margot's island. Swinging to the right after crossing the bridge we quickly arrived at Margot's drive. On the side away from the bay, the house was screened from the road by massive hedges of hibiscus and a row of Royal Palms. I pulled into the drive paved with old bricks of a soft dusty pink hue to find Margot standing there watching for us while she pinched faded flowers from the border around the front of the house. She ran to the car and was pulling open my door when it stopped.

Grabbing me in a bear hug, she gasped, "God, Jo. You told me you would be here by four but I didn't believe you could do it. You and Beth look exhausted. Let's get your bags inside and get you settled." She ran to Beth's side of the car and gave her a resounding kiss before helping me carry the luggage into her house.

Crossing the mellow terra cotta tiled floor, I was immediately struck by the open cheerful decor. Soft pinks, greens and creams in the upholstery were washed by the tropical light flooding in from French doors that opened onto a terraced pool area with a lush backdrop of a multitude of colorful blooming flowers and verdant foliage. At the end of the entryway, separated from living room by a banister and just to the left of the French doors, was the spectacular art deco stained glass windows that Maurice had salvaged from his family home and given her while they were dating. There were six of them total, three across and two deep in varying shades of greens, pinks, creams, yellows, blues and lavenders. In Beth's absence, we would jokingly begin to refer to them as the 'penis windows' due to the highly suggestive motif in the center of each of the six panels. On the large brass and glass coffee table she had carefully arranged a massive display of fresh flowers in honor of our arrival.

"I had the window built in and special lighting installed so at night it's backlit. During the day, sunlight keeps it lit up." Surveying the room, she remarked, "The house once belonged to Gloria Swanson. I fell in love with it the minute I saw it. It's not too big and it didn't take that much renovation to make it perfect for me. Come on and let me show you the rest of the house and where you'll sleep." Leading from the raised area that extended across the front of the living room, we entered a corridor and turned right into a cheerful den containing built in bookshelves, a television, a daybed decorated in rusty rose and piled high with pillows in front of rose and green print draped double windows, and more French doors leading to the right side yard.

"Beth, I thought you might like to sleep here since except for the living room, this is the only television that I have right now. Is it okay?"

"Aunt Margot, I love it. It's so pretty. And you put flowers in here for me, too."

"Of course I did, Kitty." She hugged her again. "Good. That's settled. And since your mother and I are going to laugh and giggle half the night, I'm putting her in my room with me." I wasn't surprised as whenever we stayed together, we always ended up in the same bed talking until we fell asleep. We walked to the left end of the corridor and entered her room, done in soft pink and white-striped wallpaper with festooned border. The queen-sized Italian walnut bed was covered in a white sprigged cover of pink roses and pale green leaves. Opposite the bed on the near wall was a matching dresser centered with an ornate rococo mirror. The immediate right wall contained a massive armoire. The back wall was centered by another set of sheer draped French doors opening onto the pool and barbecue area. Just pass the armoire a door led into a mirror and marble confection of a bath. I paused to admire the beautiful Lalique perfume bottles arranged on an ornate mirrored brass tray that coordinated with the gold toned fixtures.

"Look, Jo. Don't you just love these towels?"

Looking where she pointed, I fingered the scalloped pink embroidered edge of the snowy white Pratesi towels. "They're gorgeous. You know this is a deliciously feminine house. It's obvious you decorated it to be your own private haven. It's luxurious but it has an airy, informal feel at the same time. I just love it. If you're not careful, we'll move in."

Laughing, she took my arm. "That's fine with me, move on down. Come on and I'll show ya'll the other side of the house."

Retracing our steps, we crossed the living room area and through an arch, entered the dining room featuring a glass top table centered by a large Lalique bowl and supported by two huge shells made of a pickled-blond wood. The matching chair backs with the same shell motif at the top were upholstered in a slubbed white silk. On the far wall, two built-in sconces, featuring the same wood and a shell motif at the top, angled the corners on either side of a large window. I walked over to admire the Lalique sculptures and crystal champagne goblets she had placed in the sconces.

"So how do you like my Lalique? Those were all wedding gifts. At least I got to keep them." She grinned at me. "I more than earned them."

"I don't blame you. I'd want to keep 'em, too. They're fabulous."

"Okay, next the kitchen. It's my pride and joy." Turning to her left, she stood back so we could enter ahead of her.

The kitchen featured a center island with a wooden chopping block surface and a small prep sink in the far end. Over it she had hung a pot rack filled with carefully scrubbed and shined cookware. Pride of place went to a commercial sized Wolf range. Knowing how much she loved to cook, I wasn't surprised. The walls were covered in decorative food motif tiles imported from Provençe. The cabinets and refrigerator were paneled in the same wood used in the dining room.

"I love this room. It's the way I always wanted my kitchen to be. With two sinks to work at, lots of counter tops, and custom designed drawers it's so easy to cook and entertain. The arch leading to the living room means I can see what's happening around me while I'm in the kitchen. Not that it matters, as sooner or later everyone ends up in here with me anyway."

"You know, I think that's a universal truth: everyone wants to be in the kitchen to see what's happening. This center isle makes a great serving area and a bar for people to stand around while you're cooking. Have you entertained yet?"

"Better believe! I've had three dinner parties already, plus come mealtime I seem to have adopted all the stray kids in the neighborhood. I don't think any of them have mothers who cook. Just call me Auntie Mame." Beth and I both laughed with her. Knowing how much she loved people and how very charismatic she was, it was no surprise that people were already gravitating to her door.

"Okay, through here we have the guest rooms. You're family so you can't stay over here. You have to stay with me."

"That suits us. Besides this is too far away to talk."

We entered another short corridor off the kitchen that completed the 'U' shape of the house. On the right was a yellow, coral and green floral patterned bedroom and at the end of the corridor, one done in green and white. Between the two, on the left side of the hall, was a bath for the guest rooms that also served as a powder room when she entertained.

"Did you see my portrait in the living room over the fireplace?"

"I did. It's spectacular. When did you have it done?" We walked back to the living room and stood in front of the five by four foot canvas showing Margot holding Perky, her Yorkie, currently sleeping on the sofa and ignoring the new arrivals.

"Michael Volbrecht did it for me. He designed a lot of the gowns that I wore to various functions when Tony and I were married and he wanted to do this. It really is pretty sensational."

"Boy, you can say that again. That vibrant pink background that picks up the colors you have used in the room really looks great in here."

"That's why I used these colors. Now, enough 'house' already. How about a glass of French champagne for you; and Beth, would you like some 'American Champagne'? Somebody told me you really like it."

"Great."

"I'll echo that. I could use some wine and a chance to unwind. It was a bitch of a trip."

"Well, you're here now and we're going to play. I thought tonight I'd make a simple dinner for just us. Tomorrow, my friend Javier is going to come by and take Beth to the beach while you and I go grocery shopping. I've invited him and a couple of other people to come to dinner tomorrow night. After that, we'll play it by ear."

"Suits me. Now pour that champagne."

"Got it, girlfriend. Coming right up."

Perky who was as dumb as a brick but passionately loved by Margot, moved off the sofa when I settle into the down stuffed pillows with a heart-felt sigh. Beth snuggled beside me as we waited for Margot to serve us drinks and a pre-dinner nibble.

It felt great to be with her in her new home and to enjoy once again her happy spirit and familiar vibrant exuberance for life. I wondered if she had really adjusted so easily and joyfully to her single status as she seemed to have done on first inspection. I suspected she would open up and really talk at some point during our visit. If she did not, that too would tell something about her state. Dinner was delicious, as Margot during her marriage to Tony had evolved into a gifted cook. The braciole made of veal scaloppini stuffed with Parmesan cheese and herbs cooked in a succulent tomato sauce, were a hit with both Beth and me. Margot had learned the recipe from Tony's mother while staying at his Tuscan villa. The red wine, crisp baguettes and fresh arugula salad were perfect accompaniments. After dinner, Beth retired to the den to watch television prior to falling asleep. Margot and I cleaned the kitchen and went to her room where I stowed my things while she showered. Afterwards I did my nightly ablutions and we ensconced ourselves in her bed for a typical long night chat. Perky snuggled between us, obviously annoyed that I had usurped her spot. We talked and laughed until nearly two in the morning but never really touched on her divorce and the pain that she carried as a consequence. Finally I drifted into sleep while she was still talking. For me it had been an extremely long day.

Unfortunately it wasn't to be an uneventful and restful night. Perhaps an hour or so after drifting to sleep, I awakened feeling that something wasn't right. I could smell a nasty odor that in my befuddled state I could not immediately place. I felt Perky's weight pinning my hair uncomfortably. Reaching up to fluff it on my pillow I felt something damp and sticky. With shock I realized that I had stuck my hand into what could only be feces.

"Margot. Wake up and turn on the light. I think we have a

problem here."

"What?" She mumbled but didn't move.

"Wake up. Something's wrong."

With a groan she rolled over and flicked on the bedside lamp.

"Oh, my God. Margot, Perky has had diarrhea all over my hair, my pillow and this bed."

"Shit. It's all over me too, and look it's on the floor and all the way into the bathroom."

"Yeah, shit's right." Disgusted with the mess, we climbed out of bed. While she washed the dog, I stripped the bed and got things to the laundry room. Margot finished with the dog and mopped the floor. We then took turns showering and washing our hair. By the time the three of us were clean, Perky was ready to snuggle happily back to sleep on the now stripped bed, I was reluctant to join her after the recent fiasco, and Margot was wide-awake.

"Tell you what, Jo. I'll go make us a cup of coffee and some breakfast. It's after six and the room is so bright from the sun I'll never get back to sleep. We might as well get up."

Wearily I responded. "Yeah, we might as well. I'm too worked up to sleep anyway. Besides, we have a bunch of stuff to do today and your friend will be here for Beth at nine." I put on my robe and continued, "You start the coffee and I'll get the washing machine going. The towels, sheets, bedspread and mattress cover all have to be washed. Not to mention, our nightgowns. What a night, Sis."

"You can say that again. I'm afraid Perky has a nervous stomach. It really is a problem at times. I'm just sorry this one was such a big mess."

"Oh, well. Hopefully she is so empty we won't have a repeat performance for at least a little while." I commented wryly. At that point, that dog was definitely on my 'shit' list, no pun intended. I thought murder might be appropriate.

The smell of bacon reached Beth's room and she emerged, bright-eyed and eager for the day at the beach even though the idea of going with a stranger was a bit un-nerving to her. That was quickly put to rest when Javier rang the doorbell. One look at him and she had a healthy crush. I had to admit to myself that he was a one fine hunk of man. Dirty blond hair, eyes as blue as a noonday sky, perfect features, and an athlete's trim and muscular body certainly made for a fine package. I could see why Margot was enjoying the fling with him following marriage to a man so much her senior and not the most handsome around. Javier was not only a handsome man as I quickly realized, but a charming one as well. He had arrived with a bouquet of roses for each of us and a collection of compliments that would have done the best of sycophants proud. Yet he managed to make every trite phrase into a seemingly earnest paean of praise for each of us in turn. Unaccustomed to such Latin gallantry, Beth was mesmerized and I wasn't far behind. I caught Margot's eye and grinned. I knew by the sardonic lift of her eyebrow she wasn't surprised at his elaborate introduction of himself to us. Javier joined us for breakfast and chided us about the excursion to the beach with Beth while we escaped to look for a better boyfriend. His ego seemed secure enough that I didn't think he was too seriously worried about being abandoned.

He and Beth left after we ate, and Margot and I cleaned the kitchen and readied ourselves for the day. She told me to dress nicely as she was treating me to lunch at Carpaccio, her favorite restaurant in Bal Harbour, prior to grocery shopping for our evening's dinner with her friends. In nice dresses and heels and our hair swept up, we were ready for the elegant shopping center about which she had told me so much. I was eager to see all of the exclusive designer shops and drool over the fabulously expensive merchandise. I knew it was beyond my means to buy, but looking is exceedingly cost effective.

I loved climbing into the Mercedes convertible and speeding along Alton Road to the juncture with Collins Ave. and from there to Ninety Sixth Street and the entrance to Bal Harbour. The wind, blowing from the water kept the temperature perfect, and made the palms in the front parking area rustle and sway. We quickly found a parking space and sauntered into the mall itself. Entering the Neiman

Marcus store, I felt like a princess in shopper's dreamland. We walked from there all the way down the open air central mall to the Saks store at the opposite end, passing Cartier, Fendi, Bulgari, St. Johns, Pratesi, Charles Jourdan and numerous other designer boutiques. Not only were the shop windows gorgeously arrayed, but also the walk itself was beautiful with tropical flowers, palms, lush green plants I couldn't name, and splashing fountains. Happy just to look, we wandered in and out of the shops without buying anything. Margot was delighted at how thrilled I was and seeing it through my eyes, she was soon sparkling with excitement, too.

We walked back to mid-mall and entered Carpaccio's where the maitre d' all but sang with joy at seeing her. Obviously she was a well-liked frequenter of the restaurant. We were quickly seated at a prime table much to the annoyance of a line of frustrated would-be diners who were still awaiting a seat. Margot remarked that locals were generally given preference as the restaurant knew that they would be returning customers unlike tourists who came once just to see and gawk at the frequent celebrities. She had also slipped him a tip, a useful habit I had seen Maurice employ to similar good effect. Metaphorically pulling the daggers from my back, I relaxed and picked up the menu.

We had just ordered our Spaghetti a la Vongole when Margot looked up and muttered, "Oh, shit. Don't look now but a neighbor just walked in and seems to be heading our way."

Sure enough, "Hello, Margot. Gosh, I'm so glad I ran in to you. I don't have a reservation and they are reluctant to seat just one person with so many waiting. Since you have an extra chair do you mind if I join you?"

"Please, do. Marlene, let me introduce you to my sister, Jo, who's visiting me for a few days."

Marlene sat beside me, and immediately surveyed herself in the mirror that spanned the wall behind Margot. From then until the end of lunch she seemed mesmerized by her image rarely looking away when she spoke to us or we to her. I could tell there was an avid love affair going on between Marlene and the reflected Marlene. She was a strikingly beautiful woman of that mature age that is hard to guess, curvaceous but slim figure shown to advantage by a low-cut form hugging orange slubbed silk sheath, shoulder length blond hair, powder blue eyes and perfect features. I knew it cost a fortune to look like that and continue looking that way. Although she obviously wasn't stupid, her intellectual side was well concealed by the depth of absorption with herself. I was quickly bored and spent most of the lunch enjoying my food and watching the busy restaurant. With a jerk I stopped woolgathering, when Margot sharply nudged me with her toe. "What?"

"Jo, Marlene is going to make a cake for our neighbor whose wife just died and she wants me to go with her tomorrow night to offer her condolences. I don't have a thing to wear for a funeral occasion, so I guess we should pay our tab and look for something in Saks."

"Don't do that. I've got a dress with me that is conservative enough and I'm sure it will fit you, so why not use it?" Belatedly I realized that I had missed her cue to say we needed to leave to dress shop, however she recovered nicely.

"Great. That makes it easier as we still have a lot to do between now and seven."

Margot, with much relief paid the tab and we were on our way. On the ride to her grocery at the south end of the beach, she filled me in on Marlene's history. We both laughed at the obvious ploy of taking a cake to the new and fabulously wealthy widower. "I guess she's ready to be purchased by husband number six," Margot cracked wickedly.

Epicure, which Margot had quickly nicknamed "Epi-screw" or occasionally "Gyp-pidys" for their exorbitant prices, had some of the most gorgeous produce, breads, wines, flowers and meats I had ever seen. My favorite counter though was the cheese. What a fabulous array of the best from every corner of the world. I could see why, despite the prices, she shopped there: if you get the best, you pay for it. We left with the trunk of the car loaded with groceries, things I was joyfully anticipating trying, as many were then unavailable in Raleigh.

On the way home she detoured to show me Sunset Islands III and IV, just as the other two they were a testament to "the life style of the rich and famous." We talked too.

"Don't you think Javier is a bit much of a change from your ex-husband? Compared to him, Javier is a baby. But such a pretty one," I teased.

"That he is; that he is. I do like my Javier-cito even though I must say he's a spoiled brat. It's a nice change to be with a man who's young, lusty and gorgeous after dealing with a man our parents' age." She glanced over at me, "So...who's the man in your life now? You've been mighty quiet about that topic for a long time now."

I snorted, "Ha! After Ed, I decided I've had enough of men for a while."

"God, Jo, don't tell me you're turning into a nun."

"Not a nun, a 'none'." Laughing with her, I remarked, "I did meet a nice Italian guy on the plane coming back from my spring trip. He's written me a couple of times and called, too."

"Hmm, sounds interesting. You're going to have to tell me some more about this one."

"There isn't much more to tell at the moment." I explained how we had met and we laughed when I told her about him following me in the airport and forgetting his package.

"So don't you get 'wolfy' from time to time and just kind of want to date someone?"

"All right, smarty. I'm going to tell you like a told my smarmy divorce attorney who wanted to know how I was going to take care of my needs since I was divorcing...implying of course that he could assist me with it. I looked him in the eye and said 'don't worry about it, if worse comes to worse, I'm sure I can take matters into my own hands.'"

"That's rich. He must have nearly fainted."

"I don't know about that, but he surely didn't volunteer anymore services in that department." We both howled with laughter. It felt so good to be with her and share girl talk and just be silly together.

Suddenly Margot swerved to the curb and stopped the car beside a hedge bordering a magnificent estate.

"Why are we stopping here?"

"Look at that!" She pointed to a heavily fruited key lime tree.

"So????"

"So, I want some."

"I suppose you plan on ringing the door bell and asking if you can have some key limes from their nice tree?" I remarked sarcastically.

"Nope. We're going to crawl through the hedge and pick up the ones on the ground after we pick up the ones on this side." She waggled her eyebrows at me, "You game?"

"I can't believe we're doing this. Here we are dressed to the nines in a fancy Mercedes and we're going to crawl through a hedge on hands and knees and steal key limes."

"You got it girl. Come on."

So I did. We gathered all the limes along the curbside that we could and dumped them in the back of the car behind our seats. Then with a sigh, I gather my skirt to make a basket and followed her rump as she eeled through the hedge to gather as many as we could reach. Giggling like bad children, we did a reverse fanny wiggle, dumped our booty into the car and sped away. Back at the house, I surveyed our dirty knees and stained skirts but could not help but laugh at the fun we had. She was good for me as her spontaneity and zest took me out of my overly proper shell and let me play. And we had at least a bushel of key limes.

"I know: we'll make key lime pie for dessert tonight, use some in drinks and then we can squeeze the rest and freeze the juice. I make a good pie and I love it. Why don't you juice the rest for me?" Margot washed the ones she needed for the pie while I worked on the remainder. The door slammed as we began.

"Hi, Mom! Hi, Aunt Peggy! Y'all come see what Javier bought me. It's gorgeous."

"Come in here, Kitty. Your mom's knee deep in lime juice, and I'm gooey with pie crust."

Beth waltzed into the kitchen followed by Javier who was grinning like a kid himself, obviously pleased with his day babysitting her. Margot had told me that he was from a large family and adored children. Because his family lived in Lima, he did not get the chance to see his younger brothers and sisters as often as he would have liked, so Beth was a pleasant surrogate for him to enjoy spoiling. And that he had. Not only was her nose sprinkled with freckles from the time on the beach, but also her arms were full of packages that she was soon dropping on the floor and opening. He had found a cute tee shirt that was a perfect one for the beach, a gorgeous beach towel and the most exciting thing of all for Beth, a bright turquoise blue bikini.

I smiled at her excitement. "It looks to me like you made out like a bandit. Did you spend all of poor Javier's money?"

"Of course not. He told me he has lots of it and to get anything I wanted." She turned to Javier, "You wanted me to get even more, right?"

"That I did. She wouldn't though. I must say you have a charming and very well-mannered daughter. We had a wonderful time at the beach and a great lunch at a little cafe there. You girls should have come with us, too."

"Thank you so much for taking such good care of her and buying her the presents. That was more than kind of you." He wasn't paying me much attention at that point as he had Margot, juice covered hands and all, backed against the kitchen counter and wrapped in a passionate embrace.

"Are you making me a pie, Mommy?" I could tell Margot wanted to kill him for that little sally. He laughed at her expression then kissed away the danger of a sassy retort. Beth giggled.

Soon we had dinner underway, drinks and hors d'oeuvres ready, and her friends ringing the doorbell. It was a fun evening and a joy for me to meet her friends and see that they adored her and kept her busy and happily involved in their circle. Having things to do, fun people to be with, and a gorgeous man to romance her seemed a pretty good prescription for transitioning into a new life.

The three weeks with Margot were a whirlwind of activity from dinners at her house for her circle of friends, shopping for odds and ends and just hanging out together and catching up with one another's lives. Beth spent countless happy hours splashing in the pool and playing with Perky. Javier was a frequent visitor but I could tell from Margot's increasing coolness towards him that his immaturity was beginning to wear on her. Although he was an attractive male package, he seemed far happier and more in his element splashing around in the pool with my twelve year old. Margot didn't say a great deal about it, but from time to time, would allude to the drive and ambition that she had so admired in Tony and obviously found lacking in Javier.

I also found it disturbing that she always introduced herself as "Margot Marconetti, as in Mrs. Tony Marconetti." She obviously was unable to relinquish the reflected glory of his celebrity. I could not help but wonder how any new man in her life would accept the notion that she still tied herself so securely to that period of her life and to the name of her former husband. I suppose it didn't help either that Tony called constantly to tell her of his frustrations with the current woman in his life and his inability to live without one. Whether he was serious or not, he also frequently begged her to come back to him and start anew. A part of her dreamed of that, however at the time that it was still a possibility, she was too mindful of the pain of their time together and too delighted with new prospects that the money from their divorce settlement brought her to live independently and well. Even so, she told me that he remarked at the settlement meeting that he would see to it her life was ruined. She shuddered when she told me and I knew it not only had hurt, but she worried about it. Later when she was more interested in returning to him, he had moved on with his life and was no longer interested in trying to find a new relationship with her.

As we lay in bed each night talking into the wee hours, I began to realize just how painfully bitter her marriage and divorce had been for her. In some ways she was a bit like the college athlete who achieves great acclaim for a few brief years and then returns to the relative obscurity of the everyday world. She had rubbed elbows with the rich and famous, traveled in a private jet to the most posh of destinations, been fêted at the White House and blessed by the Pope. Those who had delighted to know her when she was married had now decamped and she was left to make new friends. She had become just another wealthy divorcee in Miami Beach who filled her days with lunches, friends, shopping and the social affairs of the various charities to which they aligned themselves. Because of her flair and personality, she had already been named one of the ten best dressed in Miami and featured on the cover of a local-scene magazine. That bit of acclaim helped, however it was insignificant to her following the life she had led with Tony. Margot had been seduced by the glamour of a life that she craved on one hand, but was spurned by the life she most needed: adored wife and mother. She was basically domestic. Whereas I had never craved motherhood, she hungered for it. Nothing made her happier than puttering around the house, arranging flowers, cooking dinner and entertaining. She could have been a wonderful wife for him had their mutual egos not warred, but Margot like he, had to be the center of her universe...a universe that only acknowledged one center.

I was so admiring and in some ways so envious of all she had that I felt I lacked: the out-going personality of one who had never met a stranger, the stunning beauty, the stylishly dramatic aura, the now considerable wealth, the social panache, the decorator showcase home in Miami Beach, and the life of the idle rich. My less stunning looks, schoolteacher life style and socially shy nature were a strong contrast. I wasn't unhappy that she had attained the things that she enjoyed, I even celebrated them with her, but deep down inside I accepted and mourned the lack of them in my own life. I found myself both needful of being a moon circling in her orbit and frustrated by the squelching of my own needs and personality to her more dominant one.

Beth was no more ready to leave than I; and Margot was begging us to stay, however I had to return to Raleigh and discover what was transpiring with the lawyer in Marseilles that I had contacted about Maurice's estate. The first order of business once home was to go through my mail to see if he had written. While there were a number of letter's from Alessandro, there was nothing from the attorney. Provoked, I waited until the next day and called. I could tell he was stalling and really wanted me to just disappear, however I was determined to follow through on Maurice's instructions to me. During the course of his conversation it occurred to me that I really needed an attorney to represent me. This man was cold enough to urinate icicles and far too reluctant to answer questions.

Through personal contacts I was able to procure the name of an American attorney practicing in Paris. Immediately when I hung up with Maître Tillier, I called the number of the firm in Paris for which Kirk Van Reeves worked, and was promptly connected. I explained the particulars of my case and resolved that he would tentatively represent me. He was actually just on the way to New York to visit with his mother and we arranged to have a preliminary meeting there. The next order of business was to call the airlines and arrange for a day trip to New York. Not knowing what further expenses I might incur, I didn't want to waste limited funds on hotels and restaurants.

The apartment where we met was on the lower eastside of Manhattan. It was a swelteringly hot June day and by the time that my un-air conditioned taxi deposited me in a puddle at the front door, my dress and I had both wilted. I took a rueful glance at myself in the smoked glass door of the vestibule while I mopped my face and straightened my chignon hairdo as best I could. Steeling my resolve to go forward bravely to meet this attorney who would decide to a large extent my financial fate, I asked the doorman to buzz his mother's apartment. The walnut paneled elevator emitted a gentile hum as it whisked me upward to eject me into the marble tiled foyer of Mrs. Reeves's apartment. Judging from the faded oriental carpets, muted wallpaper, original oils of previous centuries and what looked to be museum quality antiques, it was apparent that the attorney had likely been the product of a prosperous and cultured childhood.

He was tall and while not typically good-looking there was a definite aura of strong masculinity about him that exuded a sexual energy. Both his mother and he greeted me warmly as they led me to a fragile Louis XIV chair. I perched warily while discretely surveying the past elegance of the beautiful salon. Mrs. Reeves chatted while her son placed a phone call to a nearby restaurant to procure a reservation for the three of us. When he turned back to me, she gracefully excused herself. It was time to talk business. I handed him the telegrams and letters that Maurice had given me instructing what to do in the event of his death, including the name of Maitre Tillier and the bank in Campione d'Italia as evidence. He read them all intently, occasionally frowning. Finished, he pondered for some minutes in silence. I began to fidget with anxiety for fear he would tell me that I could do nothing to procure the inheritance Maurice had left me. Despite the coolness of the room, I could feel perspiration springing out on my face. Damn, I thought, I've wasted several hundred dollars to get here; just about melted to death, and it will all be for nothing.

Looking up at me, he studied me for several anxiety provoking minutes before quietly remarking, "I think you have a good case here, but there are some real caveats in French law that will impact you. Primarily, since you are not family, you cannot inherit the full estate if there is surviving family and the will is contested. His mother, who is apparently still living judging from the content of the letters, is entitled to a substantial portion. Under French law she cannot be excluded from the will in favor of a non-family heir without her consent. I also don't know what outstanding financial obligations the estate may have incurred. It is complicated by the fact that such Swiss accounts, while common in Europe, are in effect illegal. We will have to handle this discretely in Switzerland, not in France. I'll do my best for you to get as much as I can. You need to anticipate a trip to Switzerland when we get to the finalization stage of any settlement.

Now, let's collect my mother and have lunch. The restaurant is one of my favorites in New York and I always go there when I'm here. I think you'll like it too."

"Thank you for inviting me. I don't know anything here and since it's almost two, I'm getting hungry."

"Good. So am I. You have enough time before your flight that it will not be a problem?"

"I do. I made my return for seven so I'll have plenty of time to get to the airport and check in."

Lunch was as good as he had promised and the conversation relaxed. I began to regain inner calm and to enjoy myself. I could tell that he liked me and judging from several surreptitious glances, I began to think he admired my looks as well. He poured a glass of excellent wine and toasted to the three of us meeting and the success of our venture. It was a pleasure to drink to that.

Chapter 14

Van called and wrote over the coming weeks to keep me up to date with progress. It was apparent from his remarks that he was finding the Maitre no more helpful than had I. Furthermore, time would prove to us both that he was actively working with Maurice's hated cousin, Christian, to thwart my interests. I also received frequent letters from Alessandro as well as numerous postcards from his various business trips. He repeatedly asked when I would return to Europe. Other than what had become a springtime tradition I had no other plans. That would change however in early August when Van called to tell me that he had negotiated a deal on Maurice's estate and I would need to fly to Lugano, Switzerland and then back to Paris for finalization of the documents.

Not long after I replied to a letter from Alessandro, mentioning that I would be coming to Lugano in early October, he called excited that I was returning before spring and asked if he could visit in Lugano, not a terribly long drive from Bologna. On a whim, I said "sure." Although we had enjoyed one another on the plane trip and I had looked forward to his frequent letters and cards and occasional phone calls, it seemed futile to seriously pursue a relationship with someone so imminently 'geographically undesirable'. But then, I had no other flirtation in my life and it seemed relatively harmless.

Margot wasted no time teasing me about him when I called her to tell her about the upcoming trip. She was as happy and upbeat as I had heard her in years and I could not help rejoicing that she seemed to be moving in a more positive direction for her life. Javier had moved on and she had begun seeing an older man who adored her and spoiled her in a thousand ways from small kindnesses to extravagant gifts. According to her version it was more of a platonic affair than a grand romance, but he showed her a good time and helped to compensate for the time in her marriage when she had felt so undervalued.

"I *miss* you, Jo. When are you coming back for a visit? We single girls have to stick together, you know. Besides I want to see Beth, too."

"Babe, I can't just leave school; nor can Beth. Then I have to take a week in October to go to Switzerland."

"So? Come for Thanksgiving?"

"Okay. Great. I would love to come and Beth is going to be thrilled. I'll play hooky and leave a day early and be there on Wednesday. If we leave right after school, I can get as far as Jacksonville, spend the night, get up early and be at your house by noon. I'll have to leave early on Sunday though in order to drive home and get us back to school on Monday."

"Super. That's a promise and I'm counting on it."

"There's just one caveat. Daddy doesn't look well and I'm worried about him. You may want to think about coming home to see them at Thanksgiving or Christmas."

"Oh, God. I know I should, but I am just not into that right now. I really hate to face them and have to admit I made a mistake marrying Tony, knowing how much they were against it along."

"Margot, you know they know and they don't care. They just want you to be happy."

"I know, I know. I'll think about it. I really do need to see them."

I stayed busy over the coming weeks with the beginning of school and communicating with Van, Alessandro, and Margot who increasingly consumed hours of my time on the phone. I knew she was lonely and because I too was single and lonely, she felt a strong bond with me. Not only were we sisters, but we were fast becoming best friends who could share anything. She told me that although she did not regret leaving Tony, she still missed and loved him. I heard the wistfulness in her voice when she talked of him and the glory of the good days that they had had: the people they met, the places they went, and the glamour of it all. I worried that she was romanticizing the relationship to the point of excluding much of the grim reality and feared that very process would keep her trapped in the past.

In mid-August I had driven to Greenville to see my parents and was alarmed at my father's pallor and lack of energy. He had had some cancerous tumors removed from his intestines but the doctor thought that he would be fine. I wasn't so sure and I particularly did not want him to content himself with the opinion of the local doctors when there are so many fine facilities in the area around Raleigh. Despite my urging to seek an alternative diagnosis, I was ignored. I suppose as much as anything, they just couldn't face the ordeal of going out of town for possible treatment. During the following days, my parents apparently reassessed my father's lack of progress and were willing to go to Duke if I would drive to Greenville and take them.

The diagnosis was grim. Daddy had Hodgkin's Lymphoma in an advance stage. Because of his weakened condition, chemotherapy was not an option. They gave him months to live at best. I dreaded having to leave them even for the few days in October when I must go to Lugano, not knowing what I would find on my return or even if he could survive that long. As it was, following his return from Duke he went into an immediate and irreversible decline. I called Margot and told her that daddy was dying and it could not be long. It wasn't. By the time she booked tickets and arrived in Greenville, she was just in time to spend the last few minutes of his life with him, holding his hand and telling him how much she loved him.

Mama was exhausted, having sat by his bedside for a week and leaving only to eat or go to the bathroom. Whenever she tried to lie down, he would call for her and wearily she would resume her vigil at his bedside. The last name that he called was Beth's. She was so heartbroken at losing the man that had truly been like a father for her that she could not see him. He died with her name on his lips.

Margot left immediately after the funeral to return to Miami Beach. She had never given in to her grief that I knew had to be considerable as she had always been our father's favorite. I wondered what adding a new layer of sadness on top of the other unresolved ones: mourning for her marriage and the loss of Tony, would do to her. I didn't realize it at the time, but she would now turn to a new friend, Vodka.

Saddened by the loss of my father with whom I had finally established a forgiving peace, I left for Lugano. Van met me there at two o'clock on Friday afternoon and in a harrowing three-hour session, we managed to wrest a portion of the estate that Maurice had left from the grasping hands of his hated cousin, who was there to claim the estate on Marie's behalf. I wondered if she would ever see one franc of it.

Afterwards Kirk and I walked from the bank where the deal had been brokered to the Hotel Splendid Royale where I was staying, and arranged for the front desk to keep the check for my portion of the estate in the hotel safe until I could get to a bank on the following Monday morning. Sitting on the terrace facing the lake, we enjoyed a champagne toast to the completion of the first portion of the ordeal. I enjoyed his witty and slightly off-center repartee. I found him interesting in a unique way and he seemed to enjoy my own sense of humor. Van left immediately after to fly back to Paris where I would meet him on Tuesday for the completion of the paperwork on the estate.

Alessandro arrived at the hotel Saturday morning and I drove with him to Locarno where he was negotiating some kind of business deal. It was obvious from his comments that he had eagerly awaited my return to Europe and the opportunity to see me again. With reluctance, he left me to explore the shops along the Locarno lakefront while he went to his meeting. It was a dismally dreary day and the biting wind off the lake was carrying more than a promise of coming winter. In my lightweight clothing I was soon shivering so badly I knew I had no choice but to buy a sweater before I cracked my chattering teeth. I found one which was far too expensive for the quality, but that was not the prime consideration.

Following his meeting, Alessandro joined me for lunch by the slate gray water of Lake Locarno. His comments left no doubt he was interested in establishing some kind of relationship and definitely some kind of romance. I hedged, reluctant to begin something with him despite the attraction and comradery, due to his recently widowed state and the considerable difficulties of a relationship with a foreigner in a foreign country. But then he was one mighty persuasive Italian and it had been a long dry spell. I had a feeling the separate rooms, which I fully intended to keep that way for at least that Saturday night, might not get dual and separate occupancy afterwards. I debated calling Margot later that night after successfully forestalling him at my door to talk it over with her. I could just hear her telling me to "go for it" so there didn't seem much point.

The following day we spent in a leisurely tour of Lugano and a nice dinner downtown. I realized as the day progressed that while he had grown warmer, I seemed to be growing colder to the prospect of an amorous evening. It was even more difficult to put him off as it was our last night in Lugano, but I succeeded. He left midday on Monday, most disappointed that he had not accomplished his goals. I figured that was the last of him.

With the bulk of the money safely deposited and a Swissair ticket in my purse, I was in Paris by nightfall. Margot had called the proprietor of the Hotel Cambon where she frequently stayed to procure a reservation for me. What a great location: on the same street as the backdoor of the Ritz, through which Lady Di would make her ill-fated escape some years hence. I crossed the street to the Florian Cafe, had a quick pizza and then returned to my room to read, eager to curl up in the bed in the tiny attic space that I had been lucky to find and would not have, had it not been for Margot's intercession. I grabbed my book from beside the bed, adjusted the pillows and dragged the light closer in preparation for reading "Pillars of the Earth." The book was captivating and I read until my eyes were tired and drooping. With a weary sigh, I put the book down, turned off the light and snuggled in for some needed sleep. After ten minutes I felt a lot like the story of the Princess and the pea, only someone seemed to have spilled a whole pod full of mighty peas worthy of "Jack and the Beanstalk fame." It was like trying to fit my body around lumpy boulders that only seemed to grow larger as the night progressed.

Morning found me staring at the mirror with raccoon eyes. Makeup did little to hide the dark circles, but that wasn't going to stop me from shopping and blowing some money. For the first time, I was in Paris with some real spending money in my pocket, money I had held back from the check deposited in Lugano.

"Look out Paris, here I come!" I informed the grim reflection that looked back at me as I grabbed my purse to take the miniscule and creaky elevator down. I wasn't meeting Van until late afternoon, so I had time to do some damage and a little matter of baggy eyes was no deterrent. I had never had so much money in my purse in my life and despite a serious effort to blow some of, found nothing that carried the same appeal as that money. Amazed at myself and wondering about the psychological implications of not wanting something once it was obtainable, I went back to the room, squirmed around on the bed until I found a tolerable arrangement of limbs between the lumps and slept until time to dress for my meeting.

I met him at his office on the Ave. Champs Elysées to sign the final document that he needed to complete matters and of course to pay him for his efforts. Afterwards he and his wife treated me to champagne cocktails in their spacious apartment in an elegant building on the Boulevard Raspail, and then a nice dinner at a small and rustic near-by restaurant. I enjoyed their company until late and despite a less than restful evening on the lumpy mattress, was up early for my flight home the following morning. In my handbag I was carrying that lump of cash and the documents that gave me access to more money than I had ever envisioned having.

I knew I would not be able to bring it all back into the country at one time without some serious explaining, so I planned to have it sent to me in $9,900 increments. When I had accumulated enough, I was determined to make a down payment on a townhouse in a development that I had loved since its inception. The first thing Beth and I did on my first afternoon back was to visit the model home there and start dreaming about making one of them ours.   After several years of renting and avoiding the suggestive comments of my landlord as to ways to reduce my rent, I was more than ready for us to be in a home of our own. Beth wasted no time planning her decor and chattering about color schemes.

Margot called the first night I was back and talked for over two hours. Mostly she just seemed really lonely. I knew she had friends in Miami but I suspected that she did not really connect with them on a soul level. The sharing of the intimate and personal details she saved for Kat, and particularly for me now that both she and I were single.

"So, Jo, are you still coming for Thanksgiving."

"I don't think I can take that Wednesday off the way we talked about, so that really cuts into my time. I missed days from school when Daddy died and then again the time that I was away in Europe. My principal would kill me if he knew I was playing hooky. Would it be okay if we come Christmas instead since we would have so much more time to enjoy with you?"

"Shit! I really wanted you to come for Thanksgiving. Of course, Christmas is great too. In fact I'm going to invite Kat and mama, too. We'll make it a family Christmas here."

"Super. With Daddy gone, I don't think any of us was looking forward to being in Greenville for the holiday."

"That's for sure.   So why don't you just fly on down for Thanksgiving? You can afford the tickets now."

"Babe, you know getting tickets at this late date is a real problem. Hell, they're scarce as hen's teeth if you don't buy them by late summer. But I'll check and let you know, okay?"

She continued to wheedle and grumble. Finally I just asked, "Margot, just what's eating you? You seem so lonely?"

"I am. Yeah, I know people here; but some of them are just hangers-on because I have money. I wonder how many I would have if I were poor?"

"Hey. Get a grip. You were poor before and you had tons of friends. People like you because you're fun to be with. That has nothing to do with your pocketbook, you ninny."

"Okay, okay. But I still want you to come."

"I said that I'll try and I will." By the time we hung up, it was nearing midnight.

After school I immediately got on my phone and shopped airlines to find reservations. With my time constraints it was hopeless and I did not relish driving so far for such a short visit. I knew Margot was going to be upset, so I didn't call her with the news. It didn't matter: she called me at nine and chatted until after eleven. I stalled and didn't tell her that I wouldn't be coming until Christmas. When I finally did, she didn't seem surprised and told me that she had been invited to have Thanksgiving dinner with friends. After hearing that I didn't feel so badly.

Was Christmas that year ever a bear! Kat and Clint were at odds and spent the time by the pool in apparent argument. The rest of us figured out the atmosphere was as chilly as a plunge into glacial water and tended to steer clear of any incipient fireworks. Mama was as wicked mouthed as a hormonal bitch on Speed. She took one look at my new red leather pants and told me I looked like a whore and hoped I fell into a canal and the alligators got me. I suppose I did take a little exception to that remark. Beth and Kat's son, Hardiston, spent their time fighting over the remote control in the den. Margot was exasperated with trying to keep the various warring factions separate. So much for the happy little family gathering around ye old Yule log. We hit the absolute nadir at Christmas Eve lunch. Mama pitched a hissy fit over something so trivial that afterwards none of us remembered what it was, and then locked herself into the den where she made sure she wailed loudly enough we could all hear her: "I should have died with your daddy." At that point, she had more than one of us in agreement. We sat in the living room wondering how to deal with it. After listening to the caterwauling for over an hour, I'd had enough.

Picking the lock, I marched in and announced, "All right, Mama. I know you're mad Daddy died but in the end he was so sick it was a blessing and you said so yourself. He'd suffered enough."

"I know it but I wish I'd died too."

"Why is that when you have family that loves you and needs you? We miss Daddy too and we certainly don't want to mourn you as well right now."

"I don't care. I should have just crawled in the casket with him." More sobbing followed.

"Mama, remember at the funeral when you said he didn't look like himself and you didn't even recognize him? You wouldn't want to go crawling in that box to spend eternity curled up with someone you said looked like a stranger, now would you?" I knew that was a nasty one, but I was so tuckered out from the constant carping I'd reach the point of not caring. I realized that her anger was a way of diverting herself from the inner pain of the first Christmas without Daddy, but she was hell on wheels with no brakes. We'd all had enough, but as usual I being the eldest was the tacitly elected delegate to handle it. Always had been.

She snapped her mouth shut mid wail. If looks could stab, I'd have been a dead woman. I'd done what I could and thankfully the moaning and groaning had stopped. I went back to the living room and found them silently awaiting another Hiroshima. I just shrugged. Margot, Kat and I formed a subdued trio in the kitchen, preparing dinner for some friends Margot had invited over. The others decamped to the relative neutral ground of the patio and Mama sulked until the doorbell rang announcing the arrival of guests. The rest of the evening went fine although I noticed a distinct chill wafting my way whenever I was near Mama. It stayed there through the coming days and recalling her earlier remark, I suspected she was still praying for an alligator. I made a note to steer clear of any canals.

After the guests had left it was late. The soft air and the rosy hued sky with the black silhouette of swaying palms were calling me. I slipped silently from the door, determined to walk and just enjoy the peace and beauty of the night. I had barely cleared the hedge along the street, when I heard soft footsteps following me.

"Don't even think you're going to walk off and leave me here do deal with this stewpot." Margot laughed.

"Hi, Babe. Actually I'm glad you sneaked out too. I could use some fun company. It's been in sorta short supply lately."

"Fucking A! Think I hadn't noticed?"

"If you haven't, you're deaf, dumb and blind and I do mean dumb."

"Shit, you'd think we were having a meeting of the All-Time Champions of the Bitchy-Witchy Society." She sighed, "And I worked so hard to make everything nice. What a waste."

"Actually it isn't. Dear God, think how much worse it would be if we were all holed up in Greenville!"

"You got that right. At least here we can do things and go places. And it's much prettier here." She paused, "God forbid we were all trapped inside at Mama's. Here the weather is nice and we can at least go out to the patio to escape," she paused and laughed when I chuckled, "...well sometimes."

We walked to a small park-like area on the waterway and sat on the bench facing Biscayne Bay. The lights of Miami twinkled across the way, the full gold of the moon shimmered on the surface of the waves; and the only sound was the rustling of the wind in the trees. Dancing branches of Bougainvillea glowed faintly in the golden glow of a street lamp. With the heady perfume of tropical flowers filling the air, it was a paradise.

"Boy when I die, if I don't end up in Miami Beach, I'm going to know I went to hell. I love it here. I see why you came back."

We sat in companionable silence, both reluctant to return until all were calmly settled for the night so we wouldn't have to deal with them. Since we were sharing her room, sneaking in her bedroom door from the patio would assure us of even greater safety.

"Well, do you think Mama has it out of her system now. I thought she would kill you for sure when you went in to talk to her."

"So did I. Actually I understand that this is just her way of dealing with grief. I just wish she didn't have to piss the world off to do it."

"Amen, sister!" Margot laughed. "Let's you and I just have a hell of a good Christmas tomorrow regardless of what the others do."

"That's a deal!"

The next morning dawned peacefully under a perfect sky, no clouds either literally or figuratively. After a catch-as-catch-can breakfast, Margot, Kat and I worked in the kitchen to prepare the big feast planned for mid-afternoon. Beth and Hardiston were assigned patio clean-up duty. Clint busied himself staying out of the way and reading a current Tom Clancy novel. Mama stayed in the den doing who knows what, since by tacit agreement we had all decided to steer well away from her. We decided to hold the gift exchange after all the guests departed.

Al, Margot's new beau or *friend* as she made it a point to stress, arrived first. I liked him immediately. Al was fun, witty, obviously very intelligent, more than prosperous, well-dressed and nice enough looking. I judged him to be somewhere in his early to mid-sixties. After talking with him for several minutes, he reminded me that we had met ten years previously when Margot was working as manager of the lounge in a hotel on Sailboat Bay. I vaguely remembered the occasion. At the time, I was married to my first husband and had taken a mini-vacation to visit my sister for a few days. Because she had to work part of the time I was there, I had hung out in the lounge as well. Apparently it had been one of Al's favorite haunts.

We soon had him settled in the living room with Mama. He rapidly charmed her. For the first time in days, she was smiling and laughing. By the time the other guests arrived, the wine and Al's wit had combined to put us all in a festive mood. From the kitchen, we sisters breathed a great sigh of relief. Dinner went well and by the time they left, we had stalled the two kids as long as we could. When Margot suggested we do dishes after we had opened our presents, they raced like greyhounds at Hialeah to perch by the tree where they had already eyeballed the tags bearing their names. Clint did the honors for the rest of us, handing out the packages to each eager smile. We were excited too.

I had found a beautiful pair of mother of pearl inlaid opera glasses for Margot who often attended performances funded by various local charities she supported. It had been an expensive gift and I held my breath while she opened it for fear she might not like it. Fortunately for me she held them up with a genuine beam of pleasure lighting her face.

"Thanks, Jo. I love'em! They're gorgeous. I really wanted some, too. "

Kat gave her a beautiful Hermes scarf she laid atop the already opened gift from Al, a breathtaking pearl necklace with three jeweled studded clasps that allowed it to be converted to different lengths. Mama gave all of us an envelope containing money so we could each get whatever we might like. My gift from Margot was a set of Caphalon cookware she knew I wanted. Soon the living room was knee deep in cast off wrappings and boxes and everyone was busy cooing over their gifts and calling "thank you's." Mama seemed genuinely happy for the first time since we had all arrived.

Kat, Clint and I decided, since Margot had done most of the cooking, to clean up the mound of dishes waiting in the kitchen while she loaded the tape deck with Christmas music and poured champagne for us all, including a small sip for Beth and Hardiston. We all made a toast to Daddy on this our first Christmas without him. I thought of Maurice and Marie in her lonely mourning and sent a silent prayer her way.

Following our visit, Margot continued to talk by phone at least once daily, sometimes more. Beth and I made a mini break in February around President's Day and two teacher workdays I took as additional vacation days. Coupled with the weekend we had five days of which we spent almost two driving. It was a much more tranquil visit than the one at Christmas and far more fun. We generally behaved like lunatics on the loose sending Beth into gales of laughter at our antics. Al wined and dined us repeatedly during our visit, however it was obvious to me that he was far more smitten than she.

Spring break in April found me taking another group to England. Alessandro flew to England on business and took me to dinner one of the nights we were there. I was surprised that he went to the trouble after the disappointment he suffered in Lugano. But then hope springs eternal they say, not that it was springing in his direction this time either. And even though he continued to write with some regularity and to call on occasion, I was still reluctant to take it to the next step. Margot continued to tease me about what she called my coy behavior. Actually I think the term she used was cock tease. Lord, what happened to the joy of a flirtation, just a flirtation?

I returned home to a flurry of calls from Margot. She was invited to stay in St. Jean du Cap Ferrat as a guest of very wealthy friends that she had met while wed to Tony. Begging me to come, she told me that she also planned a visit to the villa in Italy courtesy of Tony and to Modena to visit friends who owned a hotel there, and that she really wanted me to be with her. Since I had never been to St. Jean du Cap Ferrat, Modena, or the villa, I was really excited by the prospect. When I discovered I had enough frequent flyer points from my tours to fly free, it was a done deal. Margot knew someone with Delta in New York who promised us both first-class up-grades from New York to Milan and back from Nice. Thrilled by the coming trip, we spent endless hours talking about what to pack and what we wanted to do.

June arrived and the end of school. I took Beth to my parents and then drove back to Raleigh, packed and caught the plane to New York where I would meet Margot. She was waiting for me in the terminal with Perky in a carrying case and a broad smile on her face. I was elated to see her and at the prospect of the coming adventure, but could well have suffered the absence of that dog. The seats were glorious in the old days of first class, reclining almost horizontally and with lots of room. The food was excellent, the wines perfect and service just short of obsequious. I loved it. The two of us talked non-stop until well after dinner. She then promptly began hours of soft snoring while I did the customary fidgeting albeit in far more comfort than what she referred to as my usual rat class accommodations. From Milan we caught a plane to Bologna where her friends had a chauffeur waiting to take us to their hotel/residence in Modena.

The husband, Umberto, was a flirtatious scamp who quickly embarked on a have-fun-with-Jo campaign. He fired the opening salvo at dinner the first night in the basement restaurant of the hotel. Not having met him on arrival, when we were introduced at the table I employed my neatly memorized greeting. *"Sono molto lieto di fare la suo conoscenza."* (I am pleased to meet you.) I inwardly smiled in smug pleasure at perfectly reciting the phrase.

To which he replied, *"Fa pompino?"*

I sat there momentarily puzzled as my limited Italian knowledge told me that he had asked if I did something involved with being a fireman. I sat there, mulling the phrase in my mind, perplexed by the guffaws from the others and his smirk. It suddenly dawned on me that he was asking if I pumped....did blow jobs. I was not amused at what I consider insufferable rudeness to someone who was a total stranger and a guest in his home. Smiling sweetly, I leaned closer in my best Southern Belle manner and cooed, "Not on this trip, Sweetie."

When the others all howled in amusement at my riposte, I knew he was not going to be too fond of me. The next evening at dinner, again I was seated beside him much to my chagrin. Trying my damnedest to make conversation, I commented on his art collection that hung in all of the public areas of the hotel.

"Do you know the artist, Guido Reni?" He asked, obviously expecting ignorance.

"Yes, I do. Unfortunately he has not been as appreciated as he once was, but I think that may be changing."

"That I hope as I have a large collection of them."

"Is that a Caravaggio in the office? And I think the small St.

Jerome above the door in the bar is a Titian."

"You seem to know your art." I noticed he neither confirmed nor denied.

"I teach art history so I am fairly familiar, especially with such famous artists."

Anna his wife, interrupted. "Jo, you would love the collection in his private apartment. That's where his best pieces are as it is too risky to hang them in public view. Although most people wouldn't realize what they are anyway."

"I would very much like to see them." I turned to her and smiled. She was so suppressed by her over-bearing husband that I found myself responding with special gentleness to her. I knew from Margot that for years she had suffered through his mistresses and casual affairs. Indeed the mistress was seated with us at dinner. I commented to Margot later that had I been Anna, a little exploration of discreetly poisoned dishes might have been an appealing addition to her rival's diet.

"She just wants to see them because they are worth a lot of money." Umberto sneered at me.

Instantly I flush red and knew my temper was about three miles past ceiling height and climbing. "That's an insult. I don't have to take any more impertinence from you or anyone else."

Margot and Anna both gasped audibly. The others sat in stunned silence. Too afraid to speak, they waited for his explosion. He wasn't accustomed to spine in others apparently.

He twisted his lips wryly and leveled a long look at me. I glared back. He was absolutely not going to cow me. Perhaps he respected that. At any rate, he announced to the table, "I will show her my collection after dinner is finished."

It was an amazing assembly of Reni's. More than in any other single place that I know. I thanked him sincerely for the privilege of viewing them, but I was glad we were leaving in the morning to go to the villa. I'd had enough of Umberto for the moment. Back in our room, Margot turned to me wide-eyed.

"I can't believe he showed you his collection. He never allows anyone to see them. I've never even seen them before and I was here many times with Tony. Plus I thought he would combust when you stood up to him."

"He made me so blasted mad, I'm surprised *I* didn't!" I narrowed my eyes in thought, "Margot, do you think there is something *illegal* about this collection? He's very touchy about it and it's not just remarkable in scope but fantastically valuable just to be hanging around here. Maybe he's just afraid of thieves, but something tells me that it's more than that."

"I've wondered about that, too."

"Are you packed and ready to go in the morning? Even if it is only one night away and we have to come back here for another night, I'm glad to be leaving."

"All packed." She smirked, "You're just thrilled that Alessandro is coming to take us. Are you going to, ah...you know, make some whoopee?"

"I have no plans to, Miss Priss. So, Good night."

"Night, Jo." Margot chuckled at me as she turned out the light.

Alessandro arrived early and made every appearance of being impressed by the hotel and its owners. It was also obvious that he found Margot very enticing. I thought to myself, so much for him. Was that a small frisson of jealousy that tap-danced down my spine?

The ride from Modena to the villa south of Siena was a long one for me as I sat listening to the two of them chatter away like old friends. I was glad they liked one another. I kept telling myself that it was not as though I envisioned any great future with him. I knew that Margot wasn't interested in him but she couldn't resist a little ego satisfying flirtation. Plus she was friendly and bubbly with everyone. But, I was secretly annoyed and my vanity wounded as I really thought he was smitten with me. I liked it that way even as I resisted giving my heart to him. I was glad when the car climbed the olive lined drive to our destination.

Magnificent ivy colored vines draping the walls of the thirteenth century structure had turned a flaming red. The villa wrapped around a central court on three sides. Beautiful arched double doors opened into sunlight flooded tiled floors. The central salon in the right wing was dominated by a stone fireplace on the back wall big enough to roast a steer. Plush camel colored leather sofas faced one another on either side, made comfortable with bright cushions. The space between was covered in a beautiful Tabriz carpet and a rustic coffee table polished to a high sheen by centuries of human contact. The dining room was large and fortunately so, as the table was big enough for a skating rink. It too was a natural wood polished by the ages. In the center a ceramic bowl held a Bacchanalian array of fresh fruit, obviously a welcoming gesture on the part of the local ladies who worked as part time staff when the villa was in use. There was a huge kitchen as well with another gigantic table for working, a granddaddy of all ranges, modern refrigeration, a wood burning oven and open cabinets filled with glowing dishes of the softest cream. The central axis of the house was a large activity room, again dominated by a massive fireplace, looking out on a pool that closed in the base of the u-shaped courtyard. Beyond the pool the cypress spiked hills of Tuscany rolled off towards the sea. The three-bedroom left wing contained two small baths, kitchen and sitting room for use by Tony's security people and chauffeur. He never visited the villa without security, but Margot had opted not to use them for this visit.

She directed Alessandro and me to the stone stair that climbed the left wall of the main salon to the upper level bedrooms of the main house. I could tell by the wicked grin on her face that she intended to ensconce the two of us in the master suite while she took one of the other bedrooms. With five to choose from all with private baths, I didn't think we needed to economize on space and if we did, it wasn't going to be with that particular grouping. I was prepared to share a room with her, not him. Before she could open her mouth and create an awkward moment, I interrupted.

"Why don't you take the master suite? Since you already have some of your things here, it makes sense. I'm sure Alessandro and I will find a couple of the other bedrooms just fine." A glance at him assured me that he too had envisioned a more intimate sleeping arrangement. Never having gone to bed with him before, I certainly wasn't going to begin with Margot in hearing distance down the hall.

Dinner that evening was at nearby San Felice, a medieval village famous for its wine, now converted to a hotel encompassing the old houses, a restaurant, and bodega. I couldn't help but wonder where the former inhabitants now lived. Margot explained that the hotel was not yet officially opened thus the owner was treating us to a private dinner. When we entered the dining room, Franco, the owner and 'gourmet chef of the evening,' gave a whoop of joy before rushing to Margot and sweeping her into a spinning hug. It was obvious he adored her. Their meeting and greeting done and introductions made, we were treated to a meal of endless courses each accompanied by at least two San Felice wines. With Franco regaling us with the hilarious and frequently painful struggles of getting the conversion and renovations finished, the wonderful food, and perfectly paired wines, we were all soon convivial, to say the least. By midway into the evening, I began to wonder if it were a good thing that it was a hotel as well, considering the dark winding road back to the villa. Alessandro apparently held his wine better than the two ladies as he drove back with remarkable ease. I kissed him goodnight at his bedroom door before entering my own room.

I was exhausted, just a shade tipsy, and more than ready to sleep. Distant thunder echoed over the silent hills as I slowly slid into slumber. Suddenly a tremendous crash jolted me into frightened consciousness. Images of Red Brigade kidnappings flitted across my groggy eyes. I debated whether to hide in the armoire, fling myself from the window and pray those flagstones below were softer than they looked, or seek protection with the others. The three of us apparently opted for the latter. Bursting from my door in wide-eyed fright, a found Margot in the hall ahead of me with a crossbar from one of the window shutters griped tightly in white-knuckled hands.

"What was that?" I mouthed to her in the moonlight. Before she could answer, Alessandro emerged into the hall as well, struggling to get his robe wrapped around him, pockets flapping like wings on either side. I didn't see any need to point out that it was inside out. I was just glad to have a man in the house.

Without a word, he took the wooden bar from her and motioned us to go back into her bedroom, which had a doorway to an outside stairs. I held onto her as we silently backed through her door and watched him creep bare-footed down the stairs to confront some unknown peril waiting in the dark rooms below.

Another gigantic crack sounded just behind us, causing us to jump in panic, mouths opened in silent screams. "What...?" I began, when suddenly another bang sounded. Turning slowly and in fear of eminent death, we caught the inward movement of the unlatched shutter just as the rising wind swung it back for another clap.

"Oh God, Jo. I forgot to latch the damned shutter and the wind is banging it. We aren't being assaulted by the Red Brigade after all."

Alessandro rounded the top of the stairs bat at the ready. "It's okay," I called.

Margot piped in, "Don't worry it's just the wind. If you'll give me the crossbar I'll latch the shutter and we can get some sleep. Sorry about the fright."

I could tell he was shaken. Again I kissed him goodnight and thanked him for trying to rescue us. When his door shut, Margot motioned me into her room. We both felt braver for the other's company.

"Well, Jo. I surely am glad you're not sleeping in there with him now. The house creaking and groaning with the wind is a little scary."

"Well, actually I was just going to go to his room and check him out. After all, you've been telling me to and it's obvious he wants to sleep with me. Don't you think I should?" I teased.

"Don't even think about leaving me alone," she giggled.

We fell asleep just as fat raindrops began to drum on the tiles of the roof. The morning sun rose to a freshly washed and sparkling day. After a breakfast prepared by the two ladies Tony hired from the nearby village, we were on our way back to Modena.

It was easy to laugh about the banging shutter in the brave light of day.

Once more Alessandro left disappointed in his romantic anticipations. As for me, I could not help but marvel at and be flattered by his perseverance. Somewhere deep inside there was a reticence to stop seeing him balanced by an equal reluctance to progress to the next level. I could not discern why that should be. It wasn't customary for me to be so indecisive and certainly it wasn't my intention to be coy.

"So why?" Margot asked as he disappeared around the corner from the hotel.

"I wish I knew." I remarked with a wry grin. "I wish I knew."

Our final night there was anti-climatic considering the previous dinner with Umberto; and we bade both he and his wife goodbye and gave our thanks for their hospitality before we went to our room. With departure scheduled for six in the morning, it was obvious they had no desire to awaken in time to see us off.

We were waiting on the front steps of the hotel at six o'clock in anticipation of the driver Umberto had procured to take us to Linate Airport just outside of Milan. At half past we were still waiting and growing a bit anxious. Margot kept glancing nervously at her watch. I knew we would be cutting it close to make our flight to Nice where we were the invited guests of friends of hers.

"Where in the hell is that guy. If we don't get going fast, there is no way we can make it." With that Margot stormed inside to the receptionist desk to demand that the driver be called and told to get to the hotel with all haste.

Driving a long cream colored Maserati sedan, he leisurely wheeled up in front of the hotel at seven, pausing to take a last puff before flicking his cigarette stub from the window and strolling around the car to open our doors. Watching him, her foot tapping up a storm, Margot was as "mad as a wet setting hen," to put it in the southern vernacular. I thought to myself, this boy has no clue what he's in for.

"Buon giorno, signore. Come Stanno?" Mistake. He really didn't want to know how we were.

"I'm sure you must not realize that you are an *hour* late?" Margot smiled sweetly. Giving him enough rope to hang himself as he loaded our luggage?

"Ah signora, no problema. Thees ees Eetalie." He all but bowed, gave an exaggerated shrug to his shoulders as a sunny smile lit his face. When she responded that smile melted off like butter in a microwave.

"I don't give a damn if it's the moon. If we are not in Linate in time to make our flight, you can kiss your job goodbye along with your sorry ass."

With that, the flirtatious grin faded, the shoulders squared and the bowed head snapped back. I caught the glimpse of a devilish glint in those dark eyes, before they were politely hooded. He closed the trunk with care, softly closed our doors, climbed behind the wheel, looked back over the seat and sweetly purred. "You weel make you flight, thees I promeese."

Holy shit I thought to myself as we laid rubber leaving the hotel; she lit a bonfire under his sassy butt. Taking corners on two wheels, we were soon on the autostrata bound at breath-taking speed for the distant airport. When I saw the speedometer register 220 kilometers, some quick calculations told me more than I really wanted to know. Approximately 125 miles an hour was a new first, and I feared it might be a fatally tragic last.

We were passing cars at a dizzying speed, road signs flying by so fast reading was impossible, and that chauffeur was hunched over the wheel like a demented demon. Margot's big blue eyes were capped with eyebrows that looked ready to climb off her face. Reaching surreptitiously over, she took my hand and the two of us gritted our teeth and just hung on. She said nothing. I said nothing. The chauffeur said nothing. But then I didn't want him to talk, as he could afford no distractions. Dodging around one car close enough to peel paint, he honked his horn, hurled an expletive I couldn't translate, and resumed flying. If that plush sedan had just had wings, we could have skipped Linate and just gone on in to Nice. I closed my eyes having seen all my nerves could stand. I knew from the frequent tenseness in Margot's hand in mine, that hers were all too open. To distract myself I created mental images of cows, birds, sheep and other denizens of the pastures and woods along the way, all swept up in the backwash from the car and spinning behind us like kite tails. It helped but not enough.

When we arrived at Linate, we both took a deep and greatly relieved gasp of air, stood on trembling legs and walked to the back of the car where the driver was hastily depositing our bags on the curbing. I was relieved that the upholstery had survived without undue stains.

"Well, I must say I've driven it in less time, but you didn't do badly." Margot announced as she handed over his tip. He looked as though he was choking, and I know I nearly did.

When we entered the terminal, she cocked a wicked brow at me and commented, "There is no way I was going to let that asshole think he scared me. But to tell you the truth, if I hadn't crossed my legs I would have wet myself."

"Just do me a favor, will you?"

"Yeah?"

"If the plane is late leaving, please don't say anything to the pilot. I've enjoyed about all the terror I can stand for one day."

We even had time to each buy a scarf in duty-free prior to walking to the gate. Later Umberto would tell Margot that the chauffeur was a test driver and racer for Maserati. That car was certainly tested that morning.

Chapter 15

He liked what he saw. She didn't. Sam Taylor was a wealthy industrialist from Akron and our host in St. Jean du Cap Ferrat. He and his wife Cheryl had been friends of Margot and her ex-husband. Sam was warm, out-going, and as friendly and uncomplicated as a puppy. Cheryl radiated jealous-wife syndrome. She was about as warm as a Siberian cold wave and as friendly as a hungry barracuda. No wonder Margot had said little about her. I could tell we were going to be as fond of one another as a victim and a hit man. Fortunately he dropped her off at the luxurious villa they had rented with another couple, Fred and Marilyn Carson from La Jolla, before taking us to our hotel. On the way to the Grand Hotel du Cap Ferrat, he explained that while they would have liked to have us at the villa, Marilyn's hairdresser and the Carson's daughter, Melissa, occupied the other bedrooms. No doubt Cheryl was going to keep all those bedrooms occupied. That was fine with us.

What a gorgeous hotel. The week there was one I anticipated with relish, as I could never have afforded it on my own. "Wow!" I explained when we walked into our room.

"Double wow." Margot replied with a grin. "Good ole Cheryl's going to shit a brick if she finds out where he arranged for us to stay."

"Well, if he doesn't tell her, you can believe I won't mention it 'cause I *like* it here." The Rococo room was elegantly furnished and grandly proportioned. The gold-fringed blue-gray drapes on the windows opened onto balconies overlooking the sea and the pine-studded garden below. Delicate Louis XV chairs bracketed a small gold gilded breakfast table. Full-length mirrors concealed a spacious closet with padded hangers and storage drawers. A huge bath with a swimming pool sized tub and French doors, opened onto its own balcony through more gold-fringed drapery.

"It's sure not shabby!" Margot remarked as she looked around.

"Well, let's unpack and go exploring. I'm dying to see this place."

We got things put away, donned shorts and walking shoes and headed out. The public areas of the hotel were even more luxurious than our room. Under the pines below our window we admired the view from the outdoor dining area. The path from there led down to a cliff-side pool with the first disappearing edge that I had ever seen. The deck chairs that lined the poolside were filled with bronzed bathers in skimpy suits. Most appeared more interested in seeing and being seen than enjoying the pool. It was obvious that the pampered bodies on display were the result of serious interventions, both physical and cosmetic, to achieve that degree of perfection.

Margot snorted, "Looks like we walked into a convention of plastic surgeons' models."

From there we ambled down the shaded street from the hotel to the old port, filled with luxury boats and lined with sidewalk cafes. It was a long walk from the port back to the hotel and the day was warm. We had just finished our showers and donned the plush monogrammed terry robes we had found behind the door, when the doorbell rang.

"Are we expecting anyone?" I asked.

"Not until six when Sam is picking us up to take us to the villa for dinner. And I don't think he would come up, just have the concierge ring our room."

Opening the door, Margot stepped back as a white-jacketed waiter entered the room with a tray centered with a small dish of canapés and two glasses of champagne. A daily compliment of the hotel, he explained. I liked that place better all the time.

"*Jesus*, what's this stuff on the tray." Margot picked up a piece and after close scrutiny, announced with a sniff, "Raw fish."

"Not for me, thanks. But I'll sure have some champagne." Back then sushi was very avant-garde and neither of us had been exposed to it before. Later she came to like it, but I never have. Fearing that the hotel would not continue our daily treat if we sent it back untouched, we flushed it. Fortunately the next day it was shrimp, cooked and we had sushi only once more during our stay.

We were dressed and waiting when Sam rang the room. Neither of us looked forward to his wife, but he was fun company, only mildly flirtatious and interesting to talk to. The other couple proved to be an odd pair. She was a former actress, still beautiful in a faded and used up kind of way. He was stern, serious, and aggressively confrontational with his wife and just short enough to have an advanced Napoleon complex. Their daughter, Melissa, in a sheer white dress that did little to hide the peaks of the artificially *grand Tetons*, looked like a forty year old teenage tramp. Slouched in an insouciant pose that would have done Michael Caine proud, her boyfriend, an apparently successful Italian gigolo, occupied himself with self-adulation once he had dismissed us as less interesting financial prospects. The hairdresser, Marcus, was so light in his loafers he needed an anchor to stay down. And Cheryl was well on her way to a buzz. It looked like an interesting evening.

It was a beautiful cliff-side villa, large and airy with the living areas opening onto a pool surrounded by a landscaped terrace. Colorful blooms spilled from artfully scattered pots; and on the left side was a cabana with rattan stools. From there, Fred supervised the bartender as he mixed drinks for the group. Since everyone seemed to be having martinis, we accepted one as well. After one sip, I knew why Cheryl was on her way to tipsy-land.

Under my breath I whispered to Margot, "This stuff must be a thousand proof!"

"Let's dump them in the potted plants first chance we get and ask for champagne. I saw some on the bar."

"That's going to be one dead flower tomorrow." She confided with a giggle as we surreptitiously emptied our glasses into a large geranium.

"No kidding."

Their maid, in crisp white apron and cap, summoned us into dinner in the palatially appointed dining room. With maid, bartender/chauffeur, chef and gardener/handyman, they were not going to have to worry about doing anything for themselves. While the dinner itself was superbly prepared, the atmosphere at the table was as frigid as the air-conditioning. Fred never missed a chance to chide his wife, obviously detested Mario the gigolo, and was openly contemptuous of Marcus, who was one of the more pleasant members of the party. I felt sorry for Marilyn who was flustered and embarrassed much of the meal. Sam chatted blithely on, oblivious to the frost emanating from Cheryl. While it was obvious she barely tolerated Margot because of Tony, Margot's ex, she purely detested me. Other than being female, I couldn't figure out what I had done, as Sam was certainly no romantic thrill and I don't make it a habit to flirt with married men anyway. Thankfully Margot was at her best and soon had the table laughing and distracted from their normal program.

We were both glad to call it an early evening and get back to the hotel. The following days were on our own, but the evenings were spent with the others. Since we went out for dinner the rest of the time, the interpersonal tensions seemed to be less. Maybe it was a reluctance to act out in public.

On Wednesday night it was apparent to both Margot and me we needed to do some hand-laundry as we were both running low on underwear. In the bathroom was a laundry bag with a price list attached. We gathered our things and stuffed them in the bag. Just as we prepared to place it on the doorknob outside our room, I glanced at the list and then Margot.

"Gee Whitakers, would you look at this! It's *five bucks* to get underpants washed." I handed her the list. "Damn. I bought at 'em T. J. Maxx for less than what they want for cleaning them."

"Hell. I'm not paying these prices either. In the morning let's go looking for an laundromat down in the port."

The day dawned with clear skies and perfect temperatures. The walk to the port was a pleasure with the wind rustling the pines, birds singing and all right with the world. Before going to the laundromat we stopped for flaky croissants and cappucino. Again, perfection on a perfect day. Next to find the laundromat and get those undies clean. It wasn't hard. A few questions of the waiter and we were on our way. Skirting some roadwork barriers on the small side street along the quayside and with only a small sign above the door to announce its presence, we had found it.

It wasn't large, maybe fifteen washers and ten driers, but more than big enough for our needs and since no one else was there, we had our choice of machines. We chose the nearest, threw our laundry in and extracting francs from our purses, made a pile of coins. Margot picked up the first franc and found it fit perfectly in the slot. She slid it closed. We punched the appropriate wash buttons and sat down prepared to stare at the little round window and watch our clothes slosh around. Nothing happened.

"Shit. It must be *broken*." She exclaimed. "Let's put'em in another one."

"Okay with me." And I began stuffing the clothes into the adjacent machine. Again we inserted the coin and sat down to wait. Nothing happened.

"Oh for crying out loud. This one is broken, too." I announced in exasperation. "No wonder there's no one else in here. Let's see if the next one works."

"Okay. I'll shift them over this time and you grab another franc." She concentrated a minute and added, "You know, it may take *two* and not one. Maybe that's why it didn't work before."

"Right. Two it is and if that doesn't work, we can add another one. Surely it isn't more than that."

Again clothes in the washer, franc in the slot, and nothing. I added another coin and still nothing. The third one produced the same. Perplexed, we looked at one another and sat a little longer waiting to see if something would finally get going. Again about five minutes of staring at the little round window, no action, no water, no slosh, not even a hum. It was about as interesting as watching a television that hadn't been turned on. We twiddled our thumbs, sighed a couple of times, fidgeted a lot and in general were totally perplexed. And then I glanced at the wall above the washer and noticed a sign.

"Hey, slick, guess *why* the washers don't work."

"Christ. We have to go to the bar on the other side of the building and get *jetons* to put in the machines. Whatever that is."

"Go get'em and I'll stay here with our clothes."

In minutes, Margot was back, red with fury and clutching a precious jeton for our machine. "Those assholes in the bar were all sitting up there laughing at us. We're on candid camera. It seems they have a television monitor to watch the laundry. They were pointing and laughing and in general having a fine time at our expense." I've never been so embarrassed in my life.

When the underwear was clean, we realized that we still needed to dry them. Having paused only long enough to buy the one jeton, Margot had not bought any for the drying. Cocking an eyebrow at me, she announced, "There is *no way* I'm going back up there, ole girl. It's your turn to get laughed at."

"Uh-uh. No way am I going, Kitty Puss. Besides, if I had not seen the sign, we'd still be sitting here with dirty clothes."

"Crap. We might as well go."

Walking out of the laundry, we once again noticed the nearby road barriers with their jaunty red and white stripes. At the same moment, we both exclaimed, ah ha. The day was sunny and beautiful so surely it wouldn't take long to air-dry our things. Extracting the bras and panties from the plastic hotel laundry bag, we proceeded to drape them on the barricade. Not wanting to return to the laundromat to watch from the window, we hunkered on the curbing to wait. That gentle breeze that had played in the trees on the walk down now picked up to a hefty blow. Suddenly our newly cleaned undies were in peril of being blown into the rubble of the roadway. Frustrated, we gathered them and walked back to the hotel.

"So what do we do now with all of these wet drawers?" Margot looked around the room. "I'm not about to drape them on the chairs for the maid to see what cheapskates we are."

"We could put them on the railing of the balcony, except I'm afraid they might blow off."

"Not only that, can you image the spectacle from the restaurant terrace if someone looks up. They'll be up here in a minute to lecture us."

"Well, we have to figure out something unless we plan to walk around in wet bloomers and no bras, wet bras and no bloomers, or neither." Always creative, I started looking for a solution. In the bath I noticed the lovely fringed draperies that we had pulled closed each night and opened each morning. "I've got it, Sis. Let's use the rod that opens and closes the drape to lace our things on and then we can wedge it in the railing of the bathroom balcony. This side of the building is just service buildings and no one can really see us from here."

"Great. I'll get a chair and climb up and unhook it. You get the clothes ready."

We stood back with pride to admire our things, neatly strung through the pole so they could not blow away. Margot smiled triumphantly, "Let's go down to the terrace and get lunch while they dry."

We ate lunch leisurely, regaling one another with the laundry saga. Soon we were both howling at the ludicrousness of it all. Our laughter quickly stopped however, when we returned to the room to find that the maid had been, opened and reattached the rod to the bathroom drapery, and neatly folded our dried laundry and laid it out on the bed for us. So much for that.

Dinner that night was in the Moulin de Mougins, a fabulous restaurant in the not too distant village of Mougins. I was glad it was our last evening as Cheryl had become increasingly bitchy towards me despite my best efforts to be pleasant to her. When I ordered my meal in French, she was really annoyed as she rarely even bothered to say *thank you* in French, and other than *oui*, knew little more. I heard her ask Sam whom I was trying to impress. He ignored her. That really lit her fuse. Even so, both Margot and I made it a point to thank her for her week's *hospitality* as well as thanking the others.

Afterwards we stopped in Cannes where the famous jazz pianist, Bobby Short, was playing at one of the hotels. Margot had met him in New York and was delighted when he remembered her. She was less delighted when he inquired about Tony and obviously embarrassed when she had to tell him that they were divorced. Although she had drunk a lot of liquor at dinner, at the piano bar she drank even more. Long before we returned to the hotel she was drunk.

When we reached our room, it was late and I was exhausted. Margot was talkative and increasingly morose. It was obvious even before she began to cry that something was really bothering her. I didn't have to wonder for long what it was.

"Jo, I went to the doctor before I came on the trip because I wasn't feeling right. I stay tired and draggy and the doctor couldn't figure out why. So they ran some tests and a biopsy on my liver. They told me that my liver is damaged from the Hepatitis I caught in Aruba years ago."

"Yeah, I remember that. You had to come home on a stretcher you were so sick. Something about drinking bad water, wasn't it?"

"Right. At any rate, the damage is serious, very serious. He told me not to drink more than a glass of wine occasionally, as my liver can't take it. I'm so worried."

"So, what on God's earth are you doing drinking like a fish all evening?"

"Because I'm so worried."

"Boy, that really makes sense." I turned the light on and sat up in bed. Turning to her, I pleaded. "Please, Margot. Just don't drink. It's not worth ruining your health for. Besides, if a glass of wine is okay now and then, that's not too bad."

"Do you know how hard it is not to drink when everywhere we go and everyone we know is constantly drinking?"

"I wish you had said something sooner. We've been drinking every day for the whole trip. If I had known, I would have helped you by not drinking anything. That way you would have some support in trying not to drink."

"I just didn't want to talk about it. I guess I think if I ignore it, it'll go away."

"I don't think your doctor is going to agree."

"I'll probably go for another opinion when I get back."

"That's a good idea. But in the *meantime*, don't you think it would be a good idea not to drink anymore?"

"Don't nag!"

"I don't mean to nag. I just love you and I don't want you to ruin your health by doing something that you don't have to do. If it's as serious as you say, it's nothing to play around with."

"I love you too. Now, good night."

And that was the end of that. We left the next day to return home. She said little but didn't drink on the plane from Nice to New York; neither did I. We separated there to fly to our separate destinations. She told me later that she had gone to another doctor who told her it was okay to drink Vodka, Scotch and wines. I wasn't sure whether to believe her or not.

Soon school started and I was back into the routine, new classes, new procedures, a new computerized attendance program to learn, and another spring trip to plan. Margot called me daily when I arrived from school and we talked for an hour or so. Then again at bedtime she called for another marathon chat session. Her phone bills were soon astronomical as she was lonely despite being surrounded by her new Miami friends. On occasion her voice seemed slurred but I could not be sure. When I ask her if she were drinking she denied it.

I had just gone to bed when the phone rang. "Jo, are you asleep?"

"Well, not now at any rate. What's up, Margot? You sound excited."

"I am. I've arranged tickets for you and Beth to come see me this weekend. There's a party I want to go to and I want you to go with me."

"I wish you had asked first. I've got a lot to do here and a mountain of laundry that I have been putting off. Get Al to go."

"Don't tell me you'd rather wash clothes than go to a party with me!" She switched to wheedling. "Come on, Josie. Come see me, pretty please. You don't want the tickets to go to waste after I got them just for you, do you?"

"No I don't." I said with resignation. "So when are we coming?"

"Thursday morning."

"Oh, my goodness, Margot, that means we both miss two days of school and I have to give a big exam Friday."

"So, don't give it. I'll bet the kids won't object to studying over the weekend."

"That's for sure."

"So you're coming, right?"

I laughed, "We're coming."

She met us at the curbing when we emerged from baggage claim. It was then that I realized she had purchased a second car to go with the Mercedes convertible. This one was a 740 series BMW sedan and she was pleased as a cat in cream. "Don't you just love my new car? I bought it yesterday so I would have something big enough for both the luggage and us. It drives like a dream, too. I love the convertible but I really needed something larger for when I have company. Is this all of the luggage? Did you have a good flight? Isn't the weather gorgeous? I am just so excited you're here and you are too, right?"

"Jesus, Margot. The car is beautiful. This is all of our luggage. The flight was great. The weather is fabulous. And we're happy to be here." We all laughed together at her excited greeting.

"I'm just *so glad* you're here. We're going to have a ball." Turning to Beth, she exclaimed. "Kitty, you're getting to be all grown up."

Beth beamed with pleasure at the compliment. "Thank you, Aunt Margot. Will I get to see Javier this trip? I really enjoyed it when we went to the beach that time."

"I'm sorry but there is no more Javiercito. But I'll make sure you have a good time anyway."

We got our things settled in the house, freshened up and were shortly off to Bal Harbor for a lunch at Carpaccio's, our favorite lunch spot. Afterwards we walked down to Saks where Margot bought Beth a pretty shirt to wear with her jeans. We ambled through the many designer shops prior to driving down Alton Avenue to Epicure to buy groceries and flowers. Margot had invited friends to join us for dinner.

Al and a couple of girlfriend's from her working days arrived at seven, followed shortly by the neighbor across the street. Judy Bloomburg was newly divorced and in time would become one of Margot's best friends and a constant companion. She had a brash freshness that I liked immediately. Despite being of the rich and pampered Miami Beach crowd, she was more down to earth and approachable than some of the others I had met. Al made it a point to talk with Beth and the two of them were soon in the floor playing with Perky. It was a fun evening and although I was concerned that Margot was drinking several glasses of wine, my worry did not spoil it for me.

Friday and Saturday were similar whirlwinds. We went out for lunch both days, Friday with Judy to Mark's Place and on Saturday back to Carpaccio's. Friday night Al treated us to a fabulous dinner at The Forge. Margot spent the evening flitting about the restaurant visiting with people she recognized at other tables. I could tell that Al was annoyed but so enamored of her that he swallowed any reproof, concentrating instead on amusing Beth and me. When she perched at the table during her peregrinations there was always a fresh glass of wine awaiting. By the end of the evening there was a distinct slur to her speech.

The Saturday event was a formal dinner followed by the featured speaker of the evening, Henry Kissenger. This was the party that had prompted Margot to invite me for the weekend. I dressed in a black formal that I had found on sale and she donned a slinky white Armani. For our wraps, she hauled out a recent purchase: one three rowed black fox wrap with three fat tails on each end and the other, an identical white one. "You take the black and I'll do the white. We can go as Frick and Frack."

"It's gorgeous. I'd love to borrow it." I wrapped it around me and cuddled my face in its silky softness.

We arrived at the Fontainebleau Hotel on Collins Avenue and joined the throng of bejeweled and gussied up people edging into the ballroom. Our table was on the right side of the stage and a row back. Three other couples were already seated when we took our assigned seats at the table for eight. Margot knew them all and introduced them to me. We chatted happily with the others while waiting for our dinner. The champagne was flowing freely and it was top drawer. I was having my share when I noted that Margot had maybe had a bit more than hers. It wasn't so much that she was slurring her speech but she became increasingly loud. I knew the others at the table had noticed as well, when the gentleman on her left surreptiously slid the bottle away from her place and placed it on the far side of his own. Undaunted, she requested another bottle from a passing waiter. I breathed a sigh of relief when the dinner ended and we could turn our attention to the introduction of the speaker. Unhappily a round of after dinner liquors had been placed on the table once the dishes were cleared.

For security reasons due to his celebrity, everyone was requested to stay in their seat for the duration of the speech. We were further instructed that no one for any reason was to leave the ballroom until he had spoken and left the room. The lights dimmed and a hush settled on the room, only to be broken when Margot laughed uproariously at some whispered remark from another table. An angry buzz of "shh's" went around the table.

Mr. Kissenger began his speech to the rapt attention of all but Margot who continued to drink. After twenty minutes when it was obvious that he was just in mid stride, she became increasingly restless. Another ten minutes went by with no ready end in sight for the speech. I knew she was preparing to bolt, so it came as no surprise when she suddenly stood up and announced. "Come on, Jo. I've got to go."

"Margot! Sit down and be quiet, please. You know we were told not to leave while he's speaking." I hissed.

"No. I'm leaving and you're coming too." She didn't bother to lower her voice and just shrugged at the angry hisses coming from not only the nearby tables but our own.

Mortified and not knowing what to do, it occurred to me that with what she had drunk, it would cause more turmoil to try to mollify her and keep her there, than for me just to acquiesce and leave with her. I just prayed security would allow us to leave without undue problems. I suppose they came to the same conclusion as I, and other than cutting a nasty eye in our direction, we left unimpeded by dark suited guards.

I insisted on driving despite her vehement objection. I said nothing on the way to her house and she said less, considering I heaved some heavy sighs and she seemed one step short of oblivious. However, when we walked in the door I turned to her and demanded. "Margot, what is this? You know you need to watch what you drink."

"Oh, for God's sake. I just didn't realize how much I had drunk because the guy next to me kept my glass full. So get off my back and let's go to bed."

Katerina paid her a visit about a month after I returned and called me immediately when she arrived home. "Jo, I don't know about your visit but mine was a nightmare."

"What happened?" I dreaded the answer.

"We went to the Forge for dinner my last night there and Margot managed to insult the waiter and leave knee-walking drunk. I was so embarrassed."

"Did you say something to her about it?"

"I did, but it just pissed her off and she told me to mind my own business."

"You know about the report from the biopsy on her liver. That's what worries me and I can't figure out what it is that is making her so horribly unhappy. I know she isn't completely over Tony and what happened in their marriage." Heaving a sigh, I added, "I've been broken hearted, and divorced too, but I didn't turn to drink."

"So have I and ditto, but she surely seems to have."

Margot called us both obsessively over the coming couple of months. Comparing notes we realized that it was generally after nine at night and she frequently seemed either tipsy or beyond. When we challenged her about it, she denied drinking.

In Early spring Kat and Margot flew to Nice and spent a week looking at villas for rent. Margot found one in St. Jean du Cap Ferrat and planned to stay from early May to late September there. As soon as school was out, I was to come over for six weeks. I arranged for my mother to keep Beth and at Margot's invitation, called Alessandro to invite him for a weekend at the villa. He seemed excited by the prospect and I looked forward to seeing him again as we had enjoyed an increasingly lively correspondence.

I wasted no time once school was out in taking my daughter to Greenville for the coming weeks. Mama was thrilled at the prospect and so was she, as there was no question about whether or not she would be spoiled rotten. Margot called when I returned home to finish packing and talked for three hours. Finally I told her that she had to get off the phone and let me pack or there was no way I would be able to make the flight the following day. Reluctantly she said goodnight.

Margot met me at the airport in Nice driving the Mercedes convertible that she had shipped over for her sojourn. With that flashy car with Florida tags and tanned good looks, she turned a lot of heads while parked at the curbing waiting for me to emerge from baggage claim. Seeing me walk out, she frantically tooted the horn and waved madly.

"Jo!" She shouted, "Over here girl!"

"Hey, babe. Haul your sassy butt out of that car and help me get my bags in."

We hugged with enthusiasm and were quickly on our way to St. Jean du Cap Ferrat with Margot chattering the whole way. It was obvious she was delighted to have company and someone she could enjoy playing with. Proudly she told me of taking French lessons, learning her way around, discovering the local weekly market and a myriad of other details of daily living abroad.

We were back in the car and on our way to Monte Carlo for dinner at the Texan, a new restaurant that had become all the rage, when Margot mentioned she had met a devastatingly sexy Frenchman who had followed her on the autoroute until she stopped at a station for gas she didn't need. There he had introduced himself and apparently made a good impression as she had begun seeing him. She grinned at me as she whipped the car into a parking space near the restaurant.

"He's taking us to dinner tomorrow night at the Chevre D'Or. I can't wait for you to meet him. He will only speak French with me since he learned I'm taking lessons, so you'll get a chance to use your French as well."

"Mine's so rusty I doubt I'll understand much."

"Don't worry, he's mostly going to be playing footsy with me and he *will* be spending the night."

"Judging by the smirk, I suspect it won't be the first time, Kitty."

"Hmmm."

After the maitre d' seated us, I continued the conversation.

"Hmmm, nothing. So tell me about him."

"His name is Jean Claude Ronsard and he's an attorney in Antibes. He's not really handsome but he's sexy in a very French way." Smiling, she added. "Very Sexy."

"Married?"

"He says he's divorced."

"Do you think there's any future in terms of a relationship?"

"Who cares! He's what I need now." Changing the subject, she asked, "So, when is Alessandro coming?"

"I told him how long I will be here and he has your phone number, so we'll just wait and see."

Dinner was fun and it was obvious that Margot was becoming

acquainted with some of the local ex-patriots who made it a point to stop by our table and chat with her. She was her relaxed vivacious self, comfortable in the center of an admiring group. While she had wine with dinner, she drank no more than a couple of glasses. I was relieved and hopeful that the summer away would prove a turning point.

The following morning dawned on a perfect Mediterranean day: sunny skies, sparkling blue water, the lazy hum of cicadas and the perfume of flowers and herbs wafting on the air. Margot popped into my room singing a silly song. I laughingly sat up as she perched on the foot of the bed.

"Time's a wasting, ole girl. Let's get going."

"Boy, you're full of energy this morning. What's the program?"

"Let's go down to the port and get some croissants and cappuccino and then I want to drive over to the market in San Remo. It's just over the Italian border so it doesn't take long. The market has the best Chanel handbags you ever saw. They look and feel *exactly* like the real thing for a hundred bucks each, instead of the thousand or more in the shops. The gypsy lady that runs the booth told me to come back today and she would have some for me. I also need to pick up some cheeses and other odds and ends."

"Sounds good to me."

With the top down on the car, the drive was pleasant except for a line at the border. Driving into San Remo, it quickly became apparent that parking spaces were at a premium. Even without the added crowds of market day it would have been a problem, with them it appeared to be an impossibility. Margot was not one to be easily daunted however, so when she found a spot downtown, the sign saying no parking was inconsequential. Or so she thought. I felt compelled to point out that no one else had seen fit to ignore it.

"This is Italy. Signs like that are just a suggestion. No one takes them seriously." She shrugged and took off in the direction of the market with me running to catch up.

The purses were as lovely as she had promised. I watched her buy eight of them in different styles and colors before I too succumbed to temptation and bought red, navy, gold and white ones for myself. It was almost my entire shopping budget for the summer but no matter, I was thrilled. The next stop was the cheese stall where we bought a bag full of different types. Then the liquor store beaconed where Margot said they had the best prices and all free of duty. She bought eight bottles. Finally we were finished and on our way back to the car weighted down and huffing.

As we rounded the corner, I spied a couple of police officers in the proximity of the car. "Look, Margot. I think the police don't like where you parked."

"Damn. Let's duck into this doorway and watch'em so we can see what they're up to."

"They act like they're waiting for something." I commented after five minutes of peeping around the corner.

"Oh my God. I'll bet it's a tow truck." She groaned, "Come on, let's go see if I can talk them out of it by playing dumb foreign Southern woman."

She plastered on a bewildered look and a demure smile and marched off with a determined glint in her eye. Good luck I thought, when I caught the smug glance of the police officers when we walked up. The one in charge, a woman, would have given Nazi storm troopers a run for their money. I didn't think she was likely to fall for Margot's brand of flirtatious charm or feigned Southern Belle helplessness. After several attempts to get her to tear up the ticket she was waving furiously under Margot's nose, Margot knew the jig was up. Switching tactics, she opened her purse and extracted about fifty dollars in lire. The officers appeared to lose a little irritation. Margot fished for more. The officers exchanged glances and were ready to accept the money just as the tow truck pulled up. They went into a huddle with lots of arm waving to punctuate a fast and furious conversation. When they emerged they quietly took the lire offered, and then led her over to the tow truck. I saw her fishing for more money, this time to pay off the tow truck operator.

A subdued Margot drove us away from the smirking officers. "Damn. For what that cost, I could have bought ten times the liquor and cheese in France. But at least I made up for some of the cost on the purses."

When we reached the villa, Margot stashed the booze in a kitchen cabinet and quickly began fluffing the villa prior to Jean Claude's arrival. I took the opportunity to redo my wind-blown hair and admire my new purses before carefully stashing them in a drawer. The chiming of the doorbell brought us both to the living room. Margot opened the door to find Jean Claude standing there with two huge bouquets of summer flowers we would end up stashing in the bathtub until we could buy vases. One he handed to her as he planted a kiss on her upturned mouth. The other he gave to me. The man certainly knew how to introduce himself to the sister.

I quickly realized that despite the flowers and the ready Gallic charm, I was going to be one very superfluous third wheel. They had eyes only for one another and to say steam radiated from them is to put it mildly. Excusing themselves, they disappeared into her bedroom. Seeking some distraction, I went to mine and grabbed a novel. Groaning, I realized it was a bodice ripping romance. I didn't need that just then, so settled on a walk in the garden on the opposite side of the house from them. Apparently the nosy landlord, who lived upstairs, had decided to prune roses on Margot's side of the villa. I watched her trying to listen surreptiously outside Margot's window. I suspected she needed a little romance in her life no matter how she got it. Just as my stomach began to growl with serious hunger pangs, the momentarily sated lovebirds emerged freshly showered to ask if I was ready for dinner.

Dinner consisted of whispered words of French between the two of them, some activity under the confines of the table that I avoided naming, a delicious meal and a great wine. The restaurant's reputation in the world of gastronomy was well merited. Even so, I was relieved when we returned to the villa. I excused myself and retreated to the privacy of my room, a cold shower and that darned book. I had barely settled in for the night when I heard the front door close with a definite bang.

Margot rapped on my door, "Hey, Jo. Are you asleep?"

"No, what's up? Oops, forget I asked that"

"Funny." She remarked as she walked in and sat on the foot of my bed. "He had to leave. And I'm pissed. It seems he has a girlfriend he lives with and she expects him back this evening."

"Great. I know that was good news. But then he said he was divorced, not that he wasn't involved."

"Oh well, it may not have lasted long but it surely felt good for a while."

"History, huh?"

"Yeah. History." She shrugged, "After all there are more fish in that ole sea."

"I'm sorry, Babe."

"No problem, really." She stood up to leave, "Night. I'm going to go read a boring book and get really sleepy."

I was asleep by the time she reached her door. Suddenly in the middle of the night there was a loud crash and the sound of breaking glass. The first thing I though was that someone had broken into the house. I lay perfectly still, listening. Dreading.

"Jo, are you alright?" Margot called. I could tell from her voice that she was as frightened as I. "I'm coming out to see what happened."

"I'll come too."

We met in the living room and reached for one another's hand for courage. Nothing appeared amiss there, and it had not come from either of our bedrooms or baths. That left only the kitchen and backdoor. Taking a deep breath, we opened the door into the kitchen and walked in fearing the worst. The fumes were over whelming. I couldn't decide if I should drop to the floor and start licking to calm my nerves, or laugh. Apparently, the shelf where Margot had stashed the day's liquor haul had broken away under the additional weight, cascading the bottles to the floor in a heap of broken glass. Liquor was running everywhere.

"Oh no.   After all that expense and hassle, all of the booze I bought is gone. Damn. Damn. Damn!"

It took us an hour to clean it all up and by the end of the time, Margot and I were both laughing hysterically about all of the trouble and parking woes we had gone to, the sex-starved eavesdropping landlady, the hasty exit of Jean Claude and then the broken liquor.

The next couple of weeks were devoted to just enjoying the ambiance of the Riviera, the restaurants, browsing the shops in Monte Carlo, the beach and sites of interests. Margot was obviously not heartbroken over the hasty end to the affair with Jean Claude and a call from Alessandro saying he was arriving on the coming weekend, soon had us busy readying the house for a guest. I assured Margot she would be sharing the room with me, as I had no plans to bunk down with him. Again she teased me and again I had no ready answer for my reluctance. I really liked him and found him appealing on many levels, but as far as a romantic relationship, I still held back.

He spent only the one night. He treated us to a wonderful dinner in Beaulieu. We laughed, talked, and caught up on events in one another's lives. All in all it was a pleasant evening until bedtime. When once again he realized that I would not be sharing his bed, he asked me to take a walk with him, obviously without Margot's company. I knew what the topic of conversation would be and dreaded it.

The evening was as soft as only a night on the Riviera can be. The wind from the water lifted my hair in a light cloud as the moon cast our moving shadows on the street. We walked on with the silence between us becoming as tangible as pea-soup fog.

Just when I thought I could stand it no more, he began. "Jo, I am disappointed that you still hold me at a distance. I have hoped for some time now that we had grown close enough that you would be ready to be more intimate with me. I think I have been more than patient. What I want to know is whether or not there is any future here?"

"Alessandro, I realize I am not being fair to you and I do know that you want more from me than I have given. I don't know. I really don't know why it is that I cannot take the next step with you? I like you. I like you a lot. I think you're interesting, attractive and nice to be with. I'm flattered that you would make the effort to be with me so many times and at great inconvenience. I don't blame you for feeling disappointed in me."

"I'm not disappointed in you. I'm frustrated by the lack of progress in our relationship."

"I understand." I could not promise more. He left the next morning and I suspected I would never see him again. It made me sad but I could not blame him.

Margot and I spent the next few days lazing at the beach and contentedly talking with one another. She was not drinking more than a glass or two of wine and assured me it was not a problem as the new doctor had told her it would be okay. So that week went peacefully until midday on Friday.

Margot received her mail from the states forwarded through Judy. She held up one of the envelopes with a puzzled look on her face. "Hey, Jo. Look. The return address is the Vatican. I wonder why they would be writing me?"

"Maybe they want a donation or something."

She opened it and began reading. I knew instantly from her face that something was very wrong. She looked at me, her mouth agape with astonished consternation.

"What is it? What's wrong?"

"That *fucker* has appealed to the Vatican for an *annulment* of our marriage."

"Why would he do that?"

"Because he's a Catholic and he can't get divorced and remarried and still receive the sacraments. I just know he's planning to get remarried."

"If you're upset, why don't you call Tony and talk to him about it."

"I wouldn't give him the satisfaction. Besides, what can I do? He's obviously determined if he would go this far to get an annulment after divorcing me. And guess *the grounds*? The asshole filed on the basis that we never planned to have children. I guess not, after he got his little vasectomy without telling me. That asshole."

"That's pretty cold. So what does the Vatican letter say to you about it?"

"They say I can appeal, *if* I can prove differently."

"So why don't you if it upsets you so much?"

"You don't understand. I'm *afraid* to fight him. He's knows too many really nasty people."

"You think he would have you *hurt* if you cross him? Surely you can't believe that?"

"Oh, but I do."

She took her letter and walked into the garden. Fortunately the landlady left her in peace, and so did I. I knew Margot was crying and needed some time alone to process the whole mess. The annulment would tear from her the last shred of the life she had loved, and the man she had loved and lost. So much of the identity that she had made and valued for herself revolved around being Mrs. Marconetti, even the ex-Mrs. Marconetti. I wondered when she walked back into the villa if she had found peace within and a final acceptance of this former phase in her life, or if it would continue to erode the essential part of whom she had become and had not moved beyond.

One look at her face told me worlds. She was no longer hurt. She was furious. I waited with bated breath to see what she was going to say or do. She hurled the letter onto the kitchen counter and screamed, "I'll show that asshole. He's fixed it so I have to be really careful what I say in public, but he can't totally shut me up."

"What are you planning, Margot."

"I met some really big talk show hosts in New York. I'll just call them up and see if they'd like to interview the ex-Mrs. Marconetti who is now the 'Mrs. Marconetti that never was.' Can you believe that? He thinks he can wipe away a marriage and a divorce just like that, as though it never happened. Well, he can't! I'm going to have one last say."

"Think on it long and hard. It's not going to change the annulment and it could make difficulties for you."

"Fuck'em!"

Chapter 16

Margot was thwarted in her attempts to appear on a national talk show. While I did my best to support her in her efforts, secretly I was glad that this venue had been closed. I could not see how any good could come of a public airing of their differences and the particulars of the dissolution of their marriage. Nonetheless, her frustrations were great and her outlets for venting them inadequate to her. In an attempt to recover some of the previous life with Tony, Margot rented an apartment on 55th Street in Manhattan. Kat went up and spent a week helping her decorate and get settled in her pied à terre. The coming months would see Margot dividing her time between New York and Miami Beach, however she seemed unable to regain entry into the circle of New York friends that she had met through Tony. This too was a painful frustration. More and more often, when I talked with her she seemed despondent and drunk.

All of us in the family began to realize that her problem with alcohol was becoming greater and we tried to talk with her about it. She protested that she was being careful, following doctor's orders and really had no problem with drinking. We knew it wasn't true but we let it slide. We had always as a family allowed her more leeway than others. I think we all lived to regret it. I know that I did. Looking back, I cannot believe that I did not see the rapid degeneration into alcoholism; and even worse than that failure, was the inability to find the words that would have stopped it all before it became so serious. I eventually stopped kicking myself when I accepted the truth that while sometimes you can save people from someone else, you cannot save them from themselves. Only they can do that.

On top of my worries about Margot, it had been a tiring and aggravating week at school. By Friday night I was exhausted and wanted nothing so much as a calm weekend with a good book. I took Beth to meet her father for a weekend visit, walked in my door and immediately went to bed. I was asleep when the phone rang at 9:30. I ignored it until I could stand the persistent ringing no longer. It was Margot.

"Where in the heck were you? The phone must have rung two dozen times."

"I was sleeping. I'm so exhausted. What a bitch of a week."

Margot went on to talk about inconsequential things for the next hour, finally begging me to come to New York for the weekend. I declined and we finally hung up at 11. I had almost fallen back asleep when the phone rang again.

"You're coming to New York in the morning. I just bought you a ticket."

"Oh, God. Margot, please tell me you're kidding."

"No way, you're coming. You don't expect this ticket to just go to waste, now do you?"

With resignation and more than a bit of annoyance, I asked, "So, when am I leaving?"

"I'm sorry but a 6:30 flight was all I could get."

"Is that a.m. or p.m.?"

"In the morning of course. If it wasn't until evening, you'd have no time here."

"Then we'd better get off the phone, since I have to pack and be ready to leave the house by no later than 5:00 if I'm to get to the airport in time."

Reluctantly she hung up. I hauled my weary carcass from bed and packed a bag for the weekend, looking ruefully at the book I had anticipated spending it with. I slept little and groaned when the alarm jangled my last nerve at four in the morning. Fortunately the trip was uneventful, a taxi was waiting at the curb with no queue, and traffic from La Guardia to the apartment was light. I walked into the vestibule at 9:30 and the doorman rang her apartment. Following his directions, I found her door and rang the bell. It was several minutes before she opened it, still in her gown and reeking of alcohol. I knew she was either hung-over, or drunk and still drinking.

"Oh Jo, come on in. I'm a little under the weather this morning so you need to entertain yourself for a while. Sorry."

She tumbled into her bed after pointing me towards the guest room. I dropped my bags, freshened up and left her a note saying that I was going for a walk. When I reached the door, Perky was standing there waiting expectantly. Suspecting she had not been out for her morning constitutional, I found her leash and the two of us set out, both more than a little annoyed at Margot. We ambled along enjoying the morning bustle of people out for shopping or whatever it is New Yorkers do midmorning on Saturday. When we returned midday, Margot was up and dressed.

"Hi, babe." She greeted me breezily as I walked in. "Let's go down to P.J. Clark's for a hamburger. It's only three blocks and they're delicious."

"Suits me."

We marked our orders on the cards that waited atop each table and leaned back in anticipation of much needed food. Ignoring my comment about her condition at my arrival, Margot chatted blithely on. Lunch was as good as she had promised. Afterwards, we walked to her grocer and to the local flower vendor for a bouquet for the apartment. That was enough walking for Margot so I went alone to the Museum of Modern Art to see the latest exhibit. I had persisted in pleading with her to come with me until she snapped at me, "Just go to hell on without me. I don't feel like it. And be back by five or so because we have reservations at 21."

I poked through the exhibit not really enjoying it for fretting over Margot and returned early to the apartment to find the flowers on the coffee table beside a newly opened bottle of champagne and two crystal goblets. Margot had donned a slinky coral caftan and was in the best of moods.

"You've got to congratulate me on my *pied á terre* Kitty. Don't you think it's great?"

It was. The location was convenient to everything. It was high enough to be removed from some of the street noise and insulated windows muted the rest. A terra cotta tiled terrace furnished with a wrought iron dining set and huge potted plants ran down one side. Although the kitchen was little more than a furnished hallway, the dining and living areas were spacious. She had found a beautiful armoire, sofas and chairs, oriental carpets and a dining set. They were perfect for the space, giving it a light and airy look while keeping a warm and welcoming ambiance. There were two bedrooms each with their own baths and large walk-in closets. Custom built-ins gave generous storage space. The draperies and bed covers were luxurious and cheerful. Obviously, she had spared no expense in furnishing this home away from home where she had hoped to regain some purpose and excitement in her life.

With many misgivings, I joined her in a toast to the apartment of which she was justifiably proud. Kat's impeccable decorating sensibilities and Margot's innate good taste had created a beautiful second home for her. On a more selfish level I was thrilled that it would also provide me with a place to stay so that I could visit New York more to see art exhibits, shows, shop and just enjoy the city in general. Margot even apologized in an off-handed way for her earlier 'indisposition.' I let it go and determined to enjoy my time with her. With most people preaching and haranguing will get you nothing but raised dander, and with her pride, I knew it would accomplish even less with her.

For dinner, Margot had purchased a stunning gray tweed Chanel suit with silver fox collar. I nearly choked when she over-casually commented that she found it on sale for $10,000. Given my teacher's salary, that was an astronomical sum for an item of clothing. I blurted before I could stop myself and prayed I had not ruined our evening, "Jesus H. Christ, Margot. That's crazy. That's a *fortune!*"

"Hey, what else do I have to spend my money on?" Her mouth made a sad little quirk.

Contritely I replied, "Just be happy, Babe." I went to my room to change into my own new outfit, a little black number I had found at an outlet for $100, considerably less than its original tag. While it wasn't as soignée as her suit, it was a flattering look on me and I was proud of it.

The two of us gathered our bags and walked out the door into the hall. Margot paused and with a melancholy look, leaned against the wall. "You know, Jo, it is so sad to have so damned much and yet so very little."

My heart broke for her and I cursed myself for the inability to find words adequate to her need for solace. For sure, that one statement of hers covered the source of her drinking and her sadness. It also had the uncanny ring of similar words Maurice

had spoken. I could only think to say, "I'm so sorry. I hope someday that you will find all of the things you need and want in your life."

"So do I, Kitty. So do I."

Margot, determined to make the evening as elegant as her suit, arranged for a limo to transport us the few blocks from her apartment to the restaurant. I loved The 21 on sight. The maître'd seated us at one of the front tables so that we had a good view of the room and the movers and shakers that dine there. Despite the gourmet meal and posh surroundings, her somber mood continued.

She carefully placed her fork on her plate and leaned back for a long thoughtful moment, silently regarding me through narrowed eyes. "You know I'm jealous of you, don't you?"

I was stunned. "Why on earth would you be jealous of me? You're gorgeous and people love you. When you walked in here every head swiveled. You've got a great personality, so much charisma, and everyone wants to be with you. I don't think you've ever met a stranger. You have two beautiful homes, gorgeous things and the money and freedom to enjoy your life. It's like that article said about you, 'you've got it all.' I'm the one that's jealous. I wish that I had all of that.

"Celebrate what you have and enjoy yourself, Margot. Find

something to do to fill your time that you enjoy and that will be rewarding to you. Do some volunteer work. And in time, if you let yourself, you'll meet someone."

"Like you have?" She snorted derisively.

"Look, we both know what a gift I have for picking Mr. Wrong. Besides finding Mr. Right is an iffy thing, but it happens to people all the time. You've got more going for you than most and you will meet someone. Hopefully someday I will too."

"You didn't ask why I'm jealous. But I'll tell you: you have a career in which you're respected, you're intelligent, you're a very good artist, and you have a child that loves you. I don't have any of that. I feel useless and worthless."

"First of all, you are one of the brightest people I know. Secondly, you can have a career and it certainly isn't too late for you to have a baby. Just get out there and take charge of your life again. You are a wonderful woman, Babe, and far from worthless. And I love you so much, not just as a sister, but as my best friend."

"But I don't have a talent and I have no degree. What kind of job could I get? I'm qualified for nothing."

"Oh, but you do have talent! Your personality is a gift. You can charm the socks off anyone you want. People love you and crave your company. Surely you must know someone from your time with Tony that could help you find a job you would enjoy doing, PR or something. You could even do it part-time maybe. As for a degree, you're far more educated from reading and travel and the people you have met than a lot of people with degrees. I may have book smarts but you have more street smarts than I could ever hope to have. Besides, you're very intelligent. Just because you don't have a degree doesn't mean you're not educated. Believe me, most of the education I have I did not get in school. I just got a piece of paper for that. When I really learned was when I pursued something that interested me, and when I had to read to learn as much as I could about artists and the times they lived in to make history come alive for my students. That just gives me knowledge in a narrow area. It doesn't help much with being smart about living. If it really bothers you, go back to school. You have the time and it's not too late."

"I know. It's just that I am so damned lonely all the time."

The coming months found me driving or flying to Miami or New York to be with her as much as I could. The hours long phone calls continued whenever I wasn't with her. I knew from Kat and our mother that they too were on the phone with her daily. We were all worried and we all visited. Nothing helped and the inexorable slide into the depths of alcoholism continued. Soon our visits were an agony. Her disease had progressed to the point that she had developed bleeding varices or enlarged blood vessels in her throat and stomach that would rupture, necessitating an emergency rush to the hospital to be cauterized to stop the hemorrhaging. She had ascites that caused her abdomen to swell to the point that she would have to go to the hospital to have gallons of fluid removed. She was frequently jaundiced and constantly irritable. She was miserable with the alcohol and miserable without it. When I could stand it no longer, I confronted her.

I was standing in her bedroom overlooking the intercostal waterway. Palm trees framed the view of the buildings along Collins Avenue across the way. Bougainvillea blossoms waving in the breeze lined the fence that separated the pool from the waterway. It was a tropical paradise and she was in hell. It had been a bad morning. I had returned from walking Perky to find her drinking vodka straight from the bottle hidden under her bed. She had been drunk even before I walked the dog. Furious, I turned on her as I unsnapped Perky's leash.

"If you're so damned determined to kill yourself, why don't you just get a gun and have at it. It would be a lot quicker and neater than this."

"You make me sick. You're so damned sanctimonious. Just get out of my face."

The door was slammed behind me and I heard the lock turning. I sat by the pool that afternoon about as sad as I could be, or so I thought. But it would get worse. Much worse.

I had been back home only a few weeks, when the family was called to rush to her bedside. She was in a coma and the prognosis was grim. We gathered around the hospital bed and held her hands praying that she would somehow come out of it, stop drinking, and turn from a *living hell* to living. The doctors warned us that even if she survived, the long-term prospects were dim. Without a liver transplant she would die of the disease. As long as she was drinking, she didn't qualify. She lay in the coma for two weeks and then one day she woke up.

In a few days more, my mother took her home and stayed with her for several weeks. Al persuaded her to go away for treatment and Margot agreed. Mama returned home and Margot flew to Hazelden in Minnesota for treatment. She had been warned it would take months. She stayed two weeks and got drunk on the plane back to Miami.

Kat, mama, and I took turns staying with her. It was November and I had been there three days with Margot rarely leaving her bed. She was so frail that we had bought a wheelchair for her and I had pushed her to the kitchen. No longer did she want to leave the house, nor did she want her friends to come. This woman who had been so beautiful and proud no longer resembled herself. She had aged decades in two years. If only before it all began I could have shown her a preview of what was in store if the drinking continued, I suspect her self-pride might have saved her. I was sitting at the table with her after making us a simple meal. In truth she could eat little as her body could no longer process her food, but we all still tried to feed her. I bit my lips and reached for her hand, struggling to hold back the tears.

"Baby, do you know what I want more than anything else in the world?"

Weakly she lifted her head and looked at me, "No."

"I want you to be well again, so we can be happy and play the way we once did."

She didn't reply, only smiled a sad and knowing smile.

I never saw her again.

It wasn't long after I returned home that mama called to tell me the news I had feared. I went through the coming days in a fog trying to anesthetize myself from the pain by keeping as much distance from the unbearable reality of my loss as I could. But the tears kept coming and could not wash it free. Then came the sad chore of closing her home and packing her things, some to give away and some for us all to keep. It fell on me to fly to New York and close down the apartment. It was a lonely job and when the last box was sealed and shipped, I was glad to leave.

I sat in the bar in the airport, waiting for my plane. It was delayed and I was weary and in no mood for the extra two hours. I pushed the glass of wine that sat on the table just at my fingertips, not sure if I could drink it after watching Margot die as she had. Feeling blue and so very lonely without her, I heaved a huge sigh and looked up.

He was like an updated version of my teenage idol, Cary Grant, moved with that same self-confident glide. My pulse raced involuntarily when I realized he was walking towards me. Stopping directly in front of me, he reached up and tucked a strand of my hair that had fallen loose, behind my ear. He leaned close and whispered, "I'm going to marry you."

Laughing, I asked, "Well, have you had a moment of epiphany or is that just a very good pick-up line?"

"Time will tell, won't it?"

About the Author

Betty J. Vaughn, former department chair and art teacher at Enloe Magnet High School in Raleigh, NC, following 32 years of teaching, launched a career as an author on retirement. She is the 2013 winner of the award for historical fiction from the North Carolina Society of Historians for her latest manuscript Run, Cissy, Run. Previously her books Muddy Waters and Turbulent Waters won the awards for 2011 and 2012 respectively. The most recent novel, Yesterday's Magnolia, is not part of the historical fiction series.

In honoring her books, in a unanimous decision, the judges commented: "It is gratifying to find an astute historian whose skills far exceed that realm; someone who can take facts and weave them together with fiction and end up with a story that actually could have happened...[It is] a wonderful story full of emotion, unexpected twists and turns, close calls and tragic moments...Mrs. Vaughn can consider herself a seasoned novelist...[Her books] are fast paced, action packed, and full of adventure...Her work simply isn't just a flurry of words, dry, and boring...She is a master of literary technique as she weaves together her tapestry of words."

A prize winning visual artist with paintings in collections worldwide, Mrs. Vaughn designed the magnet art program at Enloe where her students consistently won top honors. The recipient of a three year Federal Grant to the Wake County School System, she led Enloe Enterprises, Inc. in operating an art gallery, a summer arts camp, and an Emmy award winning television production company. As a result of the Enterprises Enloe was selected as one of the ten best art schools in the nation by Business Week Magazine. She wrote and published a monthly newsletter for the Enterprises and is the author of numerous professional articles.

She loves to travel and led study tours of Europe for many years. History, art, and books are a lifelong passion. Both as a teacher of advanced placement art history and as a writer, Mrs. Vaughn brings the story of the past alive through the people who lived it.

Other titles by B.J. Vaughn

- Paperback: 300 pages
- Language: English
- Hard Cover Book ISBN: 9781590956748
- Paper Back Book ISBN: 9781590956755
- eBook / ISBN: ISBN: 9781590956762

You would think Cecilia LaRoque has it all: a loving father, wealth, beauty, social position and a devoted suitor. She doesn't. Crushed by a cold and critical mother who soon absconds to live with a dissolute lover, 'Cissy' struggles to prove herself worthy of love and respect. She could not have foreseen in her teenage years that the genteel and privileged life she had led would come to a crashing halt with the outbreak of Civil War, a bitter struggle that would tear her world apart. Despite the hardships and inherent danger, she seizes the opportunity to forge an unorthodox role for herself as a spy.